CW01455689

Other historical fiction books
by
Paul W. Feenstra
Published by Mellester Press

First published in 2024 by Mellester Press
Copyright © 2024 Paul W. Feenstra

A Gentleman at Heart ISBN 978-1-99-118248-7 Soft
A Gentleman at Heart ISBN 978-1-99-118249-4 Hard
A Gentleman at Heart ISBN 978-1-067010-10-2 Kindle
A Gentleman at Heart ISBN 978-1-067010-11-9 epub
A Gentleman at Heart ISBN 978-1-067010-13-3 Apple

The right of Paul W. Feenstra to be identified as author
of the Work has been asserted by him in accordance
with the New Zealand copyright act 1994.

This book is copyright protected. Except for the purpose
of fair review, no part may be stored or transmitted in
any form or by any means, electronic or mechanical,
including recording or storage in any information
retrieval system, without permission in writing
from the publishers.

No reproduction may be made, whether by photocopying
or by any other means, unless a licence has been
obtained from the publisher or its agent.
MellesterPress@gmail.com

Published in New Zealand
A catalogue record of this book is available
from the National Library of New Zealand.
Kei te pātengi raraunga Te Puna Mātauranga
o Aotearoa tewhakarārangi tēnei pukapuka

With heartfelt thanks.
Cover Design by Mea
Jane Petersen

A Gentleman at Heart ©2024 Paul W. Feenstra

Published by Mellester Press

A

GENTLEMAN

AT HEART

by

PAUL W. FEENSTRA

Published by Mellester Press

This novel is dedicated to my much-loved father, Cornelis, who at 93 years old, passed away while I was writing this novel. He was a dear and considered man who was, and will always be, A Gentleman at Heart.

Since the invention of printing, no discovery has been made that has exercised so great a change and produced such remarkable and beneficial results to the whole human race as has the introduction of railways and that of steam carriages. By steam-locomotive power distance has been comparatively annihilated, and in conjunction with steam navigation, it has practically reduced the dimensions of the earth.

— The illustrated london news (october 1864)

PROLOGUE

London, England 1869

Paintings and prints of mighty rail locomotives belching steam and smoke graced the Grand Overland Rail reception office walls like trophies of conquered steel monsters. Enoch Willems gazed closely at the behemoths on each picture before stepping towards the next to examine another. He had no particular interest in images displaying endless lines of luxurious carriages; the engines spoke to him. Locomotives ran on coal, and Mr Willems was the sole proprietor and owner of Midlands Collieries Company, which supplied coal that brought steam locomotives to life.

A receptionist sat primly behind a desk and worked quietly; occasionally, her eyes flicked up and studied the distinguished elderly visitor as he perused the images while he waited.

Mr Willems turned with expectancy when a door opened, and smiled politely as a portly gentleman with a flourishing walrus moustache entered the executive reception area.

"Mr Willems?"

"Sir Ronald. Good day, sir," greeted Enoch with his hand extended.

Mrs Marsh, the receptionist, hung his hat and coat near the door and generously offered him a comfortable seat. To ensure Grand

Overland Rail was not seen as discourteous or their fine hospitality and reputation brought into question, Managing Director Sir Ronald Hewitt-Thompson insisted that tea and an assortment of cakes and biscuits were served to their esteemed guest.

"I must say, Mr Willems, your solicitor provided all the necessary documents, and I'm quite perplexed on why you insisted on coming here personally," began Sir Ronald after exchanging pleasantries.

Enoch Willems placed his teacup onto a saucer, nodded thoughtfully and studied the managing director with the same intensity as he evaluated the paintings and prints in reception. He leaned back in his chair and, after a moment, pulled his gaze away from the walrus moustache and glanced around the room before replying.

The office was large, well adorned and graced with expensive trinkets and souvenirs. On the rich wood-panelled wall to the left of the railwayman, a large gilded framed map displayed the route of Grand Overland Rail as it snaked east of Cardiff in Wales, only to have its bold black track end after only seventy-one miles at Swindon, in England. In bright red, the proposed, uncompleted track continued onwards to London. This was what brought Enoch Willems to see Sir Ronald Hewitt-Thompson. He tore his focus from the map and looked at the moustache again. "As my documents detail, I wish to purchase shares and become a minority owner in Grand Overland Rail, Sir Ronald."

The managing director smiled appropriately. What Mr Willems proposed represented a considerable sum of money, and the company needed a large influx of capital to pursue its planned expansion. He savoured the moment with barely concealed glee.

"In return, I want a seat on the board of directors. However, before I commit, I wanted to meet you personally and ensure your prospectus is valid and current. Ten thousand pounds represents a significant investment, and my solicitor has expressed concern that my part ownership of your company, although relatively modest, can create liability for me, Sir Ronald. I will only invest if you intend to purchase the last tracts of land needed to complete the line from Swindon to London." Mr Willems took another sip of tea. "It isn't just your signature and pledge I need, sir; I want to look you in the eye and feel assured as we consummate this arrangement."

Rain pattered against the windows as both men assessed each other.

The managing director leaned back in his chair, and the walrus moustache expanded outwards as he smiled. "As you can see, we have met all the council provisions and obtained permissions we've been waiting on, and all regulatory and regional requirements have also been satisfied, Mr Willems."

The elderly gentleman raised an eyebrow. "I'm impressed, sir. Obtaining regulatory approvals and permits is an extraordinary feat, and yet you can confirm they are all in order and meet all your legal obligations?"

Sir Ronald nodded. "We are most diligent, Mr Willems. That is how I ensure this company is productively managed. And as asked, we've provided you with copies. All required paperwork has been submitted and approved." He smiled warmly at his guest before continuing. "As requested, the board has approved your petition and created a position for you. Good sir, I am here to appease your apprehension and validate your wishes. However, I wish to clarify the terms of our agreement regarding the cost of coal from you. Nothing is holding us back once our contracts have been formalised, is there?" Sir Ronald eyed a chocolate-dipped wafer lying amongst the treats on a plate.

"I don't believe so, Sir Ronald," responded Enoch. "As outlined,

Midlands Collieries Company will service the entire line, and all coal will be discounted a further twenty per cent from your current costs. It's detailed in the brief you received from my solicitors," he affirmed.

"And you can fulfil our projected coal demands?"

"And more. Midlands Collieries Company has the proven historical capacity to provide you with all the coal you need," replied Mr Willems confidently.

Sir Ronald clasped his hands. "Then I'm satisfied, Mr Willems."

Enoch Willems smiled and turned to the gilded framed map on the wall. The red track indicating, *proposed,* symbolised his entire cash reserves. Excluding his home in the Regent's Park and Midlands Collieries Company, he'd sold every asset he owned, including his country estate, the London flat, liquidated other investments and sold shares from dozens of companies to fulfil this covenant. It was a risky venture, and he knew it.

When Grand Overland Rail purchased the last remaining parcels of land needed to complete the rail line from Cardiff to London, he could retire and let his son take over the business. Enoch was tired and had worked hard his entire life; with a sigh, he turned from the map and any misgivings and bent down to retrieve his satchel.

He lifted the worn leather flap, extracted an envelope, and held it carefully, almost reverently, as if he had second thoughts. The doubts were there. His solicitor, Howard Willoughby, vehemently opposed this undertaking and voiced his concerns more than once. On the front of the envelope, the seal of The Bank of England stared up at him. Britannia, the woman holding the spear and olive branch, beckoned in silent warning.

The managing director chewed the last of the chocolate wafer he'd taken and cleared his throat, a less-than-subtle reminder that time is money.

"Uh, yes. Sir Ronald." Enoch cast aside any unease and raised the envelope. "I have a *lettre d'indication*[1] for you. I'm sure, uh, everything is in order." With a slight tremor in his hand, he passed the envelope to the managing director.

"Mr Willems, thank you. On behalf of the board of directors, we welcome you to Grand Overland Rail and a fruitful and prosperous relationship." He stood and reached out a hand, and they shook.

"It's for my son."

Sir Ronald looked puzzled. "Pardon me?"

"My investment in Grand Overland Rail ... this is for my son, for when I retire," answered Mr Willems with watery eyes.

Sir Ronald smiled in acknowledgement. "Of course, sir."

Mr Willems' expression hardened, and he suddenly clutched his arm and sank back onto his chair, grimacing in pain. A sheen of sweat covered his brow, and his skin became pallid. The managing director watched in horror as his new partner looked to be in some distress.

Enoch awkwardly reached into his jacket pocket, withdrew a small pillbox, nimbly flicked open the lid and extracted a tiny silk-covered glass pearl[2]. He crushed it with his fingers to a "pop" sound and raised it to his nose.

Sir Ronald helplessly watched. "Er, Mr Willems... do ye need assistance?" he asked before turning to the door. "Mrs Marsh, fetch a glass of water - quickly now!"

Enoch leaned back against the chair with his eyes closed as he inhaled the medication. "I'm, I'm fine, thank you, Sir Ronald. Just a, a turn... Angina." He grimaced, pulled out a handkerchief and

1   *Lettre d'indication - Written in French, the language of European diplomacy, extends credit and access to funds.*
2   *Called 'Poppers' for the sound they make when crushed. They contain medication to be inhaled.*

dabbed at his forehead. "It will pass."

With a worried look, Mrs Marsh rushed in with a pitcher and glass, and the managing director pointed to his ailing elderly guest.

She immediately filled the glass before handing it to Mr Willems.

After a minute or two of anxiousness for the railwayman and his secretary, colour returned to Enoch's face, and he sat forward in his chair. "Forgive me, please. My physician informs me I am stricken with *angina pectoris*." He took another deep breath. "A disease of modern man, eh? It was just a mild turn. I didn't mean to cause you alarm." He gripped the chair's armrests and leaned forward to rise.

Sir Ronald stepped closer, grabbed an arm and helped Mr Willems to his feet. "Are you...? Er, do you need assistance or perhaps a physician?"

"Thank you, Sir Ronald, and to you, m'dear." He smiled warmly at the receptionist and dipped his head. "I am again in fine form."

The managing director assisted Mr Willems into his coat and handed him his hat. "Are you certain...?"

Mrs Marsh bent down, retrieved his case, and handed it over. "Here you go, sir. Let me hail a cab for you." She looked at her superior, who nodded in confirmation and briskly exited the office.

"Anxiety and intemperance, Sir Ronald," winked Enoch, and on senescent legs shuffled slowly towards the door. "Good day, sir."

CHAPTER ONE

Winchester, England 1870

The proprietress, as her patrons knew her, threw open the door. "Out, th' lot of ya. Out now! Th' peelers[3] be here again, and I'm tired of them. Out!" Helen Dougherty bellowed and waved a flabby arm toward the door.

All in various stages of undress, the four officers responded unkindly with a chorus of off-colour and quite impolite retorts and gestures. "Tell them to bugger off, Helen," suggested one young officer as he rolled over, exposing a partially naked female form that lay beneath him.

Already, they could hear the police pounding on the door.

"Use the back door, lads. Hurry up, will ya!" she insisted, ignoring the good-natured barbs. "They'll be inside in a tick."

The racket and raised voices coming from the front door motivated the four military officers into action as they hurriedly began to dress as moans of displeasure and disappointment came from their four female companions.

Helen stepped out into the hallway and yelled. "Hold ya bloody 'orses. I'm comin'!"

Muffled voices from outside suggested the police didn't believe her, and the thumping intensified.

Three lieutenants and a captain of the 67th South Hampshire Regiment of Foot were passably dressed and hurried to leave the

3   *Peelers - Police*

7

room. One of them, the captain, paused, turned, stumbled back into the room and planted a kiss on one of the young women.

"Oye, that one's mine," remarked an aggrieved lieutenant, hopping on one foot as he struggled to put on a boot.

The captain looked momentarily confused, then grinned. "Oops."

With his boot secured, the young officer followed his three companions towards the building's rear door, held open by Helen, and each delivered a kiss to her cheek as they fled the house.

Once in the alley, the captain paused. "I think it's time we stopped running and gave those sodding peelers some of their own medicine. Feel like some sport, lads?"

"Austin?" questioned one of the lieutenants, "It might be best to leave well enough alone, eh."

"They need a good thrashing," replied Captain Austin Willems, "Then, they might think twice before they pick on Helen and us in the future."

Without waiting for a reply, the captain raced around the side of the house onto St Clement Street, bounded through the open gate of Helen Dougherty's property and fearlessly launched himself at the nearest of Winchester's finest constables. Following only a step behind, his fellow officers vigorously set upon the other two police officers.

The constables gave as good as they received, and for the most part, fought bravely with determination, however, the odds weren't in their favour, and superior numbers and military training took their toll.

Captain Willems limped towards Serle's House on Southgate Street, where the regiment was based, and he half carried his best friend Lieutenant Charles Newbury, who'd been dazed when a constable's boot struck him on the head. The other two lieutenants suffered scrapes and abrasions to their arms when, together, they toppled into a neighbour's rose garden. The constable, who was beneath them at the time, took the brunt of the injuries and suffered a sprained ankle, a bloodied nose, and dozens of deep scratches. One constable managed to flee, while the one brawling Captain Willems was mainly spared any visible injuries when a deftly delivered right hook knocked him out cold. None of the four officers felt any lingering pain as the opium they'd been smoking earlier nullified any present discomfort.

The four friends were still in fits of hysterical laughter when they approached their regimental base. They wisely decided not to draw any attention to their antics and quietly entered the building to retire for what little remained of the evening.

A persistent knocking roused Captain Austin Willems from a deep sleep. As wakefulness descended, so did a throbbing headache. He groaned. "What is it?"

"Captain Willems, sir!" responded the voice and the battering on his door continued.

"Dear God, go away. It's Sunday," muttered Austin and reluctantly dragged himself from his bed to stand uncertainly in the middle of his tiny room. "What do you want?"

"Colonel Farwell requests the pleasure of your company at your earliest convenience, sir," answered the voice. To Austin's way of thinking, the man sounded far too cheerful and should be shot.

Austin lowered his head into his hands and whimpered in self-pity. *It's Sunday, and I'm not on duty*, he thought, then recalled last evening and the playful encounter with the police with another sorrowful groan. "I'll be right there!" he replied, trying to clear the fog that dulled his thinking.

"They're waiting for you, sir," informed the colonel's adjutant when he arrived at the regiment's offices a short time later.

The warning bell pealed inside his head, adding to the dull ache behind his eyes. The adjutant said, 'They're', and not 'he', which can only mean trouble, reasoned Austin. He spared a thought to the constables and the minor altercation from the previous evening and hoped they weren't seriously hurt.

He took a deep breath, exhaled loudly and rapped twice on the door.

"Enter!"

He thrust open the door and, masking his limp, a slight injury he sustained only a few hours previously, stepped briskly into the office and immediately felt the presence of another person in the room. He focused on his senior officer, and when Colonel Henry Farwell rose from his seat, he snapped to attention and delivered a crisp salute.

The colonel answered the salute but did not return to his chair. "At ease, Captain. I believe you are well acquainted with Mr Willoughby."

Austin turned. "Howard?" he exclaimed in complete surprise.

Howard Willoughby's face did not return the welcoming smile, although his mouth twitched slightly.

"Er, I shall afford you the privacy you both require. Gentlemen," cordially offered Colonel Farwell before stepping from his office and softly closing the door behind him.

"Uncle Howard," repeated Austin, why are you here?" He felt a sinking feeling in the pit of his stomach. "It's father, isn't it? Is he unwell?" He took two steps closer, extended his arms, and they embraced.

Howard Willoughby was not an uncle to Austin Willems, but he'd known him his entire life. He was not only Enoch Willems' oldest and dearest friend; he was also his solicitor and trusted advisor. His surprise visit didn't portend well.

They separated, and Howard looked at the young man before him. He was the spitting image of his father. Tall, not handsome in the classical sense, but had piercing blue eyes and an openness that was likeable in an audacious way.

"Austin, I apologise and wish I could be here under more pleasant circumstances." He briefly looked down at the floor, then tilted his head and met the questioning blue eyes. "He passed." He shook his head in despair. "It was his heart. I'm sorry, Austin. I know how much you cared for him."

"Oh, dear God!" exclaimed Austin and sank into one of the colonel's chairs, burying his face in his hands.

Howard dragged another chair across the wooden floor to sit opposite and close to the distressed young officer.

"When?" was all Austin could manage.

"Three days ago. He died whilst sleeping, and Nanny found him when he didn't respond for breakfast."

Elizabeth Goodhew, or Nanny, was an affectionate name given to their housekeeper when she looked after Austin when he was a boy. Someone began calling her Nanny, and the name stuck with her. Like most employees who worked for Enoch Willems, they were intensely loyal, and the patriarch treated them all like family.

"How is she?" Austin asked.

"She hasn't taken it well, unfortunately. I don't blame her, Austin; everyone feels the same. Your father was much loved and he will be missed."

Austin fidgeted with his regimental ring. "Poor father. I hadn't seen him in a while and should have made more time to visit." He looked at his father's best friend. "And how are you coping, Howard?"

Howard took a deep breath. "I admit the news struck me considerably hard. There are many issues to deal with, and it's been difficult personally and professionally."

Austin nodded. "Yes, I expect it would. Who is running the business now?"

Howard Willoughby rose from the chair and nervously stroked his moustache. "Ah, Austin," he cleared his throat. "We need to discuss your father's affairs in some detail. Can you come to the offices in London?"

Austin looked up at Howard with growing alarm. "When is the funeral?"

"In two days." He reached into his blazer, extracted an envelope, and handed it over. "All the information you need is here."

Austin rotated the envelope repeatedly in his hands but didn't look inside. The feeling of concern didn't subside. "There's a problem, isn't there?"

"Good grief, why do you say that?" replied the solicitor, returning to the chair.

"Because I know you. Was father's death suspicious? Did something happen?"

"No, no, good heavens no. Angina caused his death, Austin. But there are matters and I would like to discuss them with you privately."

"And what of father's pride and joy, Midlands Collieries Company? I'm sure the staff will be devastated."

Again, Howard stood and walked to the window to stare outside. He remained silent for a while, then turned. "Austin, I've dreaded telling you..." he sighed loudly. "And I struggle even now when I know I must."

Austin's eyes narrowed and locked onto Howard's. "Tell me what?"

"Your father no longer holds Midlands; he died, er, … while not necessarily penniless, he no longer owned any businesses and had liquidated nearly all his assets."

Austin's eyebrows furrowed. "How can this be? His businesses thrived. They were prosperous and well managed. What the hell happened?"

"That's what I want to discuss with you; it's rather, er, pivotal," Howard offered.

"Then Father's death is not without blame?"

The solicitor raised a finger in warning. "Careful, Austin, we can't make assumptions," he sternly counselled.

Austin trusted and respected Howard Willoughby as much as he did his father. Howard was not only astute, but an active mind and a curious nature ensured he was always well-informed and exercised sound judgment. If he expressed doubt or uncertainty, then it shouldn't be ignored.

"But, er, not entirely?"

Howard Willoughby inclined his head.

Behind his eyes, Austin's head throbbed relentlessly, and he felt drained and emotional. He never knew his mother or knew much about her. His father had always been evasive when he pressed him for information about her and he put it down to the pain of losing a much loved spouse and rekindling suppressed memories. One thing his father had said, was that his mother was a dear and lovely woman and that she died during childbirth, and now his dear father, the man he most admired and loved so much, had passed. He felt alone and perhaps a little insecure as a flood of emotions overwhelmed him.

Sensing his anguish, Howard edged closer and touched his

shoulder reassuringly. "I know how you feel, Austin. I loved him too; he was like my brother, but know this: I will always be here for you."

It was too much for Austin, and in an outpouring of despair, he succumbed to the agony of his emotions.

Once composed, arrangements were made, and Howard Willoughby made his departure.

Austin was about to return to his room when Colonel Farwell reappeared to reclaim his office and sat behind his desk. He cleared his throat. "I am sorry for your loss, Captain, and I can't begin to understand how you must be feeling."

"Thank you, sir. My father was a great man," replied Austin.

"No doubt you will be requesting bereavement leave?"

"Yes, sir. If convenient, I'd like to depart for London immediately."

"Of course, Captain, speak to the adjutant on your way out."

Austin nodded and was about to leave.

"Uh, one thing, Captain?"

Austin turned to his commanding officer.

"In light of the distressing news of your father, and this may not be the best time to bring this to your attention, but, uh, how would you like me to explain your actions last evening to the constabulary? I had an unpleasant early morning visit from the police superintendent, and he was a bit put out and demanded an accounting."

Austin thought quickly. "Oh, of course, sir. I wasn't going to mention it as it was nothing, but I don't expect gratitude, sir." He kept his expression neutral.

The colonel raised a single eyebrow. "Gratitude, Captain?"

"Sir, we were returning here last evening when we observed

three suspicious men attempting to break down the door of a house." He leaned forward and lowered his voice to a whisper. "Apparently, it's a bordello, sir." He managed to feign a look of disgust. "Rather than wait for the police to arrive, we decided to apprehend the villains. It was dark, difficult to see, and we approached them unseen, sir. I do apologise for taking matters into our own hands, but we successfully prevented them from breaching the building and taught the scoundrels a good lesson, sir."

Colonel Farwell's voice hardened. "Those scoundrels were constables, Captain, and two of them required medical attention for their injuries."

Captain Willems shook his head in sympathy. "Indeed, Colonel Farwell. They were fortunate not to have been severely hurt. Perhaps, next time, they could identify themselves and avoid this unpleasantness. But, sir, I've put the incident behind me and don't require an apology," he forced a smile. "Will that be all, sir?"

Colonel Farwell wasn't impressed. "We'll speak more on this when you return. Meanwhile, my condolences, Captain."

"Thank you, sir."

CHAPTER TWO

London

The funeral of Enoch Willems wasn't as dour as Austin expected. It was well attended, and people he hadn't seen in years came to pay their last respects. It was wonderful to see them again, and despite the sorrow and blur of tears, there was also laughter and good cheer. He couldn't help but feel the warmth from their good-natured gestures and sincere wishes. It brought attention to his own selfish failings, and he promised to catch up and visit them more frequently.

The day following the funeral, Howard and Austin sat quietly in the offices of Walker, Wakefield and Willoughby, Barristers and Solicitors, on Essex Street in London, contemplating the effects Enoch Willems' death would have on them both. A bottle of Glenury Royal single malt Scotch whiskey sat on a coffee table between them, and each sipped from a glass after a series of teary toasts to Enoch Willems.

Earlier, Howard Willoughby had detailed Enoch's last will and testament with cold, legal proficiency. Having concluded his professional obligations, he moved to sit on a comfortable armchair across from Austin, where they could chat informally.

"Now then," began Howard. He placed his glass on the table,

leaned back and crossed his legs. "I'm sure you have more questions, but there are a few salient points I'd like to make."

Austin toyed with the whiskey glass and looked over at Howard. "Why did you allow father to invest in that damn railway?" He wasn't happy, and his displeasure showed.

Howard raised a hand. "Perhaps it is best if I explain, then you may draw fair conclusions."

Expecting the worst, Austin maintained eye contact and waited.

"Your father wanted to provide a steady revenue stream for Midlands Collieries Company by supplying a major customer with coal," he raised a finger into the air. "One dependable customer, under contract, who would and could not renege on the arrangement." He lowered his hand. "Grand Overland Rail represented that customer, Austin. They were in dire need of cash, they listed sufficient assets, and when they purchased the remaining land to link Cardiff and London by rail, all investors would benefit enormously. For Midlands Collieries Company, it would be a windfall and essentially a win, win."

"If they actually purchased the land they needed," added Austin.

Howard nodded. "I was against the idea from the outset and urged Enoch to only purchase small numbers of shares in Grand Overland Rail until they could prove themselves. Your father refused and said he needed to buy a minimum block of ten thousand pounds of shares to obtain a seat on the board of directors. If he had a directorship, and through diligent governance, he could ensure that Grand Overland Rail would do as promised without any shenanigans and follow through on their commitments as publicly detailed in their prospectus."

"That still doesn't explain how Father lost Midlands," replied Austin.

"I'm getting to that." Howard cleared his throat. "Enoch

purchased ten thousand pounds of stocks through a private sale from Grand Overland Rail, a joint-stock company. Are you familiar with what that is?"

Austin didn't have the foggiest notion and shook his head.

"Means any Grand Overland Rail debt also becomes the responsibility of the shareholders, who can become liable.

Austin's mouth opened.

"Yes, your father knew that, as he'd been assured that company debt was minimal, they had assets and more than enough cash reserves to cover unforeseen expenses.

"So, what happened? I don't understand."

"The official and public account is that the landowners collectively wanted to drive up the value of their land, and they did this by inviting other companies to bid. Grand Overland Rail had to outbid those competitors to purchase the land they so desperately needed for their expansion."

"And they were outbid?" Austin asked.

"Oh yes, they were. But this is where it becomes interesting. The company who won the bid and purchased the land sold it back to Grand Overland Rail for slightly over twice what it was originally budgeted for."

Austin shook his head in disbelief.

"Grand Overland Rail did not have the capital to buy the land offered to them at the inflated price, and the directors voted to obtain a short-term bank loan." Howard pointed a finger at Austin. "Your father and a couple of other directors voted against it, but the majority prevailed."

Howard lowered his hand and took a sip from his glass. "Grand Overland Rail defaulted on their loan, and as a shareholder, your father was presented with an invoice to pay for his share of the shortfall. He had no capital because he'd sold all his businesses except for Midlands Collieries to purchase shares in Grand Overland Rail. He was legally bound to sell his cherished company or be in default."

Austin stared at the floor with head bowed and remained silent as he digested what he'd learned. After a minute or two, he looked up at Howard through a torrent of tears. "Seems so unfair and harsh... poor father." He had a thought and wiped his eyes before speaking. "Was it deliberate?"

Howard's lips compressed, and he met Austin's intense gaze before turning away. "I'm not sure!"

Austin rubbed his face. "For heaven's sake, Howard, why did he do it?"

Howard took a sip of his whiskey and shrugged. "Austin, I can't be certain."

"Why didn't father obtain a loan?"

"We tried. The problem was the loan amount was too great, and the banks believed your father did not have enough cash reserves and did not run his business profitably. They claimed he had too many employees and paid them too much. For the banks, the risk was too high."

Austin nodded. It was true; his father was generous. "He did pay his staff well, but it seems peculiar that Grand Overland Rail didn't secure formalised agreements with the landowners beforehand on the purchase price of the land," he thought.

"And now you're thinking like your father," Howard stated.

Austin stared at his hands and the empty whiskey glass he toyed with. He looked up at his dear family friend. "But there is blame?"

"Blame?" Howard questioned.

"Yes, father's death."

Howard Willoughby smoothed out his pencil-thin moustache. "There are no suspicious circumstances around Enoch's passing, and the cause of death was listed as heart failure."

"But, you must have uncertainty around Grand Overland Rail and what they did."

Howard tapped his fingers on the chair's armrest. He knew Austin would discover the truth sooner than later. "I'm not entirely comfortable with the business practices of Grand Overland Rail."

Austin was becoming annoyed. "Why would you say that? Have you cause? You're a solicitor, for heaven's sake. If they have done something wrong, they must be held accountable."

"All the paperwork I received satisfied all their legal requirements."

Austin looked at Howard for more answers and refilled both glasses while waiting for him to provide details.

"I warned your father beforehand and advised him not to do it."

"And what about now? What can we do? Do we have recourse, Howard?"

The solicitor took a deep breath. "I have some suspicions and reason to suspect that a separate core group of Grand Overland Rail directors, acting independently, outbid and obtained significant tracts of land that Grand Overland Rail wanted at quite a low price. They deliberately purchased the land cheaply, increased the selling price, and made a fortune selling it back to Grand Overland Rail."

"What you're saying is these directors bought the land and essentially sold it to themselves?"

Howard raised an eyebrow.

"But they would have been invoiced like father and had to pay their portion of the default loan. They would have incurred debt," Austin reasoned. "So, what would be the purpose?"

"Relatively speaking, I can only determine that each director's invoice amount was small compared to the profit each director enjoyed from buying and selling the land. I imagine they were reimbursed, and repaying the debt from profits wasn't an issue."

"Unlike father," Austin seethed.

"From what I can determine, it must have been a well-crafted plan, Austin, and it allowed Grand Overland Rail to ultimately take control of Midlands Collieries Company. I suspect it was planned. Midlands had been targeted, and your father was swindled."

Austin shot to his feet. "No, this can't be! Are you telling me this scheme was a plan by Grand Overland Rail to deceive Father and obtain his company?"

"I have no proof, Austin. I expect the directors used a separate company they created, an anonymous third party, or perhaps, and let's call it an undisclosed principal, to win the bid on the land, sell it, and then purchase your father's company with their proceeds," Howard added.

"I'm not sure I understand."

Howard rose from his chair and stretched his back as Austin watched. "I believe it was always the intention of Grand Overland Rail's board of directors to obtain Midlands Collieries Company from your father. The entire land purchase deal gave these renegade directors and their secretive company enough profit to purchase Midlands coal."

"And father didn't know?" Austin returned to his seat, helped himself to the whiskey bottle and refilled his glass again. "And all the directors were involved?"

Howard shook his head. "Some directors resigned after selling their shares back to Grand Overland Land Rail for huge losses, but Austin, how could your father have known? And what could he do? Enoch was distraught, and afterwards... well, he had suspicions all right and brought them to my attention. The poor man was overcome, and I believe that contributed to his death; his heart couldn't take it."

"Poor, dear Father." Austin drained the whisky and

shuddered as he felt the burn. "What Grand Overland Rail directors did, isn't that illegal?"

Howard grimaced. "No, it isn't illegal. While it certainly could be construed as immoral and unethical. I'd call it insider misconduct or self-dealing. Remember, the directors are liable because they aren't protected by limited liability." He retrieved his glass, up-ended the contents, and, like Austin, shuddered as the expensive whiskey burned its way down.

"Do we have recourse? Is there anything that can be done? If the board of directors used confidential company information to enrich themselves personally, that must surely be fraudulent," Austin asked.

Howard shook his head. "The Government has talked about introducing Limited Liability, but typically it's been held up in parliament."

The muffled sounds from the outer offices drifted in as both men contemplated.

"How did father establish a relationship with the directors?" Austin asked.

"From White's."

"White's?"

"That is where your father first became acquainted with principals from Grand Overland Rail. Fortified by brandy at a gentleman's club, men are only too eager to brag of their accomplishments." He laughed. "I, er, have some friends who keep me apprised of useful gossip from time to time."

"The bastards!" Austin was upset. "Father was a decent and moral man. Those directors need to face justice for what they have done."

Howard repositioned himself in his chair. "Nothing can be proven, Austin. I have no evidence of foul play, and even if I did, what could I do?"

"Nothing legally," clarified Austin. "But proof...? Do you have any information or know what land tracts were purchased?"

"I do, and it's public knowledge."

Austin rubbed his chin. "Then I shall call upon those who sold land and see if any information will be gleaned. I want names."

"Are you sure you want to do this?" Howard asked after topping up their glasses.

"I have leave for another ten days, and I might detour to Swindon and investigate further."

"And what will you do? How can you discover and prove Grand Overland Rail purchased land at an inflated rate from their directors?

Austin rubbed his chin. "I really don't know. Do you have any suggestions?"

Howard leaned forward and lowered his voice. "As your solicitor or as a family friend?"

Austin grimaced and remained quiet as Howard continued.

"There is little I can do as your solicitor, but as a friend, I'd like to see Grand Overland Rail suffer the consequences. I'm in full agreement with you, Austin, and if it's proven they did wrong, then damn them."

CHAPTER THREE

It was a slow train journey. Carriages were full, and the passengers were boisterous. Initially, he hoped he could enjoy the trip and reflect on the passing of his father or perhaps even sleep a little, but it wasn't to be. He stepped from the train with some relief and found lodgings at a nearby inn for the evening. In the morning, he would rent a horse, ride out to the addresses Howard gave him, and dig around a little. His expectations were low, and he didn't expect much from his enquiries, however, he still felt an overwhelming obligation to his father and would do his utmost to hopefully clear up any confusion and put this matter to rest.

The landscape around Swindon was flat and dominated by agriculture and small productive farm holdings. The first place he called on was Soves Farm. He rode his horse up a long path towards a house and was greeted by a farmer wielding a pitchfork outside a barn.

"Don't get many callers here, you be lost?" offered the farmer while appraising the horse Austin rode.

"Good morning. I hope I'm not lost," grinned Austin in reply. "I'm just gathering some information and hope you can assist me."

The farmer scowled. "What you be needin' then, cause I don't know much 'bout anything, except farmin'? And you don't look much like a farmer."

Austin dismounted and stepped around the horse to stand closer to the man. "You recently sold land to Grand Overland Rail."

"Aye, that land there, you rode through it to get here." The farmer pointed with a dirty hand back from where Austin rode. "Who you work for, the railroad?"

"I don't represent a company, and my visit here is personal."

The farmer seemed to relax.

"Were you pressured into selling the land at a different price than you originally wanted?"

The farmer laughed and turned to the heap of dirty hay behind him to toss it into a wagon. "Aye, there were some 'round here who wanted me to join 'em and jack the price up." He continued to fill the wagon.

"But you didn't?"

"I didn't see the point, and I reckon it wouldn't have made any difference in the end. We would never get th' full amount of what the land was actually worth. And I didn't want to end up in court or have trouble, so I accepted the low offer."

Low offer? "Why?"

"I need to plan my crop planting. I ain't gonna plant crops on land I don't own, and I needed to know one way or 'nother. Was easier for me that way. Why is this important to ya?" He stopped tossing hay and leaned on the pitchfork while waiting for the stranger's reply.

"Makes sense to me," Austin stated. "I'm trying to ascertain if there are any improprieties around the sale of land Grand Overland Rail wanted."

"Is wrong any time a man be forced into sellin' his land," spat the farmer. "But let me tell ya, there was a man, and he came by here and stirred things up a bit. Said all farmers should stick together, work as one, and we'd get more money, a lot more money. Turned out he was a liar."

Austin's curiosity was piqued. "Who was this man, and who did he represent?"

"Oh, ya got me there," stated the farmer. "He was fancy, dressed like you, he was. Let me think. Never liked him; he smiled too much."

"Did he leave a calling card?"

The farmer shook his head, then looked at Austin, inclined his head slightly and closed an eye. "You're military, aren't ya, an officer?"

Austin was taken aback. "Yes, I am."

The farmer laughed. "Your moustache and the way ya ride yer horse, your attitude."

"I'm sorry. I hope it doesn't bother you. It isn't my intention."

"You seem alright to me, but that chap, he rode like you, and he did bother me. His bloody name… is on the tip of me tongue…."

Austin waited.

"Siles! That's it, Miles Siles. Strange bloody name."

"Miles Siles," Austin repeated. "Any idea where he was from or which company?"

The farmer shook his head, speared the pitchfork into the hay, removed a clay pipe from his coat and began stuffing the bowl with tobacco. "London, most likely."

"And to clarify. This Miles Siles fellow was trying to force you to increase your price in concert with other farmers?"

"Yep, that'd be right, but he lied."

"Lied?"

"Aye, from what I hear, he claimed that if us farmers stuck together, we could get a better price. Instead, it was the other way around, and everyone had to accept less, a lot less." The farmer shrugged and partially turned his back to Austin. He had nothing further to say.

Austin was perplexed. This was turning out to be even more complex than he first imagined. "You've been most helpful, thank you very much."

The farmer dipped his head in acknowledgement, and Austin mounted his horse.

"About two miles east, there'd be a farm with a fallen tree b'side the road. A crazy Irishman owns it. Careful, he'd be a hot-head. He sided with that Siles chap along with the others, and you might want to have a wee chat with him."

"Thank you, I shall do exactly that," offered Austin. "Good day, sir."

Austin retraced his route down the long carriageway to the main road, turned left, and continued. What the farmer told him was interesting, but nothing that indicated his land sale was dubious, although he'd like to discover more on this Miles Siles fellow.

He enjoyed being outside on a horse and riding in the countryside, giving him time to think about his father and dwell on his future.

It seemed only an instant, and he saw the fallen tree as the farmer described. He turned up the track and rode towards the farmhouse some distance from the road.

"What can I do for ya?" suddenly came a voice. A man stepped out from behind a bush and stared at Austin suspiciously.

"Oh, you gave me a start," replied Austin. He never saw the man. "I'm looking for the owner of the farm."

"That be me, and what you be needin'?"

Austin described the purpose of his visit, just like he had told the farmer he spoke to earlier.

"What business is it o' yours then?"

"I'm trying to sort the affairs of my father, who recently passed and find out if this sale of land to Grand Overland Rail is what contributed to his death."

"He was a farmer then?"

"No, coal was his business."

The Irishman said nothing and just stared. "What's your name?" the Irishman asked.

"Austin Willems."

"Never heard of you a'fore."

"Were you encouraged to decrease the price of your land when Grand Overland Rail first wanted to purchase it?"

The Irishman shrugged. "Maybe. But who be sayin' Grand Overland Rail wanted to buy it?"

Austin was puzzled. "Who else wanted to buy it?"

The Irishman shrugged but wouldn't elaborate.

"Were you approached by a gentleman called Miles Siles? Was Mr Siles trying to have you work with other farmers on the selling price of your land? And, did you finally have to accept less?"

The Irishman's eyes narrowed. "I've heard nuff from you, on your way!"

"Do you know who Mr Siles worked for?"

"Don't have me tell ya again, be gone. Off me land!"

Austin paused. He had no quarrel with this man, and perhaps he should leave and avoid any unpleasantness. "I'm not trying to cause you any harm or cause ill will, sir."

The volitile Irishman stomped towards him and, without warning, attempted a vicious head butt. It was completely unexpected and caught Austin by surprise. He pulled his head back in time, and before the farmer could react to the miss, Austin quickly raised a foot and kicked out. With a grunt, the Irishman fell backwards to land on his rear.

"That wasn't very sociable," Austin shook his head. "I'm not here to cause you any trouble." He looked at the man and decided to try one last time. "Please, can you tell me anything about Miles Siles?"

The Irishman rose unsteadily and wiped his mouth with a dirty coat sleeve. He didn't look happy. "You'll be a wish'n you hadn't come here," he spat.

Austin turned to his horse, put a foot in the stirrup and hoisted himself onto the saddle. Without a word, he rode away.

"Bloody English!" shouted the Irishman.

He met with similar hostility on other farms he visited and learned nothing. Curiously, no one was willing to talk to him, and he couldn't fathom why. Austin rode on towards the tiny hamlet of Baulking and stopped at the small parish church of St. Nicholas. Outside, a vicar was pruning hydrangeas and looked questioningly at Austin as he dismounted, tethered his horse to a post and walked up towards him.

"A lovely day to be outside in the garden," greeted Austin.

"To be sure." The vicar stood upright and stretched his back. "How can I help you, sir?"

"I'm looking for anyone who might still be around here that recently sold their property to the rail company."

"Oh, most have moved on by now. No reason for anyone to stay, really," he replied.

"I just thought there may have been one or two that never left the area and moved close by." He recalled the hostility from the Irishman. "I don't mean anyone harm; it's personal, and I'm trying to tie up matters with my father's estate; he recently passed."

The vicar scratched his head and then nodded. "You are indeed correct. Forgive me, sir. The widow Dorling recently bought the cottage just up the street, and you might want to call on her." He turned and pointed up the road to a cluster of homes. "The last one on the left, Mrs Margaret Dorling."

"I shall do exactly that, thank you."

The vicar smiled and returned to his pruning.

The cottage was small, homely and bordered by a low stone wall. Austin tied his horse to the gate, entered the property, and strolled unhurriedly to the door. Before he could knock, it opened, and an elderly woman greeted him with a welcoming smile.

"Good afternoon, Mrs Dorling. My name is Austin Willems, and I do apologise for my intrusion. The vicar suggested I visit you. I wonder if I may ask you some questions about the recent sale of your land?"

She looked at him with uncertainty and said nothing.

Before she told him to leave, he quickly interjected. "Uh, I'm not representing a company. I'm here to satisfy my curiosity, and it's personal." He presented her with his warmest, most charming smile.

She nodded and looked him up and down. "Well, you had better come in. I've just made a pot of tea. Would you like a cup, Mr Willems?"

Austin grinned and removed his hat. "I would indeed, thank you."

They sat on chairs in the small living room. A teapot and a plate with scones sat on a small table between them. Austin was ravenous, and the scones looked tempting.

"I made them this morning, Mr Willems," she smiled. "Please, help yourself."

Austin needed no further urging and reached for a scone.

"Now, then, how can I help you?" she asked.

As he'd done half a dozen times earlier, Austin recounted the reason for his visit. Mrs Dorling listened and smiled when he'd finished.

"Albert was military," she said.

Austin looked at her in surprise.

She pointed to his hand. "Your regimental ring. My late husband, Albert, was an officer... he passed, bless his soul. What rank do you hold?"

"I'm a captain with the 67th South Hampshire Regiment of Foot, Mrs Dorling."

"Then I shall address you appropriately, Captain Willems."

"Thank you. Ah, yes, and, er, my condolences for your loss." He smiled politely as she sipped from her teacup. He was about to remind her of his question when she spoke again.

"Captain Willems, I was forced into selling my home. I didn't want to part with it but had little choice. That man came here and made me a ridiculous offer. He told me if I didn't accept, the courts would intervene and tie me up in endless litigation, and there was every chance I could be offered even less to mitigate legal costs. Doesn't seem just to me, Captain Willems. Do you think it's fair?"

Austin was shocked that she was willing to talk. "Uh, no, it isn't equitable at all."

"That man told me I shouldn't talk about the sale or the offer, as it could have unpleasant repercussions." She looked at Austin and laughed. "What could they possibly do to an old lady?"

"Mrs Dorling, this man, can you recall his name?"

"Oh yes, I remember Mr Siles well. I didn't like him very much and found him rude and arrogant. Like you, he was military. When I asked him if he was in the army, he denied it, but he wore a ring like yours, and I didn't tell him I knew."

"Do you know whom you sold your property to?"

Mrs Dorling looked up at the ceiling and shook her head. "I can't recall. Please, have another scone, Captain."

"Your bill of sale paperwork," he suggested.

She placed her teacup on the table and rose from her chair. "One moment." She walked from the room and returned moments later with several documents. Austin helped himself to another scone as she suggested.

"It says here that that purchaser was a gentleman called Julian De Vore. I have his address. Would you like it?"

Austin grinned. "Yes, thank you, it would be most helpful."

"18 Middle Temple Lane in London."

Austin committed the address to memory. "Mrs Dorling, when this man Mr Siles said to you there would be repercussions, what did he mean?"

"Oh, good heavens, I don't know. When he told me that, he wagged a finger at me and said to keep my mouth shut. Rather rude, don't you think?"

"So why are you willing to share this information with me if you have been warned not to?"

"Because I disapprove of how they went about it, Captain Willems," she harrumphed and folded her arms. "Threatening people with repercussions, what nonsense is that I ask you?"

CHAPTER FOUR

"Shouldn't you be back in Westchester?" asked Howard Willoughby from behind the clutter on his desk. He rose from his seat and pointed to a comfortable armchair for Austin to sit.

"I would, except for what I learned from visiting Swindon landowners who sold their property."

Howard seated himself in the other armchair facing Austin. "Then I presume your jaunt was somewhat fruitful?"

"Unfortunately, it was, which is why I decided to revert to London before returning to the regiment."

The solicitor's face clouded over. "Out with it."

Howard chewed on his bottom lip and considered all that Austin shared. "So, this Miles Siles chap tempted everyone to band together and form a group with the promise of receiving a high price for their property, and once they did, he came back and told them they would have to accept a paltry meagre offer, or else?"

"Apparently so."

"And the property purchaser, this Julian De Vore character… The name is familiar to me… Did you manage to glean any information on him?"

"Only an address, 18 Middle Temple Lane in London."

"Good gracious, that's the next street behind us," exclaimed

Howard. "I would hazard a guess the man is a solicitor, or worse, a barrister."

"And I believe this Miles Siles fellow works for him," Austin added.

Howard nodded. "Most likely, he does the sodding dirty work."

"And what do we do about it? Now, more than ever, I believe Grand Overland Rail set father up. I have confirmed that two property owners sold at a very low price, and you told me that Grand Overland Rail complained that they had to outbid competitors. Which I don't believe happened at all."

"Then it would be safe to assume that Mr De Vore accepted the bid from Grand Overland Rail, and in all likelihood, he probably works for them." He exhaled.

"I can't ignore this, Howard." Austin shook his head. "What can you do, anything?"

Howard gave the matter some thought. "Austin, look, it may not be in your best interest to pursue this–"

"–Howard," he interrupted, "something has to be done. I won't sit by and allow these rogues to continue."

Howard raised both hands in surrender. "You don't know that they are rogues - well, not yet, anyway. But I shall visit this Mr De Vore and see what he has to say for himself. Would you care to come?"

Austin was looking out the window, lost in thought.

"Austin?"

He swivelled his head to look at the solicitor. "Sorry, I was just thinking."

Howard repeated his question. "Would you care to come with me to see Mr Julian De Vore?"

"No, I do not believe this is best. I prefer that he or his staff don't recognise me for now.

Howard looked surprised.

Austin grinned and leaned forward. "Howard, I have the inklings of an idea, and it might serve me better if these people don't know about me. It might be prudent that you do not mention my name or any interest I have in Grand Overland Rail. I suggest that your excuse to visit Julian De Vore is regarding a..." Austin thought quickly. "A mystery client."

"Mister De Vore will see you now, sir, come this way," instructed the secretary. She waited for Howard to stand and indicated with an arm down the hallway.

Howard smiled politely and followed her to a suite of offices. A brass nameplate was screwed into the door, proudly stating, 'Julian De Vore, Solicitor'. He entered the office to be greeted by an extremely tall man with gaunt features, a rather lengthy beard, and bushy eyebrows that further exaggerated his elongated form.

"Mr Willoughby, I'm delighted to make your acquaintance, and we finally have occasion to meet. I've heard many things about your work, and you set a fine example for the legal fraternity, good sir." He shook Howard's hand vigorously. "Please, please, have a seat, and how can I be of service?"

Howard was surprised at the overly warm welcome, *but better to be welcomed than shunned*, he thought. He took a seat as invited, faced Mr De Vore and smiled in return with equal ardour.

"Mr De Vore, I have a client who came to me with a fairly trivial concern," began Howard with a story he and Austin concocted. "I've come to understand that there are some existing ancestral graves on the property recently sold to you in the outlying region of Swindon."

Mr De Vore's eyebrows raised at the revelation.

"And there is some discussion about relocating the graves," continued Howard.

"Er, which property? This is the first I've come to hear about this. Why was it not brought to my attention earlier?"

"Yes, good point, Mr De Vore. My client believes they did speak to someone and never heard back."

"Oh dear, that isn't proper, is it? Er, who was it they spoke to?"

Howard bent down and retrieved his case. "I have it here, one moment." He made a fuss of looking for a document and extracted a random sheet of paper. "Yes, this is it. My client spoke to a Mr Siles. Does he serve your interests, Mr De Vore?" Howard looked at the solicitor closely. He had Mr De Vore in a quandary.

"There were a few individuals whom I employed that were involved in preliminary discussions with landowners. I'd have to check my records."

"That's quite all right. I can wait," Howard smoothly replied.

"Why must you wait?"

"Oh, forgive me, Mr De Vore. Because my client failed to respond to the original query about moving the burial site, they now must go to considerable expense to have men and machinery do the work, whereas earlier, they had the available resources and labour for this unpleasant task. They have suggested litigation if no recompense is offered. If that were to happen, then Mr Siles becomes a defendant."

"As could I."

"Yes, sir, I expect you would be named. But I don't think it will come to that," appeased Howard with another smile.

Mr De Vore scratched the back of his head. "I seem to recollect, there was a gentleman who was employed by us, uh, his name was Miles Siles. I'm sure he will be able to clear up any misunderstandings."

"Yes, I expect so," Howard responded. "If my client were in error, which is entirely possible, then Mr Siles would inform you."

"Mr Willoughby, what is the address of the property in question?"

"My client does not wish to have their name disclosed yet; they value their privacy, and I'm sure you understand, Mr De Vore. But if Mr Siles recalls the conversation and details, he can suitably inform you. Saves them embarrassment if they have erred, eh."

"This seems highly irregular, Mr Willoughby," Mr De Vore shook his head.

"I agree, and," Howard lowered his voice, "between the two of us, I believe my client is mistaken." He smiled again. "Good day, sir. I shan't keep you from your important work any longer."

"How do you wish to proceed with your client's claim?"

"Mr De Vore, rather than complicate matters unnecessarily, if Mr Siles informs you and denies that anyone spoke to him about relocating a burial site, I will advise my client and ask how they wish to progress. If Mr Siles recalls the conversation, then I shall leave it in your capable hands to see the matter put right. You can send a letter to my office detailing Mr Siles' response and your appropriate course of action."

"I think that is acceptable."

"Wonderful, and thank you for seeing me, sir." Howard stood.

"Yes, anytime, Mr Willoughby." Mr De Vore unfolded his lengthy frame from his seat.

Howard turned to the door, paused and twisted to look back. "Is your client Grand Overland Rail?"

"Is this relevant, Mr Willoughby?"

"Perhaps it might be. Especially if it came to litigation."

"If you refer to who purchased the tracts of land around Swindon, then no, Grand Overland Rail is not my client. My client wishes to remain an undisclosed principal."

Howard's smile vanished. "For the time being, eh… Good day, sir, and again, thank you for your time."

Julian De Vore watched as Howard Willoughby departed and

couldn't help but feel he'd just had something put over on him, but couldn't think what.

Howard returned to his office and immediately drafted a letter to Austin outlining what he'd discovered from his meeting with Julian De Vore.

Captain Austin Willems walked from the regimental offices carrying the letter he received from Howard. He closed the door to his room and impatiently tore open the envelope to read.

Once finished, he placed it on the small writing desk, stood at the window, and considered the matter. On learning that De Vore was a solicitor, as predicted, Howard cleverly thought of a plausible reason to visit him that would have no repercussions or affect his professional reputation.

The objective was to confirm if Grand Overland Rail purchased the land directly from the landowners or through a third party. Because of the nature of Howard and De Vore's discussion, Julian De Vore had a legal responsibility to be truthful if Overland had purchased the land directly because of the potential for litigation. Most interestingly, Howard confirmed that Grand Overland Rail hadn't purchased the land. *Then who did*, he wondered? If the gossip Howard heard from White's Gentlemen's Club were true, that suggested a third party had made the purchase, and in all likelihood, it was the renegade directors from Grand Overland Rail. Secondly, they could now associate Miles Siles with Julian De Vore. This was most perplexing.

Austin had another unbidden thought, and he wondered about the name of the company that purchased his father's business, Midlands Collieries Company. Could Overland's scheming board of directors have created a separate company and, in that name, purchased the land the railway needed and also his father's company before selling it back to Grand Overland Rail?

He sat down at his writing desk, composed a letter for Howard, and outlined his concerns and beliefs. Because Howard was his father's solicitor, he would know the name of the company that purchased Midlands. Austin wagered that the same company bought the Swindon land through Julian De Vore.

Miles Siles loitered in a dark doorway and patiently waited for his employer to appear. Mr De Vore was many things, including a creature of habit, and Miles knew the solicitor would leave his offices at exactly six-thirty and then take a cab, head down The Strand to Pall Mall, and alight at St James Street outside White's, a prestigious gentleman's club.

Miles was about to check the time on his pocket watch when the unmistakable figure of Julian De Vore appeared. His height, accentuated by the topper[4] he wore, made him seem a tall wisp of a man easily blown away by a brisk northerly.

Before the solicitor could hail a cab, Miles exited the doorway and took two long strides, falling into step beside him.

"Mr Siles, how fortunate for us both as I was going to send for you," remarked Julian.

"Ah, of course, Mr De Vore, then it would be a good turn of events."

Julian looked around, found a sheltered doorway, and stepped beneath the awning to avoid the drizzle.

"How can I help?" asked Miles once he caught up.

"What's this business about a previous landowner near Swindon wanting to move family graves? What do you know about this, and why wasn't I told?"

Miles' eyebrows furrowed. "Graves? You've caught me

4   Topper – Victorian slang for Top hat.

completely on the hop. I don't know anything about graves. What's this all about, sir?"

Julian tore his gaze from pedestrians passing by and looked to his helper in consternation. "Graves, Mr Siles. What do you know of ancestral graves in or around Swindon?"

Miles shook his head emphatically. "I must apologise, Mr De Vore. This is news to me. Why would you ask?"

Now, it was Julian De Vore's turn to look puzzled. "Did anyone at any time ever ask you about burial plots?"

Miles shook his head in denial.

Perhaps Mr Willoughby was correct when he assumed his client spoke in error. "No, it matters not, Mr Siles." He made a mental note to send a letter to Mr Willoughby in the morning. "Now, what is it you wanted to see me about? Hurry now; it's damp and chilly, and I have urgent matters to attend to."

I'm sure you do, thought Miles, *Brandy being one of them.* "It's come to my attention that an individual has been asking questions about the Swindon, London land purchase, sir. He was calling on people who sold their property to us."

"Oh, really? Do you have a name, and do you know why, and what interest could he have in a land purchase made months ago?"

Miles shrugged, "Again, I don't have the foggiest notion, sir. The only name I have is Austin Willems."

"Willems!" Mr De Vore exclaimed.

"Then you are familiar with him, Mr De Vore?"

"I do believe he is the son of the late Enoch Willems, previously from Midlands Collieries Company. Why he is asking questions, I don't know. What else did your enquiries reveal?"

"All I know is that he was persistent and upset a few people."

Julian tugged at his beard as he thought. "I think it's time you visited this Willems fellow, Miles. Best if you can tactfully warn him off, eh? Let's keep this gentleman out of trouble, shall we? Come by the office in the morning, and I will give you details on where you can locate this chap."

"As always, sir, I will take care of this for you."

Julian smiled as he saw a cab approach and stuck out his arm. "Carry on, Mr Siles." He hurried from his shelter and into the cab.

CHAPTER FIVE

With little to no regard for her modesty, Austin watched the young girl twirling her skirts atop a table. Fortified by ale, and as he duly predicted, she slipped on the wet surface, lost her balance and promptly fell. Fortunately for the girl, a leering young man sitting at the table opened his arms, and, with a scream of delight, she toppled safely into them. The young man, pleased with his quick reactions and heroic act of chivalry, held her tightly and proceeded to grope her amidst further giggles and squeals. With a laugh, Austin turned away from the amorous couple, upended his tankard and drained what little remained. He belched, slammed the vessel onto the table and turned to one of his companions. "Your turn!" he shouted above the din inside the alehouse.

Two of his three friends followed suit, emptied their mugs with an exaggerated flourish and thumped their tankards onto the table. It was James' turn to buy the next round of ale.

Austin looked at Charles, his closest friend, who waved his arms and shouted. "Not for me, no more. I can't!"

"Why on heavens earth not? It's still early."

Lieutenant Charles Newbury leaned closer to Austin. "Because I must remain reasonably sober, and I am moderately concerned, my good fellow, and certainly fear I may have already crossed that murky line." He saw the disparaging scowl from Austin. "I have to go to London tomorrow and help Father," he added.

"Ahh, yes indeed. I forgot. Well, one more won't hurt, eh?"

Charles's face broke out into a broad grin. "I'm supervising the transportation of father's precious artwork from a gallery to a secure artwork storage warehouse. Father will quickly learn if I appear to show even the slightest effects of intoxication, and then I will suffer endless penance at his pleasure and will. No, thank you very much. I'd rather face a horde of charging Orientals than Fathers' wrath."

They watched a barmaid collect the empty tankards and walk away.

"You've never faced a horde of Orientals in your life. The closest you were to any angry Oriental was in Hong Kong when you refused to pay the madam for that boy."

Charles rolled his eyes. "How often need I say? I asked for a girl, and she gave me a young man; he was but a boy!"

Austin bellowed in laughter and would have fallen from his seat if Charles hadn't hauled him upright by his collar. "Then, by God, you should have availed yourself of his services!"

This time Charles gave him a shove, and Austin fell laughing from his seat to land amongst the debris and rubbish on the filthy floor. All three officers roared in delight as Austin struggled to regain his feet.

Having successfully managed the intricate manoeuvre, Austin stood. "Speaking of, and whilst I remain temporarily upright, I shall visit the convenience. He stumbled to a darkened doorway, a public toilet that allowed only men.

With his task mostly completed, Austin was floundering with the buttons on his breeches when a stranger entered.

The man ignored the army captain's futile attempts with his buttons, walked past, and turned to face him. "Excuse me, sir, are you Captain Austin Willems?"

Austin raised his eyebrows. "Normally I am, good sir, but this evening finds me a little out of sorts," he grinned.

With both hands, the stranger leaned forward, roughly grabbed the front of his tunic, and swung him around to slam hard against the wall.

"Wha–!" Austin was unhurt and sat on the floor, more puzzled than angered by the man's aggressive behaviour.

The stranger stepped up and bent down. "Best you keep away from Swindon, eh ? What happens in Swindon is none of your business, and we don't need troublemakers interfering. Take this as a warning." He thrust a finger into Austin's chest. "Next time, I will be a little less courteous."

Austin stared at the finger momentarily, blinked a couple of times, and then looked at the sneering face. He smiled, but not in mirth. "Chin up, old boy." With clenched hands, he drove them upwards to strike the extended jaw.

Miles Siles' mouth snapped shut with a loud, painful clack, and he stumbled backwards from the impact, clutching his face in agony.

It was a hard blow, and Austin knew he'd seriously hurt the arrogant man. He attempted to stand, the slippery wet floor proving too much, and he failed miserably, sliding back down the wall to the foulness of the toilet floor.

Miles Siles, on the other hand, bent double in pain and, with a hand over his jaw, ran for the door as Charles entered. He barged past the lieutenant as Austin finally managed to stand.

"My God! What happened, Austin?"

"Taught that fool a bloody lesson. Teach him to threaten me," he mumbled.

Austin wondered why he was ordered to appear before his

commanding officer, Colonel Henry Farwell. With permission from the adjutant, Austin entered the regimental office and delivered a crisp salute, ensuring he kept his expression neutral.

"At rest, Captain." Instructed the colonel after returning the salute. With a sigh, the colonel lowered himself to his chair while Austin remained standing and patiently waited.

"And again, Captain," began Colonel Farwell, "I have received complaints about your outlandish behaviour. Frankly, it is disgraceful, and you have hung a dark cloud over this fine regiment and its stellar reputation."

Austin was puzzled and had no idea what the colonel was referring to.

"I find myself in a quandary. You've been a fine officer. No, I stand corrected; you've been an exemplary officer who has shown great leadership, initiative, and bravery. You've proven yourself and fought with distinction and valour. Yet, your recent conduct has been less than satisfactory and marred a distinguished commission." He paused and drummed his fingers on his desktop.

Austin took the pause as a cue. "Colonel Farwell, sir, have I run afoul of someone or some deed?"

The drumming stopped, and the colonel picked up a document at his elbow and waved it at Austin. "When I am forced to explain the conduct of an officer serving under my command to my superiors, then *indeed,* you have done something wrong, Captain."

Austin shook his head in puzzlement.

"My superiors received a letter of complaint and admonishment from a noted and influential London solicitor that detailed your violent and unprovoked attack on a distinguished military officer, Major Miles Siles. How can you continue with such behaviour, Captain? It's totally unacceptable."

"Sir, I can explain. This account is a fabrication."

"A fabrication? Captain, you broke the bloody man's jaw!"

"It was an unprovoked attack, sir. He set upon me in the public toilets of an alehouse and assaulted me. I defended myself as is my right, Colonel."

Colonel Farwell sucked the inside of his cheek and slowly nodded. "Then you have witnesses and someone credible to support your account?"

Austin thought back to that evening over two weeks ago. "Lieutenant Charles Newbury was there but did not witness the attack on me. He entered the convenience after the incident, sir."

"As I thought. So, it is your word against the word of a Major. Is this the best you can do, Captain Willems?"

"I can only recount to you the truth, sir."

"Ah, the same truth you used to describe the assault on three constables?"

Austin defiantly lifted his chin and remained silent.

"Captain Willems, I have been influenced to begin an immediate court-martial proceeding against you. Your reckoning of this incident with Major Siles doesn't serve you well, and the outcome looks rather bleak. While I have defended you, I can no longer jeopardise my career when my superiors seek blood."

Austin looked down at the floor and tried to think of a solution or mitigating details to help. "Am I permitted to read that letter?"

The colonel scooped it up and thrust out a hand.

Immediately, Austin recognised the solicitor's name, Julian De Vore, and it all made sense. The letter detailed how Captain Willems, while inebriated, attacked Major Siles when using the public amenities at The Cotters Arms alehouse. Through physical and unprovoked violence, Captain Willems struck Major Siles around the head, resulting in a broken jaw. "May I keep this, sir?"

"I'll have a copy made, and you can keep the original," stated the colonel.

"Thank you, sir."

Colonel Farwell looked at the young captain. "Then you don't deny you struck him?"

"No, sir, I did hit him, and hard too."

"But you claim he assaulted you first."

"He threw me against the wall, and I collapsed to the ground, sir."

"Are you previously acquainted with him, and did you initiate the incident?

Austin shook his head. "No, sir, I did not. I'd never met the man before." He leaned forward. "As a point of interest, sir. Miles Siles is employed by that solicitor, Julian De Vore, who wrote the letter. Yes, that doesn't prove my innocence, but it casts some doubt on the man's integrity. He's a fixer for De Vore."

Colonel Farwell seemed to relax and leaned back in his chair with both hands clasped over his stomach. "I shouldn't, but I do believe you." The colonel sighed again. "Captain, you have two choices." He looked into Austin's eyes. "You can defend the charges made against you in a court-martial, or, and there is another alternative that might suit you better, you can voluntarily resign your commission with honours. But I cannot let this slide."

Austin's heart began pounding in his chest. He'd never considered resigning his commission. "May I think on this, sir?"

Colonel Farwell shook his head. "No, you may not. I need an immediate response."

Austin looked up at the ceiling and thought about how he could defend himself in a court-martial, and he knew he had no witnesses who saw Siles attack him; no one overheard the threat made to him; he had nothing. He lowered his gaze, squared his shoulders and held the colonels' eyes. "Sir, I will resign my commission, but I need assurance that this accusation goes no further and ends here and now. I do not want to face any judicial or military proceedings over this fabricated claim. The only reason this ludicrous allegation was made is that this Siles fellow ensured there were no witnesses when he attacked me."

The colonel's expression softened. "Does this have anything to do with your father's death?"

"I believe it does, sir. My father died of a heart condition, but he recently lost his business in a, let's say an underhanded way. I made some inquiries while on bereavement leave and seemed to have ruffled a few feathers. The letter from the solicitor you were given is the same solicitor that may be behind all this."

Colonel Farwell raised both eyebrows. "And that solicitor has some powerful friends. But again, can you prove any of it? It could help with the court-martial if you choose that option."

Austin shook his head. "No, sir, I have no evidence at all."

"I see." The colonel paused and looked thoughtful before speaking. "Austin, the court-martial is not my doing, and I have no choice but to initiate and support the proceedings. The date of your resignation will precede the date of any investigation of the allegations made by Mr De Vore; therefore, as far as I am concerned, the matter is closed."

"I understand completely, sir, and thank you."

"Come by the office in the morning, and the sergeant will have the required paperwork for you to sign. That will be all."

Austin saluted.

CHAPTER SIX

Austin's childhood home in London was a four-storied, Regency era townhouse. Enoch Willems purchased the spacious house when new because of its convenient proximity to the pleasure garden across the road, called The Regent's Park, and had lived there ever since. For a mischievous young lad, the park had been a wonderful playground. Austin enjoyed the freedom to explore the four-hundred-acre grounds, including the lake and all it had to offer with friends under the watchful eye of Miss Elizabeth Goodhew, or Nanny as she was more familiarly known.

Austin stayed at the house briefly during his father's funeral service, but after resigning his commission, he returned permanently and arrived with his few possessions late the previous afternoon.

He leaned against the window, looking out across the expanse of greenery called The Regent's Park and cradled his chin in his hand, lost in the sadness and despair of his father's recent passing and the unexpected change in his circumstances. Being back here took emotional courage to accept that his father was no longer alive, yet his memory and presence remained a welcoming and vibrant force inside the walls of his childhood home.

Money wasn't an issue; Henry Willoughby had explained that adequate financial provisions had been made for him, and Enoch had wisely ensured his only son would have no need or want. Although he was an active bachelor, Austin had also been careful and had more than enough money from investments and through Henry's wise and expert financial counsel. All combined, there was no need to work, and Austin could live comfortably as a gentleman for the rest of his life and the next if he chose. Boredom was the challenge, which was why he loved the excitement of life as an officer with the 67th South Hampshire Regiment of Foot. But those days were now over, and for Captain Austin Willems, it was difficult to accept.

When he heard a knock, he turned to face the door, and Nanny entered the room.

"Mr Willoughby is here, sir," she said politely.

Austin smiled. "Thank you, Nanny, see him in."

She dipped her head and quietly exited the room, closing the door softly behind her. No matter how often Nanny had been asked and then instructed to address them familiarly by their Christian names and to be more relaxed and informal, she adamantly refused. While Enoch, and now Austin, paid her a generous wage, they treated her as family and not staff, and no matter how much they insisted she sit and eat with them during meals or play parlour games during long winter evenings, she declined. Austin loved her like the mother he never knew, and to him, she was family. Yet, Nanny determined and set the rules; for all intents and purposes, this was also her home.

Only moments later, Nanny knocked again, opened the door and invited their guest to enter. As was his habit, Howard turned, leaned forward and kissed her cheek. "Mr Willoughby!" she exclaimed in mock protest. Austin saw her smile before turning away and closing the door to leave both men alone. She loved the attention.

"Howard, lovely to see you," greeted Austin. "Sit, make yourself comfortable."

Howard sat in his favourite chair and crossed his legs as Austin walked from the window and sat in the chair his father had typically occupied.

"I must say, your letter gave me a start, Austin. I never expected you to resign your commission."

"Nor I. Although I had little choice." Austin reached into the inside jacket pocket and extracted the letter written by solicitor Julian De Vore that Colonel Farwell had allowed him to keep.

Howard began reading the letter as Nanny reappeared with a tray of cakes. After placing the plate on a low table, she reached to a silver tray atop a credenza, put a glass before each man and thoughtfully poured a healthy dollop of whiskey into each.

"Thank you, Nanny," said Austin while Howard smiled warmly at her. Austin and his father had often talked together and believed Henry had more than a casual fondness for Nanny. Try as they might, they could never entice Howard to admit it.

After the door closed, Howard continued reading the letter and, when finished, looked at Austin. "Let me make an assumption: your commanding officer gave you two options: either resign or face a court-martial?"

Austin shrugged. "I had no choice."

"So, what really happened?"

Austin explained the details of the incident at the Cotters Arms and what he did to Miles Siles. Howard listened and asked a few questions.

"Mr De Vore shouldn't be underestimated, Austin. I believe he is a dangerous and well-connected adversary."

"And after receiving this letter, that's what I believe, too."

"Through his military connections, he may press the issue, and you could still force a court-martial, which concerns me."

Austin nodded. "Colonel Farwell said the matter is closed."

"But do you have that in writing?"

"No."

"Then we shall see." Howard took a sip from his whiskey. "You queried me a while ago about who purchased Midlands Collieries Company."

In anticipation, Austin leaned forward in his chair.

"As suspected, and you were absolutely correct, it was Mr Julian De Vore," Howard quietly replied, looking distractedly into his glass. "That's why I recognised his name when you mentioned it."

"Bloody hell! This changes everything. That means De Vore was acting in concert with the wayward directors from Grand Overland Rail." Austin saw Howard's expression. "Something wrong?"

Howard looked up from his whiskey. "When you first mentioned Julian De Vore to me, I admitted to being remiss and did not associate him as also being the solicitor representing the buyer for your father's business. It never dawned on me. I feel terrible and should have known."

"But at the time, you had no reason to suspect anything was awry."

Howard shrugged. "Yes, it looks like De Vore was behind everything. He orchestrated purchasing cheap land, sold it at an inflated rate and then, with the surplus, bought Midlands Collieries Company. But remember, Austin, not all the directors were involved. Your father was a director too but knew nothing of their plans. So, there must have been a group of them, and as you believe, a shadow board of directors who pulled the strings."

Austin was furious and downed his glass. He shook his head as he felt the burn. "Perhaps it's the remaining directors, the ones who didn't sell their shares."

"Most likely," Howard responded with his mouth full of Nanny's cake.

"Howard, you told me that father met the principals of Grand Overland Rail at a gentleman's club."

"Yes, at White's. Apparently, they're keen whist[5] players, and he would occasionally join their group, although I abhor the silly game. Why do you ask?" He wiped away cake crumps from his waistcoat.

"Perhaps I should take up whist, as I'm unemployed and a gentleman of leisure, then I could make the acquaintance of these particular gentlemen and learn more about them," Austin held Howard's gaze.

"And to what end?" Howard asked, his voice measured.

"I'm going to see justice done."

Howard laughed. "Legal justice or yours?"

"We shall see," Austin grinned. "And if you'll help me?"

The solicitor paused a moment. "All right. I shall endeavour to find out the names of the directors I suspect are part of this shadow directors' cabal. I'll do what I can. Certainly, we owe it to your father. But what will you do with this knowledge?"

"Ahh, now there's a good question. At the moment, I'm not sure. At first, my priority is identifying the board members and which ones are the rogues. Anything else depends on what I learn, and I, uh, have the time."

"That you do."

As one of London's most exclusive private gentleman's clubs, obtaining membership at White's was not a privilege to be taken lightly. Thoroughly aware of that challenge, Enoch Willems secured his son a highly prized membership by registering his name for membership at birth. Austin had been there infrequently and generally only to meet his father for a meal or a beverage when

5   *Whist – An English trick-taking card game that was very popular during the Victorian era.*

visiting London. He was largely unknown to its members, could enjoy anonymity, and was hopeful to learn more about the few Grand Overland Rail board members who acted independently.

White's Gentleman's Club card room is on the first floor, on the right-hand rear side of the five-story building on St James Street. It isn't a large room by any stretch of the imagination, yet it offers an intimate setting for those wishing to be entertained while playing cards with close acquaintances or utilising the room for more private discussions. Against one wall sits a small fireplace, and hanging from the ceiling, an oversized chandelier provides more than adequate lighting. A handful of small beige-covered tables are discreetly positioned, allowing players to play unhindered or distracted by other groups of card-playing members.

Howard told him that his contact, a White's employee, dutifully informed him that Grand Overland Rail board members typically met and played cards on Wednesday and Friday evenings. Once a month, they met on a Sunday afternoon. They preferred to sit and play at the table immediately in front of the hearth, where they could warm chilly bottoms.

Captain Austin Willems sat in the cardroom at White's, in the far corner near the fireplace, with a notebook, a slate pencil, and a healthy pile of reading material, which included everything that Henry Willoughby could obtain on Grand Overland Rail and its current board of directors and waited.

It wasn't a long wait before four gentlemen noisily entered the cardroom and saw the unexpected and unknown club member quietly reading in the corner.

"Oh, good heavens, you gave me a start. I apologise, normally it's just us in here," stated a rotund man with huge side whiskers that extended well below his jawline.

"Sorry, old chap," replied another.

Austin sat side-on, with his hand covering most of his face, offering only a partial profile to anyone entering the room. To prevent anyone from recognising him, he removed his moustache, a compulsory requirement for military officers, and was now cleanly shaven. With some confidence, he felt he appeared more unrecognisable.

He partially turned to the four men and forced a smile. "It's quite all right, and I hope my presence doesn't disrupt your game."

A somewhat obese man waddled in and took a seat. "Who the bloody hell is he?" he barked.

"George!" admonished a man with healthy walrus whiskers. "Be civil."

Austin kept his head lowered and tried to be as unobtrusive as possible. Throughout the evening, the group became more talkative and directly proportional to the brandy they consumed, and Austin listened and made notes.

Determining the man in the corner wasn't paying them any attention, Grand Overland Rail's directors began to speak without reservations. While they cleverly never used any names, Austin learned that the company was being overcharged by a London solicitor and presumed it was Julian De Vore they spoke of. Austin smiled when one director suggested the solicitor was extorting them.

Through ongoing conversations, Austin learned that one director collected fine art, and another had more interest in women and the stable of mistresses he financially supported.

Another gentleman seated at the table was Grand Overland Rail's managing director, Sir Ronald Hewitt-Thompson, and Austin knew him to be a baron of lowly peerage. His passions lay with the numerous racehorses he owned. Austin risked a closer look and identified him as the corpulent chap with the blossoming walrus moustache and a ruddy complexion. He committed his face to memory as he kept his own face obscured. By the end of the evening, he became quite conversant with each man's personality, but not once did anyone discuss coal or Midlands Collieries Company. By the time they finished their games of whist, Austin was exhausted and fought to remain awake.

He waited for quite some time to ensure they'd all departed the building, as he didn't want to encounter and be forced to converse with any of them when he departed. When he felt it safe, he kept his head low, quickly exited the club, and returned home.

Howard previously informed him that the directors would meet on Sunday. As it was only Wednesday, Austin decided not to return on Friday but go to their once-a-month Sunday afternoon game and hope to discover more.

CHAPTER SEVEN

The rules of whist are quite explicit, and no player may comment on the cards they are dealt whether to express their good or bad fortune. Vocally communicating game strategy to your partner is also strictly forbidden, thus allowing all players to chat and talk freely about anything other than their current game.

During Sunday afternoon's whist game at White's, the four directors of Grand Overland Rail's conversation ranged from the weather, racehorses, and crime in London to the remarkable talents of a few ladies of dubious character, and Austin was becoming increasingly restless.

Another group of four men played cards quietly on the far side of the room. As protocol dictated, they honoured the privacy of other club members and spoke discretely only amongst themselves.

Austin forced himself not to react when suddenly, George Dillington, the obese and outspoken director, who typically showed no restraint with his opinions and thoughts, made a simple comment about coal. He exclaimed that coal was indeed a boon to humanity when a White's employee entered the room to attend to the fire by shovelling more coal onto glowing embers.

Immediately, the managing director, Sir Ronald, added with a laugh, "I do consider, George, that Mr Enoch Willems also believed that to be the case."

"And we should give thanks to Mr Willems. Without his fine business, we could not enjoy the advantage and benefits of possessing Midlands Collieries Company," added Oscar Baker, the art connoisseur, with a hearty chuckle.

Austin gripped the armrests of his chair until his knuckles turned white.

Sir Ronald coughed. "This brings me to a point, gentlemen. I, uh, had a recent *communiqué* and, er, instructions." He paused and waited until he had everyone's full attention. "It's been suggested that Grand Overland Rail should also acquire a coachbuilder. Certainly, this would offset our expansion costs. We currently don't have enough carriages and will require significantly more."

"But we have already factored that into our budget," added Virgil Hartmann, the more reserved and softspoken of the directors.

Sir Ronald lowered his voice, and Austin unconsciously leaned over to hear more clearly. "If London Private Acquisitions makes the purchase in the same manner as we obtained Midlands Collieries, then we stand to gain enormously."

"And of the Chairman, does he approve?" whispered an unknown voice.

"No, apparently not yet. I'm told he will be apprised, and we will receive his endorsement in due course," clarified Sir Ronald.

Austin was frantically writing as quickly as possible. *London Private Acquisitions? Who was this company? The Chairman?* he wondered. What these men were talking about was simply staggering, and his blood was near-boiling.

Sir Ronald spared a glance around the room. It was almost empty, except for the card-playing group on the far side of the room and the stranger in the corner scribbling away. Since the fire had been stoked, it again blazed and provided much-needed warmth. Even though the four directors made every effort to speak quietly, they needed to talk above the roar of the fire, and they spoke just loud enough for Austin to overhear.

"It seems that a respectable coachbuilder is interested in obtaining shares and a position on the board of directors of Grand Overland Rail. Oh, goodness, it seems I am again victorious, gentlemen," exclaimed Sir Ronald with more enthusiasm than deemed sporting. "One more game?"

Austin rolled his eyes.

George Dillington laughed, ending with a series of wheezes like a locomotive leaving the station. "And as luck would have it, we do have an open position on the board," he added, dealing thirteen cards to each player.

The other group finished their game and left the cardroom.

"And how thoughtful of Enoch Willems to conveniently vacate his position," chimed in Oscar Baker. "Perhaps the coachbuilder will offer us the same courtesy." They all chuckled. "And, Ronald, who is this coachbuilder so interested in us?"

"Watson Brothers, in Marylebone."

All players stopped looking at their cards and lifted their heads to stare at Sir Ronald. Each knew the name of Watson Brothers Coachbuilders; they were a foremost leader in the industry."

"Goodness, that could be a windfall, but that's two board positions… the brothers," added Oscar Baker. "But we must exercise restraint and caution."

"And not be carried away," added George Dillington with a loud guffaw.

All four directors laughed heartily at George's dry wit and returned to studying the cards dealt to them.

"I've already spoken to one brother, but it was only a casual enquiry," volunteered Sir Ronald. "We still have a way to go before any commitment is made."

Austin glared at the distant wall, seething in silent rage.

"But how will we make money? We have all the land we need. So that ploy won't work again," asked Virgil.

"Gentlemen, come now. The Chairman has thought this through and foresees a labour dispute that will cause a costly delay in laying track, unless, of course, a loan can be obtained to appease greedy workers and their selfish demands for more money."

"Sodding labourers," added George with a grin as he threw down a card to win the trick. "And no doubt that line of credit will be available to us?"

"So it seems," replied Sir Ronald.

Long after the four directors departed, Austin sat alone in the cardroom of White's gentleman's club. In disbelief, he stared at his handwritten notes and tried to make sense of what the directors talked about. What they planned was risky, even foolhardy, and the amount of money involved would be staggering. Buying shares, invoking a labour dispute, bank loans, and shareholder debt repayments didn't bear thinking about.

One thing became increasingly clear to him. He wanted these directors who acted with such brazen impunity to suffer. Perhaps suffering was too soft, he mused. Pain was more apt, and if those four wealthy men could experience real pain and have their financial dominions collapse like a house of cards, that would serve his purpose and prevent honest businessmen like his father from falling victim to these scurrilous swindlers.

He thumped his fist on the chair's armrest, packed his notes away and departed the building. This evening, his friend Lieutenant Charles Newbury was visiting for dinner, and he was looking forward to catching up.

Nanny cleared away the dinner dishes, and Austin and Charles retired to the library, which was more agreeable. They sat in comfortable leather wing-backed library chairs and cradled a glass of Port.

"I must say, Austin, being in the house without your father is strange. How have you been coping?"

Austin shrugged. "It hasn't been easy, especially around the circumstances preceding his death."

Charles turned to look at his friend with some concern. "In what way?"

"Mostly with his business, and more than ever, I think he was swindled." he replied, staring into the fire.

"That's a bit on the nose, eh? Is this something you wish to share?"

Austin exhaled loudly and began to detail the entire story, including his visit to White's earlier today and what he'd learned. When finished, Charles remained quiet as he digested what Austin divulged.

The fire crackled in the hearth, and both men stared, mesmerised by dancing flames.

"And what will you do? I know you, Austin, and you won't sit idly by and allow these men free rein to cheat people."

Austin turned from the fire and looked at his friend. "What can I do?"

"Tell me again, what do you know of these four directors?"

Austin recounted all he knew, including their habits and personalities.

"So this Oscar Baker fellow collects art?" Charles asked.

"Apparently so. Mr Baker has some art at his various residences and others in various galleries, but most of it is in storage somewhere.

He can't stop bragging about his collection, and it's a passion very close to his heart."

"I know the sentiment; father feels the same," added Charles as he rubbed his chin. "Were you aware that there is only one credible secure art storage facility in London?"

Austin shook his head.

"Aye, and if you are a serious collector and require your art stored securely, then there is only one place to go." Charles raised his glass and gently swirled the ruby liquid before swallowing the remainder.

"And where would that be?" Austin asked.

"Finch & Gossett. I've been there numerous times. Father is too old to supervise the relocation of his art, so on his behalf, I must ensure all is well, and when required, I supervise the transportation and storage for him." Charles paused, then continued. "Colin Finch lives above the warehouse and is a most peculiar person of habit. He has a fondness for whores–"

"Then he has interests similar to our own," laughed Austin.

"Indeed," grinned Charles. "But one in particular has taken his fancy. Every Saturday evening, she visits him at his flat above the warehouse for an hour–"

"Only an hour?" Austin interrupted with a grin.

Charles opened his mouth to continue when Austin interjected. "I have heard of fine art storage, but only because people talk about a safe and secure place to store art, but why are you telling me this?"

Charles put his empty glass on the table and leaned forward. "Because, my good chap, you're going to steal his art."

Austin's mouth dropped open. "You want me to steal fine art from a secure warehouse like a common robber? You must be out of your mind," he exclaimed.

"Am I? Austin, you want to drive a stake into the heart of these four directors, and the only way you can achieve that is to get them where it hurts. Their pockets and hearts. It is easier–"

"I'm not a villain–"

"Even better. Look, if this director, whatever his name is–"

"Oscar Baker."

"Very well, then I'd wager if his prized art collection is as impressive as he says, then he can only use Finch & Gossett." Charles leaned back in his chair with a self-satisfied smirk. "I believe you can obtain his artworks with some ease."

"Me, by myself?" Austin asked.

Charles laughed. "Well, I can help. Both of us will do it. But yes, and I propose that we steal his art," he confirmed with an air of smugness.

Austin shook his head and stared into the hearth. *What Charles proposed was audacious, pure lunacy.*

"It isn't like you haven't done worse. And you and I both know it, Austin."

Austin waved his arm at Charles. "I needn't be reminded, thank you."

"Look, you want to bring financial ruin to these men. You told me that's what you wanted, so this is a good opportunity," Charles suggested.

Austin changed to a more comfortable position in his chair to better see his friend. "Yes, it is what I want. But there are three other directors, and stealing art from one of them won't bring about their combined downfall."

Both young men reflected in silence.

"Unless," began Austin, "We discredit George Dillington with the public knowledge of his mistresses and, er, steal a racehorse or two."

Charles laughed. "That's the spirit. If he is well-heeled in racing circles, his horses surely must race at Ascot."

Austin shrugged. "He did mention Ascot."

Charles slapped the arm rest of his chair. "So be it. We shall plan our annual Ascot pilgrimage and investigate these horses. What say you, Captain Willems?"

"We got into so much trouble last year," Austin laughed.

"We?" You were the instigator, my friend and like a fool, I followed," Charles added.

Both men laughed.

Charles's expression turned serious. "But that leaves one other."

"Yes, Mr Virgil Hartmann."

"And what's his Achilles heel?"

"The man is enamoured with large boats, sailboats, I believe."

"I have a sinking feeling about Mr Hartmann, Austin." Charles looked Austin in the eye, and both men began to laugh.

Once settled, Austin refilled both glasses. "Charles, it's all very well to make fanciful plans to hurt these four men, but it doesn't solve the main issue."

"Which is?"

"I want Midlands Collieries Company to be owned by a Willems again. It was Father's business, and he dedicated his life to growing and expanding it. He always wished to hand Midlands over to me, and I want to honour that."

"And so it shall be, Austin."

Austin raised his eyebrows.

"You know the plans of these directors. With careful thought, you could affect their dishonourable intentions and destroy them in the process, and then there is every chance you could buy back Midlands at a good price. And before you interrupt me," Charles raised a hand, "If Grand Overland Rail is encountering financial difficulties, then they will want to unload Midlands and other businesses they have purchased for the cash."

Austin nodded. "I agree, and I thought of that too."

Charles emptied his glass. "Rather than stumble blindly into this, we should carefully plan every phase of the Order of Battle and execute with military precision. Surrender is unacceptable," he laughed.

"And you are willing to help and be part of this?" Austin asked his friend.

"Try and stop me," grinned Charles.

It was late evening when Lieutenant Charles Newbury walked from Austin Willems' home in The Regent's Park. They'd talked long into the evening and spoke of their *campaign*, as they called it, much like any officers planning for battle against a capable adversary. They weighed risk against reward and how to overcome obstacles that lay in their path. The more they talked, the more convinced Austin became that his campaign of retribution could work.

His dear friend Charles brought light into his life, and for the first time in weeks, he slept soundly.

CHAPTER EIGHT

Austin stepped from Walker, Wakefield and Willoughby, Barristers and Solicitors on Essex Street and waited for a cab. He'd spent the last two hours explaining to Howard what he'd learned while eavesdropping at White's on Sunday.

Howard was livid and absolutely furious when he heard what the renegade directors were planning. Thankfully, he calmed down before Austin told him he would pay Mr Watson, one of the principal brothers who owned Watson Brothers Coachbuilders, a visit and warn him. Tactfully, Austin did not inform Howard of his plan conceived the previous evening with Charles. Howard believed Austin was only advising Mr Watson to stay clear of Grand Overland Rail and nothing more. Meanwhile, Howard offered to learn everything he could about London Private Acquisitions and confirm who the company's principals were, including the mysterious Chairman.

The cab delivered him to Marylebone and deposited him outside the yard of Watson Brothers Coachbuilders. Austin could see that the company occupied an enormous workshop and built various coaches and carriages of different design sizes and shapes. Through large, open sliding doors, he could see men working and scrambling like ants in and over their unfinished creations. Occasionally, the sound of a foreman yelling at some poor apprentice drifted out onto the street and didn't seem to be much different from a drill sergeant screaming at an enlisted recruit. He grinned and walked on.

He looked for offices and found a small administration building inside a yard adjacent to the workshop, where timber and other supplies were stored.

He entered the office to find it empty. While waiting for someone to attend to him, he picked up a brochure and quickly skimmed through it. He read that two brothers, Jeffrey and Harrison Watson, ran the company and were the men he needed to meet.

He was about to leave when a harried young man finally entered through a side door and looked surprised to see someone waiting.

"Excuse me, sir. Has someone attended to you?"

Austin shook his head. "No, not yet."

"Oh, dear me, I apologise." He straightened his tie and vest and self-consciously walked to the reception counter, paused and leaned forward. "Er, and how may I assist you, sir?"

"That's quite all right; my visit is unscheduled. But I want to arrange a meeting with Messer's Jeffrey and Harrison Watson." Austin smiled warmly.

The young man took on the appearance of an undertaker, and his expression changed from one of overwork to pure despair. "Oh my, I'm dreadfully sorry, sir. All executive appointments must go through our main office at 17 Garrick Street in the West End."

Austin nodded; he expected as much. "Not to worry, cheer up. I shall visit them there. When is the best time to call?"

The young man looked horrified to be burdened with such an important question. "I'd, uh, presume, ten o'clock, sir."

"Thank you, and good tidings."

The nervous man smiled as Austin opened the door. Once again on the street, he hailed a hansom cab with instructions to take him to Garrick Street.

The executive waiting room of Watson Brothers Coachbuilders was impressive and constructed like the inside of a luxurious carriage with exquisite woodwork and upholstery. This time, the reception desk was staffed, and a middle-aged woman looked at him inquisitively. "Good morning, sir. How may we assist you today?"

Austin removed his hat and smiled pleasantly at the receptionist. "Good day, er, my name is Captain Austin Willems, and I'd like to schedule a meeting with Messer's Jeffrey and Harrison Watson. It is rather urgent and, er, confidential." He smiled again, just in case she missed his earlier one.

She scrunched up her face. "Confidential? Can you provide a company name that you represent, sir? It may help."

"Please inform them I am Captain Austin Willems, Midlands Collieries Company. That should be sufficient. Are they in?"

"Yes, you are fortunate, sir. Please wait, and I shall return." With that, she hoisted herself from her seat and trotted off down the hallway, only to return a minute later. Austin saw she looked a lot happier.

"Captain Willems, this way, sir. They have time to see you briefly."

Two rather large, burly men stood in the office and faced Austin with some trepidation and annoyance. After introducing themselves, they remained standing and did not offer him the kindness of a seat.

"And how may we help you, Captain?" said Harrison Watson, standing in the middle of his office. His brother, Jeffrey, stood a yard away from his brother with thumbs hooked through his braces.

"Gentlemen, I come here this morning as a courtesy through a mutual interest," Austin began.

"And this mutual interest would be?"

These men aren't making it easy, he thought. "Grand Overland Rail."

Both brothers exchanged a look. "And what interest do you have with Grand Overland Rail, other than representing a coal company?" asked Harrison.

"I don't represent a coal company, Mr Watson. Midlands Collieries Company was founded and owned by my father, Enoch Willems, until he was forced to sell due to the immoral business practices of Grand Overland Rail."

Again, the brothers shared a look. "And what does this have to do with Watson Brothers Coachbuilders?"

Austin looked squarely at Harrison, held his gaze, then turned to Jefferey and locked eyes with him. "Because you are considering purchasing shares of Overland, and let me assume, also a directorship."

"Utter nonsense!" Jeffrey bellowed.

"That is confidential. How did you come by that information?" snapped Harrison.

Jeffrey looked at his brother in complete surprise but remained silent.

"Mr Willems, perhaps–"

"Captain Willems, sir."

"Perhaps, Captain Willems, would you care to have a seat?" Harrison raised an arm and pointed to a settee. Directly in front of the settee, like sentinels, two enormous chairs were positioned side by side. Austin nodded and sat closer to Harrison at one end of the settee, creating an imbalance.

"Captain Willems, how is it you came by this sensitive information, and what is this drivel about immoral business practices?"

Austin nodded. "Gentlemen, if you have any appointments, I suggest you reschedule; this may take a while."

Neither Harrison nor Jeffrey responded although Jeffrey looked angry and ready to explode. Austin ignored the man, shrugged and began. "My father was the sole proprietor of Midlands Collieries Company, and he sought a major long-term customer. As I've been informed, he met some of the directors of Grand Overland Rail at White's, where early discussions began, and he was offered a directorship if he purchased a minimum of ten thousand pounds of shares. Grand Overland Rail required capital to purchase land to complete their rail line from Cardiff to London, and they still needed to buy large tracts of land around Swindon. Because Grand Overland Rail was an established company with customers, assets and a prosperous future, it appeared to be a low-risk investment. Or so my father believed." Austin paused a moment to collect his thoughts. Jeffrey still fumed.

"Carry on, Captain Willems. Er, would you like a cup of tea?" asked Harrison, oblivious to his brother's demeanour.

"Yes, thank you," Austin replied.

"Cancel the twelve o'clock," stated Jeffrey, appearing more composed.

Harrison exited the room and returned soon after. "Now, where were we?"

"Some of what I shall tell you is still unclear, but I will explain what I know."

The Watson brothers nodded in tandem and listened with growing interest and concern.

"An undisclosed principal purchased the land that Grand Overland Rail needed through a solicitor acting as an agent. I believe this undisclosed principal is, in fact, a company called London Private Acquisitions. Are either of you familiar with this company?"

Austin saw Harrison's eyes widen in reaction, then shook his head.

"I think we will soon discover that London Private Acquisitions is owned by at least four men, who collectively are also board members for Grand Overland Rail. Through intimidation, London Private Acquisitions purchased the land cheaply and sold it to Grand Overland Rail at over two and a half times the budgeted cost."

"Good heavens," stated Harrison, turning to his brother for affirmation.

"Whoresons," responded Jeffrey.

"Most unfortunately, it does become worse. Grand Overland Rail did not have the capital to purchase the overpriced land from London Private Acquisitions and turned to the bank to obtain a short-term loan. When the loan was due, and because they still didn't have the funds, they had the liable shareholders pay their portion of the unpaid debt according to the shares they owned. My father, who liquidated many of his assets to buy Overland shares, had no cash on hand and had to sell his business. He sold Midlands Collieries to an undisclosed principal. As it turns out, the principal was–"

"London Private Acquisitions," emphatically stated Harrison.

Jeffrey leaned back in his chair, folded his arms, and didn't appear thrilled.

Harrison spoke for both brothers. "Aye, and, purchased by the profits they made. I presume, they transferred ownership of Midlands Collieries Company to Grand Overland Rail."

"Captain Willems, I was not aware my brother had made such inquiries into Grand Overland Rail," began Jeffrey, contributing for the first time. Austin detected a tremor in his voice and believed he was fighting to control his anger. "And I will discuss this with him after your departure. I do agree this behaviour of Grand Overland

Rail appears to be most unacceptable, but why does it concern us?"

Harrison's face coloured slightly.

"Because, Mr Watson, you will become their next victim," Austin said slowly.

"Oh, come now, you're being a little melodramatic, Captain," added Harrison.

"No, wait, let him finish. I think I know where he is headed," interjected Jeffrey.

Oh no, you don't, Austin thought.

Tea was brought in, and all three men sipped from delicate China cups, offering a dignified opportunity to reflect.

Austin placed his cup and saucer on a table and looked at each man. "I have learned that Watson Brothers Coachbuilders has enquired about purchasing shares from Grand Overland Rail. And I'm sure your reasons for doing so are sound and make fiscal sense. However, a similar fate will befall you."

"Rubbish," stated Jeffrey and shook his head. "We're not contemplating any such investment."

"How?" snapped Harrison, ignoring his brother's outburst.

"Because shortly after you purchase your shares and attain a seat on the board, a labour dispute will prevent further work on the development of laying railway tracks on their newly purchased land. To fulfil their obligations, Grand Overland Rail will need to pay an enormous sum of money in unpaid wages and costs in delays before work resumes. Conveniently, Overland will deliberately keep its cash reserves low and, therefore, not have the capital. In all likelihood, it will probably seek assistance from a bank and assume another loan that it can't repay."

The brothers exchanged a private glance when Austin mentioned the bank loan.

He continued. "Shareholders will ultimately be liable and pay the debt, so it's conceivable, without sufficient cash reserves, you may have to sell your company."

"Absolute rubbish!" exclaimed Jeffrey. "What you've told us just isn't possible." He turned to his brother in realisation. "Or is it? What other arrangements have you made behind my back?"

Harrison waved an arm dismissively at Jeffrey. "I'll explain later." He maintained focused on Austin. "These directors are also shareholders, and those you suspect who are behind this must pay the debt along with everyone else, so how will they make money from a labour dispute?"

"And the directors do pay the debt, but presumably, their company, London Private Acquisitions, reimburses them individually from their profit. As far as the labour dispute goes, Mr Watson. I'm sure you'll find that, in all actuality, workers will likely be offered a lesser cash incentive than promised to return to work. The reported amount will probably be higher than what they receive, and the difference will somehow end up in the coffers of London Private Acquisitions. Afterwards, I presume that Grand Overland Rail will own Watson Brothers Coachbuilders."

Harrison shook his head. Jeffrey scowled.

Austin thought back to what Howard explained to him. "Mr Watson, if you purchase those shares, Overland will probably place an order with you for a substantial number of carriages to build. While they may provide you with an initial down payment, you will have significant costs. Your cash reserves will be stretched, and you will become vulnerable when required to pay Grand Overland Rail's debt. That is when a solicitor, Julian De Vore, will act as agent for an undisclosed principal and offer to purchase your company."

Jeffrey Watson looked like he'd been sucking on a lemon as his mouth puckered. Harrison scratched at his ear while Austin finished his tea.

Jeffrey's face returned to normal, and he leaned forward. "Can you prove any of this?"

"Have your solicitor contact my father's solicitor. He has agreed to confirm everything that has transpired, but obviously, he cannot confirm what has yet to happen."

Harrison turned to his brother. "If what Captain Willems says is true, and in all honesty, Jeffrey, I can't think why he would lie unless there is more he hasn't told us, but the prudent course of action is quite simply not to involve ourselves with Grand Overland Rail, so cast aside your aspersions. In light of what I have learned this morning, I have no intention of pursuing this." He turned to face Austin. "I'm intrigued. How did you come by this information about us and this so-called labour dispute?"

"It makes no difference how I came by this information. I just wanted to warn you of the danger of associating with Grand Overland Rail."

The brothers nodded.

"I want to string that Hewitt-Thompson by his neck," added Jeffrey.

Harrison stared at the far wall, lost in thought.

"Can you imagine how I feel? Due to stress and anxiety, my father's heart condition worsened, and sadly he passed. He lost his business, and like you, who've worked hard for years to make your business prosper, he lost it all. Frankly, it's abhorrent," said Austin.

The brothers seethed in silence.

"However, there is more that I wish to discuss with you. Perhaps, if you feel strongly as I do, we could turn the tables on Grand Overland Rail."

Jeffrey's eyes narrowed.

CHAPTER NINE

Jeffrey leapt to his feet. "Captain Willems, we will not be a party to any illicit activities. Our business was founded on integrity and honesty–"

"Sit down, Harrison," interrupted Jeffrey. "Let Captain Willems speak before you start getting damn righteous and pompous. Seems like you got us into this mess. Hear him out."

Reluctantly, Harrison sat as instructed, and as Austin correctly surmised, Jeffrey was the dominant of the two brothers.

"My solicitor informs me that laws will soon be in effect to protect shareholders from company debt and that they will enjoy limited liability, but presently, unscrupulous men, like the select four Grand Overland board members I have identified, will take advantage of hard-working and honest businessmen like yourselves." Austin looked at Harrison to drive home his point. "But these unfettered men need to be stopped."

Both Watson brothers nodded in agreement.

"What I'm asking of you isn't breaking the law, nor will it bring Watson Brothers Coachbuilders into disrepute." To Austin, the brothers seemed to relax.

"What do you want us to do, Captain?" asked Jeffrey after a loud sigh.

"For now, I'd like you both to continue expressing interest in purchasing shares from Grand Overland Rail. I want Overland to believe you will buy those shares and obtain a seat on their board of directors as you originally sought," replied Austin.

Jeffrey's eyes narrowed. "But you wouldn't want us to do that unless you were planning something more."

"You are correct, Mr Watson. I intend to ruin Grand Overland Rail and buy back my father's business."

"I'm sorry, that just won't do," Harrison stated as he shook his head. "If Grand Overland Rail is ruined, that will affect our business, and we will lose their orders to build carriages. If we support them, we prosper."

"Harrison, think on this," Jeffrey advised. "If Grand Overland Rail folds its tent and disappears, they still own the land and the track, no doubt they'll have all the permissions, and someone else will take control of the rail route and develop it. Who knows, they may even operate and manage it better than Grand Overland Rail. We don't need their business; we want honest and respectable customers," Jeffrey stated.

"Perhaps," scowled Harrison.

Austin sat back and allowed the brothers to talk. So far, Jeffrey was doing a splendid job of making his argument for him, although he was distinctly unhappy at not knowing what his brother had done behind his back.

Harrison turned to focus on Austin. "Captain Willems, we trust our solicitors implicitly, and before we act or do anything, I would like to accept your offer and have him verify what you've told us. If our solicitors report to us and confirm what you've said and if what you say is true, then I support you and will do all we can to assist. What do you say, Jeffrey?"

"I think I have no bloody option. Yes, I agree," he replied with a grunt.

"For the time being, gentlemen, people shouldn't be aware of our association, and I suggest we direct all further communications through our solicitors," Austin looked to each brother for confirmation.

"Agreed," replied Harrison.

Jeffrey leaned back in his chair with his arms folded again and nodded.

Verrey's Restaurant, located at 229 Regent Street, was one of Austin's favourite dining establishments in London. Sitting opposite him, Lieutenant Charles Newbury devoured the last of his prime Scotch beef with gusto while Austin still had a little more of his fresh grilled river trout with almonds sitting on his plate. Charles waited for Austin to finish and then reached into his satchel, pulled out a long wooden box about ten inches long and about three inches wide, and placed it on the table in front of him.

"What's this?" asked Austin, dabbing his mouth with a serviette.

"Go on, open it," invited Charles with his typical mischievous grin.

"Don't tell me you're proposing marriage. I am impressed if this is a ring, Charles, but this box is too large and tastefully unadorned. Perhaps it contains a necklace with precious gems or, better yet, diamonds? You should have wrapped it, for then I know your intentions are truly honourable and, no doubt, you are eager to promote a long, healthy relationship," Austin laughed.

"I apologise, Austin, but my love interests lay elsewhere, firmly nestled in the bosom of my dear Antoinette."

"That hussy!" exclaimed Austin as he reached for the box.

"I'll have you know, good sir, that Antoinette is a fine and upstanding young woman."

Austin nodded, "And so says every man between here and

Watford with two bob[6] in his pocket. Although, I expect many seldom find her standing," he grinned.

Charles laughed without shame or offence and watched Austin lift the box to examine.

"I tell you what, it's bloody heavy."

"Open it," Charles encouraged.

Austin flicked open the heavy clasp and lifted the lid. He stared in puzzlement and then poked it with his finger. "What is this? It looks like clay."

Charles looked pleased with himself. "It is clay, and it is an impression box."

"Ah, and if my memory still serves me correctly, I believe these are used for imprinting keys." He closed the box with a thunk and handed it back to Charles.

"Austin, I have been requested to move some of my father's artwork from storage…" he leaned across the table and lowered his voice. "And when at Finch & Gossett's, I shall determine if your wayward director has his art stored there. If he does, then I shall make an impression of the key to unlock the cage so we can gain access to it."

Austin looked stunned. "You're absolutely serious, aren't you, and are intent…," Austin looked around the room to ensure no one could overhear, "…on robbing that bloody warehouse?"

Charles nodded enthusiastically. "With the impression of the key, I will have Jack, back at the regiment, metal forge it for us." He shrugged. "It's simple."

"Lieutenant Charles Newbury, you are indeed a rascal," laughed Austin.

"That's what Antoinette constantly tells me," laughed Charles, then his expression turned serious. "Although once we have the key,

6   Bob – English slang. A 'bob' is a shilling.

our biggest challenge still awaits."

Austin's eyebrows furrowed. "What challenge, Charles? What have you failed to tell me?"

Charles casually picked up the dessert menu and began reading. "Er, are you familiar with Dobermanns?" He didn't look up.

Austin's hand flew to his forehead. "Do you mean to tell me a Dobermann is patrolling inside the warehouse?"

"Best to keep your voice down, old boy." He placed the menu back on the table and looked at his friend. "No, not exactly, but, er, outside the warehouse."

"That complicates things."

"Yes, sort of...."

"What? What haven't you told me, Charles?"

"Ah, you see, Austin... uh, there's not one Dobermann, but two of them and in all honesty, they're not the friendliest of beasts and certainly don't qualify as being man's best friend. Actually," he shrugged, "far from it."

Austin lowered his head and stared at the tablecloth as he thought the matter through. Suddenly, he looked up. "Do you recall when we were in Kowloon, that palace?"

The boyish grin returned. "Ah yes, those bloody big dogs."

"And what did we do?"

"Laudanum," stated Charles. "Of course, why did I not think of that? We gave the dogs meat and laudanum, worked a treat."

"And we shall do so again," Austin stated.

"Perhaps we should give it to the guards."

Austin groaned. "Guards? How many, Charles? Six, ten, twenty?"

"No, no, only two; they patrol outside."

"We distract them long enough to get inside and again when we want to leave."

"A bayonet would be easier, in the gut and right up the middle."

Austin ignored the comment. "Is that their entire security, dogs and two guards?"

"They have the guards patrolling outside a fence, and once distracted, we can climb the fence and then unlock the gate from the inside. That's where we give the laudanum to the dogs. It isn't a problem. The warehouse is locked, but there is another key the guards use when they want to get inside. It's hidden nearby, and I know where it's kept. Once inside, there's an office, and the door that leads into the warehouse is usually unlocked, and we stroll in towards the cage where your friend's artwork is kept."

"His name is Oscar Baker, and he isn't a friend," Austin protested.

"Once we're inside and the artwork–"

"I think you've lost your mind," Austin laughed.

Charles grinned. "–is located, we use our key, open the cage and *voila*, grab the pieces you want, and leave the same way, except walk through the outside gate, locking it as we leave. No one will know we've been inside until your Mr Baker notices his art is missing, and by then, it's too late."

Austin scratched his head. "So, dear Charlie, how do we distract the guards?"

"A fire, a fight, a couple of randy streetwalkers... Take your pick."

"A fire might be best, but we must look first and find the best place. I certainly don't want to burn the entire building and ruin innocent people's beautiful art collections."

'Nor father's, although he is far from innocent," added Charles with a wry smile.

A waiter appropriately waited until there was a pause in the conversation and tactfully approached the table to take their dessert order.

"Let's take a cab and pass by Finch & Gossett's warehouse when we leave here. It's on North Audley Street," Charles suggested once the waiter departed. "And after, we can stop for an ale or three."

From Verrey's Restaurant, Charles instructed the cab to detour down N. Audley Street, where they passed by Finch & Gossett's warehouse. The premises were nothing more than an unassuming smallish warehouse, separated by a narrow alley between two much larger buildings. No signs or attractive frontages advertised what the building was used for. A stout wrought iron fence and gate kept the unwanted from straying onto a small area where coaches and wagons could enter and park securely whilst loading or unloading. A large sliding wooden door granted access to the building's interior, and as Charles previously explained, another smaller door on the building's front left side was for customers to enter the office or administration area.

Mr Colin Finch resided in a flat above the warehouse, and the only access to his residence was up a flight of stairs that ascended from inside. It was another layer of security because Mr Finch would undoubtedly hear anyone fumbling around inside the warehouse attempting to steal artwork he was paid to protect. Charles didn't know anything about the other partner, Mr Gossett.

Two bored truncheon-wielding guards ambled backwards and forwards in front of the fence. Occasionally, they'd stop, chat a while, and continue aimlessly. The only consideration afforded the guards was a rough shelter, constructed off to one side, that offered a seat and protection from inclement weather.

The rear of the building had one door that opened onto a service lane. It was sturdy, made of steel and completely impenetrable.

The cab dropped Austin and Charles off at a nearby alehouse, where they sat planning their mission.

"Distracting those guards is the biggest challenge, Charles," said Austin, and he raised a glass to his lips and took a hefty pull. "But I think I have some ideas."

"You always do," Charles laughed.

Austin wasn't paying attention and caught the eye of a young woman and her friend. "Make room, Lieutenant Newbury; we have company."

CHAPTER TEN

Austin still didn't know much about Grand Overland Rail's director, Virgil Hartman. He'd heard the man had a passion for sailing and owned an impressive boat. He just didn't know what type of boat and spent the following Wednesday and Friday back at White's, hoping to find out.

He learned nothing more of interest on Wednesday, and Virgil Hartman didn't even turn up on Friday. According to Sir Ronald, who explained the absence, Virgil was with his beloved *Belisha* at Tower Bridge Moorings.

Now Austin had a name, and on Saturday morning, he rose early and told Nanny he'd be back by lunch and departed to find this boat, ship, or yacht named *Belisha*.

Tower Bridge Moorings was located a stone's throw from Tower Bridge on the east side of the River Thames. A cab dropped him off near the bridge, and because of bridge congestion, he found a wherry[7] to take him across, which suited his purposes and was more convenient than walking.

The river reeked, and he hated having to be anywhere near it. Raw sewage emptied into the river, and so did everything else that floated, stank or decayed. The waterman wasn't particularly

7   *Wherry – Ferry boat, rowed by a waterman or a wherryman*

talkative, which suited Austin, and they safely crossed the river without mishap.

On reaching the other side, Austin asked the waterman to take him alongside the moored boats, and they rowed into the docks. The vessels were magnificent, especially the pleasure yachts. Austin looked at the names of each boat but didn't see *Belisha.* They exited the docks, re-entered the river, and slowly drifted past larger vessels moored on the outer side of the marina. Then he saw it. How could he not?

Austin estimated the yacht, or schooner as the waterman corrected him, was about one hundred feet long, with a beam of at least twenty feet. The name *Belisha* was engraved and boldly painted in bright *faux* gold lettering on the schooner's stern and two tall masts sprouted from its deck and reached skywards with an impressive tangle of lines and tackle.

As they drifted past the schooner and headed downstream, two men appeared from inside and climbed onto the deck. Austin instantly recognised the face of Virgil Hartman and turned the collar of his coat up and adjusted his topper to hide his face in case Grand Overland Rail's director looked down

"Take me back, please," Austin requested. "I've seen enough."

"Make up yer bleedin' mind, will yer," exclaimed the waterman. With a curse, he pulled hard on an oar, and the boat spun quickly from the schooner and angled upstream to navigate the swift current safely. Austin relaxed now that his back was turned to the schooner and planned what he would do.

He paid the waterman's tariff, added a little gratuity, and then caught a cab home.

"Sir, you have a guest in the drawing room. Er, Mr Willoughby only just arrived," Nanny informed him when he entered.

Her face looked a little flushed, and he presumed she'd been busy with Saturday cleaning and housekeeping. "Thank you, Nanny. Let me just refresh myself."

She took his coat and hat, and he quickly wandered off to wash his hands and face before entering the drawing room. Unusually, he saw Howard on the settee and not seated on his favourite chair.

"Uncle Howard, a pleasant surprise," greeted Austin.

Howard Willoughby smiled and stood. "Always good to see you too, Austin. And I hope my unexpected visit is not intruding on your plans?"

"Not at all."

"Excuse me, sir, will Mr Willoughby have luncheon with us?" Nanny asked.

Austin looked to his father's friend in question.

"Absolutely, I wouldn't miss one of Nanny's lovely meals for anything," he smiled.

Nanny blushed and left the room.

Austin sat in his father's chair, a regular habit he'd taken to and turned to Howard. "And what do I owe the pleasure of your Saturday morning visit?"

Instead of returning to the settee, Howard sat on his preferred chair. "Late yesterday afternoon, I had an appointment with Mr Browning, a solicitor representing Watson Brothers Coachbuilders, who came to see me."

"Oh my, that was fast. I only saw them a week ago."

"You certainly stirred things up a tad, Austin. After you visited with them, both Watson brothers were quite distraught."

"Good. I hoped to warn them of potential disaster."

"Well, according to what Mr Browning informed me, your ploy worked." Howard smiled. "As you instructed, I informed Mr Browning of what befell Midlands Collieries Company and how

Grand Overland Rail handled their finances concerning their debts. He was quite inquisitive and demanding."

"Typical solicitor, Austin laughed. "But thank you for seeing him, Howard." Austin crossed his legs and waited. He knew the solicitor had more to say.

"But this raises an interesting question, and I am quite perplexed. Why would you request further communication between the Watson brothers and yourself through Mr Browning and me?" Howard inclined his head. "I can only assume there is… uh, more?"

Austin nodded. "Aye, there is, Howard. I didn't want to tell you until I had more information."

"Does this have anything to do with your visits to White's?"

"Yes, most certainly."

"And?"

Austin eased himself upright, walked to the window, and gazed over the splendour of The Regent's Park. "I'm going to bring about the downfall of Grand Overland Rail and will target four directors. Mr Hewitt Thompson, Mr George Dillington, Mr Oscar Baker and Mr Virgil Hartman."

"I see," replied Howard as he rubbed his chin. "As I'm unaware of any complaints made to the authorities about them, then this surely is a personal vendetta." He paused a moment. "And your method of retribution falls outside the law?"

"I intend to legally obtain ownership of Midlands Collieries Company from Grand Overland Rail." He faced the solicitor. "And to answer your question honestly, yes, my scheme for reprisal against the directors is illicit and wholeheartedly unlawful." Austin held Howard's unwavering gaze.

A knock on the door interrupted the tenseness. "Luncheon is served," Nanny announced.

"We'll be right there," Austin replied after tearing his eyes from

Howard.

"Yes, I thought as much. And do you need my professional counsel to inform you of the consequences?

"You can inform me all you want, Howard; nothing changes. I will see this through to its conclusion. What they did to Father–"

"What they did to your father is unforgivable," Howard interrupted. "It was wrong, malicious, and disgusting."

"Then I need your help."

Howard's head shot up. "My help?"

Austin nodded.

"Then you'd better explain what you have in mind."

They sat in the dining room and enjoyed fish, spinach, and a dry and fruity bottle of *Albariño* wine. Austin explained what he would do to each of the directors and how he would somehow foil the plans of Overland to initiate a pseudo worker's revolt for better wages and working conditions. After lunch, they returned to the drawing room and sat in companionable silence.

Austin could see Howard mulling over what he'd divulged. Finally, Howard focused his attention back on Austin. "I loved your father like a brother. What they did to him sickens me, Austin, and like you, I want to see vengeance done. There are extraordinary risks associated with what you propose, and, in all likelihood and probability, we could be compromised and face justice. Are you willing to accept that?"

Austin's expression was grim. "Without question."

Howard looked intently at the son of his dearest friend silently acknowledged Austin's anger – he felt the same. Enoch Willems was a remarkable man who deserved respect and, sadly, received so much less. Austin had grown into a principled young man his father was proud of, and yet, what he intended to do was illegal – but a criminal he wasn't. High-spirited and mischievous, yes. But the law didn't protect Enoch Willems from rogues and scoundrels, and Austin was fully prepared and willing to risk it all for his cause of vengeance. He was brave and, if anything, perhaps even foolish… Howard sighed. "Very well, I will do what I can to help," he responded with a smile.

Austin was about to reply when Howard raised a hand. "Now, hear me out, Austin. Your plan has merit; however, there is a danger for you. Attacking each director separately and over time won't take a genius to decipher that someone is after them. By the time you've attacked two directors, the others will have taken precautions."

"Then, when possible, attack all at once? A simultaneous full-frontal assault and across all battle lines?"

"Indeed, that is more logical," Howard grinned. Austin always had a way of incorporating military doctrine into any challenge he faced.

"That means I have to involve more people… although it will take some time for the theft of artwork from Finch & Gossett to be discovered. I believe we can pull that heist off a day or two earlier than the others. Absconding with Sir Ronald's racehorses will need to be done on another day for logistical reasons. A coordinated attack on the other two directors simultaneously will impact them more, especially when the board members eventually learn of what has befallen the other directors."

"I agree," Howard nodded in support.

"You would have made a fine General," Austin laughed.

"But you haven't yet found a solution to the impending labour dispute. Neither do you know who or how Grand Overland Rail will entice the workers to revolt. I dare say your entire strategy falls apart if you cannot prevent it."

Austin nodded, "And that's been troubling me too, and I have been toying with the notion of hiring someone to loiter amongst the workers laying railway track. If there is any dispute or rumours of a work stoppage or strike, he would certainly hear about it and report to me."

"Do you have anyone in mind?"

"Yes, Sergeant Oliver Nagle. He lost a leg through sepsis after being inadvertently stabbed by a bayonet. He was declared unfit for duty and had to resign. Occasionally, all the regimental officers kick in and donate money to assist him. He's a wonderful chap and loyal. And above all, he is trustworthy."

"Then, by all means, I'd suggest using him if he is agreeable."

"I'm sure he will, and he is very resourceful, too," Austin grinned. "By chance, do you know how much money the Watson brothers were going to invest in Overland, and did you learn who this Chairman fellow is?"

"Mr Browning told me it was in the neighbourhood of twenty thousand pounds."

"Good heavens, that's a fortune," Austin exclaimed.

Howard nodded. "And no, the Chairman is rather elusive." Howard shook his head and then made eye contact with Austin. "What do you need me to do?"

"I need information on Sir Ronald's racehorses. Where he keeps them, their names and anything useful that could help."

"And what will you do to the horses, do you know?"

Austin shook his head. "No, not yet. I've only determined what I will do to Virgil Hartman's boat. Next are the racehorses."

"I'll do what I can. By the way, I happen to know who is George Dillington's mistress and have an address."

"How do you know that?"

"You can thank your father, he told me. Thought it was quite

95

amusing at the time," Howard added. "And one more thing. Did you know Grand Overland Rail is attempting to buy back its shares? In light of their recent debts, many shareholders are trying to unload them, and Overland is trying to repurchase them at a much cheaper rate, thus eliminating what remains of their cash reserves."

Austin's face hardened. "I just want to kill them."

"That might be taking things too far, Austin."

"Is what they bloody deserve," he grumbled in reply.

CHAPTER ELEVEN

"All this radiance is surely a gift from God." Lieutenant Charles Newbury shook his head in wonder. "Look how the heavens have opened and delivered forth such ravishing specimens resplendent in all their finest glory. Austin, look, feast your eyes, for never will you behold such visions of such perfect form and unrivalled beauty." He spread his arms wide and rotated.

"Aye, not even at Helen's in Westchester," Austin wryly suggested.

"These exquisite women, their clothes and adornments give me chills."

"Your chills are from overindulgence, Charles, and you know brandy affects you badly."

They both stood inside the main entrance to Ascot Racecourse near the public Queen Anne enclosure, having just arrived a short time earlier. Behind them and outside, a line of coaches dropped off invitees, distinguished guests, and the general public. For anyone in society, Ascot was the place to be, to be seen and to take in the spectacle of royalty, horses, and an abundance of the fairer sex because women outnumbered men four to one. For bachelors, Ascot was more than horse racing and gambling; it was an opportunity for the finest women to showcase the latest fashion trends and hopefully attract a possible suitor. However, men also needed to be acceptably dressed, especially if they wanted to enter prestigious enclosures and be noticed.

Austin wore a formal grey morning suit with tails, a waistcoat accessorised with a tie, a carnation, a thoughtful gift from Nanny, and a plain grey topper. Charles was similarly dressed, except he chose a darker colour, charcoal. As neither had an invitation to enter the prestigious Royal enclosure, their presentation adhered to the strict dress standards of the Queen Anne enclosure, which allowed them access.

Austin and Charles had attended the Ascot Races for years. It was their annual pilgrimage, and Charles had always met with partial success, temporary romance and frequently an empty wallet. Austin was more circumspect and had yet to meet anyone not affected by wealth, social standing and glamour, but not for want of trying. Anyone he met whom he later invited home to meet his father had first to pass covert scrutiny by Nanny. She never told Austin that she disapproved or approved. It was her behaviour. Any women he brought home were always treated courteously. The more Nanny disapproved, the more polite she became. It wasn't until later, when his guest had returned home that Nanny might casually comment in passing how the young lady appeared distracted or inattentive. At first, Austin was a little disquieted by her shrewd observations but later learned she was astute and saw things in these women that he did not. More recently, he ensured that any young ladies he called upon always met Nanny, and he'd find a way to leave them alone for a few minutes.

"Come, Austin, I require whiskey," Charles urged.

They threaded their way around spectators and guests, passed the door attendants' close examination, and entered the Queen Anne enclosure, where they found a table and ordered beverages.

Austin purchased a sports journal to better study the horses entered in the various races, and after their drinks arrived, he casually browsed through its pages. He wasn't a punter but liked to make a wager from time to time after studying a horse and attempting to make an informed bet rather than a random pick. Over the years, he lost more than he won, although not as much as Charles, who didn't seem to care one way or another.

Charles nudged Austin with his elbow. "Do you recognise her, Austin? I daresay that looks like Miss Sarah McDonald."

Austin looked up from the journal and grinned. "She's filled out a tad."

"Oh yes, and I think I need to present myself to her again; she is adorable."

Charles stood, straightened his waistcoat and leaned down. "Hold the fort. I'm on a reconnaissance mission. Wish me luck, old boy."

"With looks like yours, you'll need more than luck," Austin laughed.

Charles disappeared, and Austin was able to better focus on the journal. He scanned through various pages until he recognised the name Hewitt-Thompson, the managing director of Grand Overland Rail with the walrus moustache.

It came as no surprise, as there had been talk at White's about his horses and his entry for the Royal Ascot Race. But here he was, listed in bold print as the sole owner of two racehorses named Charming and Father's Pride.

Austin thought carefully, downed what remained of his whiskey and stood to look for Charles. There was no sign of him anywhere. He wasn't worried; they always planned to meet back here if they separated. With that, Austin scooped up the journal, tucked it under his arm, left the enclosure, exited the racecourse and walked across the road.

After safely navigating the road, with its confusion of carriages and coaches, he had to walk up a slight rise and down the other side to where the stables were located. The general public wasn't admitted entry, but he'd been here enough to know the guard attendants could be quite agreeable with a modest and discreet largesse.

Because he was appropriately dressed and easily identified as a gentleman of means, he slipped a few coins into the hand of the attendant and was granted admission to the stables.

The challenge was where to find Charming and Father's Pride. There were dozens and dozens of horses, easily over a two-hundred, and each horse had an individual stall.

As he approached the first row of endless stables, he noticed that each horse's name was written on a card affixed to each door. He casually strolled past each stall and read each horse's name.

As a military officer, he was a skilled and competent rider and genuinely loved horses. These exquisite animals were just beautiful, in perfect condition and health, and he marvelled at each horse as he casually strolled past their stalls. He was so engrossed that he almost missed Father's Pride. When it dawned on him, he stopped, took two steps back and looked at the fine bay-coloured mare that stared curiously at him. Suddenly, a head appeared behind the horse from within the stall.

"Morn'n, sir," came the gravelly voice."

"Yes, good morning. Are you the trainer?"

"Aye, for this one and a few others." The man finished rubbing the horse's flanks and then began massaging its thighs and legs. Within moments, his head disappeared again.

Austin took a step closer to see better. "How will she do?"

"Oh, I reckon she'll do fine if it dries out a bit more. She likes a hard track," replied the trainer.

Austin looked around. The area around the stables was busy. Owners, trainers and jockeys were discussing tactics and strategy. Others, important folk, also came to admire the horses in wonder.

Austin needed to learn more about the horse without appearing to show anything but casual interest. He nodded to a gentleman and his lady as they strolled by. When they were out of earshot, he continued. "Is the ground hard where she normally grazes?"

The trainer laughed, stood, moved to the other side of the stunning racehorse, and continued his massage. "Chieveley is a bloody bog if you don't mind me sayin'."

"Is that where the owner lives?"

"Aye, stabled at the owner's country estate, Windhaven. Why you be so curious, sir?"

"Because I intend to wager a fortune on this animal, and any information you can give me could prove useful."

The trainer continued grooming the mare. "Fair nuff," he said.

"Are you also the trainer for Charming?"

"Yep, that 'orse too, but he ain't racing this week, he'd be scratched. Got a minor injury, he does. Bloody jockeys are too hard on these animals and always think they knows best," grizzled the trainer. "Too much crop is cruel on horses," he added with a mumbled curse.

"Oh. A shame. Well, thank you, I must be off, and er, good luck," Austin offered and began walking away with a smile. Now he knew That Sir Ronald kept his prized horses in Chieveley at his country estate called Windhaven.

A dozen stalls later, he saw Charming, a grey gelding with a rear leg wrapped in a bandage. He paused briefly, memorised the horse, and continued as he planned his revenge.

From nowhere, he heard a shout, a woman's frenzied cry, and he turned around as a small white coloured dog dragging a leash bounded around the corner and ran towards him.

"Peaches!" came the exasperated cry.

Peaches? Queried Austin to himself. The dog went to run around him, but a quick sidestep and a firm foot on the trailing leash created a yelp and brought Peaches to a sudden, undignified stop. He bent down and retrieved the leash as a young woman approached, walking as quickly as she dared.

"Thank you, kind sir," she said.

Austin could see she was quite beautiful and stylishly dressed. "I don't believe bringing dogs here into the stables is very wise; I'm surprised they allowed you to enter," he cautioned with a smile as he admired her auburn coloured hair that cascaded down from beneath her hat.

"I'll consider that next time he demands I chaperone his dog. Thank you kindly, sir." He noticed her subtle look of appraisal when she raised her head. Because of the wide-brimmed headwear, it was difficult to see her face when he stood close to her.

"He?" Austin asked.

"Yes, my stepfather. He insists on bringing his dog here and then expects me to look after it."

She didn't look happy about taking care of dear Peaches. Austin nodded in sympathy.

"And just so you know, I never intended to bring Peaches here. I was having him do his, uh, duties outside near the carriageway when he ran away."

Austin dipped his head. "Then please accept my apologies for making assumptions, Miss?"

Peaches had taken an interest in his shoe.

She looked at him closely and paused a moment. "Harriet Stephenson," she finally replied, extending her hand, and he realised he still held the leash. He swapped the leash over and shook her hand. "It is delightful to make your acquaintance, Miss Stephenson. I am Austin Willems, formerly Captain in the 67th South Hampshire Regiment of Foot," he replied and awkwardly handed the leash over.

"But your moustache[8], sir," she questioned with an accompanying smile. "I wouldn't have known."

"An accessory I prefer to be without," he added. He liked this young woman and wanted to keep chatting with her.

"Excuse me for prying, Captain Willems, but you seem quite young to have retired your commission."

Austin's smile disappeared. He didn't think Harriet needed to hear about his altercation with Miles Siles. "My father recently passed, and I needed to attend to his affairs."

"Forgive me, I'm so sorry," she reached out and touched his arm.

Austin didn't need to simulate his feeling of grief. "That's quite alright, Miss Stephenson, you weren't to know."

"I do understand. My father passed five years ago, and I miss him terribly, so I appreciate how you feel, and I can see that I upset you."

Austin presented his warmest, most pleasant expresion. "You haven't upset me. My father was a warm, loving and kind-hearted man, and you reminded me of that, thank you."

She returned his smile.

"Perhaps I can escort you back?"

Harriet looked at him and nodded, then handed Austin the leash. "Yes, thank you, Captain Willems, I would enjoy that."

---

8   Moustaches were compulsory for all members of the British armed services from 1860 to 1916.

Peaches led the way.

With Peaches tugging at the leash, Austin and Harriet crossed the road, re-entered Ascot Raceway, and leisurely strolled in front of the enclosures. They wove around people picnicking on the grass and up as far as the parade ring, looked distractedly at the horses proudly on display and then walked back. They shared stories and laughed, and Austin thought she was delightful, intelligent and lively.

Unaware of time, and in between races, they crossed the track and entered the Heath in the middle of the racecourse. Under the pretext of exploring, they continued their spirited dialogue and enjoyed each other's company.

"I apologise, Miss Stephenson, it is growing late, and you have missed luncheon; your family will be concerned," Austin said after a pause in their discussion.

"I doubt it. My stepfather will undeniably be discussing business, horse racing and has forgotten about me. Mother knows I abhor the shallowness of those people and that I prefer to be elsewhere." Her look softened. "Perhaps, and in the interest of dispelling idle gossip, I should re-appear... but please, call me Harriet," she invited.

"And you may address me as Austin," he offered.

As they crossed the track and headed towards the stands, their pace slowed; neither was interested in separating or leaving and as Austin led the way to the Queen Anne enclosure, Harriet stopped.

"My stepfather is firmly ensconced in the Royal Enclosure, Austin."

Austin grinned. "Oh, how silly of me, I just assumed...."

She laughed. "It's quite alright. Where are you located in the Queen Anne enclosure?"

Austin pointed to where he and Charles's table was. "I, er, I hope to see you again, Harriet."

She looked up at him, and he saw her eyes sparkle. "Perhaps, Captain Willems. Thank you for a wonderful morning and afternoon." With that, she spun and strolled away, only to stop. To Austin's puzzlement, she turned and walked back. "My stepfather may be a little upset if I don't return with Peaches."

Austin felt embarrassed. "Er, of course." He handed the leash over and watched her walk away.

"Where the bloody hell have you been?" asked Charles when Austin returned to their table.

Austin sighed loudly and grinned.

"Who? Who is she? You saucy devil. Who is this young woman who has captured your attention? Spare nothing but the sordid details."

Austin recounted his time spent with Harriet and how much he enjoyed her company.

"Are you sure it isn't Peaches that you're more interested in?" Charles laughed.

Austin feigned kicking him under the table to a bout of laughter.

They spent the next hour or two wagering on horses, talking and laughing as two close friends do. Austin failed to win any money on races, while Charles, unusually, did quite well.

Austin's thoughts kept returning to Harriet Stephenson. He wouldn't dare admit it to Charles, but he was very taken with her and hoped to see her again before the races were over. Of some concern, he had no idea where her home was, other than somewhere in London, and it wasn't possible to call on her if he didn't know where she lived. He could have kicked himself. Not to mention, she hadn't seemed willing to see him again when he raised the topic. Perhaps he overdid it and made a fool of himself, and she wasn't interested in him at all, he worried.

He caught Charles looking at him.

"I think you are smitten, old boy."

"Why don't you tell me about your encounter with the voluptuous Miss Sarah McDonald?"

Charles grinned wickedly and leaned forward.

"Pardon me, sir," came a voice. "Are you Captain Austin Willems?"

Austin and Charles's heads whipped around to stare at a stoic white-gloved attendant.

"Yes, I am he," replied Austin, with his curiosity piqued.

"Of course, sir," answered the attendant without expression. "If it pleases you, sir, Miss Harriet Stephenson has requested the pleasure of your company and extended an invitation to dine with her and her family at six o'clock this evening in a private box at the Royal Enclosure."

Austin swallowed. Charles's mouth opened.

Austin didn't need to think and he responded quickly. "Please pass on my gratitude to Miss Stephenson and inform her that I graciously accept and look forward to seeing her at six o'clock," he replied.

Charles realised his mouth was open and shut it.

"Very well, sir. Er, may I recommend a freshen-up, sir?"

Austin dipped his head in acknowledgement. The tactful reminder about dress etiquette didn't go unnoticed. "Thank you."

"Have a pleasant afternoon, gentlemen," the attendant smiled and backed away.

Charles whistled softly. "I think you may have made a favourable impression on this Miss Stephenson, and such that you're invited to the Royal Enclosure to dine with her family. Your fake charm and silky patter have served you well this day," Charles teased.

Austin was dazed. "I can't say I expected that."

"Nor I," stated Charles."

Austin freshened up, purchased a new *boutonnière* as his carnation was looking a little worse for wear, and abandoning Charles to his own devices, he stood at the entrance to the Royal Enclosure and waited for admittance. It was precisely six o'clock, and with his heart pounding, he was led to a private box to be introduced just as another gentleman was leaving. The stranger nodded politely at him and departed.

The attendant waited for a lull in the conversation and coughed once. "May I announce, Captain Austin Willems."

Austin smiled appropriately and felt a flutter when he saw Harriet. She returned his smile, and he turned to greet her stepfather, Sir Ronald Hewitt-Thompson.

CHAPTER TWELVE

Austin fought to control his reaction as Sir Ronald's walrus moustache expanded outwards.

"My daughter informs me you chastised her for Peaches' errant behaviour," began Sir Ronald without recognising his daughter's guest.

"Sir, my concern was for the safety of the horses, and Harriet seemed admirably in control." With apprehension, he looked around the table and met the gaze of each individual. An attractive middle-aged woman sat opposite Sir Ronald, who he guessed was Harriet's mother. He dipped his head in respect and offered a congenial smile in greeting. Another couple sat at the end, who looked unfamiliar. Again, he dipped his head in greeting and finally acknowledged Harriet, who sat smiling at him. "I hope I'm not intruding…"

"Not at all, Captain. That was Sir Felix Dampierre, who you just passed, and he just popped over to say hello," replied Mrs Hewitt-Thompson with a broad, welcoming smile.

"Captain, I've been remiss. Allow me to introduce Harriet's mother, Eunice, Lord Eric Tidsbury, and of course, the lovely Lady Blanche Tidsbury," introduced Sir Ronald, whose face looked more flushed than normal; his moustache returned to its natural position. "Please have a seat and enjoy your meal as our guest."

Austin's heart continued to pound as he sat next to Harriet.

"Thank you very much for the invitation." He wasn't sure if his anxiety was from unexpectedly meeting Sir Ronald or because Harriet invited him to dine with her. So far, her father hadn't recognised him or his name, and he thought back to when he was at White's and how he avoided looking directly at the directors. To all appearances, her stepfather was over-indulging with alcohol consumption, and it seemed that his impairments also extended to his memory.

His heart slowed to only a slightly accelerated level, and he gave Harriet a quick look and felt her leg move beside his. He could feel the heat.

"Harriet informs me you recently resigned your commission," commented her stepfather before upending and draining his glass of wine.

"Yes, sir. Although not by willing choice. My father recently passed, and I needed to administer to his affairs." He saw Harriet's mother looking at him carefully, as only mothers do when analysing a potential suitor for their daughter. Austin wanted to change the subject. "And will your horses be racing tomorrow?"

Lord Tidsbury scoffed. "Not bloody likely."

Sir Ronald emptied his glass and shook his head in anguish. "One of my horses suffered a minor injury when the jockey rode her. Reckless fool. But Father's Pride is ready to lead the field tomorrow."

A waiter refilled his wine glass from a bottle.

"Where is your regiment based, in London?" asked Mr Hewett-Thompson.

Austin felt Harriet stir beside him. He sensed her becoming annoyed.

"The 67th South Hampshire Regiment is based in Westchester, Sir Ronald,"

Austin didn't see Harriet's quick look of puzzlement.

"That's enough, dear. Let's not make our guest uncomfortable," advised Harriet's mother.

"Nonsense," spluttered Sir Ronald. "Military officers are used to scrutiny, isn't that so, Captain?"

"Especially if we've been captured," Austin added, hoping to lighten the mood.

Everyone laughed.

"Remember that man from Westchester, Ronald? It was years ago," Lord Tidsbury asked.

Austin was pleased the conversation was being redirected away from him. He felt movement on his leg, and he slowly placed his hand under the table and felt Harriet's hand. His face flushed and he hoped no one noticed but Sir Ronald was deep in conversation and Harriet's mother was distracted.. Harriet pressed something into his, and it felt like a folded paper. He gently squeezed her hand and put the paper in his pocket without anyone noticing." With his heart thumping, he turned his head to look at her, she smiled in return.

To Austin, dinner was awkward and tense. Sir Ronald controlled the conversation and never allowed his wife or daughter to participate. Austin found him to be overbearing, detestable and rude. Whenever he wanted to converse politely with Harriet or Eunice, her mother, Sir Ronald, would interject or talk over him. When dinner was finally over, Austin was eager to be alone and talk with Harriet away from her stepfather, but that was most unlikely.

He thanked everyone, including Harriet's stepfather and was about to leave.

"Father, I'm just going to walk Austin to the exit," Harriet stated.

Sir Ronald just waved his arm and said nothing.

"Come," she said softly.

They walked towards the exit, and she spoke before Austin could say a word.

"Thank you for coming, Austin, and I'm pleased you did. I wish my stepfather could have been more civil, but I hope..." she paused momentarily. "Forgive me for being forward, but I hope you can call on me because I would enjoy more of your company." She placed her hand on his arm, just like she'd done earlier in the stables, looked up at him and smiled. Before he could reply, she turned and was gone.

"No!" Charles held both hands to his head in reaction after Austin told him about Harriet's stepfather being the managing director of Grand Overland Rail. "And he didn't recognise you or your name?"

Austin was lying on his bed and shook his head.

Hotel rooms in Ascot were a premium during horse racing season. To make life easier, Austin typically booked a room with two beds a year in advance, and he and Charles shared the facilities.

"The man had obviously been drinking all day and was bevvied. I was fortunate."

"Fortunate? You were bloody lucky, Austin. If he had recognised you, it could have affected your entire plan."

Austin laughed. "I was indeed lucky to have met such a captivating woman." He remembered the paper she slid into his hand and sat up.

"What now?" Charles asked.

"She gave me a note." Austin walked to the wardrobe and found the note in his suit. He carefully unfolded it and read.

25 Upper Brook Street, Mayfair

My dearest Captain Austin Willems,
If you are so inclined, I will enjoy the

occasion to have you call upon me.
You may find it convenient to consider
a Wednesday, Friday or Sunday,
and I think you will understand.

.

Your esteemed friend,
Harriet Stephenson.

"What does she say?" Charles sat up.

"She invites me to call on her and suggests either Wednesday, Friday or Sunday."

"Why, those days? I must say, she is being rather particular. Is this angel worthy of your pent-up desires, Austin? Or are you flogging a dead horse?"

"Because, dear boy," Austin grinned, "I happen to know those are the days when Sir Ronald plays whist at White's. And so you can temper your lurid thoughts, Miss Stephenson is not only exceptionally gorgeous and intelligent," he raised a hand and pointed at Charles, "A rare quality you do not seek in woman, but she happens to be delightful company and, I will gladly accept her invitation."

"May I attend with you?"

Austin threw a shoe.

The remainder of their time at Ascot was uneventful, and try as he might, Austin never saw Harriet or her family again. Charles returned to the regiment in Westchester, and the train journey back to London gave him time to think and plan.

His promising friendship with Harriet Stephenson did create a problem and interfered with his plans for her stepfather. It was an unforeseen complication that tugged at his conscience. He didn't want to deceive or hurt her, but at the same time, he couldn't tell her that he sought her stepfather's financial downfall and ruin. He knew there had to be a solution and hoped time would provide some ideas. He shifted his focus back to his plan and knew he needed to secure the assistance of Sergeant Oliver Nagle as quickly as possible and as soon as he returned to London.

He found a hansom cab to take him to the Lamb and Flag public house in Covent Garden. Austin was wary and knew gangs of youths wandered city streets, causing mayhem. Unable to work and provide much-needed extra income for their families, they roamed neighbourhoods in small groups looking for opportunity, especially from the wealthy or privileged who were foolish to enter their domain alone or unprotected. They were notorious thieves and wouldn't shy away from causing injury or even committing murder to fill their pockets of ill-gotten loot.

Coming here at night always posed a risk, and to Nanny's undisguised frown of disapproval, Austin dressed appropriately in an assortment of threadbare clothes that had seen better days. As a stranger, he'd stand out, but in the Irish pub, he hoped to be slightly less conspicuous. However, Austin had little choice in the matter; if he wanted to find Sergeant Oliver Nagle, he needed to go there during the evening.

Due to the risk of being robbed, the cab wouldn't take him any closer to the Lamb and Flag than the busy intersection of Seven Roads, and from there, it was only a brisk two-minute walk to the public house. He saw a group of four youths watching him, and they turned to follow as he headed down Garrick Street. The Lamb and

Flag was located on Rose Street, which was more of a narrow lane than a street, just over one hundred yards from where the cab left him.

The gang of youths who followed must have been disappointed when he turned left onto Rose Street towards the inn.

Heads turned in curiosity at the stranger when he entered. A few drinkers briefly paused their boisterous conversations, then resumed a little quieter. He paused and looked around, hoping to catch sight of the one-legged sergeant, but it was difficult in the dimly lit confines of the inn.

He walked to the bar and caught the eye of the publican. "I'm a friend and looking for Oliver Nagle."

The publican didn't acknowledge Austin's request and continued pouring drinks. He stepped back to see the room better and felt someone shove him.

"Door's that-a-way," said the man between clenched teeth. "Make use of it."

He reached out to give Austin another push when Austin deflected the man's outstretched arms and stepped up to him. They faced each other, chest to chest. "I'm looking for Ollie, and I'm a friend."

"Even without the tash, you look like a bleed'n officer," the man held eye contact with Austin, then turned over his shoulder and simply said, "Sarge." He looked at Austin with a scowl, "Don't you go mov'n, stay right 'ere." With that, he turned to his friends with a laugh as a man separated from the small group and walked into the gloom.

Austin waited

"See yerself out!"

Austin spun just in time to dodge a roundhouse punch that would have connected with his jaw. A thick, smaller man with no neck or teeth sneered and pulled his arm back to take another vicious swing. Austin knew he couldn't show weakness and had to account for himself. He positioned himself to retaliate and then kicked at the back of the man's leg and pushed him firmly in the chest. The man stumbled backwards to land in the arms of his laughing friends.

With fists clenched, Austin slowly turned. The noise in the pub diminished and settled to a disquieted mumble. "Anyone else?" he challenged.

Two men walked from the gloom; one returned to his group of friends, and the other walked up to Austin. "This way, sir."

Austin recognised the face as an enlisted man who'd served in the regiment years earlier. He followed him to the back of the pub and up a flight of stairs. When they reached the landing at the top, the man stopped and turned. "Sorry 'bout that, Cap'n. These blokes are a tad nervous with the mutton shunters[9] causing us bloody grief."

"That's quite alright, Thomas."

"This way, Cap'n, Sarge is wait'n." He opened the door to a private room with tables and chairs, where it was better lit, cleaner, and more civilised.

"Captain Willems, only you could cause such a ruckus at the Lamb and Flag, and I shoulda known." Sergeant Oliver 'Ollie' Nagle stood from behind the table where he sat and stepped out to greet his visitor. His wooden leg struck the floor in rhythm as he approached.

Austin grinned. "Ollie, it is always a pleasure to see you up and about when you should probably be locked up behind bars somewhere."

Ollie laughed, "Oh, Cap'n, but they'd have to catch me first," he bellowed with laughter, as did the other two men in the room.

"Get the officer a bloody drink, Thomas."

9   *Mutton Shunters – Another Victorian slang word for police.*

"Ale," Austin informed.

The captain and sergeant sat alone, nursing their third tankard of ale and caught up on old times with laughter and the spirit of camaraderie and shared experiences.

During a pause in their conversation, Ollie turned to Austin, "You didn't come by here just to catch up, Cap'n. Hows can I help?"

Austin explained about the recent death of his father and recounted how he'd lost his business due to the dishonesty of the directors of Grand Overland Rail.

Ollie shook his head. "I always liked your ol'man. He was a good sort, fair and respectful to all. Then I can only hope you'd be planning something. Revenge, Cap'n?"

"Aye, Ollie, and I need your assistance."

Ollie grinned, and Austin explained what he had in mind. When he was finished, Ollie leaned back in his seat. "Well, now, seems we may need a few people to lend us a hand, eh? I can get them, sir, but they will want a shiny coin or two."

"That's what I expected, Ollie, and you'll do all right from me too.'

"And when do you want to do this?"

"I think soon. I still need to check on a few details and arrange for another, er, gentleman to assist me."

Ollie's face broke out into a smile. "Don't tell me Lieutenant Newbury will be helping?"

Austin smiled. "I believe he will. But not a word, Ollie, keep this quiet until the last possible moment."

"You can trust me, Cap'n,"

"I know, and that's why I'm here. I will send word to you. Do I leave a note with the barman?"

"Aye, he's a good man, but he just doesn't show it. As long as the messenger tells him it's for Sarge, there's no problem, sir."

Austin stood. "It's late, and I should be returning home."

"Then I shall see you soon, Cap'n. An don't worry about the lads outside. They've been told to keep an eye on you so you don't get into trouble. They'll follow you just to keep guard," Ollie informed.

CHAPTER THIRTEEN

It was a non-descript residence in the Soho area. The street was once fashionable, but fourteen years earlier, an outbreak of Cholera forced the aristocracy away, and many of the once lovely homes now needed repair and love. Austin stood in a sheltered doorway and leaned casually against a wall with a newspaper held up to his face as he pretended to read.

He was waiting, if not somewhat impatiently, for someone to appear from number thirty-five. Specifically, he hoped, a woman named Mildred Cannock.

He'd never met Miss Cannock and knew not her age, appearance or countenance, so his visit was exploratory, or in military jargon, a reconnaissance mission. Howard Willoughby had obtained her name and address from his father. How his father came by her information, he didn't know, but it was valuable all the same.

George Dillington, similar to the other three directors of Grand Overland Rail, also had a passion. It wasn't sailing yachts, fine art, or thoroughbred horses; his delights were more carnal, and if Austin believed what he'd overheard from the directors while playing whist at White's gentlemen's club, his compulsion was for women.

Mr Dillington was grotesquely obese, his outward demeanour was undeniably loud and abrasive, and he couldn't have presented himself to anyone, let alone a woman, in a more distasteful way. Austin found it difficult to believe that any woman could endure his company for any length of time, let alone five minutes. More astounding was the fact that amorous George was also married to Pearl.

Typically, a man's hobbies might be tolerated by his wife, and if a man chooses to have an affair outside the bonds of marriage, that might be frowned upon or even vehemently discouraged. However, George Dillington's challenge lay in keeping his recreational pursuits a secret from Pearl, and Austin believed Mildred Cannock was his hobby.

When George Dillington first met Pearl, his wife-to-be, he was only a bank manager and somewhat slimmer. Somehow, a thread of romance had endured, strengthened and blossomed into love, and George not only married Pearl, which gave him access to her considerable family wealth, and by all accounts, lucky George had done well for himself. Needless to say, if Mrs Pearl Dillington had learned of her husband's hobby and habitual infidelity, George's luck might have run its course and the purse snapped shut.

Austin needed to confirm George and Mildred's relationship. Was it just casual or more of a sexual nature? He needed to be absolutely sure.

He had spent part of the previous afternoon in an enclosed coach, parked on the street, and peeking from behind curtains hoping to see if Miss Cannock ventured outside; she didn't. Today, he abandoned the coach and waited across the road, hoping to see her. It was relatively early, but so far, the only thing he'd noticed was the curtains of number thirty-five had been opened.

Austin reached for his fob watch from his waistcoat and looked at the time, he'd only been here for an hour. He returned the watch to its pocket and opened the newspaper to an unread page when his eyes flicked up when he caught sight of movement.

A woman appeared behind the door carrying a basket and proceeded to walk down the street. She wasn't exceptionally stylish or beautiful and more closely resembled a youngish maid, but he needed to confirm what he believed. He hastily folded the paper, tucked it under his arm, and followed her from across the road.

He guessed she was headed for the markets, so he quickened his stride, passed her and arrived at the produce markets two streets away before the woman did. To his relief, she appeared and began browsing and shopping. He positioned himself strategically so their paths would cross.

Austin turned and collided with the woman. "Excuse me; I'm so sorry. I was careless and had eyes only for apples," he stated. He noticed she wasn't as young as she first appeared, although she had a remarkable figure.

She collected herself and smiled. "I should have been paying more attention, sir."

Austin inclined his head slightly. "You look familiar to me, are you Miss Cannock?"

She looked uncomfortable, and half turned to walk away. "I'm sorry, sir, I don't believe we have met."

"Don't you recall? It was with George; he introduced us," Austin added with a lusty sneer. She blushed and couldn't help but smile at him, and he knew she was Mildred. Now came the challenge: he needed more information.

"Er, perhaps, but sir, I don't know your name."

"How rude of me. Miss Cannock, I'm Miles Siles."

She acknowledged him with a slight dip of her head.

Austin looked into her basket and saw she had quite a few vegetables, and he presumed she was cooking for more than one. "Is

George visiting this evening?"

"Oh, good gracious." She raised the basket so he could see. "No, this is for Ginny and Olga. It's my turn to cook."

He smiled. *Who were Ginny and Olga? Her children*? he thought. "Your daughters?" he asked.

"Mr Siles," Mildred blushed again. "I'm sure you've met them," she inappropriately leaned into him and lowered her voice. "At one of our parties."

Austin thought Mildred was a little over-familiar and improper and quickly decided she was a strumpet. He took a step closer so their shoulders touched and whispered, "Miss Cannock, I'm a little embarrassed. I, uh, don't remember names well, and If my memory serves me, we were a little pre-occupied, weren't we?" he grinned.

She giggled.

"I'll have to ask George when he's having his next get-together so I can reacquaint myself."

"Like always," Mildred whispered, "Sunday evening for guests."

"George is correct. You are a naughty girl."

"Oh, Mr Siles," she blushed again.

.

"Captain Willems is up to something, Mr De Vore," said Major Miles Siles awkwardly. Since the injury to his jaw, he'd had difficulty chewing and talking, but in the weeks since the pain and discomfort had diminished considerably, and he could again eat with care and talk as long as he didn't try to open his mouth wide. "As you asked, I followed him, and he's involved in some shenanigans. I just don't know what."

"And you failed to see whom he met in Soho?" Julian De Vore was rather displeased.

"All I know is he went to the Lamb and Flag, nothing more. And that woman he met in Covent Garden is nothing, just a trollop, Mr

De Vore."

Julian De Vore tugged at his beard as he thought. "You said he went to Ascot? Did he socialise or meet anyone?"

"He was with a friend, Lieutenant Charles Newbury, from his regiment. Nothing odd there, sir, they're good friends and have been for years. However, he met a striking young woman and had dinner with her and others."

Mr De Vore shook his head in frustration. From the core of his soul, he knew Austin Willems was scheming against Grand Overland Rail, but the true purpose of his activities eluded him. Not to mention, it cost a fortune to have him followed. He wasn't concerned about being reimbursed. He was required to detail and justify his expenses to his client. He sighed, "Who was this woman?"

Major Siles consulted his notes. "Er, a Miss Harriet Stephenson."

The name meant nothing to Julian. "And who did Captain Willems dine with? Miss Stephenson and…?"

"I have it here," Miles flicked a page or two on his notebook. "Uh, of note was Lord Eric and Lady Tidsbury…"

A minor lord of no consequence thought Julian.

"…and Sir Ronald Hewitt-Thompson and his wife, Eunice."

Julian's eyes snapped open, and his mouth suddenly felt dry. "Did you say Hewitt-Thompson?"

Miles nodded.

Julian reached for a glass of water. He had ensured that Major Siles did not know who his principal contacts were at Grand Overland Rail. And judging from the major's response, he was still completely unaware of his relationship with Grand Overland Rail's managing director.

"Did you need me to enquire further on Miss Stephenson, Lord Tidsbury, or the other chap, Sir Ronald?" Miles asked.

Julian placed the glass of water back on his desk. "Without

incurring huge costs, Major Siles, a little background on Miss Stephenson might prove valuable. ”

"Of course, sir."

"How were you able to obtain the names of those people?"

Miles shrugged. "It's amazing what a guinea can do, sir. But, when Mr Willems had dinner, it was at a private box in the Royal Enclosure. Since admittance is by royal invite, I use a telescope to observe, sir. Then, when they've gone, I approached the attendant and spoke to him. Two guineas will encourage people to talk, sir."

"Yes, I'm sure it does," Julian distractedly replied, wondering who the young woman dining with Sir Ronald and Captain Willems was. The Lord and Lady would be easy to learn about. He looked down at Major Siles. "When you can, continue to watch Mr Willems, and if anything peculiar happens, inform me immediately. Is that understood, Major?"

"Yes, sir."

"Now, I need you to return to Swindon and follow through with the workers laying track. I need their combined support very soon so we can consummate this deal. It represents an enormous sum of money for my client, and like our earlier arrangements, this new deal must go through as planned." He looked down at the sheet of paper Major Siles gave him, which detailed all Austin Willems's recent activities and whom he had met. He couldn't see a pattern, and there was no common association or logical explanation. "Very well, Major Siles, that will be all, carry on."

Miles eased himself from his seat, gathered his notebook and left the solicitor's office. Julian watched him go, poured himself a hefty whiskey, leaned back in his chair and thought more about Captain Austin Willems.

In the quietness of his office, the answer came. It was the only possible solution and would rid him of the pest plaguing him and interfering with his work and that of Grand Overland Rail and their objectives.

He walked from his desk, grabbed his coat and hat and entered reception. "Cancel my afternoon appointment and reschedule for tomorrow morning, Mrs Dutton."

After concluding a frustrating meeting with division staff, Lieutenant General Alexander Wardlow enjoyed his well-earned luncheon. With him sat his two *aide de camp*s, who were almost finished with their poached salmon.

When the general looked up and saw the lanky frame of Julian De Vore approach, he grunted quietly in annoyance. His two aides, familiar with their superior's nuances, knew this didn't portend well. The grunt they heard set alarm bells ringing, and they hurried to swallow the last vestiges of their meal.

"Lieutenant General Wardlow," exclaimed Julian in mock surprise as he approached the table. "How fortunate we should run into each other. May I have a seat?" Without waiting for an invitation, he slid a chair from the table and seated himself. "How is the salmon today?"

The two aides dabbed at their mouths with napkins. "Sir," said the *aide de camp* closest to the general. "We really do need to complete the assessments, er, with your permission…?"

The general scowled and nodded. His aides were tactful enough to know when their presence wasn't required. He waited for them to leave before focusing on his unwelcome visitor. "Why, Mr De Vore, you do have a knack for ruining a splendid lunch, and then what could have been a most glorious day?"

Julian ignored the slight. "I have a problem, General, and I believe you can be my saviour."

"If I were indeed your saviour, I'd have you shot to rid myself and others of the misery you bring."

"Captain Austin Willems," simply stated Julian.

"A letter was sent to his commanding officer outlining my disgust at his behaviour as you requested, De Vore. What more could you possibly want that won't draw attention to our fragile and most temporary liaison?"

"He resigned; that was it, and he wasn't punished. Captain Willems was not court-martialled, and he voluntarily resigned his commission. He enjoys the distinction of his service with honours, and that, General, is totally unacceptable."

Lieutenant General Wardlow toyed with his dinner knife and considered stabbing the detestable man before him in the throat. He smiled as he imagined the solicitor lying on the floor with blood spurting from a fatal wound on his neck as he took his last gurgling breath. "And what do you need me to do?" he stared malevolently with hooded eyes and waited for an answer.

"I want your office to court-martial Captain Willems."

"De Vore, you underestimate Captain Willems. He is a fine officer with a remarkable service record. He has attained recognition for his bravery and selfless actions on the battlefield, which have been acknowledged with honours. Your insistence is not only inappropriate but will only draw attention to the perceived failings of command and bring disrespect to the regiment – that it doesn't deserve."

With a sigh, Julian met the hostile gaze of the General. "It needs to be done soonest. See to it."

His lips compressed into a thin white line as the dinner knife moved from hand to hand. General Wardlow leaned forward and said nothing, but his expression spoke for him.

Unaffected by the implied physical threat, De Vore spoke. "I apologise, Lieutenant General Wardlow. I'm unable to dine with you today as I have other important matters to attend that require my attention." Julian kicked back his chair as he stood. "Good day, General." He turned and stalked off.

Lieutenant General Alexander Wardlow sat still and silently cursed his weakness and Julian De Vore.

As he'd done in the past, the General had considered resigning his commission. It would spare the 67th South Hampshire Regiment the humiliation of seeing one of its finest officers in an absurd spectacle of a court-martial and additionally bring unnecessary attention to why a divisional officer is involved in such a trivial matter. If he resigned his commission, he'd also be spared the ordeal of blackmail and the perverted influence of Julian De Vore. He wondered if there was another way to solve his dilemma and not bring attention to himself.

CHAPTER FOURTEEN

Austin sent a message to Harriet Stephenson, informing her that he would call on her Wednesday afternoon. He believed her stepfather wouldn't be home, which suited him fine. He certainly didn't want to meet him again, and the last thing he wanted was to be recognised—a distinct possibility if the man was sober.

He arrived at 25 Upper Brook Street in Mayfair with a bouquet that he hoped would brighten Harriet's day and, feeling a flutter of apprehension in his chest, stepped briskly from the cab. In the two weeks since he'd seen her last, she may have decided that she was no longer interested in him, and his visit to see her was unwelcome.

With his heart flutterering, he firmly gripped the door knocker, rapped twice and waited.

Moments later, a matronly servant opened the door. "Good afternoon, sir," she said politely, glancing at the flowers he was choking.

Austin took a cleansing breath. "Good afternoon, I am Captain Austin Willems. I believe I am expected."

She smiled. "Please come in." She opened the door wider, stepped back, and allowed Austin to enter the home of Sir Ronald Hewitt-Thompson. "May I take those, sir? I'll find a vase."

"Er, of course, thank you."

He'd only just sat on a chair in an expensively furnished drawing room when the door opened, and Harriet appeared. He stood quickly, and his mouth dropped open. She was…. She was beautiful and so radiant.

"Austin, how thoughtful of you to come and visit." She held out her hand and dipped her head. "Thank you for the flowers, a thoughtful gift."

He shut his mouth. "Harriet, it is lovely to see you. Er, you are beautiful, and you look so different." He forgot to release her hand.

She smiled and gave a little laugh. It sounded like the heavens had opened, and angels heralded the arrival of a divine being.

"Please be seated," she offered.

He stood mutely as all his faculties had deserted him, and he lost all sense of direction. Mrs Hewitt-Thompson entered. "Good afternoon, Captain Willems; it is a delight to see you again. We've been looking forward to your visit, haven't we, dear?"

"Mama," Harriet admonished.

Clarity returned in a rush, and Austin felt his cheeks redden. "Mrs Hewitt-Thompson, it's a pleasure and thank you for making me feel welcome."

She smiled warmly. "I have a few matters to attend to and will return shortly." She turned and left the room.

"Mama is so thoughtful to allow us a little privacy."

Austin couldn't disagree. "How have you been, Harriet? It feels like an eternity since Ascot, and admit, I looked forward to seeing you."

They talked and forgot about the time, and Mrs Hewitt-Thompson appeared occasionally and mindfully allowed them time alone. Eventually, she entered the room, stood with hands clasped and looked at Austin. "Captain Willems, it is a glorious day, and Harriet and I often enjoy a stroll in the park. Would you care to join us?"

Hyde Park was only yards away from Harriet's home. Austin looked at Harriet, who gave a subtle nod. "Of course, I'd love to, Mrs Hewitt-Thompson."

Harriet slid her arm through his, and her mother followed a few steps behind. It was unseemly for an unmarried woman to walk with a man unchaperoned in public. They entered Hyde Park, and Harriet encouraged Austin to walk towards a sheltered seat where Eunice promptly sat.

"Come, Austin," Harriet tugged his arm.

Austin turned to her mother for approval, and she smiled in return.

They strolled in the warmth of the afternoon sun, always within sight of her mother, and Austin enjoyed every minute. After a while, Harriet stopped. They were relatively close to her mother but far enough away not to be overheard. She gently eased her arm free and looked up at him. "Austin, there is something on my mind, and I admit to being a little puzzled, but this has been sitting uneasily with me."

Austin's eyebrows furrowed. "Oh, is there something I can do?"

She bent down, plucked a daisy from the grass, and toyed with it. "Yes," she said. "At Ascot, when I invited you to dine with us, my stepfather asked where your regiment was based. Do you recall that?"

Austin was puzzled. "Of course. And I replied that the regiment is based in Westchester."

"But you said more. Austin, how did you know my stepfather's name? I had not told you his name, but you knew it. I thought you might bring it up later during our conversations, but you didn't." She looked down at the tiny flawless flower she toyed with before looking up and meeting his eyes."

His heart began thumping in his chest as he sought an answer. He looked down at her and held her questioning gaze. Her face was perfect, unblemished and innocent. Yet she was quick of mind and, as he discovered, astute.

He fought the impulse to wrap his arms around her and hold her close.

Deceiving or lying to her was the last thing he wanted to do. "I am a member of White's, the gentleman's club where your stepfather is also a member, and I overheard his name while he played whist."

"But why did you not mention that to him at dinner? Why wouldn't you have told him if you are both members of the same club and share common interests? I admit to being a little vexed, Austin."

"It's of no real consequence, Harriet. As he did not recognise me... I felt it unimport– I did not incline to bring it up."

"I see," she replied. "Then you won't mind if I tell him that? He'd be interested in learning about your association at White's. It puts you in good standing with him, does it not?" she smiled.

Austin's heart thumped almost uncontrollably. He was in a dilemma, and poor Harriet had unwittingly stumbled on his secret. He thought of his father and how Sir Ronald and the other three directors had destroyed him. He had no choice; he had to tell her something...

"Harriet, when we met at Ascot, I did not know you were the daughter–"

"Stepdaughter," she clarified.

"Yes, the stepdaughter of Ronald Hewitt-Thompson. When I

arrived at your table at the Royal Enclosure, that was the first I knew of it." He twisted to look behind and saw Harriet's mother reading from a small pocket-sized book. He turned back to face Harriet. "I accepted the invitation to dine with you because I met a wonderful woman I am deeply attracted to. If I am forward, forgive me, but I shall not lie or offer deception as I respect you too much. I came here to Mayfair to see you, only you." He took a deep breath and squared his shoulders, to show her he was determined. "I would enjoy seeing our relationship develop and grow, Harriet. Your stepfather does not factor or play a part in my interest in you."

She looked thoughtful. "But Austin, you have not answered me. How do you know my stepfather? And I can only presume you don't want me to tell him that you know who he is?"

He nodded and felt contrite as his shoulders relaxed. "Because, Harriet, your stepfather and his businesses are linked to my father's death."

She gasped, and her hand flew to her mouth.

"I think it is time I went home, Harriet." He turned away from her.

She reached out to hold his arm. "Austin, what happened? Please, tell me."

He could feel the warmth of her delicate hand... he exhaled. "Harriet, I'm unable to tell you more at this time. All I can say is that my intentions towards you are honourable, and I wish you no harm or ill will. I want to see us become good friends and possibly more, and your stepfather adds a complication that will only come between us."

"Austin, please, let me talk."

"I ask a kindness from you, Harriet. Please, please, do not under any circumstances mention me, my White's membership or my family name to him. It's all I ask."

Her expression changed, and he saw a dark cloud slowly descend over her. He turned away and walked towards her mother, who'd been studying them.

Harriet followed a step behind. "Captain Willems has to return home, Mama."

"I will escort you back," offered Austin.

Unseen and partially concealed by the trunk of a stately oak, Miles Siles observed from the shadows afforded him by the expanse of its branches and leaves. He lowered his small pocket telescope, extracted a notebook and hastily scribbled some notes.

Austin returned home totally devastated. Harriet Stephenson deserved so much more than what he offered. He couldn't tell her about the vileness of her stepfather and how he and other associates schemed and plotted to deceive so many people, and obviously, he couldn't share his plans on how he would seek retribution.

He'd met the woman of his dreams. She wasn't a wallflower, a passive socialite seeking to impress. Harriet differed from all the other women he'd met or had short relationships with, and now that he'd found her, he'd destroyed any chances of developing a romance. He fumed as he entered his home at The Regent's Park.

Nanny knew immediately that something was wrong. After taking his hat and coat, she gripped his elbow and led him to the kitchen. "I just baked a cake, and I think it would serve you well to sit quietly and enjoy a piece; what say you, sir?"

Austin knew it was futile to disagree and allowed himself to be led to a familiar stool in the kitchen. The same seat he sat at when a boy when she made him a snack or lunch. The same stool he sat on and pouted when scolded by his father.

He couldn't help himself, and while he enjoyed her cake, he poured his heart out to her. She listened and tut-tutted and offered the benefit of her wisdom and advice. As he always did, he felt remarkably better.

When they heard a knock at the door, she wiped her hands on a dishcloth and hurried to greet the caller. She returned shortly after, looking a little flustered. "There is a gentleman at the door. Definitely military, and he refuses to give his name and insists on seeing you, sir, and he won't divulge the nature of his call."

Austin wondered who it could be. "See him seated in the drawing room, Nanny, and I'll be there momentarily."

"As you wish, sir." She trotted out and heard her welcome his guest and show him in.

"Good afternoon, Captain Willems. Excuse me for my unexpected visit, but it is of some importance that I speak to you."

Austin walked to his chair and tried to recall where he'd seen the man before. He was familiar, and as Nanny accurately guessed, obviously military, but he couldn't put a name to the face. "That's quite all right, Mister?"

"Captain, my visit here is unofficial, and if my superiors knew I was here… well, it wouldn't bear thinking about."

Yes, military, definitely an officer, but who? "Then, considering the risk you put yourself in, I hope I can help," Austin smiled congenially.

The officer leaned forward on his chair and played with his fingers that were steepled together. "Captain Willems, it has come to my knowledge that an individual seeks to illegally influence a senior officer to initialise court-martial proceedings against you."

Austin straightened in his chair. "For what offence?" he blurted out.

"Outwardly, it appears to be battery, and you assaulted a retired officer, Major Siles and broke his jaw or committed some other ungodly injury."

Austin looked horrified.

"But I am not here to serve you an official notice. As I said, I'm here of my volition."

"Please continue," Austin encouraged.

"Are we able to talk in confidence?"

"There is no one here but Nanny and the two of us. Anything you say stays within these walls unless we deem otherwise." Austin could see the man was nervous and highly agitated.

"I have come to understand that, as I said, a senior officer is being blackmailed by a civilian. This senior officer was instructed to draft charges for your subsequent court-martial."

Austin shook his head in disbelief. "All right, can you tell me who this civilian is?"

"I can, a solicitor named Julian De Vore."

Austin placed his hands over his face.

"Then you are familiar with him," stated the officer after seeing Austin's reaction.

"Indeed," Austin removed his hands. "Although not personally. Do you know what Mr De Vore is blackmailing this senior officer about?"

"I'm a little uncertain and have some limited information. I'd need to do a little research to confirm."

"Look, unless you can tell me who this senior officer is, then there is nothing I can do, and to be candid with you, sir, I don't know why you came here. I've resigned my commission."

The officer nodded in understanding. "I came here because what Mr De Vore is doing is wrong. It's illegal. As you are no longer a commissioned officer, you can investigate and make inquiries and possibly end this for him and yourself. Captain, I know with absolute authority that the senior officer never believed you had committed any crime of significance to warrant a court martial or resign your commission; perhaps you deserved a verbal reprimand, but nothing more."

"Does this senior officer know you've come here?"

The man shook his head, "No, not at all; he has no inkling."

"Then who is it? For God's sake, man, give me something if you want me to help. Tell me his name," Austin appealed.

The man grimaced. "Lieutenant General Alexander Wardlow."

"What!" Austin exclaimed. "Good heavens. Now I know your reluctance." The general was a powerful man and commanded the division. He looked intently at the officer. "We have met before… Then you are his *aide de camp*, Major Ryan, er, Seth Ryan."

The man continued his grimace. "I'm one of two *aide de camps*."

"But why come to me?"

"Because, Captain, other than the General, you have the most to lose. A court-martial will see you discredited, and you will lose your rank and honours. Don't for one moment believe you'll receive a fair and just hearing; you won't. The outcome of your court-martial has been pre-determined."

Austin stood. "What do you believe General Wardlow has done? Give me your thoughts, what you suspect."

Major Ryan stood and stepped close to Austin and lowered his voice. "A Molly[10]."

Austin looked aghast. "The General?"

The Major shook his head. "No, his son is a Molly-Boy and was caught, and the General paid someone to ensure his son didn't face criminal charges."

---

10   *Molly – Victorian slang to describe a homosexual or gay man.*

"And somehow, Julian De Vore caught wind of it?" Austin asked.

"Yes, that's what I believe, but I cannot be certain."

Austin rubbed his chin and then looked at the major. "I understand now, and you're here because of Julian De Vore. Somehow, you know that I have an association with the man."

Major Ryan nodded. "Colonel Farwell was defending you to General Wardlow, and I overheard him say that Julian De Vore was behind the baseless accusation and had something to do with your father's death. I was also there when De Vore came to see the General when he demanded the court-martial."

Austin walked back to his chair, and it all made sense to him now.

CHAPTER FIFTEEN

It hadn't been a good week for Austin; he felt disheartened about Harriet and worried endlessly over the possibility of a court-martial. While he was no longer a serving member of the army, his voluntary resignation gave him distinction. However, if he was court-martialled, he could lose respectability in the eyes of the community. He didn't give a damn if he could or couldn't use his military rank; what concerned him was upholding his good name and character. A court-martial would be more than a slight blemish on his career; it would be an indelible stain.

He explained his meeting with Major Ryan to Howard Willoughby and outlined what he'd been told.

"Extortion and blackmail are a pervasive scourge, Austin. A conviction for committing homosexual acts can lead to capital punishment. However, the courts seldom rule so harshly these days, so I fully understand the position of General Wardlow and feel a measure of sympathy for the man and the need to protect his son."

Austin nodded in agreement. "And that detestable Julian De Vore is blackmailing the General to ensure I'm court-martialled and found guilty. What can I do? I can't go to the police because that will impact his actions to protect his son. Can you report De Vore to someone?"

"With what evidence? If I go to the Law Society, it becomes his word against mine."

Austin shifted in his seat to a more comfortable position. "Then tell me, Howard, how can I get out of this unscathed and protect the General and his son?"

Howard chewed on the stem of his unlit pipe, and only the sound of a ticking clock disturbed the silence.

Austin leaned forward with his elbows on his knees. "Howard?"

The solicitor removed the pipe from his mouth and raised his head.

Austin continued. "Then I shall employ some unethical tactics and turn the tables on Mr Julian De Vore. I can even use it to my advantage and achieve a favourable outcome regarding Grand Overland Rail."

"As your friend, I advise you to think carefully and act wisely, Austin," Howard frowned.

Austin's expression was grim. "I have little to no choice."

Austin sat alone on a seat at Victoria Embankment Gardens that fronted the River Thames. He checked his fob watch and saw it was almost four o'clock. Punctual and on time as ever, he saw the distinctive gait of Sergeant Oliver Nagle as he approached.

They spent the best part of an hour chatting. Austin explained the situation around his impending court-martial and General Wardlow's son. After a while, Ollie rubbed his thigh just above his stump. "Don't think I'll ever get used to havin' one leg, Cap'n. Is worse in the bloody cold." Ollie shifted his gaze and focused on Austin. "When do you want to do this?"

"The sooner, the better. How about tomorrow?"

"Then I need to get busy."

Austin reached into a pocket, extracted some money and handed it over. "This should be more than enough."

"You don't be need'in to do this, Cap'n."

"I do. Fair is fair."

"And you're positive, sir, that this De Vore character ain't gonna recognise you?"

"He won't recognise me; the only one who can is this Major Miles Siles, the officer I told you about. I need to make sure he doesn't turn up or interfere."

"Very well, sir. I'll make sure this bloody Major Siles and anyone else don't stick their beak in. There'll be plenty o' lads around."

With a grunt, Ollie stood, and Austin eased himself from the hard seat. "For the regiment, eh, Ollie?"

"And for good friends, Cap'n," Ollie grinned and hobbled away.

Julian De Vore finished writing in his daily journal and was about to begin his next task when the receptionist knocked on his door and entered. He looked up at her in curiosity.

"Mr De Vore, this just came for you." She stepped forward and handed her employer a folded message.

As she left his office, he unfolded the document and read.

Please come soonest, urgent matter to discuss. I
will wait for you at the Inner Temple Gardens.
M.S

He turned the document over and saw nothing on the back; it was blank. It was apparent that the M.S initials could only be Miles Siles. The Inner Temple Gardens were close by, less than a two-minute walk, but what on earth could be so important there? He wondered.

Because some of his business practices were a little questionable, there was always a possibility something may have gone wrong, and as Mr Siles was his intermediary, then it was prudent to take the message seriously.

With some haste, he snatched his coat and hat, told the receptionist he would be out briefly and exited his building onto Middle Temple Lane. He stepped across the road, beneath the arches and past the Crown Chambers. He turned right and paused momentarily, hoping to catch sight of Major Siles.

The lawn was mostly deserted, and he walked down towards the trees where he hoped to find him.

The tall figure of Julian De Vore was unmistakable, and behind him and unseen, youths appeared, street lads, who quickly spread out and began loitering near the arches and the access lane to the small park in the other direction. Their murky presence was enough to dissuade anyone from venturing into the gardens. Had Mr De Vore been more attentive, he would also have seen more lads near the walkway beside the River Thames, and they, too, prevented anyone from wandering anywhere near where the solicitor was headed.

Not that far away, Julian could see three men approaching, and judging from the awkward gait of one of them, appeared to have a wooden leg. However, neither looked like Mr Siles, and they would pass by him. He walked under the branches of the trees, and in the shadows, he saw a lone figure with his back to him. He briskly walked over, annoyed at the untimely disruption of his day.

"Mr Siles, I find your methods of communicating rather– "He stopped midsentence as the figure in front of him suddenly yelped and fell forward with arms outstretched onto a tree trunk for support. His unfastened trousers slipped down, and with one hand, he reached behind and held his lower back.

"Mr Siles!" exclaimed Julian as he took the last two steps towards the stricken figure and stood near his feet.

At that exact moment, the man cried out. "Please, don't bugger me, Mr De Vore, not again, please!" he wailed in pure torment.

Immediately, Julian knew it wasn't Miles Siles but an imposter. He swivelled his head to see who was playing a prank on him and saw the three men he'd seen earlier standing frozen and watching in obvious disgust.

The man leaning against the tree straightened, hoisted his trousers and refastened his buttons. "Don't bugger me anymore, Mr De Vore!" he cried.

"Mr De Vore! What vile and disgusting behaviour is this?" yelled Howard Willoughby.

"It isn't what you think!" Julian said with growing fear. "I know you, … er, Mr Willoughby."

"The police need to be informed," added Austin.

"No, no, stop, this is a set-up!"

"Police! Police!" yelled Sergeant Oliver Nagle in his loud parade-ground voice.

The clean-cut and very handsome young victim finished tucking in his shirt and ran as quickly as he could towards Howard, Austin and Ollie. "He was buggering me, sirs. He made me–"

"Rubbish and utter nonsense," Julian quickly responded.

"Police! Police!" continued Ollie.

"Mr De Vore, I find your behaviour disgusting and shall inform the police of what I witnessed. Shame on you," Howard stated.

"I know what I saw, and the Police will be keen to learn what I have to say," replied Austin with a stern look.

"Police!" yelled Ollie.

"Gentlemen," appealed Julian as he stepped closer to the three men and pointed to the victim, "This man will tell you I committed no crime. Go on, tell them, damn you!" he shouted in frustration and anger.

Howard shook his head in mock sympathy, "Mr De Vore, by my accounts and that of my associates, what we witnessed is despicable, and frankly, I find it difficult to feel any compassion for you, let alone this poor young man." He waved his arm at the victim, who turned his face away from Julian and addressed him. "Perhaps, sir, as the constabulary have yet to arrive, I could provide them with your name and address so they can investigate the matter. As luck would have it, I am a solicitor."

The victim, a well-dressed young man, wiped his teary eyes, reached into his pocket and handed Howard a business card. "I feel so ashamed…"

"M, Mr Willoughby," stuttered Mr De Vore, "let's not act hastily now. This man is nothing more than a scoundrel and deceiver with intentions to extort me. I'm an innocent man caught in an unlawful scheme." Suddenly, he lunged for the victim. Austin, who, as planned, had remained relatively silent, stepped in between them.

"The three of us witnessed a sexual perversion, sir, and I fully intend to explain this to the police. Best you do not threaten the victim; it wouldn't look good to have that added onto the police charges," Austin warned.

"I can explain everything. This is a farce—"

Howard reached for his fob watch, flicked it open, glanced at it quickly and snapped it closed. "Mr De Vore, I have an appointment I must attend. I suggest you come by my office tomorrow afternoon, say, er, five o'clock, and we can discuss how to proceed. Is that equitable?"

"I want the bastard locked up!" shouted the victim. And kind sir, as you are in the legal profession, could you be my legal counsel?" asked the victim.

"Let me remind you, I'm a solicitor, young man, but my legal practice retains barristers who can advocate for you."

Julian De Vore looked like he was going to explode.

"Mr De Vore?" Howard asked.

"Yes, yes, damn it. Tomorrow at five."

"Saw a constable," Ollie suddenly said and pointed towards a crowd of people far in the distance.

"Splendid, and about time," said Austin.

"Er, I must be going. I, too, have an appointment," said Julian as he turned and gave the victim a disparaging look of pure hate. He began striding quickly back the way he came. The lads who'd prevented anyone from straying near them had discretely vanished.

No one said a word until Julian De Vore walked beneath the arches and disappeared from view.

Clarence Hurst, the victim, bent over with hands on his thighs and loudly exhaled. "Good heavens," he gasped.

Ollie laughed, "Clarence, that was quite a performance."

The unemployed theatrical actor looked up at Ollie and grinned. "My best yet."

"Bravo! Bravo, and thank you. Thank you so much. What you all did was perfect. Do you think we have him, Howard?" Austin asked.

"I don't know; perhaps we do. He is certainly aware of the precarious situation he now finds himself in. Let's see if he turns up at the office tomorrow."

"Since when did you have a bloody business card?" Ollie asked Clarence.

"I don't. It was one of Mr Willoughby's; he gave it to me earlier, and I just handed it back as we arranged."

Ollie laughed and clapped his friend on his back.

"I think it best we all split up and best we aren't seen together," Austin suggested.

"And we'll talk more about your other stuff later, Cap'n."

"I'll contact you in a few days," Austin replied.

Howard and Austin watched Ollie and the actor walk away.

Howard shook his head. "If I may say, Austin, that was a very believable scenario. That actor Clarence pulled it off admirably."

"And Ollie's lads kept everyone else away, and fortunately, there were no witnesses other than the three of us." Austin glanced around. "Time we departed, Howard, and we can discuss it further over dinner tonight. Nanny is expecting you."

"My heart is still racing," stated Austin over dinner.

"I admit, if it wasn't for that stellar performance from that actor, I don't know if we could have pulled it off," Howard replied between mouthfuls. "I'm too old for this sort of thing, but it does get the blood pumping."

"And what happens tomorrow?"

"There are several factors in our favour. Three witnesses. A solicitor, a gentleman, and a retired army sergeant observed the crime. De Vore will be conscious of that. He seemed convinced we were legitimately passing by and not part of the conspiracy because we were walking to my office on the next street. It was happenstance."

"Pure bad luck," grinned Austin.

"If he turns up at the office, I will remind him of the witnesses and present him with an offer he can't refuse."

"What happens if he does refuse?"

"Then, my dear boy, we may have to go to the police and inform them of the extortion and expose the General's son. Just remember, your head may yet be on the chopping block.

CHAPTER SIXTEEN

After the drama of the previous afternoon with Julian De Vore, the anxiety he felt over Harriet returned. Austin felt increasing guilt over how he treated her, and try as he might, he couldn't stop thinking about it.

As an eligible bachelor, he'd called on many young women and had no success developing a genuine long-term romantic interest. His father had spoken of romance and encouraged him to seek love because, he explained, love was the unbreakable bond that held a relationship together. Even during the hard times, love will prevail. Infatuation and lust will always pass, he cautioned with a wink.

He'd encouraged his son to call on women to enjoy their company without becoming embroiled in fanciful desires of wealth, status or power. You will know the woman of your future when you meet her because nothing else matters.

The wisdom of his father never seemed more appropriate. Meeting Harriet at the stables that day in Ascot was revealing; it brought attention to his failings and misgivings and his selfish belief that love lay purely within the illusory imagination of poets and performers.

Was love an abstract concept sought by the hopeless? He didn't think so, not anymore. Being with Harriet was different, and if reciprocal love was possible and tangible, then he had never been closer to experiencing that when he was with her.

What he told her at Hyde Park was the truth. And as much as he despised her stepfather, Ronald Hewitt-Thompson, and if he had a future with Harriet, then he didn't see the man playing much of a role in his life. Sir Ronald was irrelevant and inconsequential, but to Harriet, he was her stepfather. He had to honour and respect that relationship if he wanted to be honest with himself and her. However, considering how he last spoke to her, a future didn't seem likely, especially since he had no intention of stopping his crusade against Grand Overland Rail directors, including her stepfather.

Austin sighed, rose from his seat and walked to the window to gaze over The Regent's Park. Happy couples strolled arm in arm, a few men returned home from work to their families, and keenly watched by a protective nanny, two boys played joyfully with a ball. Lost in thought, he observed them as he considered his plans of retribution.

He needed Charles's help here in London, but that wasn't possible because the regiment was currently training in the countryside, and he had to wait for the meeting outcome with Julian De Vore.

He also needed to decide what he would do with the stolen artwork. He had no interest in selling or displaying them, and his intention was nothing more than to hurt the directors and let them experience the pain of losing something close to their hearts.

The same went for Sir Ronald's horses. Where would he keep them, and what to do with them? A solution would come; he knew it would.

At this time of the afternoon, more people were outside walking in the park. Austin's gaze wandered closer to the road, where he saw a man beneath a tree in front of his home. His movement caught his eye as he unexpectedly appeared from behind the trunk and began walking away. Austin casually watched and was surprised when the man turned his head to look at something. Even from a distance, he recognised Miles Siles.

How long had Major Siles been spying on him, and was his every move being watched? This posed a problem, and Austin was deeply concerned.

With Miles Siles on his mind, he turned from the window and glanced at the clock. It was half past two. Howard's meeting with Mr De Vore was at five, and Howard asked for him to attend.

Refreshed, dressed and looking presentable, Austin stepped from the rear entrance to his home, generally used by servants and tradesmen. He looked both ways and searched for any clues he was being observed. Seeing none, he walked briskly up the service lane onto York Gate, turned right and looked for a cab. Thankfully, no one followed.

He exited the cab on Kingsway, a few streets away from Walker, Wakefield and Willoughby, Barristers and Solicitors, on Essex Street. To ensure he wasn't followed, he took an erratic path to Howard's office and arrived at half-past four.

Howard was pleased to see him and appeared a little apprehensive. As he reminded, what they were doing was illegal, and if caught, the repercussions would be severe and impact them both. Howard's main concern was for Austin, and as the ageing solicitor clarified, he didn't need to work and only did so as not to become idle and bored, while Austin was a young man with a rosy future ahead of him.

The clock on the wall showed four fifty-five when Howard's secretary informed him that Mr De Vore was waiting in reception.

"Are you ready?" Howard asked.

Austin nodded.

"Show him in, and then go home, dear."

"Thank you, Mr Willoughby."

Austin didn't rise or offer a greeting when Julian De Vore entered. Howard was professionally courteous and indicated for him to be seated. Austin deliberately sat slightly behind and to the side of Mr De Vore. If the solicitor wanted to communicate with Austin, it would prove awkward.

From his mannerisms, Austin could discern that De Vore appeared nervous and fidgety, and it was confirmed when without pleasantries, he came directly to the point.

"What's this all about then? You–" he twisted to look behind. "– both know I was stitched up. I committed no lewd or illegal acts of a sexual nature, and that man, that accuser, he, he, is nothing more than a swindler and–"

"Mr De Vore," began Howard calmly and with confidence. "At this time, your opinion matters little, and the fact is you've been accused of buggery." Howard shook his head slightly to emphasise his disapproval and disgust."

"Has he gone to the police? Has he made a complaint?"

Howard's expression turned grave. "You are most fortunate, and for the time being, I have advised my client not to go to the police."

"But I did nothing; I committed no crime," appealed Julian.

"Not from where I observed, Mr De Vore. To me, it was plain, and you appeared to be, er, quite intimate with the victim."

"He isn't a bloody victim, I am!" De Vore raised his voice in anger. "Anyway, why is he here?" De Vore pointed over his shoulder at Austin.

"Just in case any matters need clarifying. He isn't here in any legal capacity and is only a witness to an alleged crime." Howard smiled.

Julian De Vore's anger simmered.

"As I stated, Mr De Vore, I'm quite happy to put this unpleasant business behind us, as I'm sure you are too." Howard smiled benevolently. "However, my client has been adamant and wishes this law firm to advocate for him and see the incident reported to the authorities."

Julian De Vore gripped each chair's armrest with whitened knuckles and looked like he would launch himself at Howard. Austin tensed and prepared himself to move quickly.

"However, this raises an interesting issue, Mr De Vore," Howard continued. "It has come to my attention that you could do yourself and another client of mine a great service."

Julian's eyebrows furrowed, and he relaxed a little. "What service?" He twisted uncomfortably to spare a glance at the stranger seated behind him.

"I am convinced I can prevent my client from making a complaint against you to the police. In return–"

"In return?" loudly questioned De Vore. "What is this, blackmail?"

"In return," Howard ignored the accusation and continued, "you will cease all attempts to seek a court-martial against my client, Captain Austin Willems, for allegedly striking your employee, Major Siles."

"I have absolutely no idea what you are referring to. This is ridiculous, utter nonsense! What are you insinuating?"

"I'm not insinuating anything, Mr De Vore. I'm simply suggesting that you notify General Wardlow and inform him that you've changed your mind and will forget any alleged improprieties his son may or may not have committed and forever drop the matter."

Julian again looked like he would leap from his seat as he throttled its armrests.

"And, instruct General Wardlow that you prefer Captain Willems is not court-martialled."

"This is extortion!" exclaimed Julian. "I was right; this is a stitch-up! How dare you…"

Austin smiled; the irony seemed lost on De Vore.

"Mr De Vore, your professional conduct has left much to be desired, and you discredit the legal profession through your actions. You know as well as I that a man in your employ attacked my client without cause. Your, Mr Siles, viciously assailed my client, who only defended himself. Why you chose to target Mr Willems, I don't know. But it–will–stop!"

Austin watched in awe as Howard's theatrics intensified. It was masterful.

"Mr De Vore, I witnessed an abhorrent act that repulsed and sickened me. If you give me the opportunity, I shall see you judged, convicted and receive a well-deserved custodial sentence." Howard stood and leaned forward with his arms on his desk. "I will use all the available resources at my disposal to–see–it–done!"

Julian's mouth opened.

"Do you doubt me, SIR!" Howard yelled.

Julian shot from his chair and stood glaring at Howard. "I don't know what you are up to, Mr Willoughby, but something reeks."

Austin had heard enough. He rose from his seat, strode toward Julian and paused threateningly before him.

Julian took an involuntary step backwards.

Austin decided it was time he contributed. "Let me remind you that Lieutenant General Wardlow is a distinguished and respected senior officer in the service of Her Majesty. Captain Willems has had an exemplary career with honours. The unfortunate victim who we witnessed you buggering ostensibly comes from a well-heeled and influential family. Now, if this were to go to court, then tell me, Mr De Vore, as a man who makes his money advising clients on legal matters, how do you believe the court will react when they hear the testimony from these upstanding gentlemen?" Austin tightly clenched his fists. "Sit down, Mr De Vore!"

De Vore looked from Austin and faced Howard. "Who is this man, and why is he here? Is he in the military and working for the General?"

Austin's hand snaked out and tightly gripped Julian's elbow. With a twist and a painful yelp, he forced De Vore's arm into an unnatural position. He had no choice but to obey as Austin stepped to the side and pulled down, forcing him back onto his seat.

"You can't do this!" Julian cried out.

"I can, and this is what you fully deserve," hissed Austin between clenched teeth. He returned to his chair.

Wisely, Julian didn't react and looked down at his arm as he massaged his elbow.

"Your decision, Mr De Vore," stated Howard.

"I believe I don't have a choice in the matter." A vein on his neck pulsed rapidly.

"Mr De Vore?"

"Damn it, as I have no choice in the matter, I'll do as you ask."

"You will immediately notify General Wardlow. Is that understood?"

De Vore nodded.

"Then that concludes our business, Mr De Vore."

"For now," said De Vore quietly.

"Pardon me?" Howard asked.

"Mr De Vore," Austin interjected. "Your immediate concern is to ensure the General knows he is no longer being blackmailed, and he should abandon any court-martial proceeding against the Captain. Beyond that, my advice to you is to secure your safety. London is a dangerous place, and accidents do happen."

De Vore's face distorted. "Am I now being threatened?"

"Consider it an advisement," replied Austin.

Howard stood and offered a professional smile. "Mr De Vore, thank you for coming to see me today. It was a fruitful and productive visit. I shan't keep you any longer, as I'm sure you have other things to do that require your attention."

Julian De Vore stood, glaring at Howard and Austin before storming from the office, leaving the door ajar.

Howard followed and waited for him to exit the building before returning. He exhaled loudly. "That was a tad stressful, was it not?"

"De Vore is detestable and pure evil. Even when confronted about what he has done, he showed no contrition or even acknowledgement. Aye, even we have soiled our hands, Howard, but that creature is the worst."

"I was fearful you would assault him."

Austin grimaced. "I apologise, the man upset me. It required all my willpower not to strike him. He turned to Howard, who began pouring whiskey into two glasses. "Do you think he will do as we ask?"

Howard handed Austin a glass and sat down before taking a sip. "When De Vore came here, he believed that you and I were just witnesses and that it was merely a coincidence that Sergeant Ollie, you and I happened along. De Vore believes he was framed. How could he not? But it doesn't change anything. And how it hasn't dawned on him who you are does surprise me."

Austin held the glass to his lips. "Be careful, Howard. Miles Siles is following me, and perhaps he will have someone follow you, too."

"What?"

"Obviously, under instructions from De Vore, Miles Siles is watching me."

"That is bothersome."

"It won't continue," Austin added.

CHAPTER SEVENTEEN

The postman delivered a letter from Lieutenant Charles Newbury, and to Austin's delight, Charles said he would arrive in London the following week to enjoy a period of leave and cryptically wrote that he had a present for him. Austin guessed the gift was a key made from an impression by the master craftsman, old Jack, one of the regimental armourers. The key would gain them access to the secure room at the art storage company Finch & Gossett. Austin grinned; his dear friend Charles came through with the forged key, which now gave Austin the impetus to begin planning earnestly.

The next day he met with Ollie at the Lamb and Flag pub in Covent Garden, and the two of them went over details, plans and how many other individuals they'd need to rob Finch & Gossett and destroy the boat at the Tower Bridge Moorings. They also established that it was impossible to steal the horses belonging to Sir Ronald on the same evening. Windhaven, Sir Ronald's country estate in Chieveley, was too far away and would require a train journey and on arrival, he would need accommodation and suitable transportation. Thankfully, the discovery of stolen artwork from Finch & Gossett wouldn't be noticed until much later, Austin decided they would take the artwork first, then the boat at the mooring and lastly the horses a day or two later.

With his head spinning, Austin returned by cab and entered the doorway to his home to be greeted by Nanny.

She took his hat and coat. "You have a guest in the drawing room, sir," she simply said.

Austin looked at her in question, as he wasn't expecting any visitors. "Oh, who is it?"

"I suggest you freshen up, sir. You smell like you've been in a swamp." She swatted some lint and other foreign matter from his coat and turned to walk away.

"Who is the guest?"

"You mustn't keep a lady waiting," she replied over her shoulder.

Perplexed, Austin wondered who this female caller was. He rushed to his room, cleaned himself, combed his hair, and, feeling somewhat presentable, returned downstairs, entered the drawing room and froze.

"Harriet, what a pleasant surprise. I, uh, I had no idea you would visit. Did you come alone?"

She stood and politely extended her hand. "Yes, Austin, I came alone, although Mama is visiting a friend in the neighbourhood. It was convenient for me to slip out."

"Please, have a seat. Nanny told me I had a guest but didn't say who it was. But, er, does your mother know you are here?"

"Her friend lives a few houses down the street and she knows I am here."

"Had I known you would visit, I would have arrived sooner. I hope you weren't waiting long?"

She smiled. "I was helping Nanny in the kitchen, and we baked a cake."

"You did what?"

She laughed, "When I arrived, she was preparing to make a cake, and we began talking, and one thing led to another, and I helped."

Her laugh was delightful, and he smiled warmly in return. If Nanny had been speaking to Harriet for any length of time, that was most unusual. But to have Harriet in the kitchen helping her was unheard of.

Harriet fidgeted with the cuff of her dress sleeve. "Austin, I came here today to speak frankly." She raised her head and looked at him. "Will you permit me?"

"Of course, I am pleased you chose to visit, regardless of your reason. I wasn't sure–"

"When you departed Hyde Park, you did so after telling me about how your father's death is linked to my stepfather. Is this not so?"

He nodded, "Indeed."

"Yet you did not allow me the opportunity to speak."

She continued to look at him closely, and he felt captivated by her. "And I apologise, Harriet. I acted hastily and have regretted it ever since."

Typically, by now, Nanny would have made an appearance and offered tea and cakes. Austin had a feeling she knew not to interrupt.

"As have I, Austin. But I want to comment on what you said, and I can only hope you won't think badly of me."

He wanted to reach out and embrace her. "I don't think that is possible, Harriet. I could never think ill of you."

She nibbled on her bottom lip, and he could see that whatever she wanted to say was difficult. "You told me that you have an interest in my stepfather, but I think it's fair to warn you about him. He is a detestable man, Austin. He is corrupt, immoral, and a beast." She maintained eye contact with Austin. "His presence causes me distress and even fear."

"Fear?" Austin croaked. He couldn't believe what she was saying.

"Yes, he has hurt Mama and threatened me. His temper and violence worry us both. If he is somehow caught up in your father's death, then I am so sorry. I could never doubt what you said because I think he is capable of that – and more."

Austin imagined how his father must have felt and lowered his head into his hands. She rose from her chair, dropped to her knees on the floor and eased over to sit directly before him. She reached up and enveloped him with both arms. He lowered his head and could feel the softness of her hands on his neck, her breath on his face, and breathed her in.

They stayed that way a while before he pried her arms away, helped her to her feet, and offered her a seat beside him on the settee.

"Tell me, Austin, what did my stepfather do?" her voice was soft and insistent.

He'd detailed all he knew about Grand Overland Rail and how his father invested heavily only to lose everything, including his life.

She turned away, and Austin could see that she felt ashamed. "It isn't your fault, and you cannot be responsible for what he has done," he reassured.

A small lacy handkerchief appeared, and she dabbed delicately at her eyes. "He repulses me, and you have every reason to feel as you do about him. I wish there were something I could do to amend for his actions, But I can't, Austin. I must think of Mama first."

The sound of the clock striking the hour disrupted their thoughts. Its chiming stopped after the fourth strike.

"Oh my goodness, the time. I must go, Austin. Mama will worry."

"Harriet, I would never expect that you turn against your family. My feelings towards your stepfather have no bearing on you or your mother, and I would never do anything that would come between you and her."

She held his gaze. "Thank you, Austin."

They both stood and embraced and to Austin, it felt terrific. "Will you allow me to see you again?" he asked.

"Can you visit on Friday, he–"

"He's at White's playing whist," he finished her sentence. "And yes, I will arrive at three o'clock if that is acceptable?'

As they walked from the room, Nanny appeared, carrying her coat.

"Thank you, Nanny. I enjoyed our talk," said Harriet.

"And I hope to see you again, Miss Stephenson," Nanny replied, then wandered away, leaving them alone.

"What a dear, wise woman."

Wise? he wondered. "She is indeed," Austin agreed.

Harriet stood on tiptoes, lifted her head and pecked Austin on the cheek. "Good day, Captain Willems."

With that, she was gone, and Austin stood on the doorstep, grinning from ear to ear until he saw Miles Siles in the park under the branches of a tree. He gave no impression that he saw him, and fighting to control his anger, he watched Harriet walk away and hoped Siles wouldn't follow her. Thankfully, he didn't, and Austin re-entered his home and shut the door.

He sat on the settee where, not long ago, Harriet had sat and thought about what she had told him.

The door opened, and Nanny appeared with a teapot and cake. "I thought you might like a cup of tea, sir."

"And some cake that Harriet helped make?"

"Yes, sir, but I didn't ask her to. Miss Stephenson insisted that she should help while waiting for you to arrive."

"And have a natter?" Austin asked with a broad smile.

Nanny didn't immediately respond, and Austin waited. "Yes, we chatted, as women do."

Austin laughed. "Let me guess, women's affairs and matters of the heart."

Nanny looked uncomfortable. "Er, I have dinner to prepare, sir. Do you need anything else?"

"Thank you, Nanny. I'm pleased you were here for Harriet and could talk."

She quietly left the room, and Austin recalled how Harriet called Nanny wise. How much advice could a barren spinster offer a beautiful young woman? As far as he knew, Nanny had never been married or had a male caller or male friend. But one thing was evident: Nanny was taken with Harriet and had given her tacit approval. He leaned back on the settee, placed his hands behind his head, and allowed time for the tea to steep.

Dusk had descended over Regent's Park when Austin stepped through the rear door of his house and walked up the service lane. Any neighbours would have been aghast at the sight of him as he was not dressed respectably as a gentleman should. He more closely resembled a labourer and certainly did not look like he belonged in the affluent neighbourhood.

He walked quickly up the lane, turned left, crossed over Ulster Terrace, where he lived and continued down York Bridge into the park.

Few people were about, and once inside The Regent's Park, Austin walked parallel to the road and back towards his house. It was dark beneath trees, and anyone looking would have difficulty seeing him. He crept stealthily from tree to tree, closer to where Miles Siles loitered.

From gas lamps illuminating the street, he could see Siles waiting, and with patience, he stalked and narrowed the distance separating them. He was directly in front of his house, and through the window, he could only see the vague outline of a person near the drawing-room window. It was Nanny, and he'd asked her to move randomly near the window to hold Miles Siles' attention.

He grinned as he watched Nanny don his topper. Even from behind the curtain, it looked convincing and would appear to anyone watching that a man was dressed and ready to go out.

Austin eased closer to Miles, and they were only separated by ten yards. Up the street, a horse and carriage clip-clopped down Ulster Terrace, and the noise masked any sound he made. When the carriage passed directly in front of them, Austin sprung forward.

Miles Siles was caught entirely unaware when suddenly Austin's arm snaked across his throat. Miles spun and tried to throw off his assailant, but Austin held on tightly. Of similar build and height, the advantage moved to skill.

Austin yanked Miles to one side, then the other, and finally, with a desperate heave, Miles lost his balance and fell. Austin maintained his death grip around his throat as Miles thrashed on the ground. With both legs wrapped around his torso, the Major couldn't do much to free himself. He tried to reach up for Austin's face, but it did little good.

Unable to breathe, Austin felt Miles' strength wane as he began to slip into unconsciousness. Still maintaining his grip, Austin rolled over the top of Miles, released his arm and placed a knee firmly on his chest pinning him to the ground.

As soon as he could breathe again, Miles began to struggle. With the full weight of his body, Austin pushed his knee down harder.

"Enough," wheezed Miles. "Stop."

Austin eased the pressure and looked down at the man who'd been outside his home watching him. "Why are you spying on me?" he hissed.

Miles shook his head as he tried to clear the fog.

"Tell me, why are you spying on me?" he repeated.

Even in the darkness, he could see Miles scowl. Austin delivered a hard punch to his temple, and Miles grunted.

"Tell me!" Austin asked again. He received no response and, without waiting, struck him again in the same place. It was a hard punch, hurting them both, and Austin shook his hand to relieve the pain. Miles was unconscious.

Austin was fully aware that he'd previously broken his jaw, and it wouldn't take much to re-break it as it had yet to heal fully. He'd chosen not to hit him on the mouth, but he would if Miles didn't respond to his questions.

With his knee, he applied pressure to his chest, and with a cough, Miles regained wakefulness. Austin lowered his head and spoke slowly. "If you do not answer my questions, I will hit you on your jaw. You wouldn't want that now, would you?"

He heard a groan in response.

"Why does De Vore want me followed and watched?"

"He, he believes you're interfering," Miles mumbled.

"Interfering with what or who?"

"I don't know; he doesn't tell me."

"With Grand Overland Rail?"

Miles tried to sit up and push Austin away, but a knee pressing painfully onto his chest changed his mind.

"I, I don't know. He doesn't tell me those things."

Austin tried to think. He believed it was possible Siles wasn't told why he was tasked to follow him. But he certainly knew more than he was letting on. "You will tell De Vore I won't tolerate being spied on. It ends now. I will come for De Vore and you if I catch you or anyone else following me again. Ensure my message is passed on."

Austin relaxed pressure on his chest and went to stand when Miles' fist shot out and hit him on the side of his head. Austin saw stars and, in reflex, swung his arm and struck Miles firmly on the jaw. He felt rather than heard the jaw give. Miles let out a painful howl.

Miles had no fight left in him, and Austin let him go. He watched him leave Regent's Park, holding his hands to his face as he tried to hail a cab. Austin felt no pity and doubted he would see the man again.

CHAPTER EIGHTEEN

The luncheon invitation came as a surprise to Austin, and it was the last thing he expected. Ever curious, he set out in a hansom cab with instructions to the driver to take him to St James Square in Pall Mall.

An attendant led him into the Army & Navy Clubhouse dining room, where Lieutenant General Alexander Wardlow was seated along with Major Seth Ryan, one of the General's aides-de-camp. Austin recognised the major from when he visited his home, and while he knew General Wardlow by sight, he'd never had to speak to him other than a cordial greeting in passing.

Both the general and the major stood when Austin approached.

"Lieutenant-General Wardlow, Major Ryan, may I present Captain Willems," announced the attendant with formality.

Both the general and major extended their hands in greeting and warmly shook Austin's hand.

"Take a seat, Captain," instructed General Wardlow.

"Thank you, sir."

"Please, and as my guest, enjoy your luncheon. A waiter should appear momentarily, and I, uh, recommend the poached salmon," he informed.

"It is our favourite," added Major Ryan with a grin.

They discussed the 67th South Hampshire Regiment and tactfully did not stray into sensitive areas that could prove awkward while the three officers enjoyed salmon during their informal chat. After the plates were removed, General Wardlow looked at Austin intently. "May I speak candidly, Mr Willems?"

Austin recognised the deliberate omission of his rank, which presumably meant General Wardlow would not be speaking as a senior officer.

"Of course, sir."

General Wardlow sucked at a tooth before continuing. "I wish to extend my heartfelt gratitude to you. I don't know how you did it, but by golly, De Vore called off the dogs." He paused a moment to collect his thoughts and then continued. "As a father, my concern is for my son's well-being. Being extorted by a reprobate solicitor is abhorrent and explicitly disgusting." He cleared his throat. "I would also like to apologise to you for having the dark cloud of a court-martial hung over your head. I was wrong, and agreeing to pursue that course of action against you was immoral. Believe me, young man, I'm reminded of it every day. What you did is remarkable, and I am, sir, forever in your debt."

"Sir, I–"

"One more thing, Captain. Your resignation was made under unfair duress, and If you wish to make an official complaint against me, as is your right, then please do so–"

Austin quickly glanced at Major Ryan, who remained silent.

"–I will not seek favour or privilege and accept full responsibility for my actions. If you wish to return to military service, that is your choice and an option to reflect on."

Austin was silent for a moment. "Thank you. May I consider your offer?"

"Of course. And Captain, if I can ever be of help and if I can do anything… Please, Major Ryan will always ensure you have my ear."

Austin nodded his gratitude. "I have no intention of filing any complaint, General Wardlow. I agree with you that Julian De Vore is a most odious man, and I believe that his influence on power is extensive and far-reaching. It certainly has affected my life."

"Most unfortunate, really," added the General. "But as I said, if I can help you in any way…."

"Actually, sir, there might be two ways."

Major Ryan shifted his position to listen more easily.

"There is a gentleman who does De Vore's more unpleasant tasks. I would like to know more about him. This is important to me, and I hope you might be able to help, sir."

"Who is this man?" asked the general.

"Major Miles Siles."

General Wardlow nodded to his aide. "Can you call on a favour or two and find out more about this chap?" he asked.

"Of course, happy to do so, sir," stated Major Ryan. "Captain Willems, do you have any other information, his regiment, when he retired?"

Austin shook his head. "I'm sorry, that's all I know."

"And the second matter?" General Wardlow asked.

"Yes, sir, uh, this request is a little more delicate."

Austin outlined what he wanted as General Wardlow leaned back in his chair. When Austin finished, the general pondered the request. "Major Ryan, perhaps you could give us a moment?"

"Of course, sir, I shall avail myself of the convenience," the major replied, dropping his napkin on the chair as he walked away.

General Wardlow leaned forward and kept his voice low. "What you propose, does this have anything to do with Julian De Vore?"

"Very much so."

"But what you intend to do isn't legal, or is it?"

"Well, sir, uh, not entirely. But not for self-gain, I might add. I intend to destroy De Vore and the people he works for."

Again the general sucked on a tooth before he spoke. "I will speak to Colonel Farquharson

privately, but ensure that he and the Queens' Royal Hussars believe that what you are doing is above board and beyond scrutiny."

"I wouldn't want to tarnish them or their fine reputation, sir," Austin replied.

"Good, but I admit if you can pull off this daring feat and bring down De Vore and his masters, I will enjoy that tremendously."

Seeing a pause in the conversation, Major Ryan returned to his seat.

"Captain Willems, if I may ask, how was it that you could convince Mr De Vore to, er, change his mind?" asked Major Ryan.

Austin suppressed a smile. "Mr De Vore is entirely comfortable serving his needs through underhanded and deplorable means. Let me just say that I used his strategy and turned it against him."

General Wardlow leaned forward. "It might be prudent to let the matter rest. Let's leave it there, shall we?"

"Yes, sir," Austin replied.

Austin departed the Army and Navy Clubhouse in Pall Mall soon after and had a cab take him to Howard's office.

It was late afternoon when Austin arrived, and as always, Howard was pleased to see him. Austin stood at the window and recounted the incident with Miles Siles in the park, and Howard grimaced when Austin described striking him on the jaw.

"Poor Miles won't be of much value to De Vore with his jaw broken again, will he?"

"I wouldn't think so," Austin replied.

"Do we know whom De Vore is liaising with?" Howard asked.

"I can only presume it's Ronald Hewitt Thompson," Austin replied.

Howard was placing documents in his case. "There will be others."

"Others?" Austin questioned.

"Yes, more than ever I'm convinced there are others. If De Vore is the point person for the directors and their little company, London Private Acquisitions, other people may be on the peripheries. Why would De Vore have Miles Siles follow you? It's costly, and what is the point? It makes no sense unless there is more that he doesn't want you to discover."

Howard's suggestion was a possibility he hadn't considered.

Austin recalled a conversation he overheard. "I heard one of Overland's directors refer to 'The Chairman' I previously told you about. Could that be who you refer to?"

Howard stroked his chin. "Possibly, and I'd enjoy knowing who this Chairman chap is. But let me warn you, it will be wise to watch Mr De Vore and see who he meets," Howard suggested.

"Or perhaps, whom Hewitt-Thompson meets," Austin added.

"I agree. And have you decided when you will action your plan of retribution?"

"Charles will be on leave and arrive in London next week. I'm waiting on confirmation from Ollie that he has the people and a few resources we need," Austin added.

"Just be careful, Austin and don't take unnecessary risks. I don't want you in court facing a host of criminal charges. I don't believe you'd fair well incarcerated."

"Yes, I can't say I'd look forward to that."

"And this Miles Siles, chap. Austin, I dare say he can't be thrilled with you. It might be best to look over your shoulder."

"Yes, that occurred to me, too."

With Howard's comments reverberating, Austin decided to detour to Covent Garden on the way home. He saw small groups of youths observing him. It was always four young lads, and Ollie had informed him that more than four attracted too much attention from the constabulary. But they didn't bother or threaten and kept their distance shadowing him.

"Do you have any people who can follow Julian De Vore?" Austin asked Ollie once they were seated upstairs at the Flag and Lamb Pub.

Ollie rubbed his chin. "Cap'n, I can have anyone followed at any time. That ain't the problem." Ollie looked apologetic. "It's the cost."

"Until we have completed our plan, I think we should keep an eye on Mr De Vore. Howard believes following him may prove useful in finding out who he is in regular contact with, and I need to know names."

Ollie nodded.

Austin handed over some money.

Ollie raised his eyebrows. "Cap'n, that is more than enough."

"If your people learn anything important, have someone slip a message under my door."

Ollie nodded.

They reviewed the details of their plan for when Charles arrived. As far as Austin was concerned, everything was ready. Ollie had obtained a sufficient amount of paraffin that Austin asked for and a covered wagon. For safety reasons, Ollie kept them hidden at Austin's recently rented warehouse. There couldn't be any mishaps, and Austin was very concerned that no one was hurt deliberately or through an accident.

Austin was satisfied; everything was going to plan, and Ollie would ensure his lads would follow Julian De Vore. Charles would soon be arriving, and tomorrow, the highlight of his week would be calling on Miss Harriet Stephenson.

It disturbed him to think that her stepfather was violent. But to what extent? Was he physically violent towards her and her mother, or was he prone to just temper tantrums and throwing the odd brandy glass across the room? It was unfortunate that Harriet had to leave his home when she did, as the nature of their relationship seemed to have pleasantly changed.

He'd underestimated her and made a terrible mistake by leaving the park when he did. She should have been allowed to speak, and he hadn't done that.

CHAPTER NINETEEN

House staff placed the flowers he brought into an elegant vase and brought the colourful display into the drawing room, where he sat with Harriet and her mother, Eunice. It was a spectacular bouquet, and he had deliberated on the colours to best compliment the room for quite some time.

While drinking tea and nibbling treats, they politely talked of trivial things, social events and people of interest. To Austin, Eunice appeared very tense and anxious, although he felt no hostility or resentment from her at being in their home. She made him feel welcome, and he believed she was sincere.

After a short while, she excused herself and informed them she would return, leaving Harriet and Austin alone.

He wanted to be careful about how to broach the subject of her stepfather. It was a sensitive matter and not his business to pry, but he had questions and was concerned for Harriet and her mother if they were in any physical danger. As if reading his mind, Harriet raised the issue and spared him any awkwardness.

"I do not normally share personal information about my family with suitors," she lifted her head slightly to gauge his reaction, and he saw her cheeks colour slightly.

"Actually, Austin, eligible bachelors who have come calling

have nearly always sought favour with my stepfather than fawn over me." This time, she smiled, and he felt slightly embarrassed.

"But you have been different, and for some reason, it is comfortable to talk naturally and share with you." She smiled warmly to put him at ease.

Austin listened carefully and felt she had prepared her monologue in advance.

Harriet took a moment and looked down at her hands nestled in her lap. "I told you that he was a violent man, and I know he is capable of hurting others." She looked up and met Austin's questioning eyes. "Yes, even to hurt your father. I do not doubt that my stepfather's actions contributed to your father's passing. He has hurt Mama. She hasn't told me, but I know. I've seen the painful marks of his brutish behaviour on her. I, too, have suffered bruises on my arms and felt the lash of his vile tongue. But I worry about Mama. His intemperance opens the door to reveal a dark and troubled man and that frightens me." She looked down at her hands again.

Austin moved forward to sit on the edge of the chair.

"You may wonder why she affords me such freedoms. Why she isn't seated with us now or allows me to visit your home unescorted?"

"Er, yes, I had wondered."

"Because I asked her, and she trusts me. Our neighbours have heard my stepfather's obscene rants and heard Mama's cries of pain. Yet they do nothing to inquire about our well-being or see if we are maltreated. However, they are quick to lift their noses in disapproval or offer an unsavoury opinion of me because I am alone or wish to talk privately with you. Idle gossip is of no consequence to Mama or me and their opinion matters nothing, but Austin, be warned, when sober, my stepfather is menacing; when inebriate, he is unpredictably dangerous."

"Harriet, does my presence here put you in harm?"

She laughed. "No, Austin, for he has no interest in you because you are not a horse breeder, a railwayman, or have political influence. No offence to you, my dearest, but he has already forgotten you exist."

"That is why he never recognised my name at Ascot?"

"He cares not for Mama or me, and what is closest to his heart are his confounded horses and Grand Overland Rail. As you have no apparent interest in either, you are no use to him. As I said, he's forgotten you already."

Austin guiltily looked away. He'd been selfishly thinking about his father and what he suffered through, and here, in this room, sat a beautiful young woman and her mother, being abused by an unrestrained and aggressive man. He turned his attention back to her. "I'm sorry, Harriet, I've been self-absorbed. Is there anything I can do?"

She shook her head. "No, nothing. We must endure."

Austin looked pensive and stared at the flower arrangement before continuing. "Why are you so forthcoming and tell me these things about him."

"Because peculiarly, Austin, I feel responsible for what happened to your father. You have a right to know the type of man my stepfather is." She lowered her voice and leaned closer. "And if you plot against him, you are now forewarned."

Forewarned? "Why do you believe I seek retribution?"

"Because, Captain Willems," she smiled with an impish, mischievous expression. "Why else is it so important that he doesn't recognise you? If I were in your position, I would be concerned."

Austin leaned back into the chair and rubbed his chin.

"Am I wrong?" she asked.

"Harriet, I fear for your safety. Suppose your stepfather is, as you say, unpredictable and violent. Then you put yourself at risk if and when he learns of me. Or, *if* I am planning something...."

She batted her eyelids. "Are you?"

Austin laughed.

"You haven't answered my question."

He looked into her eyes. They were unwavering, focused and clear. He saw it in her and knew she wouldn't let this go.

She demanded an answer from him. "I want to see him suffer, Austin. He has caused us so much pain, humiliation and continued torment. He deserves to fall – and hard, and you laugh? Do you believe I am nothing more than an offended schoolgirl with a petty grievance?"

He was in a bind. *Can I trust her*? He continued to hold her gaze. She had proven herself, and he had no reason not to believe in her. He came to a decision and nodded slowly. "Yes, Harriet, I will see his downfall. But I will ensure you do not become involved. You must trust me in this."

She sat up, reached for his hand and squeezed.

Julian De Vore packed away his papers, placed them in his satchel, checked his office one last time to ensure no sensitive documents were left lying about, pulled on his coat and hat, looked at the clock, and saw it was six-twenty-seven. He stepped from his office, locked the door and, with his satchel under his arm, stepped from the building to be greeted by Major Miles Siles.

"Good Evening, sir," mumbled Miles with his jaw clenched.

Mr De Vore looked disapprovingly at the major, who had a bandage tightly wrapped around his head and under his jaw to prevent his mouth from moving. "What was that?" asked De Vore, leaning forward to better hear.

"Good evening."

"Ah yes, Good evening. You'll need to speak up. I can't hear you with that confounded bandage across your jaw." Julian looked around and saw the alley between his offices and the neighbouring building was clear. "Come, we can talk more privately there."

He entered the alley and turned to face Miles. "Now then, I'm glad you found time to meet me. "I'll make this quick."

Miles looked at him expectingly.

"I no longer require your services, Mr Siles. I'm unhappy with your recent performance, and obviously, I've placed far too much faith in your abilities. Much to my disappointment and distress, you cannot cope with the basic tasks I've hired you to perform, and it just won't do." He shook his head to emphasise his point.

"But, Mr De Vore–" slurred the major.

"What?" De Vore asked.

"You can't. We have agreement," Miles managed to say.

"Ah, an agreement, you ask?"

Miles Siles nodded.

Two lads peeked from behind a stationary hansom cab across the street and watched.

"I'm terribly sorry, but our verbal arrangement is null and void, and must I repeat myself? You are unable to undertake the duties that I hired you to perform, and I don't believe any outstanding monies are owed, so that concludes our *modus vivendi*," offered De Vore with a condescending smirk. He went to push past, but Miles reached out and firmly held Julian's arm.

"Mr Siles, please remove your hand."

"We have deal," muttered Siles through a clenched jaw.

"Perhaps you misunderstood me, and the blow to your head also affected your hearing, Mr Siles. We have no arrangement!" He jerked his arm free and went to push past when Miles stepped in front of him and gave the gangly solicitor a most ungentlemanly shove.

Julian backpedalled a few steps but managed to remain standing.

"Money," hissed Miles. "You need – pay me."

"Money? Money!" replied Julian loudly. "I'll not see you receive another penny from me. I'll have you rot in hell first."

Miles reached into the pocket of his overcoat and extracted his .442 calibre Beaumont-Adams service revolver that faithfully served him during the Crimean War and levelled it at Mr De Vore. "Pay me what you owe."

"What, what did you say?" questioned Julian as he stared at the pistol. "And you have the audacity to point a firearm at me. How dare you!"

Miles tried again. "Money. Pay me."

"Pay you?" he laughed. "That will be the day."

The bandage wrapped beneath his jaw and around his head had moved through excessive mouth movement and was about to slide from the major's head. Instinctively, he raised his hand to reposition the bandage when Julian saw an opportunity.

De Vore lunged forward to push Miles away, misjudged his timing and collided with him. The revolver dropped from Mile's hands, along with Julian's satchel that fell from beneath his arm. Conveniently for Mr De Vore, the Beaumont-Adams revolver fell at his feet. While inconvenient for Miles, he had to turn to look for it.

Julian scooped up the revolver and wasted no time. He raised his hand and squeezed the trigger just as Miles pulled his arm back to strike him. The retort was deafening in the confines of the alley, and when the smoke from the discharge dissipated, Miles lay on his back. Blood already began seeping through his clothing as Julian looked in horror at what he'd done. The revolver slipped from his hand and clattered to the cobblestones.

It took only a heartbeat to recognise his untenable predicament, and he panicked. Without a thought for his satchel, he turned and fled down the alley and away from any spectators drawn by the resounding discharge of the firearm.

Immediately, the two brazen lads ran from concealment, crossed the street into the alley, quickly retrieved the Beaumont-Adams revolver and Julian's satchel, and followed the fleeing solicitor. When they emerged at the far end, Julian De Vore was gone.

The elder of the two youths hid the revolver in the waistband of his breeches, and with the satchel in their possession, they ran.

They knew the streets, narrow lanes and shortcuts and wisely avoided places where constables were known to loiter. Like a well-drilled team, they handed their loot to another group of lads, who then split up and disappeared into the growing darkness of London's filthy streets.

Austin was at home thinking about Harriet. He'd enjoyed his time with her, and the afternoon passed by quickly. She was an extraordinary, spirited woman, and he delighted in her company.

As expected, Eunice finally asked about his intentions toward Harriet. He explained his feelings towards her and was surprised at how easily he could share his emotions. With her mother's approval, it was agreed that he could call on her regularly. All the while, Harriet listened quietly, and when Eunice turned to her, she nodded once and said she felt the same before bursting into tears.

He felt guilty and didn't know what he'd said to upset her, so he turned to Eunice to apologise. As he learned, Harriet's tears weren't of despair but happiness. He just couldn't understand women.

A loud knock on the door interrupted his reflections, and as he had earlier told Nanny she should retire for the evening, he went to see who the caller was.

"Evening, Cap'n," greeted Ollie.

"Er, Sarge, it's late. What are you doing here?" He saw a hansom cab parked out front. "You'd better come in."

Austin sat, and Ollie preferred to remain standing. "Now then, I see you're worked up into a lather; what ails you, Ollie?"

"I wouldn't be here unless it was important, Cap'n. But gots some interesting news."

Austin was seated on the edge of his chair. "Continue."

"I had a coupl'a lads following Mr De Vore like ya asked. Well then, he meets 'nother gentleman outside his bleed'n office in the Temple district, and he had a cloth wrapped around his head." Ollie circled his head with his hand to demonstrate.

"That would be Major Miles Siles. I, uh, had another minor disagreement with him and, uh, struck him a little hard, Ollie." Austin winced.

"Aye, of course, sir. Unfortunately, that can happen from time to time. Er, I don't think his jaw will be a bother'n him anymore, sir."

"Why is that?"

"He'd be very dead."

Austin shot to his feet. "Good God! What happened?"

"Me lads says they'd be arguin' over money. Mr De Vore pushes Major Siles, next thing, they scuffle, and Siles drops his service revolver. Mr De Vore picks it up, shoots him once and takes off like a robber's dog, sir."

Austin stood. "Good heavens. And Major Siles is definitely dead?"

"Aye, very much so."

Austin poured two glasses of whiskey and handed one to Ollie as he thought. "Do you know if Mr De Vore has been charged with his murder or a crime?"

Ollie shook his head. "Nope, he got clean away. Me lads say that no one actually saw him shoot except them."

"Where are they now?"

"I brought em here, they'd be in the cab, sir. In case you wanted to speak to them."

"Bring them in and send the cab away, Ollie."

Ollie left to bring in the two youths, and Austin thought about how this new complication would affect his plans.

"Er, Cap'n, this be Lenny, and he'd be Cat," said Ollie once he'd returned.

"Nice to meet you both, smiled Austin as he appraised the two dirty youths. He determined they must have been about fifteen years old but were probably younger. They looked around the room in wonder, as it was unlikely they'd ever been in such a grand and spacious home.

"Sir," replied Lenny in acknowledgement.

The other received a clip across the back of his head for only nodding.

"He was a Captain of the Sixty bloody Seventh Regiment. You call him Captain or Sir. Got it?"

"Aye, Sarge, and, er, Captain," replied Cat.

"Why do they call you Cat?" asked Austin, doing his best to hide a grin.

"I like cats, er, sir, Captain." Cat gave a quick sideways glance towards Ollie, expecting another clip across the head.

"Very nice, Cat. Now, please tell me what you witnessed, and uh, before you do, why do you have a satchel?"

Cat looked at Ollie for support, who nodded for him to continue. "The toff[11], he ditched it a'fore he scarpered."

Ollie pushed Cat in the back. "Go on, give it to the Cap'n, then."

11   Toff – Victorian slang for gentleman

Cat took a couple of steps to Austin and handed over the satchel. "Did you take anything from it?"

Both boys shook their heads.

"Good." Austin opened the satchel and saw nothing more than documents with Julian De Vore's name on them. It confirmed who the satchel belonged to. "Can I keep this?" he asked.

Cat looked again at Ollie, who nodded. "We came wif Sarge to give it to ya, Captain."

"Thank you, Cat, well done."

Ollie cleared his throat and gave Lenny a shove in his back.

Austin watched as the older of the two reached into his waistband and extracted a revolver. "Uh, careful, Lenny," stated Austin, looking apprehensive.

Lenny casually handed it over, and Austin broke open the revolver to ensure it wasn't loaded. Ollie stepped forward and handed Austin the shells.

"This be the gun he used, Captain," Lenny volunteered. "Th' toff dropped it."

Austin was astonished. He had the murder weapon and evidence linking De Vore to the death of Miles Siles.

"Can you please tell me, from the beginning, what you saw?" Austin asked.

The youngest boy, Cat, spoke for them both and recounted what they witnessed.

"T'is the same story they told me, Cap'n," confirmed Ollie when he finished.

Austin rubbed his chin. "I don't see any reason for them to lie," he added.

To their immense pleasure, he gave each boy 10 shillings, reimbursed Ollie for the cab, and stood on the doorstep as the three departed.

Even before they left, he had an inkling of how to use this to his advantage. Things were looking up.

CHAPTER TWENTY

"I apologise, Captain Willems. Mr De Vore has cancelled all appointments for the day. I'm unable to help you," the receptionist smiled disdainfully.

No surprise there, Austin thought. He reached into his coat and extracted a plain, unaddressed envelope. He handed it to the receptionist. "Please hand this to Mr De Vore. When he sees the contents, I'm sure he'll make time to see me."

With a loud sigh, she took the envelope, walked down the hallway and returned moments later. "Apparently, Mr De Vore does have a few moments to see you," she coldly said without a smile.

Austin followed her to the solicitor's office. She paused at the door and, with an extended arm, waved him in. He stepped into De Vore's sanctum and was greeted by a mask of pure hatred. Julian De Vore stood behind his desk with fists clenched and seethed. "I should have known you were somehow behind this. I should have guessed," he snarled when the door closed. "What do you want, and where is my satchel?" he snapped.

Without an invitation, Austin looked around the office and chose to sit in one of the comfortable armchairs. "Mr De Vore, it might be best to sit." He pointed to the other chair, crossed his legs and waited.

"Where is my satchel?" De Vore demanded as he sat.

"Mr De Vore, most fortunately, your satchel came into my possession last evening. Shortly after you shot and killed Major Miles Siles.

"What you suggest is preposterous, pure nonsense," spluttered De Vore.

"I also have the weapon you used and two credible witnesses. Considering that Major Siles was a distinguished retired officer, the constabulary would be quite eager to see my evidence," he informed. "Don't you agree?"

Julian just stared at him for a moment or two. "What is it you want, Mr Willems?"

"You don't look at all well, Mr De Vore. Are you sleeping at night?"

Austin saw a vein throbbing on the neck of the solicitor and knew the man was near breaking point. He felt no sympathy. "Address me by my rank, Mr De Vore. In spite of your efforts, I'm still entitled," Austin smiled. "However, and for now, I just want information. Do you understand?"

Julian swallowed and nodded. "But you could go to the police anyway."

"I could, but presently, it serves me no purpose."

Julian De Vore shrugged. "I want my satchel."

Austin ignored the request. "Good, then we have an understanding. Firstly, you will answer some questions." He uncrossed his legs and leaned forward. "Besides Grand Overland Rail, do you also represent London Private Acquisitions?"

De Vore nodded.

"Who are the principals of London Private Acquisitions?"

"Why are you doing this, Mr, er, Captain Willems?"

"Answer the questions," Austin's voice hardened and contained an edge.

Julian grunted. "George Dillington, Oscar Baker, Virgil Hartman and Sir Ronald Hewitt-Thompson."

"Anyone else?"

Austin could see the hesitation.

"No, er no, I don't believe so, damn you."

"Then there could be more directors?" Austin pushed. "Who is the Chairman?"

De Vore shook his head. "I don't know of any Chairman."

Austin saw the reaction and knew De Vore was lying, but what he said mostly confirmed what he knew. Now for the more probing questions. "Who will pay the increased wages for the navvies[12] working on the Swindon to London rail expansion?"

"How do you know all this?" De Vore shook his head in helpless anguish.

"Answer the question!"

"They are not a union. It is only an agreement, a labour contract with the navvies who work for Grand Overland Rail. However, London Private Acquisitions will essentially purchase the labour contract and sell it back to Grand Overland Rail for a large profit."

"Using money paid by Watson Brothers Coachbuilders for shares? How much will this labour contract cost Grand Overland rail?"

De Vore looked stunned that Austin knew so much. His face looked ashen.

"Perhaps Fifty thousand pounds."

Austin whistled. "Correct me if I'm wrong, Mr De Vore. Grand Overland Rail will not be able to afford to pay the labour contract and be forced to obtain a loan because they have no cash reserves,

12   *Navvies – General term for workers laying railway track, building bridges and tunnels. Originally comes from the word Navigator that referred to those who built the canals.*

and shareholders will, in all probability, be burdened with repaying the loan."

De Vore sighed. "It really is quite simple. Let me explain. Any large purchases that Grand Overland Rail needs to make, then London Private Acquisitions makes that purchase at a low cost and on-sells it back to Grand Overland Rail at a much higher price. The balance of the money retained by London Private Acquisition, or their profit, is then divided equally and disbursed to the directors.""

Austin observed carefully and saw the man was actually proud of the deception.

De Vore couldn't help himself and continued. "If Grand Overland Rail cannot afford to purchase from London Private Acquisitions, then a line of credit or a short-term loan is arranged. If Overland cannot repay the loan amount, then the repayment burden falls to its shareholders. Once the loan has been repaid, the directors are reimbursed for their portion of the debt repayments from profits by London Private Acquisitions."

"And you facilitate all these transactions?" Austin asked.

"It sounds complicated, but it is just about transferring money from one bank account to another."

Austin had a thought. "Then that requires a good relationship with a bank, does it not?"

In response, De Vore shrugged his shoulders. "Of course."

"Which bank?"

"Bank of England."

Austin was puzzled, and something was still unclear. "Why would Grand Overland Rail buy a labour contract?"

Julian sighed. "The workers agree to be represented by London Private Acquisitions, which promises them higher wages and better working conditions. In theory, if Grand Overland Rail wants the workers, they must pay the fifty thousand pound labour agreement."

"And the navvies don't know about that?"

De Vore nodded. "In the end, they'll be offered less than they were promised."

"Just like the land purchases in Swindon." Austin fought to control his anger. "To clarify, Grand Overland Rail is unlikely to have any cash reserves after purchasing the labour contract from London Private Acquisitions." Austin looked closely at De Vore. "Why haven't other directors asked questions and challenged those decisions?"

"Because, Mr Willems, there are no longer any other directors. But before, when they still had more, they were outvoted or given other, er, somewhat tepid explanations."

"Untruths, lies or fabricated information?"

"If that was required," shrugged De Vore.

"Just like how my father was misled and swindled," stated Austin.

"His death was unexpected but became convenient," added De Vore. "But you forget, Grand Overland Rail is still a successful enterprise and continues to make money. This is why it's been a good investment."

Austin's eyes narrowed. "And?"

"Your Father was questioning the directors of Grand Overland Rail and accused them of being inept and corrupt. He became a problem."

Austin eased himself from the chair. "I have heard enough, and this sickens me, Mr De Vore." He thrust a forefinger towards the solicitor. "I will return, and you will continue to do your work, and then, at the appropriate time, you'll be given instructions. You needn't be told what will happen if you breathe a word to anyone."

"What instructions?"

Austin strode to the door and departed.

"Mr Willems!" yelled De Vore.

"How can the shareholders afford to keep paying Grand Overland Rail's debt?" asked Austin.

Howard Willoughby wiped his mouth with a napkin. "They can't, Austin. The remaining directors have been purchasing the shares from shareholders at ridiculously low prices. Shareholders are only too keen to unload them, as they are a liability."

"But they can't continue with their plan forever because what shareholders they have left will be destitute, and Grand Overland Rail will have purchased most of their shares."

Howard nodded. "You are correct. Their deception isn't sustainable."

They sat in Austin's dining room and enjoyed a wonderful meal that Nanny prepared.

"I loathe Julian De Vore. He is a vile man," stated Austin, pushing his empty plate away.

"I also received correspondence from Watson Brothers Coachbuilding's solicitor. They have been receiving pressure from Grand Overland Rail directors to buy their shares," informed Howard. "They need the money."

"Because the share price is low?"

Howard wiped his mouth with a napkin and nodded. "A bargain."

Nanny entered to take away the dishes.

"That was a splendid meal, Nanny. Your skills are remarkable," Howard complimented.

"Mr Willoughby," blushed Nanny. "I hope you have room for pudding?"

"Only if you made it," he replied.

"Thank you, Nanny," stated Austin, turning his attention back to Howard. "I think you should reply to their letter and tell Watson's to promise payment but delay for another fortnight. In two weeks, we should see Grand Overland Rail's scheme crash down around their ears."

"Then you are still keen to begin your personal crusade against the directors?"

Austin smiled. "More than ever, Howard. Other than a few final details around Sir Ronald's horses, we are all set."

Nanny re-entered with two dessert plates. She placed one in front of each of them and quietly left the room. Austin noted that Howard had received an extra dollop of cream.

"And Lieutenant Newbury?" asked Howard as he feasted his eyes on the sponge cake pudding.

"Charles will be here in two days."

Howard leaned back in his chair, "That was divine."

Austin used a finger to wipe away the last remnants of cream from the dish and licked it clean. He wiped his hands on a napkin and looked at Howard. "Miles Siles is dead."

"What?" Howard leaned forward. "What do you mean dead?"

"Dead. Was shot by none other than the esteemed Julian De Vore."

"Dear God." Howard shook his head in confusion. "How is this possible? What happened? Tell me…" He paused, and his eyes narrowed. "What is your involvement, Austin?"

Austin placed the napkin on this lap and raised both hands palms out. "I had nothing to do with it. As I've been informed, De Vore and Siles had an altercation in an alley beside his office. Siles had the handgun, and somehow, he dropped it after a scuffle. De Vore picked it up, shot Siles and ran. Oh, and that reminds me…" Austin stood, "Come with me."

Howard followed Austin into the library and sat as instructed.

195

"I have this." He reached from behind a writing desk and handed a satchel to Howard.

Howard was puzzled and looked to Austin in question.

"When De Vore shot Siles, he ran and forgot to take his satchel. This belongs to De Vore." Austin stood with arms folded and looked down at the solicitor, grinning. "Go on, have a look, open it."

"This belongs to a solicitor. It's unethical for me to—"

"But not for me. Have a look," Austin encouraged.

"It's wrong." Howard held up the case for Austin to take it away.

"Julian De Vore is a scoundrel. He is immoral, licentious, and a rogue who sought the downfall of my father and God knows how many other honest businessmen. He swindled people out of money, and to this day, he continues to deceive." Austin was becoming angry. "Go on, open it, and see what De Vore is up to, for I cannot make head nor tail of the legal jargon."

Howard looked contrite and lowered the satchel to his lap.

Austin turned his back on him, walked to the window, and stared across the gardens. After a moment, when he turned back, he saw the satchel open and Howard pulling out files and documents.

"Good heavens!" exclaimed the solicitor. All previous reservations were gone as he excitedly thumbed through the paperwork. "These … these are meeting minutes, bills of sale, and court documents." Howard swallowed. "There is nothing in here that we don't already know, but it does confirm everything we suspected." He looked up at Austin. "You can't keep this. Some of these signed documents need to be submitted to government agencies, and failure to do so would draw attention to why he didn't or couldn't file them. That could bring attention to you or us."

Austin walked from the window and sat at an adjacent chair as Howard returned the files to the satchel. "You understand that if this case were discovered in your possession, then you could be implicated in the death of Mr Siles, not to mention a host of other charges."

Austin scratched his chin as he considered the solicitor's advice. "Yes, the activities of Julian De Vore have to appear normal if we want to bring down Grand Overland Rail."

"And I couldn't agree with you more, Austin. Return the case as soon as it is convenient. Please, I implore you."

"Is there anything of value that we can use? Are any of those documents about the labour contract?

"Er, I saw a few referencing the labour contract, but I'd have to read them fully to know."

"Then take the satchel to your office, have a proper read-through, and as soon as you've finished, I will return the satchel to its rightful owner."

Howard shook his head. "No, not to the office… Er,…"

Austin understood Howard's reticence. I will have the satchel delivered to your home. No one will see you with it. Rest easy."

CHAPTER TWENTY-ONE

"You wished to see me, sir?"

Detective Chief Inspector Tobias Bird, from the Metropolitan Police Service, looked up from the tedium of reports he was reading and stared blankly at the detective sergeant before it dawned on him what he was referring to. "Ah, yes. Is here somewhere." He rummaged on his desk to retrieve the document he sought, and once found, he quickly glanced over it again to refresh his memory. "You were called to the scene of a shooting in the temple district a few days ago."

"That's correct, sir, a robbery gone awry. Most likely scuttlers[13], sir," said the detective sergeant with a measure of youthful self-assuredness.

The Bow Street police station was busy, and people always came and went through the large central office area, causing a commotion. Above the general hubbub of police station conversation, someone was shouting, another person laughed at some bawdy humour, and from another room, someone was loudly protesting their innocence.

Choosing to leave his tiny office door open, Detective Chief Inspector Bird successfully ignored the noisy distractions. He looked up at the detective sergeant while attempting to remove an errant piece of tobacco with his tongue that had lodged between his

13   *Scuttlers – Slang name given to gangs of working-class youths who committed petty crimes.*

teeth. "A robbery gone awry?" He raised an eyebrow. "You stated that the deceased still had money in a crumenal[14] that was found on the body, so how could you surmise it was a robbery – gone – awry?" He stabbed at the document with a finger to emphasise his point.

Detective Sergeant Roggin suddenly lost his air of confidence. "Well, sir, the robbers were interrupted before they could liberate the victim's purse - they hightailed and fled, sir."

Detective Chief Inspector Bird drummed his fingers repeatedly on his desk as he considered his response. "And yet the victim sustained a serious injury... presumably they had time to scuffle..."

"Yes, sir, the medical examiner stated the deceased had a previous injury that was unhealed, and he suspects the victim sustained another immediately prior to being shot. The er, fracture was to his jaw, sir."

"I know it was his jaw; I can read, Detective." He waved the medical examiner's report in the air like a royal pendant. "Do you for a moment believe a man with a broken jaw has it rebroken and then almost immediately after is shot and killed by scuttlers – and, is the victim of a robbery-gone-awry?"

The young detective awkwardly shifted position under the intense scrutiny of his superior. "Um, well, sir, since you put it that way, it does seem a little far-fetched, sir."

The piece of tobacco stuck between his teeth was a nuisance. Detective Chief Inspector Bird paused a moment as his tongue was otherwise occupied. "If it was a robbery, removing the victim's purse would take only seconds. Even if killing him wasn't the intention, it wouldn't have taken but a moment to take his money. But they didn't, did they?"

Detective Sergeant Barnabus Roggin shrugged.

14   *Crumenal – Small bag or pouch used to hold money*

"So what did they take, Detective? Because you don't shoot someone for no reason."

"Er, I see your point, sir."

"What makes it more interesting, Detective Sergeant Roggin, is that the unfortunate victim happened to be military, a Major Miles Siles. How is it possible some lads, mere boys, could break the jaw of a military man so easily, then shoot him and scarper, as you put it, without taking his money? Doesn't something seem a little peculiar to you?"

Detective Sergeant Roggin nodded enthusiastically. "From your perspective, I agree, sir."

"I'm thrilled you agree with me, Detective, and Mrs Bird will sleep more soundly at night knowing that," the Detective Chief Inspector presented his version of a smile. "You will return to the location of the shooting and find out what really happened. It wasn't scuttlers, blackguards or lads; something is happening, and I want to know what."

"As you–"

"Dismissed."

The detective turned to leave.

"Detective Sergeant Roggin?"

"Sir?"

"Before you go, bring me all the possessions found on the victim."

"Aye, sir."

Detective Chief Inspector Bird leaned back in his chair, paced both hands behind his head and stretched. There was something inherently fishy about the circumstances around the death of Major Miles Siles. The location where the shooting took place isn't known as a high-crime area, and it took place during the late afternoon, early evening while still light. He removed his hands and placed a finger between the collar of his shirt and neck. It was uncomfortably tight. He liberated the piece of tobacco, spat it out and reached for his pipe as Detective Sergeant Roggin hurried in and deposited a box on his desk.

"Will that be all, sir?"

Detective Chief Inspector Bird struck a match and sucked as the flame briefly disappeared into the bowl. Within seconds, his face was obscured in a cloud of blue smoke. "That will be all, Detective Sergeant."

With his teeth biting down on the stem and the pipe hanging from his mouth, Detective Chief Inspector Bird read the Police Property Inventory log attached to the box and lifted the lid to peer inside. He saw a handkerchief, a purse, a dog-eared notebook and a pencil stub. When he lifted the notebook, he saw a house key beneath it. A single ordinary house key.

He flicked open the notebook, hoping to learn more. The jottings contained abbreviated sentences, written like a stricken, harried man with no time at his disposal. The penmanship was untidy and almost like a code. He flipped through half a dozen pages to read the last entries Major Siles made.

AW location 1
AW dep at 10
AW arrive 11
HW arrive 11.30
HW dep at 1.30
HS arrive 14.15
HS dep at 16
AW dep at 16.30

It was a log of sorts, and the numeric entries certainly related to time, military time? The capitalised letters were... The Detective

Chief Inspector randomly flicked back through some pages and saw a pattern emerge and considered that the alpha letters might be initials. Therefore, HW, whoever that was, possibly departed the location at a specific time and returned at the other logged time. He removed his pipe and stared at the far wall as he tried to make sense of the notes. *Where was the bloody location*, he wondered.

Perhaps the first entry, AW, is the place of business or the residence of whomever AW is, and the second entry is AW departing at 10.00 a.m. HW might be another person altogether... Therefore, this Miles Siles fellow was watching someone and keeping tabs on them. *Was he observing them covertly*? If *so, then could his discovery have been the motive for murder*?

Detective Chief Inspector Bird straightened his legs and again slouched back in his chair. *What had Mr Siles been doing when killed and why?*

None the wiser, he shook his head, returned the notebook back to the box, withdrew the purse and opened it to inspect its contents. It held a total of £7/1/- in various coin denominations, a membership card to the Army & Navy Clubhouse, various old receipts for horse and carriage rentals and a sliver of paper with JD written on it. JD mused the Detective Chief Inspector, a woman, a mistress?

He'd been a policeman for long enough to know when something wasn't right, and the death of Miles Siles gave him an uncomfortable twitch.

Ollie watched Captain Willems walk away into the darkness, and as they usually did, his lads would watch and ensure the captain wouldn't attract any trouble. He waited a moment longer and then turned to the young boy who stood behind him and slightly to his side. "There's a good lad. Fetch me Cat and Lenny, be at it, now," instructed the ex-sergeant. "I'll be in the cosy upstairs."

"Aye, Sarge," said the boy before he scampered away with abundant energy.

Ollie turned, and the rhythmic cadence of his wooden leg clacked into the night as he disappeared into the Lamb and Flag Pub in Covent Gardens.

The pint glass at Ollie's elbow was almost empty as he sat, slouched in a chair upstairs, away from the din of the bar below him. Lost in thought, he never heard the two lads enter the room.

"Ya wanted to see us, Sarge?" Cat asked. It was always Cat who spoke first, he was a likeable lad, full of confidence and the nous to know when to take a risk.

Ollie raised his eyes and kept his head motionless as he considered the two boys. Cat was a natural leader, cocky, confident and also fearless. He had a home and a bed to sleep in, but his mother worked extremely long hours as a seamstress, and his father had been a perpetual drunkard and beat his wife for sport. If Cat, the couple's only remaining child who still lived, had the misfortune of being around, he would also get a painful thrashing.

The last time Cat received a pasting, the old man had struck his son too hard, and Ollie was convinced the thrashing had done more damage than what the eye could see. Cat wasn't ever quite the same again, but he was the sort of fella you warmed to.

Lenny's story wasn't that dissimilar, except his mother was a strumpet, and Lenny was constantly beaten by the unsavoury characters she brought home. Both young boys' lives would have been considerably shortened without Sergeant Oliver Nagle's intervention.

After a visit by Ollie and a couple of his mates, Cat's father was encouraged never to return, and Lenny's mother was offered a job in a textile factory. If she returned to her previous vocation, Ollie warned her, "I'll spread word you have pox, and you'll never see your son again."

Ollie took Cat and Lenny under his wing and many other boys with similar stories and harsh lives. While Ollie's activities may not all have been in full accordance with the law, he never abused the lads or victimised the poor.

Ollie raised his head, reached for the pint glass, downed what remained, and wiped his mouth with his sleeve before speaking.

"You both did well with that shooting the other day, and I'm proud of ya." He beamed like a delighted father.

Cat and Lenny grinned from ear to ear. They valued praise from the Sarge, and receiving his tribute was like earning a medal.

"Now then, the reason I called for you…"

Eager to please, both boys shuffled a step closer to the table.

"I gots a wee caper for ye both." It's on North Audley Street."

"Where'd be that?" Cat asked with furrowed eyebrows.

Lenny shook his head, he didn't know either.

"Aye, it's a wee ways away, just north o' Hyde Park and Mayfair," Ollie informed. "But worry your pretty heads not, 'cause the job ain't for a few days yet, but ye need to keep ya noses clean till then."

"I knows where, it's near that park where we nicked from them toffer's a while back," suddenly remembered Cat.

"Did ya hear me? Ya can't be getting into mischief."

Both boys nodded in earnest.

Satisfied they understood, Ollie continued. "Aye, that's the street," he affirmed. "Now, whats I need ya do is important, and ya can't go makin' a cock-up of it."

Cat and Lenny exchanged glances of excitement.

"What we gotta do, Sarge?"

Ollie explained in detail what he required the two lads to do.

They needed to understand the timing and exactly what was required of them. One challenge was for them to get to North Audley without attracting the attention of other street gangs and to be able to return safely.

"Worry yourselves not; you'll be travellin' by cab, and I'm gonna have Buster an his lads shadow you. If you get into strife, you scarper and let Buster's boys clean them up."

Both boys nodded.

"And we ain't nickin' nuffink?" Cat confirmed.

"Nope, not this time, lads, but you'll each pocket a canary[15] for your trouble."

"Aye, Sarge," the lads replied enthusiastically in tandem. A canary was a lot of money.

"Good, now make yerself useful and fill me jar up, eh?"

When Lenny returned after refilling Ollie's pint glass, He sat them both down and went over their mission again and again so they fully understood what they needed to do. One of the best things about these young lads was their natural ability to adapt to a changing situation, which Ollie counted on. By the time Ollie was satisfied they fully understood the job, their attention had begun to wane.

"And in case ya forget, we'll go over it all again before ya go out. Got it?"

"Aye, Sarge."

He sent them out onto the street to earn money. How else could he afford to make sure they were fed and clothed? Their own families couldn't, and while Ollie encouraged them to sleep at home, his lads often brought food and a shilling or two with them to help a hardworking mum.

15   *Canary – Slang for a Sovereign coin, which equals a pound.*

CHAPTER TWENTY-TWO

A cab dropped Austin outside Harriet's home at 25 Upper Brook Street in Mayfair, where he would take Harriet and her mother to lunch as his guests. He straightened his jacket, ensured the cuffs on his shirt were straight, and armed with another bouquet of flowers, marched up the steps and rung the bell. He could feel his heart racing in expectation. He was smiling broadly when the door partially opened.

"Good morning, sir," said the servant woman, the same one who'd greeted him on his previous visits. The door hadn't fully opened, and she wasn't smiling.

"And good morning to you too, Maggie," Austin replied cheerfully. "Miss Stephenson is expecting me."

She didn't open the door.

"I regret to inform you that Miss Stephenson has to cancel her engagement with you this morning. A message was sent to your home, sir..."

Austin looked downcast. "I didn't receive anything ... I left home early." He looked up. "Is everything well? Can I speak to Miss Stephenson?"

"I'm sorry, sir, that won't be possible. If you'd like to leave a message, I'll ensure she receives it."

Austin looked down at the bouquet of flowers he grasped.

"Is there anything else, sir," the servant asked and began to close the door.

"No," he said barely above a whisper, his disappointment evident. "Yes, actually, there is Maggie. Can you tell Miss Stephenson I shall return tomorrow at 4 o'clock? If it isn't–"

The servant's look softened, and she quickly looked over her shoulder to ensure no other domestic staff were nearby before she spoke. "She won't be here, Mr Willems. The Mistress, Mrs Hewitt-Thompson, will be at Windhaven, at their country estate."

"In Chieveley?"

Maggie nodded.

Austin was perplexed. Harriet had discussed her plans with him, and leaving for Chieveley today wasn't one of them. She was supposed to go at the end of the following week.

"Has something happened, Maggie? Is Harriet unwell or–?"

Maggie looked uncomfortable and lowered her voice. "Mr Willems," she began, "It ain't Miss Stephenson, it's Mrs Hewitt-Thompson."

"Mrs Downes?" came an authoritative male voice from inside.

"I haves to go, Mr Willems. You knows what's right."

"Mrs Downes!" repeated the voice with urgency.

Maggie gave him a wink and went to shut the door.

"Wait, take these, Maggie, and thank you." Before she could protest, he handed her the flowers. As the door closed, he saw the hint of a smile.

Austin walked back down the steps and paused. *This is most peculiar*, he thought. Maggie had said, 'You know what's right.' *But what is right? What did she mean?* He shook his head in puzzlement. He'd need to get a message to Harriet.

He turned to look down Upper Brook Street towards Hyde Park when the front door partially opened, a hand was thrust out, and an envelope was placed on the top step. Austin's head swivelled from side to side. No one else was around except a woman and her dog walking up the street and away from him. He faced Harriet's house and looked at the upper storeys. He saw her framed in the window and immediately felt his heart flutter. Harriet gesticulated with her hand and pointed down towards the door. The envelope.

He ran up the steps to retrieve it and saw his name scrawled across. He ran down the steps and looked back at the upper window, but she was gone.

He felt disappointed as he strolled towards Hyde Park to find a seat. He'd been thinking of nothing else but seeing her again, and now... he felt let down and empty inside.

He held the envelope in both hands and stared forlornly at it. If he never opened the envelope then he couldn't feel the disappointment that was sure to come. Whatever the missive contained, it wasn't good news. Good news was always delivered in person with a cheery smile. Bad news was always dispatched by letter, whereas ink was like poison to the unwary.

He inhaled deeply and, with a thumbnail, tore open the envelope and extracted the letter. He couldn't help himself, so he brought it to his nose and breathed her in. Her delicate fragrance brought a smile to his face, and he pushed aside his negative thoughts as he unfolded the document.

> *My dearest Austin,*
> *I apologise for failing to uphold our luncheon engagement together. I'm writing this letter in some haste as I know you'll be here at the door soon and I want you to receive it and not leave saddened and uninformed.*

I am leaving for Chieveley early this afternoon with Mama. Our journey is unplanned, and I need to explain to you why. It is important that I see you soonest, not just to satisfy my desire to be near you, but to inform you of what has happened.

I hear you at the door and must finish. Please, Austin, can you come to Chieveley tomorrow afternoon around 5.00 pm and dine with us?

You'll be warmly received.

With fondness

Harriet

He re-read the letter with relief and then again before gently folding it and placing it in his inside coat pocket. He knew that going to Chieveley could upset his carefully laid plans, especially at such short notice. However, he could change them, and it gave him an idea. The more he thought about it, the better he liked it. He rose from the bench seat in Hyde Park and walked towards the street to hail a cab.

As usual, the door to Detective Chief Inspector Tobias Bird's cramped office was open, and Detective Sergeant Roggin knocked on the doorpost to attract his attention.

"Yes?" the inspector didn't look up.

The young detective entered the office and stood loosely at attention. "Sir, I have the report you requested."

Detective Chief Inspector Bird raised his head. "Which report?"

"Here, sir," the detective sergeant stepped forward, placed the document on his superior's desk, and stepped back.

The inspector's head moved incrementally from side to side as he read. Once finished, he leaned back in his chair, placed his hands behind his head and stretched out his legs.

"What's your conclusion, Detective Sergeant?" asked his superior.

'Ah, sir. My investigation determined that two lads, known members of a criminal gang, were seen er exiting from the alley. Around the same time, an unidentified gentleman was also seen leaving in some haste."

"And?"

Detective Sergeant Barnabus Roggin shifted his feet. It wasn't normal for the chief inspector to ask for his opinion, and he felt uncomfortable. "Well, sir, after a more thorough investigation, I don't believe it was a simple robbery. There hasn't been a robbery reported in that immediate area in some time, and that begs the question, why were the lads there? However, sir, I find it odd that an unidentified gentleman was seen fleeing the alley, and if he was a victim, he would have notified the police, but he hasn't, not yet. As of today, there hasn't been an incident report filed." Detective Sergeant Roggin took a deep breath. "I believe the gentleman was implicit and may have shot Mr Siles. Why the lads were there," Roggin shrugged, "I don't have the foggiest notion, sir."

"But you do know the identity of the lads," confirmed Detective Chief Inspector Bird.

"Aye, sir. Actually no. Only the one, and he is known by the name Cat. I don't believe that is his real name, though."

"Cat, eh." replied the Detective Chief Inspector. He stared at the far wall a moment.

"We may not know who he is, but someone will. Ask around the station. Other staff may know … and put the word out on the street. I want this young scuttler spoken to. I have a feeling Cat may know the identity of this gentleman, and I bet you a guinea the lads didn't shoot Mr Siles." Detective Chief Inspector Bird removed his hands from behind his head and sat upright in his chair. "Well done, Detective Sergeant. I agree with your assessment. Now we need to catch a murderer, eh?" He grinned.

"Er, thank you, sir." Roggin was puzzled why his superior sneered at him.

"That will be all, and uh, I'd prefer you provide me with an update before the week's end."

"As you wish, sir." He turned and strode from the detective chief inspector's office.

Austin informed Nanny that he'd been temporarily called away on urgent business and would be absent for three nights. If anyone came calling for him, she would inform them that he'd not told her the details of his unscheduled trip.

"Of course, sir. But ye haven't told me where you'll be."

"I'm visiting Miss Harriet Stephenson at her family's country estate in Chieveley, Nanny. I shall confirm lodgings at a nearby hotel and depart by train shortly," Austin responded.

She looked distracted.

"Nanny, is there a problem?"

"Oh, good heavens no, sir. Forgive me, I, I was, er, just thinking about what I was going to prepare for dinner, but as you will be away, then it won't matter, will it?" she smiled.

"I wouldn't think so, and you can have some free time. You deserve it. Go out and enjoy yourself."

"Of course, sir."

He doubted she would go out, she never did. Her life revolved around this house and caring for his father and himself… his father… He felt the sadness.

Austin arrived in Chieveley mid-morning, secured lodging at a village hotel and with his bag deposited in his room, he immediately set out and rented a horse. Once mounted, he departed the village and headed for the training grounds and barracks of the renowned Queens' Own Hussars, where they were stationed just outside of Tidworth, about a twenty-mile ride away. It was quite a journey, and he had to hurry if he was to dine with Harriet later; he hoped the horse was up to the lengthy ride.

As he departed Chieveley, he saw the Hewitt-Thompson estate with its extensive manicured grounds and beautiful horses grazing on thick, lush grass. He saw no sign of the treacherous bog the groom at Ascot had warned about. On reaching the outskirts of the village, he spurred his horse into an easy lope and wondered if Harriet and her mother had yet arrived.

It was sometime later when he arrived at the barracks and training area for the Queens' Own Hussars, and once he arranged for the horse to be watered, fed and rubbed down, he immediately sought the Hussar's commanding officer.

"Captain Willems, A pleasant surprise. I wasn't expecting you for another day or two," welcomed Colonel Farquharson," as he reached out a hand and vigorously shook Austin's arm.

"I apologise if I inconvenienced you, sir. I had an unscheduled change of plans, and it's kind of you to see me unannounced," Austin replied after his hand was eventually released.

"General Wardlow speaks highly of you, and that's good enough for me, young man. Please, be seated." He waved Austin to a comfortable chair in the spacious office.

Austin took the proffered seat as the colonel continued.

"The general gave me a brief summary of what you need, and of course, I am happy to oblige him and assist you in any way I can."

"Thank you, sir. The general is a good man," Austin added.

Colonel Farquharson visibly relaxed. "Now, do tell me, what's this all about?"

Austin explained the details of his unusual request, and the colonel listened attentively. When finished, the commanding officer of the Queens' Own Hussars reached for two small glasses and a bottle of port and poured a healthy measure into each glass.

"I see no problem, Captain. We will be conducting exercises during that time, and it will not be an inconvenience to my staff, and I will ensure they are prepared and ready for you."

Austin grinned and drained his glass. It was a good drop.

On the return journey, he paid particular attention to landmarks and places where he could rest and water his horse, as the next time he rode along this road, he'd be in a hurry. It was late afternoon when he returned to his room at the hotel in Chieveley and had just enough time to bathe and wash away the filth of the road before dressing and heading to Windhaven.

He'd been thinking about Harriet, and again, he wondered what had caused her to unexpectedly change plans. It had to be Sir Ronald, and Austin hoped Harriet's stepfather wouldn't be dining with them. He saw no pleasure at the thought of being scrutinised and questioned by the man.

CHAPTER TWENTY-THREE

As Harriet's note promised, he was warmly received at Windhaven and, on arrival, was immediately led through the impressive manor and onto a terrace overlooking a beautiful expansive floral garden. Although it was late afternoon, the sun shone warmly, and he was invited to sit. Once comfortable on exquisite outdoor rattan furniture beneath an imitation Hindu pagoda, a house servant presented him with a generous selection of fine beverages to choose from. Appropriately, he decided on a refreshing gin mixed with quinine water over ice and garnished with a wedge of lime. He was suitably impressed; obtaining ice was a luxury few could afford, and the outdoor setting was nothing short of spectacular. He leaned back in the chair, sipped his drink and breathed in the fragrance of so many flowers while waiting for Harriet.

He didn't have to wait long.

"Austin!" she welcomed.

He never heard her entrance, and he shot to his feet, turning to greet her. To his surprise and dismay, she looked tense and fatigued.

"I'm so pleased you could come, and I apologise for dragging you all this way from London." She extended her arms, and they embraced.

"It's my pleasure, Harriet, and you didn't drag me away from London. I looked forward to seeing you." He suddenly thought of her stepfather and glanced back inside.

She sensed the reason for his apprehensiveness. "Austin, he isn't here and won't be coming." Harriet looked down at her clasped hands and then back up at him with a forced smile. "Please, be seated."

They both sat in adjacent chairs as a servant brought a refreshment for Harriet.

"Austin, I apologise for cancelling our lunch."

"No need to apologise. I'm sure you had good reason…"

She reached out and grasped his hand tightly. "Mama and I, we had to come here… we had to leave Mayfair."

Austin's expression hardened. "What happened, Harriet, tell me?"

She released his hand, and as if by magic, a *foulard* appeared, and she dabbed at her eyes. "It's Mama, she's been hurt."

"Hurt? Did she have an accident, a fall?" Austin's eyebrows furrowed together in puzzlement. "Has she been injured? What happened, Harriet?"

Again, she extended her hand to firmly hold his and, with the other, dabbed at her eyes. He could see the exaggerated rise and fall of her chest as she fought to control her breathing and emotions which reinforced his concern.

"It was him, Austin, my stepfather … a beastly man." She swallowed and took a deep breath before continuing." As usual, he was intemperate and accused her of disrespecting him by failing to acknowledge his many business achievements. I was in the next room and overheard everything. He struck her repeatedly about the face, and I heard Mama cry out–"

Austin was shocked by the revelation and stared at her in disbelief.

"That's when I ran into the parlour and saw him with a handful of her hair as he tried to drag her into the hearth. It was–"

Into the hearth? "Did he strike you, Harriet?" Austin interjected.

"He grabbed my arms and pushed me aside; that's when Mama was able to regain her feet and come to my aid as I'd fallen against a chair and it toppled backwards … I, I can still hear him laughing."

"Were you injured?" Austin asked, his voice a mere whisper.

Harriet didn't immediately answer, and he feared she didn't hear him. He was about to repeat the question when she finally spoke. Her voice quivered. "I was concerned for Mama – she had blood – she had blood streaming from her nose, and she – she cared not for herself, but only for my welfare."

It was all too much and she broke down weeping uncontrollably. Austin sprung from his seat and knelt before her, wrapping his arms around and pulling her close. He stroked her hair and whispered words of comfort as her anguish slowly subsided. His heart thumped, and his vision reddened as he felt consumed by hatred for Ronald Hewitt-Thompson.

He could hardly speak. "Where is he now?" he finally managed to ask.

"He had Maggie pack his bags and left the house shortly after you were there … I don't know where he went and couldn't care less, but I expect he has returned to Mayfair now that Mama and I have departed. Austin, he frightens me."

Austin believed Hewitt-Thompson wouldn't travel far and remain in London because of all his business interests. Harriet had earlier explained that the Mayfair residence had always belonged to Sir Ronald, while Windhaven had been inherited by her mother after the death of Ambrose Stephenson, Harriet's father.

He pried himself from her tight embrace and held her gently by the shoulders, looking for injuries and, to his relief, saw none. Your mother, has she been seen by a doctor?"

"Yes, a doctor came shortly after we arrived here. She has contusions, inflammation, and abrasions on her face and arms." She held his gaze as her bottom lip began to quiver.

He drew her tightly to him as she began sobbing again. Austin was furious and desperately wanted to find the man and dispense some well-deserved justice.

Shadows lengthened, and they spoke quietly as the afternoon's warmth surrendered to the coolness of evening. Harriet shivered from the night-time chill just as a servant informed them dinner was being served. Austin helped Harriet to her feet, and she paused, staring at him.

"Austin, you must promise me you will not retaliate for what he has done."

He went to interject, and she raised a hand.

"You must promise me. You can't involve yourself because anything you do could reflect badly on Mama. She will seek legal counsel, but I'm no expert in legal matters, and have been told there isn't much that can be done."

"Is there something you're not telling me, Harriet?"

She lowered her eyes to stare at the ground.

"Harriet, there is more, isn't there?" he pleaded

She raised her head and took another deep breath. "Austin, we think he will claim Mama is of unsound mind, which will aid him in gaining ownership of Windhaven and other assets belonging to her. We have yet to seek legal counsel but believe he has the legal right to her money and property, and we fear he will exercise that right."

Austin's mouth dropped open.

"This is why you cannot become overtly involved because it may support his claim. Austin, this is why I asked you to come here today. If you do anything to harm him or retaliate for what he has done to her, then he will argue you were either taking misguided direction from her or possibly influencing her."

Austin's head spun. "Is it possible can he claim ownership of Windhaven?"

"That is what we fear, but with the laws as they are…" she shrugged, "We just don't know."

Harriet's mother, Eunice, remained cloistered upstairs, and feeling unwell, she sent her apologies and, understandably, due to her injuries and self-consciousness, didn't venture down. They were left alone. After dinner, they moved to a smaller room where a fire blazed, and they sat talking and enjoying the privilege of unfamiliar intimacy. It was very late when Austin was driven to his hotel in a carriage.

He struggled to find sleep as twisted thoughts of revenge repeatedly spun through his mind in a maelstrom of half-concocted ideas. He was never more certain Ronald Hewitt-Thompson would suffer by his hand. He turned his thoughts to more pleasant visions of Harriet, the softness of her skin and the heat of her lips. He smiled at the recollection of the evening they'd spent together when Morpheus eventually descended over him.

Austin paid for three nights' accommodation at the hotel in Chieveley but checked out a day early. With the receipt secured in his pocket, he caught the early train back to London and would return to visit Harriet the following week. When he arrived in London, he'd book another, nondescript hotel for a few nights before returning home and tell Nanny he'd be away for five nights.

Detective Sergeant Roggin prepared himself for what was to come. He had new developments for Detective Chief Inspector

Bird, and as he always did, the inspector had a way about him that made the young Detective Sergeant doubt his abilities. He'd always leave the inspector's office feeling inadequate and less than capable. Barnabus Roggin looked at the office and saw Detective Chief Inspector Bird was still speaking with another man. Roggin shifted his feet nervously and waited.

"What is it, Detective?" he shouted from within his cramped office.

Barnabus Roggin hadn't seen the other man leave, and the Detective Chief Inspector was already barking at him before he'd even stepped one foot inside.

"Good day, sir," he began, standing at the foot of the inspector's paper-littered desk.

Detective Chief Inspector Tobias Bird looked at the young man and remained silent. His expression revealed he was curious and fully expected to be briefed, however, dispensing pleasantries wasn't the way of the man.

"Sir, I have news, er, developments, sir." His rehearsed briefing wasn't going according to plan.

Detective Chief Inspector Bird raised an eyebrow.

"The young lad who I believe witnessed Julian De Vore murder Miles Siles was–"

"Alleged."

"Alleged, sir?"

"Alleged until judged guilty. Unless you have an irrefutable motive, a weapon, even a credible witness or better yet, a confession, then alleged seems more appropriate, does it not?" Detective Chief Inspector Bird leaned back in his chair and fought to hold back a smile. He felt sorry for the Detective Sergeant because he was pedantic, but the young man needed to learn to remain calm and focused even when pressured. It would prove to be valuable when interviewing or interrogating suspects.

"Indeed, sir." Roggin consulted his notes quickly as the interruption had caused him to lose his train of thought.

"You have some developments for me, Detective Sergeant Roggin?"

"Sir, you will recall that two youths, both suspected of having ties to gang activity, were seen fleeing the location where Mr Siles was shot."

Detective Chief Inspector Bird nodded.

"We have managed to confirm the identify one of them, sir. His name is Cat. We don't know his family name, but I found that he is often seen around Covent Gardens."

"Covent Gardens is some distance from the Temple district where Mr Siles was slain. What was the boy doing so far away from his patch?" the Detective Chief Inspector questioned.

"Er, I've been wondering that too," replied Detective Sergeant Roggin.

"And what have you concluded?"

"There is considerable gang activity in that area, and we can link Cat to a…." Roggin consulted his notes. "A Mr Oliver Nagle, sir."

Detective Chief Inspector Bird's jaw tightened, and his eyes narrowed.

Detective Sergeant Roggin saw his superior react. "You are acquainted with this man, sir?"

"I am indeed. For the most part, Sergeant Oliver Nagle isn't your normal kidsman[16] and…" the inspector glanced through the door into the outer office. "Shut it."

Detective Sergeant Roggin did as asked and turned back to his superior with a quizzical expression. The office door was never closed.

16   *Kidsman – Organiser of child thieves.*

"You will not repeat what I'm about to tell you to anyone. If I hear you've opened your bloody gob… you'll be hunted to the ends of God's green earth. Do–you–understand, Detective?"

Barnabus Roggin's head rapidly bobbed up and down. "Aye, sir."

"Good. Sarge, or Ollie, is a friend of the Metropolitan Police. He informs us of any activity that would be of major concern to our governors. We allow Ollie some latitude, and he conducts his activities at a minor level, and we ignore him."

"But he is still a crook, sir."

"Let me put it this way. He takes children off the street and gives them money to buy food for their families. From what we can determine, Ollie's lads target only the wealthy and often those doing illicit things. His lads are incredibly loyal and will never speak ill of their beloved Sarge. If one of Ollie's lads is involved in a murder, then this is a surprising turn of events."

"Should we question him?" Detective Sergeant Roggin asked.

Detective Chief Inspector Bird returned to leaning back in his chair and steepled his hands beneath his chin. He remained silent for some time as the young Detective Sergeant sat quietly. Eventually, he separated his hands and laid them flat on his desk. "I'm not sure that will serve our interests, Detective. The death of Mr Siles and the involvement of Ollie's lads leads me to believe something is going on that dear old Oliver Nagle doesn't want us to know about. Otherwise, he would have told us. He hasn't, and he might be up to something, and talking to him may be fruitless or put him at risk." Detective Chief Inspector Bird raised an eyebrow. "It wouldn't be prudent to do that for now, would it Detective Sergeant Roggin?"

"Er, no, sir."

"I thought you'd agree. However, we probably need to chat with him, but not until we understand a little more. Now, here is what we shall do. Beginning this evening, you assign someone to observe

Ollie and his lads from the Lamb and Flag pub in Covent Garden. If Ollie or this Lenny character leaves, follow him. I want to know who they meet and what the bloody hell they're up to. You've done this before, Detective, and I know you're capable. However, you must exercise caution as his lads will be watching, and if your man even appears suspicious to them, they'll be on to him. If anything of interest to us happens, send word to me immediately. Do you understand?"

"Aye, sir, but, sir, wouldn't it be better to have someone else with him? If he's alone…"

"If he's alone, there will be less chance of discovery. Two will attract unwanted attention. And whatever you do, do not breathe a word of this to another living soul. Oliver Nagle should not be underestimated, and he has friends everywhere, I suspect even here within the Metropolitan Police." Detective Chief Inspector Bird glanced through the office window and turned to face the young officer. "That will be all Detective Sergeant."

CHAPTER TWENTY-FOUR

London was decidedly cooler than Chieveley. A damp chill permeated the night, and high overhead, thick clouds raced across a darkened sky obscuring a waning moon. Sensible people remained inside where it was warm and safe, while undoubtedly, those who ventured out hastened to their destination. It was a perfect evening for a heist, remarked Austin to his long-time friend, Lieutenant Charles Newbury.

All preparations had been completed, and both men sat upon a covered wagon, along with two other men, trusted friends hired by Ollie. The clip-clop of a single horse on cobbled stones broke the silence as they plodded a short distance from a small warehouse Austin had rented towards the Finch & Gossett art storage warehouse. Not far away, lights burned in a factory where workers toiled through the night in harsh conditions, but few were out in this part of London, and noticeably, the streets were deserted. Austin checked his pocket watch and determined, with some difficulty due to the darkness, that they were on schedule.

As Charles had repeatedly detailed, at 9.00 p.m., a woman of dubious character would arrive at Finch & Gossett's, and the two guards would allow her entry into the yard where she would be greeted by her amorous client, Colin Finch. Without wasting time,

Finch would escort his lovely, upstairs into his private quarters where they would occupy themselves for generally an hour, and sometimes longer if she felt generous. In pursuit of his lusty passions, Mr Finch would be preoccupied with his strumpet while she occupied considerable real estate on his well-used bed. Or so Austin and Charles hoped.

During that time, they would need to avoid the guards, two dogs, and gain entry into the Finch & Gossett warehouse to steal prized artwork belonging to Oscar Baker, one of Grand Overland Rail's directors.

Two lads loitered in a doorway approximately one hundred yards from the Finch & Gossett warehouse, and as the wagon approached, they stepped out from concealment and watched for the prearranged signal. All the focus was on the right-hand side of the street, and Austin saw the youths as they stepped out but failed to see a solitary man, hidden in a doorway on the left side of the street, who had more than a casual interest in what the two lads were up to.

Ahead, Austin saw a cab trotting away after depositing Mr Finch's Saturday night entertainment. From the light of an oil lamp hanging from a small covered shelter outside the fenced area of the warehouse, he saw the two baton-wielding guards escort the woman inside. "Are you sure you want to do this?" he asked his best friend after the guards returned to their posts.

"For your father, Austin." It was too dark to see his face, but Austin knew Charles was grinning.

"So be it." He gave the signal, and without pause, the lads sprinted off. Austin and Charles watched and anxiously waited.

Both lads ran silently towards the unsuspecting watchmen, and before they could react, Cat deftly snatched a baton, similar to a police truncheon but longer, from one of the guards while he was twirling it in the air. Simultaneously, Lenny deliberately knocked the oil lamp hanging from the shelter's wall, where it fell and smashed onto the footpath.

This was wholly unexpected, and Austin wondered what Cat and Lenny were doing. *This wasn't the plan.*

Even from a distance, he heard the guards yell in fury and immediately set off after Ollie's boys, who taunted them. The last thing Austin saw was the lads disappearing down the alley beside the warehouse, closely followed by the two enraged guards.

Now, it was Austin and Charles's turn. Charles leapt from the wagon and ran to the fence to be met by two snarling guard dogs. He threw meat marinated in laudanum over the fence, and the dogs immediately went to investigate. Austin prepared to scale the fence and open the gate from inside as soon as the animals were under the effects of the opiates. As predicted, the aggressive dogs devoured the tasty meat within seconds and were content to lie down and ignore their surroundings. He silently prayed the guards didn't return.

With agility, Austin scaled the fence and, with one wary eye on the dogs, opened the gate from inside. By now, he expected to see the glow of fire rising from behind the warehouse, but there was nothing. No smoke, no flames and no panicked yells of alarm. He was concerned that without the distraction of the fire, the guards could return at any moment. He contemplated calling the whole thing off, but Charles, unfazed by the change in the plan, ran to the warehouse door and slipped the large key made by the regimental armourer into the lock. With the muted sound of grating metal, the lock turned, and the door opened. They were in.

Charles knew exactly where to go and, in total darkness, navigated around shelving to a large cage where fine artwork was secured. He found the hidden key and began fumbling with the lock.

Mr Finch had wasted no time with his guest, and from upstairs, the rhythmic banging of a bed against a wall was a testament that he was getting his money's worth and thoroughly enjoying himself. Periodically, a muted squeal would drift down to them and, combined with the banging, masked any sound from the warehouse below. With the cage successfully unlocked, Charles entered and walked to a shelf with numerous partitions containing valuable fine art.

"Here, this row belongs to your Mr Baker," whispered Charles as he carefully slid a painting from the shelf and handed it to Austin. With care, Austin ran as fast as he dared and was met by one of Ollie's men near the wagon, who took the painting just as Charles ran up with another painting and handed it off to the other man.

The bed banging stopped just as Austin was about to run through the warehouse with his second painting. A moment later, the door to the flat upstairs opened, and Mr Finch was framed in the doorway at the top of the internal stairs. His nakedness was less of a shock than his unexpected appearance, and Austin froze. Charles crept silently behind him, and they both watched and waited. They'd drop the paintings and run at the first sign of discovery. Thankfully, Mr Finch returned inside and shut the door; seconds later, they could hear squeals of delight. With his heart pounding, Austin raced to take the remaining artwork.

In total, there were thirty-three paintings, some small, others quite large, which required careful handling so they wouldn't be damaged. Austin had hoped for more, but some must have recently been relocated. Quietly and efficiently, all Mr Baker's paintings were removed, wrapped in blankets and stowed securely in the wagon while Colin Finch enjoyed his Saturday night frolic. The fire, so meticulously planned for, never eventuated, and Austin was apprehensive. Not only did he fear for the safety of Cat and Lenny, but for himself, Charles and the two helpers, as the guards could have appeared at any moment. So far they hadn't.

The cage was locked, the main door was closed and relocked, and out in the yard, the dogs were again becoming interested in their surroundings. Austin was only too pleased to be away, and they were fortunate not to have been caught. However, something didn't sit right, and he couldn't put his finger on it. The darkness made it difficult to see, but Austin scanned the streets as best he could. It was just a feeling, nothing more; he shrugged as the wagon continued up the street, turned down a side street and headed back towards his warehouse where the paintings would be carefully offloaded.

As instructed by Detective Chief Inspector Bird, Detective Sergeant Barnabus Roggin assigned a junior constable to follow the lads, Cat and his friend from the Lamb and Flag pub, until they reached a main thoroughfare where they caught and paid for a Hansom cab. To the constable's way of thinking, that was most unusual, and he quickly hailed a passing cab and followed from a safe distance until they alighted in an industrial area on the outskirts of Marylebone about one-and-a-half miles away.

It was becoming late, and the constable was agitated as he firmly believed the two lads were up to no good. He followed them until they paused and melded into the darkness of a doorway. They were waiting; that much was obvious, but for what? From the opposite side of the street and only twenty-thirty yards away, he watched, however, the darkness made it difficult to see any detail.

When a covered wagon appeared, the lads ran off far too quickly for him to follow and remain undetected. He was deciding what to do when he noticed the wagon's occupants acting suspiciously. They'd stopped outside a nondescript warehouse, and if not mistaken, he was witnessing a robbery. They weren't there very long, perhaps fifteen minutes, and departed. He'd lingered a while, but the two lads never returned and feeling like he'd somehow failed his mission, he went home to get some needed sleep and report to Detective Sergeant Roggin in the morning.

A hansom cab dropped Austin outside his home, and he let himself through the front door. He'd given Nanny a few days off, and he wasn't sure if she'd be home, especially as he came home a day earlier than expected. When he stepped into the hallway, he heard voices. He dropped his bag and entered the dining room to find Howard seated at the table with Nanny having breakfast. She shot to her feet.

"Sir, I, I didn't expect you home," she stammered.

"It's quite alright, Nanny. I came home earlier than anticipated. Howard, what brings you here so early? Have I missed something?"

Howard dabbed at the corners of his mouth with a napkin before speaking. "I came to see you, Austin and was dutifully informed you were away. I couldn't resist the temptation of Nanny's company, her superb culinary skills and stayed for breakfast." He turned to Nanny and gave her a warm smile.

Austin looked towards Nanny, whose face turned crimson. She picked up her plate and utensils.

"Er, I have some washing to do… would you like some breakfast, sir?"

"No, thank you, Nanny, but I'd like tea."

"Very well, sir. Mr Willoughby, a tea?"

"Thank you, m'dear, that would be lovely," Howard replied.

Austin sat at the chair Nanny just vacated as she hurried to the kitchen. "I'm pleased I caught you, Howard. On Monday, I want you to contact the solicitors for Watson Coach Building and have them withdraw their expression of interest in purchasing shares of Grand Overland Rail. You must do this on Monday."

Howard smiled and picked up a slice of bread, "There will be hell to pay when they find out."

"That's exactly what I hope for, Howard."

"And your, er, your heist was it successful?"

Austin grinned. "Indeed."

"Then you will go through with the rest of your foolhardy scheme?" Howard asked between mouthfuls of toast.

"After last night, most certainly. Mr Oscar Baker is completely unaware his valuable art has disappeared. It was a complete success, I'm thrilled and relieved to say."

"What about the art? Where is it now?"

"In that warehouse you urged me to rent. It's dry, undamaged and safe. No harm can come to them."

Howard nodded and wiped his hands.

Nanny entered with a tray carrying a tea pot and cups. Austin noticed she was more composed. "Thank you, Nanny, and please, have the rest of the day to yourself. I won't be eating here tonight and will be home late."

Nanny lowered her eyes before looking at him. "I have washing to finish, sir."

Austin knew it was pointless to argue. "Very well."

She poured the tea, and took away the remaining dishes, leaving the two men alone.

"Tonight, Howard. I'm going to destroy a boat."

"By golly, you're really doing this, aren't you?"

"For father," Austin replied.

Howard's expression saddened. "For Enoch."

"And no burglaries have been reported?" the detective chief inspector questioned.

Detective Sergeant Roggin shook his head. "No, sir, not yet."

"Yet the owner of the Warehouse, A Mr Fitch–"

"Finch, sir," corrected Detective Sergeant Roggin.

"–has not reported any theft – at all?"

"No sir, he was in the warehouse the entire time with a guest, er, a lady friend, sir."

Detective Chief Inspector Bird scratched the back of his head as he considered the report given to him by the Detective Sergeant. "And is there a link of this occurrence to the murder of Miles Siles?"

"Not that I can determine, sir," replied the detective sergeant with a shake of his head.

Detective Chief Inspector Bird was perplexed. "Amongst the storage facilities Mr Finch offers his customers, is there more, anything else of interest?"

Detective Sergeant Roggin shrugged. "Inside the warehouse, he has a lock-up where valuable items, including fine art, are held in secure storage. That is why he has guards and dogs. Apparently, gentry pay a premium for his storage facility and service."

"Yes, no doubt," remarked Detective Chief Inspector Bird. "Let me understand the events as they happened as you witnessed. Correct me if I err."

"Very well, sir."

"The two lads arrive at the location and hide in a doorway until a wagon arrives, at which point they scarper and upset the two guards who give chase."

"Aye, sir."

With the guards gone, the wagon pulls up outside the warehouse entrance, and you say four men?"

"Definitely, four, sir."

"These four men have gained admittance to the warehouse and were seen carrying items and placing them in the wagon?"

The Detective Sergeant nodded.

"What about the dogs? They must have been barking."

"Er, no, sir. Not a peep from them. Later, when I spoke to Mr Finch, the dogs were acting normal, but they're are quite fearsome beasts, sir."

"These four men were loading their wagon for about ten minutes before they departed, is that correct?"

"Actually, sir, the wagon was parked outside the warehouse for exactly sixteen minutes. The men were inside the warehouse for twelve minutes, sir."

Detective Chief Inspector Bird eased his large frame upright from the chair, turned, and looked through the small window behind where he sat. Detective Sergeant Roggin patiently waited for the inspector to speak. After a minute or two, he was rewarded when the inspector turned.

"You will visit the warehouse and take that constable with you. Once there, you will inform Mr Finch he was a victim of a burglary and insist he perform an inventory and determine and itemise what was stolen and who the owner or owners of that merchandise are. The lads distracted the guards, and the dogs were likely medicated, so they didn't bark. You will search for evidence and report back as soon as you have verification. Is that understood, Detective Sergeant?"

"Aye, sir."

"Good, now, see yourself off."

CHAPTER TWENTY-FIVE

Like the previous evening, there was a nip in the air and rain threatened. If anything, being on the Thames felt colder than being ashore, especially when on a small boat trying to navigate the river, contend with choppy waves, and remain dry.

Ollie made arrangements to purchase a suitable boat from a friend, which was quickly brought down the river and tied to a pier. A couple of his lads kept watch over the small craft until it was needed. As the *Belisha* wasn't far away and only moored at Tower Bridge Moorings, Austin didn't need a local guide, and besides, he felt concerned that a local wherryman could be recognised and may talk to the authorities if questioned. To mitigate risk, Ollie also provided Austin with a trusted young man named Peter, who was in prime physical condition, an experienced oarsman and anonymous in this part of London. For Austin's needs, Peter was ideal.

Austin spent considerable time going over the plan with Peter. While the art heist had been a clandestine operation, setting fire to a large yacht would be a dynamic event and not go unnoticed; it would be a public spectacle, or so he hoped. Once the *Belisha* was alight, and to avoid detection and allay any suspicion, they needed to leave the scene as quickly as possible and not loiter to watch.

Ollie suggested that he have his lads positioned at strategic places along the river who could assist Austin and Peter if they needed to disappear quickly. An observant member of the public or a diligent constable could complicate matters, and having contingencies seemed prudent.

With everything in place, Austin and Peter safely crossed the Thames, drifted beneath Tower Bridge, upstream of the *Belisha*, and began to make their way down towards Tower Bridge Moorings.

With minimal effort, Peter kept the small craft as close to the right-hand bank as possible. Every now and then, there'd be a bump against the side as they drifted into a mysterious decaying carcass that reeked of foulness.

"Com'n up, sir. Just ahead," said Peter, barely above a whisper.

"Just don't bang against the side. If anyone is aboard, I don't want them alerted by us crashing into the hull," Austin warned.

He saw her then, painted on her stern in *faux* gold; the name *Belisha* was easily read. Peter pulled an oar expertly, and the little dinghy spun and swerved into the open space directly at the stern of the schooner, where he held the small craft steady.

Austin already had a large bottle of paraffin in his hand, and he cautiously rose from his seat and leaned forward to grasp a stanchion. It was a precarious move because if Peter didn't keep the dinghy in place, Austin could fall into the toxic and polluted river.

With his free hand, he upended the bottle of highly flammable paraffin oil, which poured onto pristine teak decking and quickly spread. When the bottle was empty, he silently lowered himself back to his seat and dropped it over the side, where it disappeared into the filthy water.

Peter manoeuvred the small rowboat away from the stern and

down the side, about midway down its one-hundred-foot length, where Austin repeated the process. The second empty bottle was silently dropped into the Thames, and Peter let the row boat drift down near the upswept bow. It was difficult for Austin to reach the deck as the bow was considerably higher than the hull further aft as the paraffin began to spread over the deck. The unstable rowboat moved unpredictably in the choppy water, and Peter fought to keep it steady. With Austin struggling to maintain balance, the dinghy was pushed away from the Belisha, and the gap widened noticeably and Austin was fully stretched out. His feet were hooked over the dinghy's gunwale, and with the small rowboat bobbing erratically in the river, he couldn't pull it in and stand fully upright. Peter's efforts to close the gap were ineffectual. There was only one safe option. He released the bottle, spilling potent oil down the hull and with a grunt, grabbed a handhold on a reachable cleat securely fixed to the deck. He unhooked his feet from the dinghy, and immediately, his legs swung towards *Belisha.* The force of motion only pushed the dinghy further away, and Austin was hanging by his hands, with his feet in the water, just as he feared could happen. The dinghy was now about three yards from the *Belisha* and already drifting downstream.

Peter expertly turned the small boat and bent his back, pulling hard on the oars with some urgency as the dinghy slowly began to make headway against the current. Austin had one hand on the cleat and another on a stanchion as his feet dangled in the water. If he slipped and fell into the Thames and wasn't immediately rescued, he knew his life could be in danger from the poisons and toxins that thrived in the polluted river.

Other than Austin's grunt, neither of them had made a sound. Peter knew exactly what to do, and he pulled hard on the oars to bring the small craft close to Austin's dangling legs. Austin twisted his head to the side, grimacing as he watched the dinghy close the distance. His hand clinging to the rail hurt, and he knew he couldn't hold on for much longer. It seemed to take an age, but Peter had responded immediately, and the dinghy inched closer.

He grimaced from pain; his right hand was in agony from the stanchion which was cutting into his palm when he felt Peter grab his legs and pull them into the dinghy. Using remarkable skill and strength, Peter kept the small boat stable and pulled Austin safely inside the small boat without it capsizing.

Austin rubbed his hand to restore circulation as Peter continued to hold the craft in position. Impatient to leave the area, he reached into a pocket, extracted a box of matches and, careful not to set himself on fire, lit a match and flicked it onto the deck. With a low whoosh, the entire deck was instantly ablaze from stem to stern and they were clearly illuminated.

"Let's go," Austin whispered.

Peter needed no urging, and the oars bit into the water. Aided by the downstream current, the flimsy dinghy gathered speed and angled across the Thames to a rickety pier on the opposite bank where they'd abandon the dinghy and then vanish.

Austin twisted on his seat to look behind; the *Belisha* was truly alight, and already flames were consuming furled canvas sails, lines and licking at both masts. He heard a shout or two as people came from homes and other boats to watch the spectacle. The fire was too large to extinguish unless pumps were used, but down at the river, it was unlikely that even a bucket brigade would affect the outcome. The *Belisha* was doomed.

Once they arrived ashore on the opposite bank. Peter said farewell and was soon absorbed into the darkness. Austin was grateful that Ollie had provided him with a good and reliable man because he had plans to use him again.

Cautiously, Austin threaded around some ramshackle buildings and reappeared on the riverbank to watch the *Belisha* struggle to remain afloat. The hull was burning fiercely, and from the light of the blaze, Austin could see hundreds of people had come out to watch. Many probably felt as he did, although few enjoyed seeing such a beautiful yacht destroyed. As the first raindrops began to fall, Austin turned up the collar on his coat and disappeared into the night.

When he arrived home and stepped inside, Nanny informed him he reeked of paraffin and insisted he remove his clothes and sodden shoes. She never asked why he had paraffin oil all over him, but he suspected she knew the reason and probably approved.

With his clothes soaking, she heated water and filled a bathtub. As Austin eased himself into the hot water, he thought of the next phase of the plan.

At approximately 10.00 a.m. tomorrow, Mrs Pearl Dillington would receive a package from an unknown messenger dispatched by Ollie. The contents would be most revealing to George Dillington's wife, and she would not only discover about her husband's infidelity but that he owned a house where he kept a revolving stable of mistresses and hosted parties that were less than wholesome. The packet would contain correspondence from George, where he invited select male friends to join in an evening of debauchery and frolic with an assortment of exotic beauties who would eagerly cater to various eclectic tastes and depravity. Motivated by some currency, Mildred had been quite helpful.

Austin had no real issue with George Dillington hosting parties of a raunchy nature; he'd been to a few of them himself. The fact of the matter is that amorous George had virtually no capital of his own, lived well beyond his means and was utterly dependent on his wife's money, which he enthusiastically spent. Pearl unknowingly paid for his lifestyle and extravagances, and by all accounts, she was an upstanding Christian woman, and he doubted she would have supported financing her husbands lurid hobby. According to Howard, who had sources that were acquainted with Pearl Dillington, the repercussions to follow would be extreme, and Austin believed those measures could see lover-boy George destitute and hopefully tossed from his conjugal home.

The package Pearl Dillington received would contain all the evidence a rational woman needed to be both judge and jury, and George Dillington's future looked decidedly glum.

Clean after a hot bath, Austin retired to his bedroom, anxious. As Pearl Dillington learned of her husband's constant infidelities, he would be on a train heading for Chieveley to complete the last of the personal attacks on the directors of Grand Overland Rail. He was anxious to see Harriet, who was expecting him, however, she had repeatedly warned him not to seek revenge against her stepfather for the violent acts committed against her mother and herself. When she learned of what he was going to do, he feared the nature of their relationship could change.

Detective Sergeant Barnabus Roggin was entering Bow Street Police Station as Detective Chief Inspector Tobias Bird was leaving. They nodded in greeting and passed each other.

The Detective Chief Inspector had a thought. "Oh, Detective Sergeant?"

The young detective paused and turned to face his superior. "Sir?"

"Have you learned anything more about the warehouse theft?'

"Er, not exactly, sir. But you were correct; it was a robbery, although I've not spoken to the victim yet. I've been unable to reach him at his residence and arranged to interview him at the offices of Grand Overland Rail on Monday afternoon. I was going to update you afterwards, sir."

"Good, see you do. Now, I can't dally here. It seems we have an arsonist with a penchant for setting yachts alight that requires my attention. Carry on, Detective Sergeant."

Austin felt the stress, but after tomorrow evening, he could relax and move on with the next phase of his ambitious plan. He tried to push aside any negative feelings and instead focus his thoughts on Harriet, and he sincerely hoped that his crusade against her stepfather's business wouldn't come between them.

He was drawn to Harriet like no other woman he'd ever met. He thought about her constantly, and in her presence, he marvelled at her wit and intelligence, and when he looked at her, he hungered for her touch. The fragrance of her hair, her breath on his neck – how he longed to hold her tight and caress her again. He'd not known her long, yet through adversity, they'd bonded and become close, and if it came to a choice, could he put aside his desire to have a healthy relationship with her in exchange for seeing the downfall of Grand Overland Rail?

The rhythmic clack of railway tracks was calming, and he felt his eyelids grow heavy. *What will I do if I have to choose – Harriet or revenge?* He was almost asleep and having lurid thoughts about kissing her when suddenly he opened his eyes, sat up, and stared out the coach's window at the passing countryside. The repetitive clackety-clack spoke to him; it wasn't an ominous or dark message but gave him clarity and purpose.

Pulled by a massive steel behemoth, a tribute to the evolution of modern engineering, locomotives powered by coal merely towed a chain of subservient carriages – nothing more. Steel carriage wheels raced over miles and miles of endless tracks, and yet, without coal, the steel monsters were dead, inert and useless. Carriages transporting goods for commerce or filled with people would be motionless with the absence of coal. Coal brought life – and this was his father's legacy; this was his endowment, or should have been. His dear father... Perhaps it was the tension or tiredness, but Austin's resilience dissolved, and he raised his hands to his face, consumed by grief and despair. His love for his father was unquestioned and profound, and his emotional state was appropriately wakened by the clackety-clack of wheels on tracks. Enoch Willems had been more than a father ever could be. He was kind, generous, and loving. Austin had always looked up to his father with respect, and as he grew older and understood more about life, he came to admire the man. Now Enoch was gone – dead, and while Austin had precious memories to cling to, he also had the means to resurrect his legacy – if he chose, and if for no other reason, he owed his father that.

Austin believed stealing expensive racehorses from Grand Overland Rail's managing director, Sir Ronald, represented the most personal risk. His relationship with Harriet complicated things immeasurably. When police investigated the theft, he knew he'd be considered a suspect and interviewed. After all, on the evening the horses disappeared, he'd been a dinner guest of Harriet at Windhaven in Chieveley.

He'd given the matter a lot of thought, and while he admitted to himself that stealing racehorses on the same night he was at the estate was foolhardy, he also believed he would have been interviewed anyway because of his other recent visit.

Tonight, he would enjoy dinner with Harriet, return to his hotel room at a decent hour, and ensure the hotel proprietor was fully aware he'd returned intemperate. He'd make some noise in his room, a few inconsiderate crashes and bangs before lowering himself down from his balcony using a rope he'd brought. Before daylight, he would return unseen to his room by climbing the rope and appear for breakfast shortly after. His bleary-eyed appearance would only support the belief that he was just another spoiled ex-military gentleman showing the effects of an evening carousing.

Charles Newbury had kindly offered to go with him to help, but Austin was determined this was a task he needed to do himself and, due to the danger, not put anyone else at risk.

CHAPTER TWENTY-SIX

Windhaven was spectacular. A long carriageway began at Chieveley's main road, continued directly towards the mansion and looped around a large fountain at the main entrance. Manicured grounds with colourful borders of late summer blooming flowers were strategically placed to provide a flash of brilliance in contrast to well-maintained lawns dissected by symmetrical garden paths and low hedges. Even though he was familiar with the extravagance of wealth, Austin was suitably impressed, and each time he visited here, he was struck by the beauty of horticultural splendour, and amazingly, it was even more impressive at the rear of the mansion. However, the magnificence of flowers and fauna did little to quell his anxiety as he was unsure how Harriet would receive him.

When he alighted from the carriage, Harriet came outside to greet him with a warm smile and hug, and yet, despite her best attempts to hide her fatigue, he could see the tension and weariness on her face. All was not well. The coach departed, rounded the fountain and trotted down the lengthy carriageway. As arranged, the coach would return for him at 9.00 p.m.

Mrs Hewitt-Thompson was comfortably seated in the sunroom sipping sherry and reading from a book when they entered. An abundance of indoor plants and greenery filled the sunroom, adding depth to the contrast of dark wood-stained floors, while richly textured tied-back drapes hung in grandeur before oversized windows that looked onto the gardens.

She rose from her seat and offered her hand as Austin walked towards her, dipping his head respectfully. "Mrs Hewitt-Thompson, how lovely to see you again." He felt it appropriate not to mention the beating she'd received from her husband. "I hope you're feeling better?" He released her hand, and she lowered herself back to the chair before replying.

"It's good to see you again, Austin. And yes, I'm feeling much better, thank you for asking." She smiled at him, but he saw she was far from well. Powder did little to hide the lingering discolouration of bruises beneath her eyes, and she looked to have aged considerably since he had seen her last. He thought of her husband striking her and fought to control his anger.

A fashionable mantle clock positioned above the hearth chimed the hour and seemed obtrusive in the awkward silence.

Harriet stepped up to Austin and slid her arm through his. "Mama, we shall stroll in the garden," she said with forced cheerfulness.

Eunice smiled at them both. "Take a stole, dear; there is a freshness in the air." She opened her book and continued to read as Harriet led Austin outside.

"How is she coping?" he asked once they were in the garden and could talk privately.

Harriet shook her head. "It seems the wounds she suffered are not just physical; she struggles daily, and while that dreadful man hasn't shown his face here, he's persistent and sends messages instructing her to return to London.

"Will she?"

"She told me she has no intention of returning to him, not in fear of her safety, but of mine." She gripped his arm tighter, pulling him in close. "She is resolute, Austin. However, he is capable of making life very difficult for her, and all he cares for is gaining control of her finances." Harriet stopped and looked up at his face as she grasped both his arms. "You mustn't jeopardise this Austin."

He turned his head away and looked towards the stables.

"I know what you want to do, and I believe you intend to take his horses tonight. Am I right, Austin?" She released his arms and stepped back.

He tore his gaze away from the stables approximately two hundred yards away and focused on her as she continued.

"I thoroughly detest the man… he is greedy, violent and overly ambitious, and I understand your need to seek retribution, Austin, but your actions could put Mama's and my welfare in an untenable position." She held his gaze and saw a vein pulsing on his neck.

Austin felt the tension and exhaled loudly. He didn't know how to respond or what to say. Whatever he said wouldn't sit well with her. He took another deep breath and reached for her hand. "I understand, Harriet, I truly do–"

"And?"

"And what?"

Her face hardened, "You did not answer me."

Ahead of them, a fountain lay silent. Carved from stone, figurines of sprites, gnomes and imps stood motionless with dry, fixed, mischievous expressions, staring insolently down at them from the edge of a pool that typically held ornamental fish. Austin licked his lips. His mouth felt as dry as the small statues that mocked him with their frozen, waggish smirks.

He shook his head. "I don't know any more, Harriet. I want to do what is right for you, but I am torn–"

"Then you have decided," she stated.

"Harriet, your father–"

"Step-father," she corrected.

"I'm sorry, and I do apologise, Harriet. But I can't be so dismissive. He and three others sought to destroy my father's life and took his business, his wealth and his legacy through deceit and dishonesty. A legacy of a wonderful, kind, and gentle man who is now dead. A man you would have enjoyed meeting, Harriet." She'd touched a nerve, and he responded ardently. "And your step-father and associates continue unabated with their fraudulence. They use their peerage and exemplary reputations to lure victims to open their purses and invest in tawdry schemes designed to fail and constructed only to cause pain. Should they be allowed to continue Harriet? Should these men circumvent laws and use their influence and intimidation to achieve their lofty goals? Is it right?"

He was breathing hard and felt terrible for raising his voice. "I, er, forgive me, Harriet, I'm not cross at you. What he continues to do to your mother and to you is wrong at every level, and is no different than what he has done to my family, but I cannot and will not ignore my father."

With her arms folded protectively against her chest, she slowly circumvented the fountain, briefly disappearing behind the elves and imps as he watched in frustration. As she silently reappeared, he saw the expression on her face, and he felt his heart plummet as she stopped six feet from him.

"I think you should leave. You're unwelcome here, Austin. It appears our paths are no longer aligned."

"Harriet," he appealed. "We can discuss this."

"You still have your hat and coat, and I think you know the way out. Good day." She turned and walked from the garden towards the house, leaving him alone beside the ornate taunting fountain. He was devastated and imagined hearing impish laughs and jeering at his back as he watched Harriet enter the manor.

"Harriet, please!"

She'd displayed a different side of her personality to him; was it resoluteness or just plain stubbornness? But he couldn't be angry at her for showing strength and loyalty towards her mother. *She's an impressive woman*, he thought and quietly admitted that he may have said something similar had their positions been reversed. Still, she offered him no opportunity for discussion, which was disappointing.

Despondent and confused, he walked from the garden, around the side of the manor and onto the carriageway. He could have requested a carriage return him to Chieveley, but the thought never occurred as he forlornly trudged away.

The alehouse in Chieveley offered him a little emotional solace as he ordered another ale. Truth be told, it was the ale that deadened the hurt. The alehouse provided nothing more than a venue to numb the pain of being spurned. He'd lost count of how many he'd had, but it mattered not. He'd devoted the remainder of the day trying to decipher the abstract logic of a beautiful and intelligent young woman and was no closer now than when he first entered the establishment. In the turmoil of his mind, one thing had become clear: he would continue with his plan and steal Ronald Hewitt-Thompson's two finest racehorses, and if Harriet chose to inform the police, then let her, they'd have a difficult time proving it.

He emptied his mug, wiped his mouth with the back of his hand and looked across the room, catching Peter's eye. It was a subtle nod; no one in the alehouse would have noticed, but it was a signal. Without wasting time, the young man upended his mug and headed for the rear entrance door as Austin made his unsteady way towards the front door and his hotel.

It was dark when he woke from his stupor and, for a second or two, believed he'd overslept. With his head thumping, he slowly undressed, placed his clothes on the bed, changed into another set of clothes more suited to a farmer than a wealthy and newly unattached gentleman, and filled his pockets with a few apples he'd previously purchased.

Thankfully, the street was deserted when he looked outside. From his balcony, he watched for movement in case anyone loitered in the shadows, but he saw no one. He carefully tied one end of the rope to a stout column and threw the coil over the balcony rail. With his head still feeling the effects of his excessive alcohol consumption, he cautiously lowered himself down the side of the building without anyone seeing him and made a devout promise never to drink alcohol again.

Once down, he positioned the hanging rope so it blended into the vertical lines of the building and was hidden from casual view. He doubted anyone would see it easily, even if they knew where and what to look for. With his collar turned up, cap pulled down and hands buried in his pockets, he wandered away.

Only a short time later, he saw the distinct form of a man and horse standing beneath a tree near the outskirts of town. He paused to observe briefly and, feeling satisfied Peter was alone, walked towards him.

Peter didn't talk much, and when he did, it was only when necessary. He didn't comment or say a word in the way of a greeting and just nodded his head when Austin arrived. Austin walked up to the horse, rubbed its neck with his hand, expertly felt along the animal's flank hind quarters and walked around the off-side.

"It's a good horse, Peter, well done."

In the darkness, Austin saw the white gleam of Peter's teeth. He must have smiled.

"You know where to meet me?"

Peter nodded.

Austin had carefully reviewed the plan with the young man and fully expected to return from his journey early in the morning when it was daylight. No one must see him, especially on horseback, so Peter would meet him further down the road, take the horse and return it to the stables from where it was rented later in the day.

"Good luck, sir," Peter offered, throwing the reins over the horse's head and passing them to Austin as he mounted.

Austin touched a hand to his cap. "See you in a few hours." He squeezed his legs, and the horse responded eagerly.

There was another less grand entrance into Windhaven, which provided access for house staff, deliveries and other farming or pastoral needs. From a substantial wrought-iron gate, the carriageway curved from the main Chieveley road about three hundred yards from the estate's principal entrance. It was a direct path past the expansive stables and a cluster of sheds that presumably stored farming equipment before reaching staff housing, and it was to this secondary access road where Austin headed. All employees who lived on the property were housed in staff quarters separated from the manor and tactfully divided by large hedgerows to ensure privacy for all.

Austin unlatched and swung open the heavy gate and entered Windhaven, leaving it open behind him. If he had to make a hasty retreat, he didn't want to have to dismount to open the gate, and he believed it was doubtful anyone would notice it was open at this time of night. He had to hasten, knowing he had a long night ahead.

He led the rented horse up the carriageway towards the stables, where he knew the thoroughbreds would be. He'd learned that trainers and groomsmen did not sleep in the stables and were billeted in the staff quarters along with everyone else a short distance away. It suited Austin perfectly. However, he needed to be quiet.

On arriving at the stables, he tethered his horse to a rail and entered. The smell of horses was distinct and calming to Austin. The musty smell of many horses confined in a small area mingled with the odours of leather, oil, and hay was not offensive, and for a fleeting moment, he was reminded of his past military career. He pushed aside his thoughts and felt for a lantern where he knew it would be hanging and in no time had it lit.

The stables housed about twenty thoroughbred racehorses. The more valuable ones had permanent stalls closer to the entrance, and with the lantern held high, he slowly walked to the first stall. As he approached, he heard movement but nothing to cause alarm. The horses sensed the presence of a human and, disturbed from their slumber, they shifted position.

He needed to find Charming and Father's Pride. Then it dawned on him. Those are professional racing names, mere pseudo-names, and he could have kicked himself. Written in chalk on each stall was the actual name of each horse, not their professional name. The first stall had the name 'Honey' scrawled on the wall. Could Honey be Father's Pride? He thought back to the day at the Royal Ascot when he was in the stables and tried to remember. Father's Pride was a bay-coloured mare, as was this horse.

He moved to the next stall, held the lantern high and saw a grey gelding. He recalled Charming, and he was a grey gelding, and this horse was certainly Charming. The name scrawled on the stall simply said Prince. Austin chuckled.

He found halters and quickly had them cinched securely on both horses, attaching lengthy lead ropes to each. With the stall doors open, he led both horses from the stables towards his horse, still tethered to the rail.

Thoroughbreds were naturally skittish and excitable animals, and while Austin had been calm and relaxed in their presence, speaking to them in soothing whispers, they were understandably agitated, having been roused from their sleep, taken from the comfort of their stalls by a stranger and now being led away. In protest, they began sidestepping and pulling on their leads.

Austin had fully anticipated this, and he reached into his pocket and gave each horse an apple. It helped and gave him enough time to untether his horse and mount.

Once astride the saddle, he turned to look at the thoroughbreds one last time before setting off and saw the outline of a person watching.

CHAPTER TWENTY-SEVEN

Austin froze. In the darkness, it was difficult to see who silently observed. If he couldn't see them, they couldn't see his face and identify him. He turned his head away and prepared to quickly ride away.

"Austin."

Harriet? His head swivelled around as the two thoroughbreds began pulling on the leads again.

"Austin!" she repeated.

His horse was becoming jittery, and he fought to maintain control. After a few calming words, the animals settled, and he turned back to her in question.

"I apologise for my earlier behaviour, Austin. I've been insensitive and rude to you. Will you allow me to help?" She stepped closer and saw she was leading her saddled horse. She was appropriately dressed in riding breeches and a jacket.

Why is she here? He wondered. It was never his plan to involve Harriet in his scheme, and if something went wrong, she'd be implicated, her life ruined. A risk he was prepared to take for himself but not for her. But neither could he stand around here and argue. He thought quickly. "Take this horse."

With remarkable agility, Harriet mounted her horse, adjusted her feet in the stirrups and then urged her horse to come alongside his. She was grinning as he leaned over and handed her one of the thoroughbred lead ropes.

"We must hasten, Harriet," he said quietly before squeezing his heels and setting off. Even though the service lane wasn't paved, four horses still made considerable noise, and he was concerned someone would hear them leave. But there were no cries of alarm or shouts, and they entered the main road to Chieveley, where he waited for Harriet to catch up and closed the gate before riding off.

Perplexed, Stable Master, Elias Pickenbury scratched his head and waited a few moments longer before entering the stables to determine which horse were missing.

"Chieveley is this way," she said.

"Who said I was riding to Chieveley," he crisply replied. His evening had taken a surprise turn, and the gloom of the afternoon and early evening dissolved into concern and annoyance as he now had Harriet to contend with. He felt responsible for her.

Two abreast, each trailing a thoroughbred, Austin brought his horse to a slow canter, and Harriet followed suit. The racehorses were calm and content to be led and caused no further problems.

It was pitch black, although the moon occasionally peeked through the clouds and provided illumination to offer some help. Still, the country road was wide enough for two horses to ride abreast if they didn't encounter anyone riding in the opposite direction.

He knew Harriet was an experienced horsewoman and a masterful rider, and to his relief, she was entirely at ease on horseback, leading a spirited thoroughbred down country roads in the dead of night. He wanted to talk to her and ask why she had a change of heart, but he had to wait. In thirty minutes, he would rest the horses at a stream, and then he could talk and instruct her to return home.

They almost rode past the bridge. He was lost in thought, thinking of Harriet and her change in attitude, when he recognised the landmark and instructed her to slow to a walk. This was the first planned rest stop. Beneath the short span of the bridge, a stream gurgled sedately over rocks and was a suitable place to allow the horses water and a few minutes of rest. They dismounted near a stand of trees and led the horses to the stream. The trees provided cover so they could remain out of sight from the road in the unlikely event a traveller happened by.

All four horses were allowed to drink, and as he and Harriet stood side by side on the bank, he turned to her. "I want you to return home, Harriet."

"I will do no–"

"If you are missed at home, how will you explain your absence? he interrupted. "You could become a suspect when they discover two racehorses have vanished. If we are caught, you face judgement and punishment, you'll be a criminal, and your life as you know it will forever change. Your reputation…"

She didn't immediately reply, and he allowed her to reflect.

"Austin, she began, her voice merely above a whisper. "I was wrong and behaved like a selfish schoolgirl this afternoon. I thought only of myself. I, I, realised the hurt I caused you when I watched you walk away towards the road… I can't live with that. I knew then that I wanted to be part of your life." She took a steadying, deep breath. "Perhaps I am too forward and speak inappropriately, but how do you know how I feel or what is in my heart if I do not speak of these things to you?"

Austin couldn't find the words to reply and allowed her to continue without interrupting.

"Here, this evening, being with you and, …er, doing this," she laughed. "If we are to be together, then I accept that happily – and will be part of it, not just for tonight, but forever – if you'll have me."

"But Harriet, this isn't me, this isn't normal." He saw the wetness of her eyes as she stared up at him. "I only seek retribution

257

for the wrongs committed against my father. When this is over, then my life returns to normal."

She wiped away the tears. "Then that is what I want, Austin Willems."

The moon briefly appeared through the occasional gaps in the clouds, and Austin stared at her silhouette with his mouth open. Her directness and openness were unexpected, and if he understood her correctly, she'd just stated that she'd accept a marriage proposal. His heart raced. He closed his mouth as she approached him and lifted her chin. He saw the glint of moist eyes that reflected her feelings.

"Is that what you want?" she breathed.

Time seemed to stop as a thousand thoughts raced through his mind in an explosion of revelation, acceptance and emotion. For the briefest instant, he felt detached from his body and heard himself answer, "Yes."

He lowered his head, and their lips met. He felt it then as she pressed against him; it was complete emotional and physical surrender.

He wanted her here; he wanted her now, but he couldn't. "Harriet…" He swallowed. "We must continue; we have to leave."

She reluctantly pulled herself away, but she wasn't angry. "I know."

They still had some distance to cover, and he was conscious of tiring their horses. Once he'd delivered the thoroughbreds, they'd need to return as quickly as possible, and the goal had always been to be back in his bed before hotel staff went about their daily duties. It now seemed unlikely that would happen unless they could make time up.

They never rode faster than a slow canter, then slow, walk for a while, return to a canter and repeat the cycle. When walking, he and Harriet could converse, and he explained his concerns to her.

"And where are we going? Where will you take these prized valuable beasts?" she asked again.

"You will have to wait and see," he teased.

They were nearly there, and if everything went according to plan, they could return to Chieveley soon.

Although it was too dark to read, Austin knew the large sign stated 'The Queen's Own Hussars, Regimental Headquarters. It was with relief when he turned to Harriet, "We have arrived."

She pulled her horse to a stop beside him. "This is where you are leaving the horses?"

"And m'dear, do you know how many horses the regiment has?" He didn't wait for an answer and continued. "Even while the regiment is away, they still have almost a hundred, and these two beautiful beasts will blend in quite well for a week or so until I decide what to do with them."

"Oh my, Captain Willems, you are indeed a devious man," she stated with a laugh.

"Why thank you, Miss Stephenson, but now, I must hand them off. Can you hold them while I talk to the guard?"

Austin rode to the guard shack and explained who he sought. Immediately, one of the guards ran for the buildings as he anxiously fidgeted.

In a short time, the guard returned, followed by a dishevelled soldier. "Captain Willems, sir, I knows all about the 'orses and been told whats to do wif them. They'll be in good 'ands and no need to worry yerself," said the soldier with a thick London accent.

The guard returned to his post, uninterested.

"They couldn't be in better hands, Fitz."

The halter leads were handed over, and Austin watched as the soldier, leading two beautiful thoroughbred racehorses, walked into the darkness. He turned back to Harriet. "We must return as quickly as possible."

Sunlight speared over distant hills as Austin crept into his room exhausted. It had been quite a night. On the return ride, they'd encountered a few people, but no one had seen them with the thoroughbreds during the evening. This part of the plan worked well, and Austin was pleased. However, he found it difficult to focus on anything other than Harriet. What she'd said to him… it was astounding. She insisted that she would raise the alarm that the racehorses were missing under the guise of discovering empty stalls when going for an early morning ride—something she did frequently.

As arranged, he'd handed his horse to Peter, who would return the animal to its owner later in the morning. Then, he returned to his hotel, climbed the rope back into his room, and thoroughly cleaned himself. He was dressed appropriately, looking bleary-eyed and seated for breakfast at precisely 8.00 a.m..

After breakfast, he would call on Harriet Stephenson and her mother, Eunice Hewitt-Thompson, before departing for London on the afternoon train.

Elias Pickenbury was Windhaven's Stable Master and had held that esteemed role for many years after being promoted from head groom. He'd spent most of his life at the sprawling estate and was an intensely loyal and devoted employee.

His room was in the employee's hall and had a prime view of the service lane and the stables peeking out from above the hedgerows.

He could sleep undisturbed through a storm, but if any sound came from the stables that weren't part of any regular activity, he would wake and be instantly alert to any shenanigans that would invariably happen from time to time.

Last evening had been such a night, and Elias had awoken by a noise or noises. He wasn't sure what he'd heard and couldn't identify the cause, but fully aware that his stables housed extremely expensive racehorses, he dressed and dutifully ventured outside to investigate.

As any employee of such a grand estate will tell you, if the Master or Mistress wants something, if their needs are unexpected or peculiar, then it's the employee's responsibility to assist, be discrete and not ask questions. Elias crept unseen towards the stables with that awareness foremost on his mind. *Perhaps the Mistress or Miss Stephenson was at the stables and wanted privacy...*

As he silently approached, he stepped into the foliage of the hedgerow and waited. He heard voices and recognised Miss Stephenson's voice. He had a soft spot for the young lass. She always treated the horses kindly, had a gentle hand, and never spoke harshly to the horses or his staff. However, the same couldn't be said for her stepfather, Master Hewitt-Thompson.

He felt relieved when he recognised her voice. At least it wasn't someone up to no good, and at that time, he could have returned to his bed, but to be sure, he lingered a moment longer and saw the outline of a man and then, much to his horror, two horses on lead ropes. He couldn't tell which horses, and within moments, Miss Stephenson and the stranger had disappeared down the service lane, leading the two horses away.

Assured they wouldn't return and catch him, Elias ventured into the stables and quickly discovered two empty stalls. Prince and Honey were gone! Usually, if horses were to be relocated, someone would have spoken to him through the Estate Manager or directly from the Master. No one had spoken to him, and Elias was quite confused. As Miss Stephenson was involved, there must be a rational explanation, and Elias returned to his bed, somewhat confident all would become clear in the morning.

"Mr Pickenbury, Prince and Honey are not in their stalls. Do you know where they are?" Harriet dismounted and handed the reins to a waiting groom.

Elias lifted his hat and scratched his thinning palette. "Beggin' your pardon, Miss Stephenson," he shrugged. "Aye, they'd be gone." He looked at her closely, but she gave nothing away, nothing to indicate she'd been involved.

Harriet gave an appropriate look of concern. "Then Mr Pickenbury, I suggest we inform Mr Harkness of their disappearance, and he can notify the police."

Elias didn't move or respond as his mind was in a shambles. He wasn't sure if he should say anything to her about what he'd witnessed during the night. Mr Harkness was the estate manager, and once he became involved, all hell would be let loose.

"Mr Pickenbury?"

"Sorry, Miss. Aye, of course. I'll inform him now."

Harriet smiled. "Can you ask him if he could spare a moment and come see me after breakfast?"

Elias placed his hat back on his head and ran off to find Mr Harkness.

All of Windhaven's employees were fully aware of the relationship between their Master and Mistress. Gossip was rife, and word quickly spread of the latest beating Mrs Hewitt-Thompson had received from her husband. Support favoured Eunice, as most employees had run afoul of Sir Ronald's volatile temperament at one time or other, and all had complete sympathy for their Mistress, including Elias. Staff were generally pleased Sir Ronald had not been at Windhaven for some time, and all privately hoped it would remain that way.

Elias didn't consider himself a clever man; he wasn't educated but knew numbers and could write enough to get by, and he deduced if Miss Stephenson didn't want anyone to learn of her role in the horses' disappearance. He would keep his gob firmly shut and, for now and wouldn't say anything about what he'd witnessed.

CHAPTER TWENTY-EIGHT

Grand Overland Rail director Oscar Baker was in a foul mood and made no attempt to moderate his disposition, and was nothing short of rude to Detective Sergeant Barnabus Roggin. In fact, the timing of the interview was most unfortunate as all directors had arrived at the offices in response to Sir Ronald, who had some rather distressing news for them that would impact the company severely.

Three directors were impatiently waiting for the detective's interview with Oscar Baker to conclude in the conference room so they could have their unscheduled meeting.

As requested, Mr Baker provided an itemised list with a comprehensive description of each stolen painting from the storage warehouse to Detective Sergeant Roggin. The total value of the paintings stolen was enormous and he fought to remain impassive when he read the document. He quickly understood this wasn't a simple opportunistic theft, but a well planned heist.

His interview at Grand Overland Rail offices hadn't gone to plan and began late as another meeting in the conference room had not finished on time. When Detective Sergeant Roggin was finally allowed to begin his interview, the conference room was untidy and smelled of sweat and stale cigar smoke. In pursuit of his duties and responsibilities, the detective asked basic questions about who had keys, access to the paintings, and who knew that he stored fine art at Finch & Gossett's warehouse. While Mr Baker had been cooperative, as he should have, his attitude changed after constant interruptions by the other directors, and within a short time, Mr Baker's temper flared.

Initially, Detective Sergeant Roggin attempted to ignore the snippets of conversation he overheard from outside the room, but after a while, his curiosity took the better of him, and he recorded what he'd heard by making copious notes as he questioned Mr Baker.

It proved to be a fruitless exercise, and eventually, Mr Baker was less than kind and, through a litany of profanity, demanded the Detective Sergeant vacate the premises forthwith to locate the thieves and his precious paintings. Not wishing to further inflame the situation, he terminated the interview, exited the board room and loitered in the reception area, tidying his notes. He overheard more frantic chit-chat from employees before reluctantly departing and returning to the Bow Street station.

Detective Sergeant Barnabus Roggin knocked on the open door. "Detective Chief Inspector Bird? A moment of your time?"

With a loud sigh, the inspector looked up from the incident report he'd been reading, placed the document into a folder and waved the Detective Sergeant in.

"Sir," began Roggin, "I interviewed the victim, Mr. Oscar Baker, at the premises of Grand Overland Rail. If you recall, he had his art stolen from that warehouse in Marylebone." He handed his report, along with the inventory list given to him by Mr Baker, to the Detective Chief Inspector.

When he finished reading, the inspector whistled. "One hundred thousand pounds is substantial. Have you any leads? Seems to me it could be an inside job."

Detective Sergeant Roggin shook his head. "No, sir, nothing yet, and I concur, but there is something else."

Detective Chief Inspector Bird tore his eyes from the list of stolen art and looked at the young Detective Sergeant, who seemed quite agitated. "Continue."

The victim, Mr Baker, is a board member of Grand Overland Rail, and because of a number of, er, some unpleasant developments at the company, a meeting of some board members was called while I was there, and company directors began arriving. I was conducting my interview with Mr Baker in the board room, and the other directors were outside in the hall talking and carrying on, which escalated into shouting, sir." Detective Sergeant Roggin could see the Detective Chief Inspector was losing interest. "I overheard quite a bit, which included one of the directors, a Mr... uh, I have it here, sir..." Detective Sergeant Roggin referred to his notes. "A gentleman called Virgil, don't have his family name, sir, was grousing that his yacht called *Bell -sa* was sabotaged and destroyed–"

"*Belisha,*" interrupted Detective Chief Inspector Bird, his interest piqued, "The yacht is named *Belisha,* and its owner is Mr Virgil Hartman."

"Is this related to the recent fire at the moorings?" asked Roggin.

"Very much so. And?"

"Oh, er, but sir, I have more."

Detective Chief Inspector Bird sat a little straighter as the detective continued.

"Er, another board member, I know him only as Ronald, had two extremely valuable racehorses stolen from his country estate last evening. He was presented with the unfortunate news while I was there, and the man was quite upset."

"Understandably," replied the Detective Chief Inspector, "and no doubt the racehorses are worth a king's ransom?"

"Er, I believe so, sir." Detective Sergeant Roggin's expression changed, and he grinned. "Uh, Mr George Dillington, another board member, is presently seeking new lodgings. From what I gather, his wife discovered his numerous infidelities and not only demanded he vacate their home, but she also left him penniless, denying him access to her credit line. It appears, sir, that all four directors are victims."

Although the inspector did not mirror the Detective Sergeant's expression, he did scratch his nose. "Have you more, Detective Sergeant?"

"I'm uncertain, sir. I only heard portions of the conversation, and I believe this was the main reason for calling the board meeting. Grand Overland Rail was expecting an influx of capital from a potential investor. The investor withdrew his interest and pulled out, and, accordingly, Grand Overland Rail is in a financial bind of sorts. They're unable to meet their financial obligations for some sort of expansion. That's all I know, sir."

Detective Chief Inspector Bird leaned back in his chair, steepled both hands beneath his chin and considered what he'd just heard. It began with a slight nodding of his head and developed into a vigorous up-and-down bobbing. "Excellent work, Detective Sergeant." The head bouncing stopped. "From what you've told me, it seems a group, perhaps a gang, has targeted this railway company and its principals. Perhaps they seek its demise, could be a competitor, or an aggrieved customer, and we must find out who. That could be our biggest lead. We know that rail businesses are fiercely competitive... Did you happen to learn where the racehorses are kept? Here in London?"

"I think I overheard Chieveley, sir. The gentleman called Ronald has a country estate there."

"I see. Then I presume this gang is well-funded and organised." The Detective Chief Inspector leaned forward and scrawled a few notes. "I will make an inquiry to Chieveley and obtain a copy of the police report on the missing horses. Meanwhile, Detective Sergeant

Roggin, you will find out all you can about this railway company and its directors because there may be more unpleasant incidents that will befall them."

"As you wish, sir."

"Inquire. Has the railway company made any enemies of late? These isolated events are not a coincidence, Detective. Whoever is behind these crimes has a motive, as they certainly aren't crimes of opportunity. They were well crafted and seem scrupulously planned if my knowledge of the *Belisha's* fire proves useful."

"Very well, sir. And sir?"

Detective Chief Inspector Bird looked up.

"My other duties?"

"I'm sure you'll find the time and adapt, Detective Sergeant. That will be all."

Sir Ronald's fist slammed onto the conference table with a bang. Cups in saucers rattled, and the three board members recoiled at the managing director's aggression. His face was crimson, and spittle gathered on his walrus moustache and at the corners of his mouth as his tirade went unchecked. "No, there will not be a disbursement of funds. London Private Acquisitions is not liquid and has no capital, George. Like the rest of us, you'll have to make do!"

"I'm destitute. Penniless. I have nothing," George Dillington appealed.

"Stay at that little love nest of yours in Soho," suggested Oscar Baker. "Then you can gorge yourself in sex as you think of a way to have Pearl take you back."

George Dillington looked like he would explode. Stretched tightly over his ample stomach, his vest appeared to have reached the limit of its durability as buttons threatened to ricochet across the board room. His face, distorted in anger and as red as Sir Ronald's, made his eyes appear small and beady as he glared at Oscar in pure, unfiltered rage. "How dare you speak to me in such a manner. I'll have you know, SIR!" he yelled, "the ownership deed to that residence is in my wife's name. I can no longer avail myself of its amenities. So kindly keep your sentiments to yourself, perhaps your time would be better suited to better management of your artwork," George sneered. His face remained unnaturally red as he seethed.

Oscar Baker shot to his feet. "I will not be–"

"Enough!" bellowed Sir Ronald. "We need to find another investor."

"What about Watson Coach Builders?" Virgil asked.

"I have received word they have no intention of investing in us," Sir Ronald replied.

George glared at Sir Ronald. "Who has done this to us? Why have the Watson Brothers reneged on their deal? Can anyone illuminate me?" He searched the faces of the three board members. They all shook their heads.

Sir Ronald continued, "We've all had something taken from us, and we will find a way to recover. Now, we must regroup, focus and find out who is behind it all."

"Are you suggesting the Watson Brothers and the destruction of my *Belisha* are tied together?" asked Virgil Hartman.

Sir Ronald shrugged. "Perhaps. Is it a mere coincidence?"

"Have you spoken to the Chairman?" Oscar asked.

The room fell silent, and Sir Ronald paused before answering. "Only through a missive I just received." He paused to collect himself. "I'm told the Watson Brothers never intended to invest."

"No!" retorted Oscar Baker.

Sir Ronald cleared his throat. "The Chairman is adamant we must find another investor. Although I'm sure he'll summon me to provide an accounting," he replied in a more subdued voice.

"At least his wealth wasn't taken," quipped Virgil.

George laughed but not in humour.

"You all sit here with priggish expressions, yet you have no notion of my financial state. My yacht represented my life. *Belisha* recently underwent a refit, which cost a fortune, and now she's gone, sitting as an abandoned, blackened hulk on the bed of the Thames. I may not benefit from a wealthy spouse," he looked at George Dillington, who was still breathing heavily across from him and then at Sir Ronald. "But my finances are limited, and I cannot continue. I just can't, I can't." he shook his head in despair.

"I'll tell you what we aren't going to do. We will not sit back and do nothing," declared Sir Ronald. "I propose we allow Mr De Vore to dirty his hands. He has the connections and the resources to investigate on our behalf. Whoever did this left clues, and by all that I deem holy, I will go to the farthest corners of this earth to find them, and when I do, they will suffer."

No one reacted to the managing director's impassioned speech. Again, he turned to each face for support. One by one, they nodded. "If you have business with me, speak now, for I will meet with Mr De Vore, and later tonight, I leave for Windhaven."

"Going to look for your nags?" George asked.

Sir Ronald stood, placed both hands on the table and leaned towards George. "Because London Private Acquisitions has no capital and we aren't receiving our expected disbursement, I need to put Windhaven on the market. Like you, George, I have little available resources and have no clear option but to sell my country estate and stock." Without another word, he straightened and stormed from the board room.

"Perhaps, gentlemen, Grand Overland Rail should consider liquidating some of its assets," simply stated Virgil Hartman.

A short time later, Sir Ronald was at Whites Gentleman's Club enjoying a brandy to ease the accumulated tension while he waited for Mr De Vore. He was on his second refill when the lanky form of the solicitor loomed over him.

"Be seated, Mr De Vore, and don't bother ordering a beverage; you won't be here long."

Julian folded himself into the armchair and kept his expression neutral. From Sir Ronald's demeanour, something was up, and he was instantly on guard. He didn't offer a greeting, looked at Grand Overland Rail's managing director, and waited.

"We have a problem, Mr De Vore."

We? Silently questioned Julian.

"We have been attacked. Last evening, two of my best and most valuable racehorses were stolen from my country estate. Mr Dillington was challenged by his wife about his extramarital activities, and she promptly requested he leave their home and withdrew access to funds and the allowance he normally receives."

Julian De Vore instantly thought about his recent spate of bad luck.

"Are you listening, Mr De Vore?"

"Please continue." Julian's eyebrows furrowed as Sir Ronald Hewitt-Thompson pressed on.

"Mr Hartman had his yacht destroyed at Tower Bridge Mooring–"

"The same yacht that spectacularly caught fire on the Thames?" asked Julian.

"The very same." Ronald paused and downed what remained of his brandy. He caught the attention of an attendant and had his glass refilled. "To add to the crime spree, Mr Baker's fine art collection was stolen from a secure warehouse." Sir Ronald shook his head. "And if that wasn't enough, the Watson brothers reneged on the investment opportunity."

Julian swallowed. This didn't bode well at all. "Good heavens," he squeaked after suddenly losing his voice.

Sir Ronald swivelled his head to glance around the room to ensure no one was eavesdropping. He leaned towards the solicitor. "You will make enquiries you deem necessary, determine who did this to us, and report back to me soonest. Is that clear, Mr De Vore?"

Julian nodded enthusiastically. "Oh yes, perfectly clear."

"Use whatever resources you have at your disposal, I-don't-care how you do it, just find out. I'll be in Chieveley for the next few days; if it's urgent, send a message."

Sir Ronald rose from his seat, and Julian followed suit, unwinding himself from the armchair and facing the railwayman. "I'll get to the bottom of this, sir. Trust me."

"Oh, I do trust you Mr De Vore, I do."

Sir Ronald took an uncertain step, recovered quickly and exited White's gentleman's lounge. When it was safe, Julian lowered himself back onto the chair and rubbed his chin. Sir Ronald didn't know those attacks weren't just directed at Grand Overland Rail or its board members. The attacks also extended to him, and he believed the perpetrator was none other than Captain Austin Willems.

CHAPTER TWENTY-NINE

On Harriet's urging, Austin decided to stay in Chieveley for the next few days. No pressing business in London required his attention, and after their candid discussion the other night, he was keen to delve deeper and learn more about Harriet's thoughts and where he fit into her plans. He also needed time to digest what she'd revealed about her feelings towards him.

Chieveley was peaceful. He kept his hotel room, and when he was there, it offered him time to reflect and think about his future. Something he'd previously been reluctant to do until he'd fulfilled his promise to exact retribution on the directors of Grand Overland Rail.

The police had come and gone and been diligent and thorough in interviewing everyone about the theft of the racehorses. The first employee they spoke to was Windhaven's Stable Master, Elias Pickenbury.

Elias had a sleepless night as he tried to make sense of the theft and what he'd say when the police came. He knew that what he witnessed could implicate young Harriet Stephenson and her consort, Captain Willems and that placed him in an unenviable dilemma.

Stacey, one of the cooks, inadvertently provided the solution for him at breakfast. She'd vehemently spoken out against the violent behaviour of their Master, Sir Ronald, in the privacy of her kitchen. The physical marks on the face of the mistress, Mrs Hewitt-Thompson, were a frequent topic of healthy conversation amongst staff, and most felt sympathy for the mistress and what she'd endured. Additionally, the master had demonstrated his aggressiveness to many employees and, on numerous occasions, been most unkind. When the master was absent, as he was now, things ran smoothly; everyone was happy, and no one was in fear.

Stacey said without reservation, "My loyalties lie with the mistress, and I couldn't care less if the master never came back." She waved a kitchen knife in the air like a weapon. "He's a bully he is. A'fore my James ran off with that floozie, he used to beat me senseless an' for no reason at all. If the law ain't gonna protect us, who will, Mr Pickenbury? That's the last I'll say on the matter." With some pent-up aggression, she continued slaughtering carrots in preparation for tonight's dinner.

Elias silently agreed. The master had been boorish to most staff at Windhaven, and Stacey had stated the obvious: Sir Ronald is a bully. It was undeniable. *Suppose Miss Harriet was involved in a scheme to hurt the master somehow. Then, I'd prefer to keep my trap shut and stay outa trouble,* he wisely thought.

Later that morning, when the police questioned him, he never mentioned what he saw.

"The police are none the wiser, Mama," Harriet said. "The detective told me there is no logical explanation why anyone would steal those horses. No one saw or heard anything."

Eunice Hewitt-Thompson looked up from her embroidery. "The theft makes me uncomfortable; what next will they take?" she asked.

Austin felt awkward and was about to offer a comforting remark when a house servant entered the parlour and said, "Ma'am, Sir Ronald is arriving."

Austin saw Harriet's mother's immediate reaction.

Eunice recovered quickly. "Thank you, Amelia," she said, touching her chest.

The servant girl dipped her head and silently left the room.

Harriet reacted quickly. "Come Austin, let's enjoy the garden, shall we?"

Austin needed no urging, and he didn't want to be near Harriet's stepfather as he feared that while sober, he may recall his face from his visits to White's Gentleman's Club. Something he'd previously spoken to Harriet about.

They'd just left the parlour when the door was thrust open, and Sir Ronald stepped in.

"Why is he here?" Austin asked when they were outside in the garden and could talk freely without being overheard. "Because of the horses?"

Harriet shrugged. "I have no notion. But most likely, it will be about Windhaven and money."

Austin could see Harriet looked apprehensive. He squeezed her hand. "Nothing will happen to you while I'm here," he reassured.

"I'm concerned for Mama, Austin." She looked into his eyes, and he could see how worried she was.

"Let's not wander far, eh? That way, if needed, I will be close."

Harriet looked over her shoulder back towards the house.

They began to walk back and sit beneath the pagoda when they heard loud voices. It was unmistakable, Sir Ronald's voice thundered.

It was embarrassing, and he felt pity for Harriet and her mother.

Her stepfather had only just arrived and, within minutes, was already in a loud argument with his wife.

"You *will* sell Windhaven! I am your husband, and you *will* do as you're bloody told!"

"Leave!" was Eunice's stressed reply that drifted out to them.

Harriet turned to Austin. "He will hurt her, and this is how it always begins." She released his hand and brought her hands to her face as she began to weep.

He was in a quandary. Ronald Hewitt-Thompson's behaviour went against everything he believed in, and he fought the urge to rush in and come to Eunice's aid. However, while they argued, it was none of his business. He couldn't interfere. If Sir Ronald struck his wife and beat her, then Austin felt he had a moral obligation to come to her assistance at the risk of being recognised, but he didn't want to wait until she was beaten.

The argument continued and escalated. "Let me go!"

Austin had heard enough. "Stay here, Harriet."

With his jaw clenched, he ran inside towards the parlour. He passed two house servants who stood with heads buried in their hands, sobbing. "Go to the kitchen," he instructed them as he ran past.

He stopped at the open door and looked into the room just as Sir Ronald grabbed his wife, hauling her roughly upright from the chair she sat on.

"You will sell if it's the last bloody thing you ever do!" he struck her on the cheek with a an open hand. It was a firm slap, delivered by a grossly overweight man with no skills, which knocked her backwards to collapse on the floor. He never heard Austin step up behind him as he glared at his wife in pure hatred. "You trollop!" he spat as he stood threateningly over her with both fists clenched.

Sir Ronald never saw the person who hit him. One moment, he

was standing over his wife, ready to deliver another thrashing; the next thing, he was opening his eyes and being manhandled into a coach. Waves of intense pain washed over him, and his vision blurred. He couldn't think. Nothing made sense… his mind addled. He closed his eyes and allowed his body to succumb to darkness.

With the help of three stout men, all Windhaven employees, Austin deposited Sir Ronald on the coach's seat. Before closing the door, Austin placed a hastily written note into Sir Ronald's pocket. With the door shut, he signalled the coachman to depart. With a healthy gratuity, the coachman was instructed not to converse with his passenger and deliver him to the railway station, leaving him there. Under no circumstances was the coachman to return to Windhaven with his passenger.

Austin turned to the three men who stood with hands on their thighs, breathing hard. "Do not speak of this to anyone. If Sir Ronald learns of your names, your livelihoods could be in jeopardy." The men looked genuinely fearful, and he doubted they would talk.

Eunice had been assisted to her bedroom and attended by one of her staff.

"Is she badly hurt?" Austin asked when Harriet returned downstairs.

"This can't continue, Austin." She sat beside him. "She will have swelling and bruises, but the damage is more than physical."

"I'm sorry I couldn't prevent him from hitting her, Harriet."

"And I'm grateful you did what you did. I only hope it doesn't happen again," she added. "He's such a, a, Pig!"

"I left a note in his pocket, a warning."

She looked at him and smiled, then leaned forward, her lips inviting him to kiss.

Sir Ronald Hewitt-Thompson returned to London somewhat worse for wear. He sported a large purple bruise accompanied by swelling around his right eye. Someone unseen had struck him on the right side of his head, and from the pain and aftereffects, he determined it must have been from a candle holder or club. He didn't know who the thug was that assaulted him, but he'd discovered the hastily written note in his pocket while waiting for the London train which simply said, *Stay away or suffer worse*. It gave him a chill and robbed him of any self-confidence. The handwriting was unfamiliar and could easily have been a Windhaven staff member, but Ronald freely admitted to himself that he wasn't a brave man, and the thought of returning to Windhaven to receive another thrashing had no appeal. For the moment, he had a rather severe headache, and from time to time, his vision blurred. He'd called for a doctor and was expecting him soon.

He was seated on his bed when he heard the door chime and was pleased the doctor had come quickly.

"Excuse me, sir, you have received a message. I have left it downstairs on your desk," informed the servant.

Ronald Hewitt-Thompson opened his eyes and groaned. "Bring it here, and be quick about it." With his fingers, he massaged the bridge of his nose as the feeling of nausea enveloped him.

"As you wish, sir," replied the servant, who quickly disappeared.

When the servant returned, he was instructed to read it aloud.

"Of course, sir. Er, uh … attend to me tomorrow, at the usual place, usual time. Er, that's all, sir." The servant flipped the paper over to see if anything more was written on the back. Seeing it was blank, he folded the note and handed it to his master.

"That will be all," replied Sir Ronald as his stomach tightened.

The Chairman had summoned him. He vomited.

Sir Ronald wiped his mouth with a cloth and focused on what remained of the day and what he needed to do before he met with the Chairman. The directors had named the secretive individual who provided guidance, resources and protection to their shady activities as the 'Chairman'. Only Sir Ronald knew the real identity of their benefactor and, by the Chairman's explicit wishes, kept it that way. In return for their successful business enterprises, their benefactor received a healthy stipend. The regular payments weren't negotiable and were a required and necessary expense. Typically, the directors were ambivalent about those remittances. However, at their last meeting, two directors wanted to defer payment as it was a hefty sum and that money represented the last of their disposable cash reserves.

Sir Ronald shuddered at the thought. He knew their benefactor was a powerful and influential man, and if he caught wind of any plan to withhold money, retribution would be swift and inevitable.

Before meeting the Chairman, he needed to speak with Julian De Vore, as the solicitor facilitated the payments to their benefactor and needed authorisation. But Grand Overland Rail's managing director also wanted updating on any developments on who was behind the recent thefts and attacks. With a sour taste lingering in his mouth, he scrawled a quick note requesting a meeting around 11.00 a.m. and, through a messenger, sent it to the solicitor's office.

The wood-panelled room wasn't lavish by any stretch of the imagination. The walls were covered in paper and bulletins, mostly notices and updates of policy changes typical of a metropolitan police department. At one end, two filthy windows allowed filtered light to illuminate the room, but no abundance of daylight could ever add cheer to the gloomy space. The room's centrepiece was a sizeable, unimpressive table. Adding to its lacklustre, less than magnificent appearance, it was covered in scratches, ink spills, and other marks, their provenance long forgotten. Mismatched chairs were placed around the table, and usually, they were always a few short when a meeting was called, but today, chairs were plentiful as only two were occupied. Detective Chief Inspector Tobias Bird and Detective Sergeant Barnabus Roggin were seated, discussing and disseminating the recent events that had befallen Grand Overland Rail's board of directors.

It was too early for the Detective Chief Inspector to draw formal conclusions from all the information he'd received. However, as he enjoyed doing, Detective Chief Inspector Bird espoused various improbable scenarios and sought evidence to support them. It wasn't unheard of for the inspector's fertile mind to solve a perplexing riddle, and he tested the young and pliant detective sergeant with a barrage of unsupported presumptions.

To his credit, and as time passed, Barnabus felt less intimidated by his superior, forcing the Detective Chief Inspector to think more carefully before allowing his subordinate to pick holes in his fanciful stratagems. Detective Chief Inspector Bird wouldn't admit to it for the present, but he found the Detective Sergeant's mind to be agile, logical, and quite astute.

"Think back to when you were interviewing Oscar Baker; what did you overhear – what did you see? Were there documents you saw? There must have been something?" prompted the detective chief inspector.

"When I began the interview, the conference room had just been vacated because another meeting had just finished, and the room was untidy. No one came in to clean it. There were documents. If I recall correctly, there was a tray that contained papers; they were of a legal nature, and I felt it inappropriate to read them."

"But you did, didn't you," encouraged the Detective Chief Inspector. "You couldn't resist,' he grinned.

Barnabus paused. "Not so much read, sir. But er, I did glance."

"Of course you did. You are naturally inquisitive, and the temptation was too much." Detective Chief Inspector Bird leaned forward and placed his arms on the table. "What was the nature of those documents, Detective?"

Detective Sergeant Roggin exhaled slowly. 'I recall something about a labour agreement. It was about a planned agreement. I know it was legal because, at the bottom of the document, it had a bright red stamp; perhaps from a lawyer or someone."

"A lawyer or a solicitor," clarified the Detective Chief Inspector. "Was it an official court document because you've seen them a plenty?"

"No, sir, not a court document. The name at the bottom was Justice or Justine D–Vo–"

"Perhaps it isn't important," the Detective Chief Inspector reassured his subordinate and scribbled notes into his notebook, writing *D.V – Lawyer, Solicitor*?

"Can you identify and name everyone you saw at Grand Overland Rail's offices? An employee probably has a grudge," he continued.

Detective Sergeant Roggin shook his head. "All employees I spoke to were rather circumspect. I believe the managing director runs a tight ship, values loyalty and does not suffer torpor or fools, sir."

'That in itself could be a reason…" began the Detective Chief Inspector as he began to outline another supposition. "An aggrieved employee, seeking revenge…" After a moment's pause, he shook his head. "Most unlikely, it would need to be a major incident for an employee to go to such great length and expense to satisfy minor offended sensitivities. And you've determined there were no recent altercations with employees…" Detective Chief Inspector Bird shuffled some papers. "This is what I require you to do, Detective."

CHAPTER THIRTY

Austin decided to return to London as Harriet needed to look after her mother, and he didn't want to loiter in Chieveley if Sir Ronald discovered who assaulted him and lodged a formal complaint with the police. Although he didn't fear the man, it was prudent to keep Howard appraised of these unfortunate developments, and his counsel was appreciated. There were other matters to attend to that required his attention, and he departed Chieveley with assurances from Harriet and her mother that they were quite safe from harm and Sir Ronald was unlikely to return.

The injuries sustained by Eunice would heal, and Harriet promised to return to London as soon as conveniently possible. Her main concern was for her mother's emotional well-being. The swelling and discolouration to her face would disappear, and the emotional scars may never heal, she'd explained to Austin. On consultation with a doctor, a nurse was hired to care for Eunice, but Harriet was reluctant to leave until her mother was again stable.

They said their tearful goodbyes, and Austin boarded the train for London, wondering when he'd see her again.

Nanny was overjoyed to see him when he returned home and chastised him for not informing her of his whereabouts or plans. "How can I run a household when I don't know if and when you'll return, sir?" she scolded.

Austin hugged her, "I missed you too, Nanny, and I promise to let you know in future," he reassured. "I'd like to invite Howard for dinner this evening. Do you have time to prepare something special?"

Her expression changed. "Indeed, sir, do you have anything in mind?" she beamed.

"No, I'll leave it up to you, Nanny."

"Then I need to get busy, sir."

A Hansom cab stopped outside The Carlton Club at 94 Pall Mall in London and a helpful concierge rushed over to open the door and offer assistance so the solitary gentleman inside could alight. Sir Ronald, conscious of the bruising on the side of his face, stepped from the coach and entered the premises, and while not a club member, he identified himself and was escorted upstairs to meet Sir Felix Dampierre or, as he was known, the Chairman.

The tastefully decorated room did not exude opulence, but certainly, it was understated comfort, hosting two large fireplaces and attentive staff to cater to the needs of its exclusive clientele. Approximately twenty chairs were arranged in small groups throughout the room, and seven were presently occupied. As usual, the gentleman he sought was seated in a corner on a comfortable green leather chair and far enough away for conversations not to be overheard. Typically, Sir Felix was immaculately dressed and groomed. His expensive clothes were tailored to suit his trim physique and six-foot, two-inch frame, and even from a distance, Sir Ronald could see the abundance of arrogant confidence that oozed from every pore of his body. He intensely disliked and feared the man he was about to meet.

A white-gloved attendant greeted him with a smile. "This way, sir."

Sir Ronald reluctantly followed a step behind the young man towards the far corner of the room and passed by hunched club members deep in subdued conversations. He recognised the faces of many and knew them to be politicians, and immediately, he wondered what devious plans were being concocted that would affect his business interests. Sir Ronald had no affinity for politics and was naturally distrustful of these well-heeled, shifty-eyed servants of the Crown who could radically change his fortunes with a simple pen stroke. This was not the place to be; he was more comfortable in the world of commerce and enterprise and like-minded entrepreneurs with a penchant for making money – not policy.

'Sir Felix, your guest has arrived," stated the attendant.

Sir Felix waved an arm toward a chair and placed a cigar securely between his lips before striking a match.

"Would you care for a beverage?" the young attendant asked.

Sir Felix managed to nod before his face disappeared into a cloud of blue smoke.

"Brandy," stated Sir Ronald as he descended into the green upholstered wing-backed chair.

"Of course, sir," stated the attendant before quickly bowing his head and backing away.

Out of habit, Sir Ronald tweaked his walrus moustache and focused on his host. There was a fastidiousness about the man that made him feel wary. It wasn't his impeccable sense of style; it was how he overtly scrutinised people like he was assessing them for flaws, weaknesses and for the opportunity to devour.

"You know, they say these cigars are rolled on the inside thigh of a virgin," Sir Felix began after pulling his gaze from the attendant and giving his full attention to the glowing tip of his expensive indulgence.

Grand Overland Rail's managing director adjusted his seating position to the accompanying sound of creaking leather and looked away from the man. Making eye contact was like admitting weakness and exposing his failings. He said nothing allowing Sir Felix to continue.

"I daresay, and I wonder if anyone would notice if it were rolled on the wrinkly thigh of a crone," he added before tearing his eyes from the cigar and focusing on his guest. "Do you think people are aware of small details, Ronnie?" He raised a single eyebrow in question before continuing. "I mean, the minor things."

Sir Ronald reluctantly turned his head back and found the unblinking scrutiny unwavering. He compressed his lips in unease and growing tension as he considered his reply. "No, I believe people see only what they want to see."

Sir Felix gently exhaled a lengthy stream of smoke before replying. "And pray tell, what do you see, for the question I ask is, do you see what I see?"

Beverages arrived, and Sir Ronald wasted no time raising the glass to his lips and enjoying a healthy sip to calm fraying nerves. "Yes, we see the same, although past experiences influence our judgement. Is this not so?"

Sir Felix laughed, but his controlled outburst contained no mirth. "Oh, I doubt it, Ronnie. Let me tell you what I see. I see a man floundering on the brink of financial collapse, and the company he's been delegated to manage will soon follow suit. I see its trusted board of directors scrambling to unflatteringly comprehend some minor inconveniences that have suddenly befallen them..." Sir Felix shook his head in mock sympathy. "And selfishly put themselves before their responsibilities to govern Grand Overland Rail. What say you, Ronnie? How do you respond?"

Sir Ronald was taken aback. *How did he know? Who told him?* This was serious. He put the glass to his mouth and took another generous sip of brandy; its slow burn offered a little measure of comfort but no respite. "We are all dealing with the thefts. It's a temporary setback, sir. It caught us by surprise, and we are responding accordingly–"

"–At what cost?" interrupted Sir Felix. "And let me inform you, there will be a quick and decisive response, but not by you. Oh no, no, I am losing faith in your abilities and will manage our retaliation myself." He brought the cigar to his lips and, with a pucker, drew in the smoke. He held it briefly, enjoying its full-bodied flavour before releasing it. His eyes narrowed as he again made eye contact with his guest. "And as you sit here squirming like a school girl before an unyielding teacher, your nemesis remains unknown to you and continues – unabated and unpunished."

"I, I cannot take action if I don't know who is behind these incidents," proclaimed Sir Ronald a bit louder than he intended.

"Decorum, Ronnie, show some self-discipline," warned Sir Felix as a few curious heads turned in their direction.

"The matter is being investigated, and I will soon learn who is behind these deeds," continued Sir Ronald in a more moderated voice.

"Like, who hit you?" Sir Felix asked, pointing his cigar accusingly at the discolouration on Hewitt-Thompson's face.

"A minor altercation of no consequence," he responded testily and turned his face, self-consciously away from his host.

"While you wallow in self-pity and Grand Overland Rail flounders on the brink of ruin, I have taken appropriate steps and will, from this point forward, deal with this so you can, and will, focus on putting things in order with Grand Overland Rail and London Private Acquisitions. As public opinion sways on this, political perspectives also change." He leaned over and pointed his cigar at Sir Ronald. "You, Ronnie, will ensure no loose ends remain.

I want a most fruitful and productive conclusion that will hold up under a robust criminal or political inquiry. Am I understood, Ronnie?"

Sir Ronald looked beaten.

Sir Felix's eyes darted around the room before settling on Grand Overland Rails' managing director. "Yes, I have learned who is behind these personal attacks, and I will take steps to safeguard our venture so it doesn't continue. I will end them once and for all."

Sir Ronald stared at the rich textures of the navy-blue carpet and jerked his head up at the revelation. "Who, who did these unspeakable things?"

Sir Felix leaned forward in his chair, gently placed the cigar into the ashtray and carefully tapped it with his manicured finger. With the excess ash removed, he glared at his guest with piercing blue eyes. "Captain Austin Willems."

Sir Ronald's eyebrows furrowed together. "Willems? Enoch Willems, son? How do you know?" It dawned on him then, Julian De Vore. The solicitor was acquainted with Sir Felix, and it was Sir Felix who'd made the initial introductions and recommended the services of De Vore. *De Vore must have told him,* he thought. Then, another memory invaded his consciousness. Captain Willems was calling on his stepdaughter. He'd never devoted time to thinking about her or what she did with her life. But now he wished he'd had and felt his cheeks colour as rage threatened to consume him.

"Settle down, Ronnie, have a drink. I can't have you going off half-cocked."

Sir Ronald needed no further urging and downed what remained of his brandy.

"There is another most important matter, Ronnie," began Sir Felix after closely inspecting his cigar. "De Vore informs me there has been a delay in my payment…"

"Yes, a few details required clarifying, but all is well."

"See it doesn't happen again, eh? I am on a strict timetable, and it is most imperative that Grand Overland Rail begins work on the Swindon to London line within the next three months."

Sir Ronald looked puzzled. "This is a new development. Why, what has changed, Sir Felix?"

"Because, dear Ronnie, I will side with my Minister in support of a new bill in Parliament to protect registered companies with limited liability."

"What!" Sir Ronald blurted out. As before, a few heads in the room turned to look. "You can't be serious." He shook his head in disbelief. "Liability is the basis of how we have succeeded, and you are killing the golden goose."

Sir Felix toyed with a piece of tobacco caught on his lip as he considered his response. Coming to a decision, he removed the offending fleck and leaned forward. "The bill, the Limited Liability Act, will pass. We have gained a timely advantage, albeit temporary, and when that door closes, Grand Overland Rail must be liquid and managed without reservation." Sir Felix was enveloped in another cloud of smoke. He knew Sir Ronald was no longer up to the task, but he'd deal with that on his terms.

"But that was never the plan, and we discussed this."

"Times change, Ronnie, and we must adapt accordingly."

An attendant made his presence known and stepped up to Sir Felix. "Your table is ready, sir."

"Thank you." Sir Felix licked his lips and turned back to his guest. "How timely, dinner." He smiled. "Lovely to see you, Ronnie. We must chat more often. Please give my regards to your wife, and I hope she recovers quickly." His smile disappeared, and he held eye contact for a moment.

Before Sir Ronald Hewitt-Thompson could respond, Sir Felix

jammed the cigar into the ashtray in a shower of sparks, stood and walked from the room. Through his stately position and out of respect, other members paused from their hushed conversations and nodded as he glided past.

Sir Ronald watched Sir Felix walk away. He was in an unenviable bind, and without consultation, Sir Felix had imposed an unfair deadline on him. By the end of the year, laws would change that would offer companies liability protection. Purely from a business perspective, he thought it was a good thing. However, he and his associates took advantage of current laws that allowed them to bilk investors from enormous sums of money, which would soon be no longer possible. The goose that laid the golden egg was dead.

As of today, Grand Overland Rail and their shadowy company, London Private Acquisitions, were not liquid; they had no cash reserves, and neither did the other principals, Virgil Hartman, Oscar Baker, George Dillington, and himself, although he had no idea of Sir Felix's financial position.

Over the last few years, they lavished on their ill-gotten gains. They spent enormous sums of money on lifestyles they'd become accustomed to by purchasing expensive yachts, art, racehorses and extravagant lifestyles. And now that had all come to an end. On a primarily reduced income, they couldn't maintain the cost of their exorbitant lifestyle unless they liquidated assets.

Options had been available to purchase assurances that if assets were lost or destroyed, the policyholder would receive recompense on a pre-determined and agreed-upon value. Assurance companies had deemed that racehorses, fine art and yachts were high risk and that premiums to purchase assurances were unrealistically high. No one had believed it worthwhile, and they, he included, had foolishly declined that protection.

Sir Ronald tweaked his walrus moustache and wondered how to convince his wife to sell Windhaven. Perhaps he wouldn't have to directly approach her with his demand and put that quandary in the hands of his solicitor. It would give him something useful to do for a change. Marrying Eunice gave him financial control over Windhaven, and he knew the courts would rule favourably.

Legal action was a last resort, something he'd been reluctant to do because it only drew attention to himself, and people would ask, why? Why was it so important to sell Windhaven? London society would conclude that he needed the money, and therefore, Grand Overland Rail was not profitable, and this would reflect poorly on his professional reputation and character.

He had no alternative and would seek immediate legal counsel. If an arrangement could be made out of court, a settlement agreement, then his name and good standing may never be questioned. He needed someone willing to dirty their hands, and only one name came to mind. He would seek an appointment with the gangly solicitor as soon as possible.

He rose from the comfort of the green leather armchair and wandered from The Carlton Club, thinking about how that bastard, Captain Austin Willems, had deceived them all.

CHAPTER THIRTY–ONE

Howard Willoughby listened intently as Austin detailed how he and Harriet managed to take the racehorses from Windhaven without being seen, but his demeanour soured when Austin recounted the abuse Harriet's mother received from the hand of her husband.

"Most unfortunately, Sir Ronald has the full support of the law, Austin." Howard dabbed at the corners of his mouth with a napkin. "Of course, there are always exceptions, and without speaking to her, Harriet's mother has little recourse."

"Then why resort to beating her?" Austin asked.

"Why do men beat their wives, Austin?" Howard quickly replied.

Austin was saved from answering when Nanny entered the dining room.

"Do you have room for pudding?" she asked.

Howard patted his stomach, "If prepared by you, then by the Gods, I'll find room," he stated with a warm smile.

Austin watched the interaction. Nanny always blushed when complimented by Howard, and typically, he noticed, she'd prepared his favourite dish. His charms provided results. He smiled as she carried away empty plates.

"What will you do now, Austin? What's the next step in your audacious plan?" Howard asked. "You hurt Grand Overland Rail and their directors with a mortal blow. Do you intend to take further action?"

Austin's expression changed as he leaned forward. "That's what I wanted to discuss. I want you to find a suitable solicitor with no ties to me, you, Father, or Midlands Collieries Company. Use your discretion, Howard, but whoever you select cannot be linked to me."

Howard's eyes opened wide as Austin continued.

"This solicitor's primary task is to monitor Grand Overland Rail and, at the appropriate time, make a low-undervalued offer to purchase Midlands Collieries Company. I expect they will need an influx of capital, and even a low offer may be enough to entice them to accept."

"We'll need to review your finances and determine your limit," advised Howard.

"It won't be an issue, I can promise you that," Austin grinned. "It's important to obtain father's company at a much lower price than they paid for it without Hewitt-Thompson learning who the purchaser is. This time I will be the undisclosed principal." Austin leaned back in his chair with a satisfied smile as Nanny returned with dessert. "Can you begin to find a trustworthy solicitor next week?"

"Aye, and I think I have just the person," added Howard as he stared at dessert.

Both men looked up as they heard the door chime.

"I wonder who that could be?" queried Austin.

A moment later, Nanny appeared. "Sir, you have a caller."

Detective Sergeant Roggin waited until he saw Chief Detective Inspector Bird was alone in his office before he knocked.

"What is it?" growled the inspector without looking up.

"Er, sir, I have a name."

"Of course you have a name—"

"Forgive me, perhaps a name to link Major Miles Siles to the murderer, sir," informed the young detective.

The inspector looked up. "…and?"

Detective Sergeant Roggin stood a little straighter. "Captain Austin Willems, sir."

The inspector didn't react. "Well, then, are you going to keep me in suspense? How did you come by this name, as I have never heard of him?"

"It's in my report, sir."

"Your words, Detective. Tell me." Chief Detective Inspector Bird ignored the report on his desk, leaned back in his chair, and as he habitually did, steepled both hands beneath his chin.

"Of course, sir. You'll remember we identified a lad, Cat, who was seen running from the crime scene. It turns out he got caught red-handed trying to stick his filthy mitts into the pocket of a topper. The victim held fast to the boy's wrist and dragged him, kicking and screaming, to the station. The detective knew I'd previously asked about Cat and sent for me."

"And you interrogated the boy?" the inspector asked.

"Yes, sir, but to no avail. He wouldn't say a word, kept his trap firmly shut."

Chief Detective Inspector Bird raised a single eyebrow in question.

"So I sent a constable for the lad's mum, told Cat if he didn't come clean, I'd arrest her for robbery. We had an unsubstantiated report she may have received stolen goods, but is her word against his, and to be honest, I believe that the, um, complainant wasn't being entirely honest."

"She's a whore?"

"No, not anymore. She now works in a textile mill."

"But?"

"Yes, but." Detective Roggin took a deep breath. "Poor Cat was fearful when we brought his mum into the station for questioning, thinking she'd be charged with robbery. He opened up and sang like a canary."

"And you believe him?" The inspector asked.

"Have no reason not to, sir. Seems that Cat and another lad named Lenny witnessed the murder of Major Siles. The shooter, described as a tall man who they couldn't identify, dropped his satchel and scarpered. Lenny and Cat ran into the alley and retrieved the pistol and the satchel."

"But you said a captain was involved?"

"Yes, sir, and this is where it gets interesting. Only a short time later, Lenny and Cat were told to bring the satchel and pistol to a gentleman's home in The Regents Park, who took possession of them. According to Cat, this gentleman is Captain Austin Willems."

Chief Detective Inspector Bird rose and began pacing in his cramped office. "How did they know? Who instructed Lenny and Cat to deliver the satchel and firearm to the captain? Most perplexing.... The satchel must have contained something of immense interest."

"But there is more, sir. They were accompanied to the gentleman's home by Sergeant Oliver Nagle, who is acquainted with Captain Willems. They served together, sir."

"Damn it! What's Ollie doing involved in this? He's supposed to be informing us, and now... Instead of passing on what he knows, he's keeping his mouth shut." The inspector shook his head. "Continue."

"I confirmed, sir, that Captain Willems was not at the murder scene, but Cat believes the captain knows the identity of who killed Major Siles."

"Do we know what was inside the satchel?"

"No, sir," replied Detective Roggin.

"When were you going to speak with Captain Willems?"

"Tomorrow evening, sir."

"And what have you learned about him?"

Detective Sergeant Roggin consulted his notebook. "Er, he recently resigned his commission with the 67th South Hampshire Regiment of Foot after his father's death. He has no prior history with us, sir. The only link we have to tie Captain Willems to the murder is the satchel and pistol and the word of a couple of street lads. In fact, not much if he denies knowledge of the satchel."

The inspector turned at a file cabinet and strode three steps towards the other wall and another file cabinet. "We need to talk to Ollie, er, Sergeant Oliver Nagle, but if we do, he could alert the captain. Ollie is no fool, and if he knows we have Cat detained and suspects anything, he'll get word to the captain." The inspector took another step before stopping and facing the young detective. "Captain Willems needs to be interviewed before he receives a warning that we are on to him. Go now, Detective, waste no time."

Sir Ronald ordered another cognac and one for his quest, Solicitor Julian De Vore. Both men watched the waiter depart before they resumed their conversation. No one sat near them, and they weren't in danger of being overheard.

"What news do you have to report Julian, and hopefully you've begun legal proceedings to take possession of Windhaven?"

"Payment was made to, er, the Chairman," replied the solicitor.

Sir Ronald felt some relief at that news. The last thing he wanted was to antagonise Sir Felix further, "And of Windhaven?"

The solicitor shifted position on his chair, scooting closer to his client. "There is a complication, Sir Ronald…"

"No, no, don't tell me there is a complication. I don't need more complications, as there's been enough of them already," Sir Ronald testily retorted.

The waiter returned with drinks.

Julian De Vore looked down at his feet for a moment before he continued. "Your wife, Eunice, isn't the owner of Windhaven ... er, as such."

Sir Ronald glared at the solicitor." As – such?" he slowly repeated and felt his cheeks redden.

"Before his death, her previous husband, Ambrose Stephenson, took the liberty of placing Windhaven into a trust. Windhaven cannot be awarded to you, or anyone, unless a prepared trustee resolution has been created which essentially documents the decision by the trust to dispose of the property."

The walrus moustache seemed to shrink as Sir Ronald's frustration and anger increased. "And whom are the trustees? Oh, let me guess, Eunice and that incorrigible daughter of hers, Harriet."

"And one other, her solicitor," added Julian De Vore.

In despair, Grand Overland Rail's managing director leaned over and covered his face as Julian coldly observed. "Oh dear God, what will I do?" he mumbled. He lowered his hands. "Can I force Eunice and Harriet to turn Windhaven over?"

Julian shook his head. "You can intimidate or coerce all you wish, Sir Ronald, but unless all trustees agree, there isn't anything you can do."

"Then why, why, damn it, wasn't I told of this when I married that, that vile woman! She told me it was hers. The whore!" A few guests in White's gentleman's club lounge turned their heads at the outburst."

Julian had no answer and stared mutely at him. Sir Ronald didn't respond, and Julian leaned back in his chair and sipped his cognac.

"Damn it." Sir Ronald shook his head in frustration. "I'm in a rather delicate and unenviable situation, a temporary one at best. I need capital, Julian. Without an influx of capital, I stand to lose everything I've worked so hard to achieve. It will all be gone."

"There is another option open to you," stated the solicitor.

"What option is that?" Sir Ronald asked with a scowl.

Julian thought Sir Ronald would burst into tears. "Approve the sale of select Grand Overland Rail assets," advised his solicitor.

"Confound you, De Vore!" Sir Ronald thumped the armrest of his chair with a clenched fist. "You know Grand Overland Rail cannot progress with the Swindon to London line because of that accursed labour strike!"

He was breathing hard, fighting to maintain control of his emotions. Julian had heard rumours about his temper and lack of control and now believed the prattle about Mrs Hewitt-Thompson and the beatings she'd received.

"And to progress, we must leverage our assets to meet the demand for higher wages," concluded Grand Overland Rail's managing director in a more subdued manner.

Heads were craned, and everyone in the lounge stared at them.

"Settle down, Sir Ronald, people are gawking. If you need personal capital, you will have to sell other assets. Quite truthfully, sir, you have no alternative."

"Unless I petition for bankruptcy..." Ronald Hewitt Thompson looked despondent. "And mark my words, Captain Willems has unfairly brought me to near ruin, and believe me, I will seek retribution against him."

Julian De Vore silently agreed. He had no love for Captain Willems either.

"Julian, create a list of assets that can be sold and another that lists which assets we leverage to obtain credit and see to it at once."

Julian nodded in agreement. "I presume the other directors are experiencing similar financial difficulties?"

Sir Ronald looked like he would attack the gangly solicitor. After a moment, his face returned to a normal colour. "Indeed."

Julian De Vore wanted to leave and, after downing the last of the cognac, scooted to the edge of the chair to rise.

"Before you go, Julian, are you sure nothing can be done to obtain title on Windhaven?"

"As I advised earlier, Windhaven is held in a trust, and your wife is not in a legal position to transfer title of ownership unless all trustees agree." Julian inclined his head. Although, she may hold other assets in her name. it's entirely probable she wasn't aware of the trust. Her solicitors would manage her affairs on the instructions of her former husband without her involvement."

Sir Ronald brought a hand to his face and twisted his moustache and grunted. "Please send me a list of her assets that can be liquidated as soon as possible, Julian. I'm not in a position to delay this."

"Of course, Ronald." Julian stood, "I shall be in touch soon."

Sir Ronald sat back in his chair and considered the unfortunate news about Windhaven and believed there was something he could do to influence that bitch of a wife, Eunice, and her daughter to transfer ownership of Windhaven to him. He just couldn't think of how.

CHAPTER THIRTY–TWO

Nanny knocked once and opened the door to the library. Her expression conveyed some concern. "Detective Sergeant Roggin is here to see you, sir."

Austin glanced at Howard and winked. "I shall speak to him here, show him in, Nanny."

"Are you sure you want to do this?" Howard asked while they waited for Nanny to show their guest in.

Austin smiled, "Rest assured, Howard, as I said earlier, I always knew the police would come, and I believe I am prepared and ready." He lifted his glass of port and took a sip as Nanny knocked and entered the library with the detective following.

Austin stood. "Good evening, Detective, I am Captain Austin Willems and this," Austin pointed to Howard, who rose politely to his feet, "is my solicitor, Howard Willoughby. I'm sure you don't mind if he stays." Austin studied the detective carefully. He appeared very young and had a healthy mop of dark hair, a full, well-trimmed beard, and smooth, unblemished skin. It was his large expressive eyes which hinted at naivety and youth."

Howard smiled and returned to his seat as Austin pointed to a fine leather settee, "Please have a seat, Detective. Would you care for a cup of tea?

"Thank you, Captain Willems, but no."

"Thank you, Nanny, that will be all."

Detective Sergeant Roggin sat as invited and extracted a thick dog-eared notebook from his pocket.

"Had you come a little earlier, you could have shared dinner with us," Austin smiled and returned to his seat. "What brings you to The Regents Park, Detective? How may I help the Metropolitan Police?"

Detective Sergeant Barnabus Roggin evaluated Captain Austin Willems carefully. He was cordial, even friendly and didn't appear apprehensive at being unexpectedly called on. Of note, the captain did not favour the moustache military officers typically chose to wear. He was tall, easily around six foot, give or take an inch or two, and trim. To women, he'd be considered handsome in a rugged way. However, his eyes were penetrating, reflected intelligence and were all-seeing. Barnabus instinctively knew he'd have to be careful.

Detective Sergeant Roggin cleared his throat. "Thank you for seeing me, Captain Willems. This visit is of no real consequence, and as I was passing, I thought I would stop in and just clear up a few details over a case I've been tasked with."

"Of course, Detective," Austin smiled at the young man. The detective's youthful appearance probably caused him some grief. However, if he attained the position of detective sergeant burdened with the appearance of boyish naivety, then he must have skills. Austin decided to be cautious and not underestimate the young man.

"How are you acquainted with Major Miles Siles, sir," began Detective Sergeant Roggin.

Austin considered his response a moment. "I'm not acquainted with the Major, Detective. He first came to my attention when he attacked me in a urinal. If I recall, it was the Londoner, an alehouse in Soho."

"I hope you weren't seriously hurt," stated the detective as he wrote Austin's responses into his notebook. "Do you have any notion as to why he did that?"

"Mostly my pride, but as to the reason, I can only speculate, Detective."

The detective looked up, waiting for Austin to continue.

The questions were exactly what he'd expected. As long as he didn't appear a little too eager. "This is personal, Detective and I–"

"I understand, Captain, and of course, we respect your privacy."

Austin looked uncomfortable.

"It's quite alright, Austin," assured Howard.

"Recently, I began to call upon a woman, er, romantically," Austin began. "The standing of her family is important to me, and there were some questions about her stepfather's respectability. I had concerns, Detective, and made some inquiries into his business affairs, and I seemed to have hit a nerve. Soon after, I was being watched and observed by a man under the employ of a solicitor working for her stepfather. It was then, when I was assaulted, that I learned that the gentleman watching me was Major Miles Siles. I believe the assault at the Londoner was to warn me away from Miss Stephenson, and then later I caught Major Siles, here in the park," Austin raised an arm and pointed outside. "Loitering beneath a tree watching me. I admit, I was rather put out and confronted Mr Siles. Again, he tried to attack me. This time, I was prepared, and in defence, I struck him only once, injuring his jaw."

Detective Sergeant Roggin furiously scribbled into his notebook. "May I have their names, Captain? Er, the woman you were seeing and her father."

"Stepfather, Detective," Austin corrected. "I am calling on Harriet Stephenson, and her stepfather is Sir Ronald Hewitt-Thompson," he replied.

Detective Sergeant Roggin briefly hesitated with his note-taking.

He knew the name Ronald Hewitt-Thompson. Detective Chief Inspector Bird had mentioned it to him the other day. The man had a couple of horses stolen, and other railway company directors had been targeted… *was there a link between these men and Captain Willems,* he silently questioned. "You stated a solicitor employed Major Siles. Do you know his name?"

Austin saw the detective's reaction and knew he'd somehow made a connection to himself and Ronald Hewitt-Thompson. "Yes, I do because I returned a satchel and pistol belonging to him, which was handed to me by an ex-colleague. The solicitor's name is Mr Julian De Vore."

"And the name of your colleague?"

"Oliver Nagle."

Detective Sergeant Roggin paused. The response to his question was unexpected. He quickly documented both names and looked at the captain. "When was the last time you saw Major Siles?"

Austin answered quickly, "A week or so before his death, Detective."

Detective Sergeant Roggin placed his notebook beside him and looked at Captain Willems intently. "The question I must ask, sir, why was the satchel brought to you and not the police?"

"Perhaps I can answer that question, Detective. If I may?" asked Howard.

The detective turned his head to look at the ageing solicitor. "Proceed, sir."

"Because Julian De Vore's office is close to my own, as I am a solicitor and we are brethren of the legal fraternity, then it seemed more than convenient, it was logical to return the satchel and pistol to Mr De Vore."

"But why bring them to this address? I presume, Mr Willoughby, you're not a resident here?"

Howard smiled, "The satchel contained time sensitive legal documents. If they were in police possession the delay in processing those documents could create many complications. Detective, I am not just the Solicitor for Captain Willems, I am also a family friend and spend a great deal of time here. I was also solicitor to Captain Willems' father before his passing."

"Howard is like an uncle," Austin added. "But if you're wondering why Ollie brought me the satchel and pistol, it's because he was concerned his lads may be accused of stealing them when they didn't, they found them discarded and Mr nagle correctly identified the satchel's contents as legal documents as Mr Willoughby stated." Austin adjusted position on his chair. "Detective, Sergeant Oliver Nagle is fully aware of my relationship with Howard, and once he had determined the satchel belonged to a solicitor, then it was the obvious course of action. I didn't question it at all."

"And you didn't question how Sergeant Nagle's lads came across the satchel and pistol?"

"Obviously, I did and was told they found them in an alley."

"And nothing more?" pressed the detective.

"No, is it relevant?" asked Austin.

"Perhaps. Major Miles Siles was shot and killed in that alley, Captain Willems."

Austin shook his head. "I knew he was dead but wasn't aware the body in the alley was him. I read about it in the newspaper but had no idea the satchel and pistol were linked to his death." Austin's eyes narrowed. "That explains why you've come here."

"Tell me what Oliver Nagle said to you when he brought you the case and gun, Captain Willems."

"Oh, I'd have to think back." Austin scratched the back of his head. "I believe he told me his lads could be in a spot of bother, that they found a satchel and hand-gun and on opening the satchel, they saw legal papers and thought they were too important to keep, and they wanted to ensure they were returned to the rightful owner as they feared being accused of theft."

The room was silent as Detective Sergeant Roggin continued to make notes. After a minute or two, the detective looked back at Austin. "Explain why you didn't notify the police about the original assault on you in the urinal and when you received the satchel and pistol, Captain?"

Austin leaned forward. "There were no witnesses. Detective, I spent many years in the military, and it's not uncommon to have a stoush, a slight misunderstanding every now and then. We learn to deal with those incidents in our own way - which we are used to doing. As far as the satchel goes, once it had been returned to Mr De Vore, there was no reason to involve the police, and felt I had done my civic duty."

"But you said," Detective Sergeant Roggin flicked some pages in his notebook. "Yes, you said earlier that, 'I was being watched, observed by a man under the employ of a solicitor working for her stepfather,' and you believe that solicitor was Julian De Vore. Then, you must have felt some animosity towards the man. After all, he'd hired someone to watch and observe you, which must have rankled you a bit, yet you returned lost items to him without thought."

Howard opened his mouth to speak.

"No, Howard, let me," interrupted Austin. "Detective, I was being watched and investigated, and returning those items to their owner showed I was a good person, that I wasn't vindictive. It was an opportunity for Miss Stephenson's family to know this about me."

"I see… and if I may be so permitted, are you still calling on Miss Stephenson?"

"I am," Austin smiled. "I'd like to add that I have no animosity towards Mr De Vore. He is a solicitor facilitating the wishes of his client – nothing more. If I feel any animosity, it's towards Sir Ronald."

"And why is that, Captain?"

Austin's expression hardened, and he glared at the young policeman. "Because, Detective Roggin, he beats his wife senseless, and I take extreme offence at that type of behaviour."

For the briefest of moments, Detective Sergeant Roggin allowed his feelings to show. "Oh. Er, thank you, Captain Willems, Mr Willoughby. I've held you up long enough, and thank you both for your time. Is it permissible to contact you again if I have further questions?"

Austin stood and extended a hand. "Of course, Detective Roggin, anything I can do to assist." Austin smiled. "Let me see you to the door."

"Oh, one more thing, Captain."

Austin waited.

"Where is the revolver?"

"I have it, one moment." Austin retrieved the handgun and ammunition from the library and handed it to the detective while he waited at the door.

Roggin inspected the revolver carefully before placing it in his pocket. "You have a lovely home, Captain. Thank you again."

Austin watched the Detective walk down the steps before closing the door and returning to the library.

"Well then, how do you think it went, Austin?"

The library door opened, and Sergeant Oliver Nagle stepped in.

"How did I do, Ollie?"

"Oh, you'd make a fine thespian, Captain. From what I heard, it was a perfect performance. Let's hope that puts Julian De Vore behind bars for the murder of that toad, Major Siles."

Howard was lost in thought.

"And let's hope I'm not required to do an encore performance." Austin laughed.

"Oh, that reminds me, Austin," Howard interjected as he sat up in his chair. "I have two extra tickets to see The New Philharmonic Society performing Bach at Hanover Square next Saturday evening. Would you and a guest like to accompany me?"

"Glad you's ain't askin' me," laughed Ollie. "Bleedin' boring."

"Yes, that would be lovely, Howard. I shall ask Harriet if she would like to attend the performance with me and have the pleasure of being chaperoned by Mr Howard Willoughby. Not that I'd detest spending an evening listening to delightful music with Ollie. But if he were to come, he'd be grousing all night and fall asleep on my arm," laughed Austin. "I shall enter that date into my diary," he replied, giving Ollie a wink.

CHAPTER THIRTY–THREE

The Permanent Under-Secretary of State of the Home Office, Sir Felix Dampierre, wasn't in a jolly mood, as many could attest through their recent interactions with him. Dour at the best of times, Sir Felix was not blessed with a sense of humour and tended to undertake his duties and obligations with a droll, single-minded determination. In his work, he was efficient, meticulous to a fault, and expected the same from his subordinates, of which there were many. As undersecretary, Sir Felix was charged with running the day-to-day affairs for the Home Department, which included law enforcement, prisons, issues concerning immigration and a host of other responsibilities. Sir Felix's superior, the Home Secretary, believed Sir Felix did a splendid job and was irreplaceable.

However, as much as Sir Felix preferred structure and order around his life, there was a single forbearance, a pleasure of immoderation that he could not shake, and that fulfilment extended to his love of attractive young men and women. It was his Achilles' heel, and Sir Felix was fully aware of the consequences should his immoral and rather excessive passions be discovered. The burden of shame and the harm to his reputation would have been incalculable, yet he was fully prepared to exercise his cravings and take the risk. If his wife and children knew of his natural desires... but he'd convinced himself that the pleasures far outweighed the penalty if discovered. That was until he had made the intimate acquaintance of another gentleman, who also held a very influential Government position, at a rather depraved gathering hosted by George Dillington.

The gentleman who'd partook and shared in his intimate indiscretions had also stumbled upon his elevated and very senior position in government and suggested that they form a clandestine alliance to create an investment company, London Private Acquisitions, which could assist a smallish and mostly inconsequential railway company, Grand Overland Rail. The gentleman would provide financial strategy and funding pathways, while Sir Felix ensured various government departments gave favour and precedence to the ambitious little rail company.

Sir Felix had genuine reservations, but his new partner was rather persuasive, and he'd reaffirmed that the extra income could fund their extracurricular activities. Their employers and family would never learn the true extent of their lurid social get-togethers and somewhat questionable, sometimes illegal perversions. A temptation neither could resist.

As promised, it was a delightful arrangement, and money was plentiful with relatively little to no risk. His partner insisted on one non-negotiable demand – that his identity could never be revealed; he must remain completely anonymous. When questioned about his preference to remain undisclosed, he'd been told that it was to assure that he could influence ongoing favouritism and borrowing options for the rail company. In contrast, any hint of impropriety and the arrangement would fail with consequences. Sir Felix couldn't disagree, and as far as Grand Overland Rail and London Private Acquisitions were concerned, Mr Phineas Grosley didn't exist.

But change is constant, and the income stream had all but

evaporated. London Private Acquisitions had been a windfall, but unfortunately, greed and mismanagement had seen the well of wealth dry up. Phineas Grosley had instructed Sir Felix to tidy up loose ends and ensure that those dubious financial activities would never be traced back to either of them.

Sir Felix was astute and didn't need to be reminded of what needed to be done. Holding a critical position in government that afforded him power and authority was certainly motivation to close the books on London Private Acquisitions once and for all. Although he was somewhat relieved the closure of London Private Acquisitions wouldn't affect his other robust passions. On the bidding of his anonymous partner, Phineas Grosley, he sought a suitable candidate who had no objection to soiling his hands and could be trusted to remain discrete. What was required was illegal, rather distasteful but nonetheless essential. Unlike other tasks he'd agreed to do for Phineas, where he could assign another and delegate, this time, he chose to personally select the appropriate candidate and determine his suitability himself.

The sun had already descended behind London's skyline, and with it went its warmth. Sir Felix Dampierre found a seat in St James Park, turned up the collar of his coat, and buried his hands deep into pockets while waiting for his candidate to arrive and make himself known. The view over St James Lake was always calming, and this part of the park was beautiful. Two men, minders, were positioned far enough away not to draw attention to him and overhear his conversation but close enough to come to his aid if required.

In annoyance, Sir Felix reached for his pocket watch and flipped open the cover– the chap was tardy, and in disgust, he snapped it closed and returned his hand to the warmth of his pocket. A minute or two later, a man joined him on the seat, and before he could chastise him for his rudeness in keeping him waiting, he spoke.

"We agreed to meet alone. Why do you have two guards, eh?"

The accent was thick, a Frenchman decided Sir Felix, and thus, the rudeness explained.

"Merely precautionary. The unruly wander these walkways and pose a risk to gentlemen such as ourselves. The two men you see are for my protection. It would not serve me to have them confront you," explained Sir Felix as he swept a small fallen leaf from his coat sleeve. "Fear not, you are quite safe."

The Frenchman didn't reply, and both men silently watched three ducks in V formation fly overhead and noisily descend to land in the lake with a splash.

"You have need of me?"

"Perhaps, but are you skilled to perform the, er, tasks without recriminations?"

The Frenchman laughed. "The people I work with do not make good referees." He folded his arms and stretched out his legs. "Let me tell you this, *monsieur*, since the Crimean War, I have travelled throughout Europe and have two dozen achievements attributed to me, and I still have my freedom and can sit with you and enjoy the view, *non*?"

Sir Felix wasn't satisfied. There were others, and he had a list of suitable men, but then, he'd have the same problem with them as he did with this man – verifying authenticity. "What do I call you?"

"*Le Taureau.*"

If Sir Felix had a sense of humour, he would have laughed. "The Bull?" he grimaced. The Bull sounded so uncouth and coarse, as appeared the man sitting beside him. Indeed, he was far from a gentleman. His swarthy appearance, lank, oily hair, and ungroomed moustache did little to suggest refinement. His hands, resting on his lap, were large, like peasant hands, and he wasn't tall, and if anything, he was squat with a thickening middle. A man who could disappear in a crowd. He looked unremarkable in many ways. Nothing about him stood out … nothing to remember if you inadvertently encountered him, just a faceless stranger. Although Sir Felix found the Frenchman distasteful, he inherently understood he might be suitable after all.

"I want two men… er, taken care of in a way that does not arouse suspicion that they were targets. Their respective deaths must appear to be random accidents. More importantly, you must be discrete. Is that understood, *Monsieur* Taureau? In fact, I'd prefer that after you complete your assignment, you immediately depart England for France, or better, disappear to some other God-forsaken place, far, far away."

More ducks flew overhead to land on the lake.

"For the right amount of money, I can do anything."

I'm sure you can, thought Sir Felix. "One hundred pounds."

One hundred pounds was a great deal of money, *Le Taureau* acknowledged after two seconds of thought. "All of it paid in advance."

Sir Felix turned his head from the lake to look at him. "Is it not customary to pay half in advance and the remainder upon completion?"

"Perhaps, but I intend to be far from London when I complete the mission. This reduces discovery and contact–"

"And adds to the risk I take," Sir Felix interjected. "I could pay you, and you could just disappear."

"And that wouldn't help my reputation. After all, my reputation led to this meeting, *non*?"

Sir Felix conceded the Frenchman had a valid point and nodded in agreement. "Tomorrow, meet me here at the same time, and you will receive full payment and information on who the targets are. Failure will not serve you well, *Monsieur* Taureau. My reach is lengthy and not to be underestimated."

"Tomorrow," confirmed the Frenchman as he stood and wandered away.

Sir Felix watched the man walk into the darkness and felt a tinge of apprehension. Two men would die because he instructed and paid for them to be killed. If there was any consolation, it wasn't his decision. It had been Phineas Grosley's idea.

Austin invited Harriet and her mother to stay with him for a few days. Eunice could socialise with her friends, and Austin and Harriet could enjoy each other's company, which suited everyone. According to Harriet, her stepfather was dealing with a financial emergency at Grand Overland Rail, and thankfully, returned to his home in Mayfair, there was little chance of him leaving London any time soon.

Nanny was excited as Austin at having Harriet and her mother stay with them. The house needed cleaning, food needed to be ordered, and Nanny insisted on having one of the guest rooms re-wall papered as, in her opinion, it looked tatty. It had been some time since the Willems household had ladies stay as formal guests, and work was to be done before their arrival.

Austin had things to do, and to avoid getting underfoot and an inevitable confrontation with Nanny, he left matters with her as he made himself scarce.

Conscious that police had temporarily identified him as a person of interest, he took precautions to ensure he wasn't followed and took a cab to Savile Row in Mayfair, where he wanted to be fitted for new evening wear for his night out with Harriet at the concert.

Once that task had been completed, he ensured no one followed him before taking another hansom cab to Covent Garden.

The interview with Detective Sergeant Roggin had gone as expected, and Austin anticipated that the detective was busy researching and gathering facts. Undoubtedly, the detective would reappear for another interview, and this time, he expected to be interrogated as a suspect. From the inspector's point of view, having him watched seemed prudent.

He wandered around Covent Garden for a while and once confident he wasn't being observed, headed for the Lamb and Flag to talk with Ollie.

He was thirsty and downed the first ale quickly. Austin wiped his mouth and turned to the ex-sergeant. "I need Peter, Ollie. Can you find him?"

"Thought you were done wif 'im?"

"I believed so. However, I was thinking, and need to make a few changes to my plan."

"T'was that bleed'n copper, wasn't it?"

"That detective isn't foolish, Ollie, and he can't be underestimated. He may look like a boy but has a sharp mind."

"Then ya reckon he'll be back?" Ollie asked.

"Most certainly, and perhaps you could spend more time with Lenny and Cat, make sure they stick to their stories."

Ollie nodded. "Already doing that, Cap'n. They'd done good so far."

"Good," Austin reached into his pocket and handed over some coins. "Make sure they receive this, a little encouragement," Austin smiled.

"They're good lads and will do as asked." Ollie pocketed the coins. "When do you want to see Peter?"

"As soon as possible, perhaps tomorrow? But not here. I don't think I should be seen here for a while, Ollie. I suspect the police will be watching me."

"Tell Peter to meet me tomorrow morning, eleven o'clock, at Trafalgar Square."

"As you wish, Cap'n."

Detective Sergeant Barnabus Roggin had begun to receive crucial information he sought and Chief Detective Inspector Bird had approved the cost of assigning more staff to aid in the investigation. As a result, the young detective began to sort through the intelligence he received enthusiastically and briefed his superior in a room in the Bow Street Police Station dedicated to the investigation.

Names on pieces of paper were pinned to a large corkboard affixed to a wall inside the room, and Chief Detective Inspector Bird stood, cradling his chin with his hand as he stared at the wall. "Then we should question this Julian De Vore immediately about the murder of Miles Siles," he announced.

"Aye, sir, but we must also determine his relationship with Sir Ronald and Captain Willems. We have the theft of Sir Ronald's racehorses, the destruction of the yacht on the river and also, of most interest, Mr George Dillington, also a board member of Grand Overland Rail who is dealing with some unpleasant personal issues. A person unknown informed Mr Dillington's wife of his infidelities and the flat he kept on the side to host lewd get-togethers. His wife, who controls their wealth, wants nothing to do with the man and denied him access to funds."

"But not illegal, Detective—"

"If I may, sir, uh, Captain Willems is the only link between Julian De Vore and Grand Overland Rail. Somehow, he is involved

– I know he is."

"But you have no facts," replied his superior.

"Except that Captain Austin Willems was in Chieveley on the night the racehorses were stolen."

"And can he account for his whereabouts that evening?"

"Don't forget, sir, Captain Willems is calling upon Sir Ronald's stepdaughter and gives him a valid reason for him to be in Chieveley on the very night the horses were stolen, sir."

Chief Inspector Bird scrunched his face. "Is circumstantial at best."

"Chieveley police are making enquiries, so I should know more in the next day or so. But, sir, I'd like to question Julian De Vore, which I believe will lead to his arrest for the murder of Major Miles Siles. I would also ask him about his relationship with Captain Willems and Ronald Hewitt-Thompson.

Chief Detective Inspector Bird turned away from the wall and the various names and sat on a rickety chair beside a table cluttered with files and more scraps of paper. "Very well, interview De Vore and bring him in if you feel he is behind the murder. Talk to him about those relationships, and if – if, mind you, Detective, Mr De Vore divulges anything of value that supports your theory that Willems is involved, then waste no time and interrogate him."

"Of course, sir," replied Detective Sergeant Roggin."

"I also think it's time we had a quiet chat with Mr Ronald Hewitt-Thompson."

"I concur, sir."

"What of those street lads?" asked Chief Detective Inspector Bird."

"We brought them both in for further questioning this morning and learned nothing of value."

"Regardless, good work, Detective." Chief Detective Inspector

Bird rose from the chair, rubbing his bottom. "Carry on and report back to me the moment you return."

Roggin smiled.

"Oh, one more thing, Detective."

"Sir?'

"Have someone retrieve from property evidence, the possessions of Major Siles."

Detective Sergeant Roggin looked perplexed, "Of course, sir."

They were brought into the room a short time later, and with curiosity, the young detective waited while his superior rummaged through the contents inside the box.

"Here, yes, here, look at this, Detective."

The Chief Detective Inspector held up the notebook. "Ah, as I thought." He pointed with a finger at the notes. "Previously, we couldn't determine the code. Captain Willems said Major Siles was watching him. If you look at these pages and these entries ..."

> *AW*
> *AW dep at 10*
> *AW arrive 11*
> *HW arrive 11.30*
> *HW dep at 1.30*
> *HS arrive 14.15*
> *HS dep at 16*
> *AW dep at 16.30*

"A.W is Austin Willems. This supports what Captain Willems said." He passed the notebook to the detective, reached for the scrap of paper with the JD initials scribbled on it, and held it up. "And whose initials are these?"

"Must be Julian De Vore, and, uh, this connects Miles Siles to Julian De Vore, sir."

"Indeed it does, but by itself, it isn't proof of anything but helps us," replied the Chief Detective Inspector.

The young detective was again looking at the notebook. "Sir? These other initials HW can only be Captain Willems solicitor, Howard Willoughby."

"Time to get busy, Detective," instructed Chief Detective Inspector Tobias Bird as he turned to read the names written on paper pinned to the corkboard again.

CHAPTER THIRTY–FOUR

Julian De Vore was just finishing a consultation with a client when his secretary knocked on the door and indicated she wanted to speak with him privately.

"It's the police, sir," she whispered to him in the hallway. "Two men have asked to see you immediately."

"Have them wait. I'll just finish, and shan't be a moment," Julian told her as he felt a knot of fear twist at his stomach.

In reception, Detective Sergeant Roggin waited with a constable. Outside on the street, a constable was positioned near the front door, and a third was at the rear entrance if Mr De Vore decided to flee.

"Good day, gentlemen, and how may I assist you?" greeted Julian after his secretary escorted the two policemen into his office.

"Good afternoon, Mr De Vore. I am Detective Sergeant Roggin, and this is Constable Northcoat." Constable Northcoat nodded once and remained impassive. "We apologise for not arranging an appointment but we have a few questions we need to ask and believe you can help us with our enquiries."

"Of course, er, please be seated," Julian waved to chairs and seated himself behind his desk. Constable Northcoat remained standing near the door while Detective Sergeant Roggin took a seat and extracted his well-used notebook.

Julian De Vore placed both hands flat on the desk and looked at the detective quizzically.

"Mr De Vore, can you please explain your relationship with Major Miles Siles?" began the detective without preamble.

Julian almost threw up. He removed his hands from the desk and folded his arms defensively as he leaned back in his chair. "Er, I've had occasion to hire him from time to time. Through my work, you understand. I have a need for people with good investigative skills. Why is this important, Detective?"

Detective Sergeant Roggin finished writing in his notebook and ignored the solicitor's question. "And can you describe the nature of your relationship with Mr Sir Ronald Hewitt-Thompson?"

Julian relaxed a little. "He is a client, or more accurately, I am retained by his company, Grand Overland Rail, and as managing director, I deal directly with him."

The young detective scratched behind his ear with his pencil. "Mr De Vore, why would Grand Overland Rail want surveillance on Captain Austin Willems?"

Julian thought furiously. *This fresh-faced detective knew a great deal of information. What else does he know?*

"Mr De Vore?" reminded the detective.

"I wish I could help you, Detective, but I must honour my client's privacy."

"Then you can confirm you hired Major Siles to surveil Captain Willems on behalf of Sir Ronald Hewitt-Thompson?"

Julian was caught. He couldn't acknowledge that Willems had been investigating the land purchases made by London Private Acquisitions as that would open up a new line of enquiry. He placed both arms back on his desk. "Detective, there are times when I'm asked to perform a duty on behalf of a client and not told the reason why. I facilitate the hiring, retrieve information and pass it on without knowing the purpose, and I don't ask – Perhaps it's commercial sensitivity, I really don't know." Julian felt relieved as his answer appeased the detective as he continued notetaking.

"Describe to me the relationship between Sir Ronald and Captain Willems."

Julian shook his head. "I couldn't begin to guess, Detective."

"Of course, Mr De Vore. Then please tell me about your relationship with Captain Willems?" This time, the detective closely watched the solicitor's face for a reaction. He wasn't disappointed. De Vore looked troubled.

Julian's mind raced. Every possible answer he could provide opened the door to a new line of questioning that would create further complications and implicate himself. "Yes, Captain Willems… er… he isn't a client. Er, I only know that he is a privileged young military officer. Detective Robin–"

"Detective Sergeant Roggin," he corrected.

Julian nodded. "Detective Sergeant Roggin, these questions seem unprofitable, and it appears you are fishing. Is there a point to, uh, what is it you really want to know?" Julian asked while waving his arms in the air in annoyance."

The young detective was unfazed. "I'm just trying to understand the nature of your relationship with Captain Willems."

"I don't have any social or business interaction with the man if that's what you're alluding to."

Detective Sergeant Roggin didn't respond and waited quietly for the solicitor to say more. The silence was awkward.

"I suppose I know of him through his solicitor Howard Willoughby, a partner in Walker, Wakefield and Willoughby, Barristers and Solicitors, uh, they're on Essex Street only a short distance away."

The detective continued to write his notes, then looked up at the solicitor. "When did you last see Major Miles Siles?"

"Tragic, wasn't it?" Julian shook his head in sympathy. "His death hit me hard, poor chap. But when did I see him last? Oh, that would be… er… It would have been a day or two before his death. It was here – we met here in the office, actually," Julian offered the detective a polite smile.

"Are you sure? The circumstances around his murder may have been upsetting to you, and your recollection a little hazy."

Julian turned to a diary at his elbow and flicked back several pages. "I'm, uh, I'm quite sure it was, uh, yes, it was three days before, uh, before his death, Detective." His finger stabbed at an entry in his diary for emphasis.

Detective Sergeant Roggin spoke slowly. "And that was the last time you saw him?"

Julian's head nodded in agreement. "I believe it was."

"You believe? Mr De Vore, I need to know with certainty."

"It was definitely three days before."

Detective Sergeant Roggin repositioned himself on the chair. "Mr De Vore, can you please explain the circumstances around your missing valise and pistol?"

The air seemed to suck from his lungs, and his heart beat furiously as he wondered how to reply. His mind was blank; he had no answer, and he knew then the crafty detective had set him up. Constable Northcoat, at the door, took a tentative single step closer to him.

"Mr De Vore," repeated the detective, "can you please explain the circumstances around your missing satchel and pistol?"

The silence in the room was oppressive as Julian De Vore tried to formulate his thoughts. *How did he know*? He couldn't think – his mind was numb.

Detective Sergeant Roggin and Constable Northcoat exchanged

glances.

"Mr De Vore, please answer the question."

Julian shook his head. "I would…" He swallowed away the bile that rose in his throat. "I, er, I would like to consult with my lawyer."

Detective Sergeant Roggin nodded to Constable Northcoat, who stepped behind De Vore's desk. "I would like you to accompany us to the police station for further questioning around the death of Major Miles Siles."

Julian De Vore raised his hands to cover his face. "No, no, you can't do this," he appealed.

"Please come quietly, sir," advised the detective.

"No, NO!" yelled Julian. "This is wrong, you can't, you can't do this," he pleaded.

Constable Northcoat grabbed the solicitor's arm and pulled him to his feet. "You have to come with us, sir."

Constable Northcoat led solicitor Julian De Vore down the hallway of his offices. People stood in doorways and stared open-mouthed as the distraught solicitor was taken away. As the small procession reached reception, Julian's faculties seemed to briefly resurface. "Find my lawyer, Arthur Barrington, tell him to come!" he cried over his shoulder to his receptionist.

Slightly over one and a half miles away from Bow Street Police Station, on Marsham Street, Sir Felix Dampierre, The Permanent Under-Secretary of State of the Home Office, had just concluded a meeting and was reviewing the following day's schedule before leaving for home when a secretary entered his office.

"This just came for you, sir. I thought it important," and handed him the sealed envelope.

"That will be all, thank you."

He waited until she left his expansive office before slitting open the envelope, extracting and unfolding the document inside. His eyes narrowed, and with his jaw tightly clenched, he read the short message in total disbelief. He stood and looked out the window before re-reading the note.

Solicitor arrested for alleged murder of investigator.
Has been relocated to Bow St.
See to it with haste.

Fin.

The note was sent by Phineas. When together and socialising, he affectionately preferred to be called Fin. This unforeseen development altered his plans considerably. What would De Vore divulge to the police? To a certain extent, the solicitor was not fully aware of all the details, but he did have an association with the man, which posed a problem. Was that connection enough for the police to turn their attention on him? Damn Austin Willems, the meddling fool. Why did he have to involve himself? All for a misguided sense of loyalty to his deceased father. He should have left well enough alone. With De Vore in custody, the police must surely re-focus their investigation back onto Austin Willems, or so he hoped.

Fin was correct. It was time to tie off all loose ends once and for all. Sir Felix turned away from the window and returned to his seat. He impatiently snatched a blank piece of paper from a desk drawer to write instructions, as he would need to meet with *Le Taureau* as soon as possible.

It was dark, damp and chilly. Sir Felix buried his hands deep into his pockets and stood near a wall overlooking the Thames at Horseferry Playground. This time, he had no guards to protect him, he was alone and waited anxiously for *Le Taureau* to show.

"You wish to cancel our arrangement?" came the unexpected voice.

Sir Felix never heard the man arrive, and when he spoke, it gave him a start. "I'd prefer you didn't sneak up on me in such a manner," warned Sir Felix."

It was too dark to see *Le Taureau's* expression, but from the silence, he presumed the man expected an answer. "No, I do not want to cancel. I wish to alter our arrangement, Mr Taureau. I have a new target to add to your list."

"Another? *Monsieur,* this venture of yours is proving to be expensive, isn't it?"

"I'm perfectly willing to pay for your services, but this new person takes priority over the others."

"But I have already set in motion plans, and I cannot prevent them from happening, *Monsieur.* Is it important to you if another on your list is, uh, seen to first?"

"As long as your new target takes precedence, Mr Taureau."

There was no reply, so Sir Felix continued after ensuring no one else was near and could overhear. "His name is Julian De Vore, and he is a solicitor currently held in custody at the Bow Street Police Station, but I don't know for how long. How you do it, I care not, just see to it immediately. Do not disappoint me, Mr Taureau." he paused briefly to let the information digest. "Have I made myself clear to you?"

Sir Felix could feel *Le Taureau* lean in towards him.

"Abundantly," replied the Frenchman.

Sir Felix could smell garlic on the man. He found the odour repulsive and took a step away to increase the distance between them. "Here, I have an additional twenty pounds." and extended his hand.

After a moment or two, the Frenchman took the money. "It isn't enough, *Monsieur*. There needs to be more."

"I will not stand here and argue with you. That's a total of one hundred and twenty pounds for three men, which is ample and more than sufficient. See to it that Mr De Vore is appropriately and permanently dealt with." Sir Felix walked away. He knew the assassin would take the money and do the job.

He returned to his office only a short distance away and tried to think of other loose ends that could implicate him. The novelty of extra income had quickly worn off with the current problems surrounding London Private Acquisitions, and the demands placed on him by Fin were becoming demanding. He thought it had become less of an amicable arrangement and, now, more of a burden he wished would go away.

Nanny fussed over Harriet and Eunice like they were visiting royalty. The house had been scrubbed from top to bottom, floor to ceiling, and new wallpaper hung in a guest room and a hall. Flowers sprung from vases strategically placed here and there, and Austin had to tread carefully lest he inadvertently knocked an arrangement to the floor.

He was thrilled at her arrival, and even Eunice looked recovered from her ordeal and seemed no worse for wear. His home was filled with happiness and joy, which warmed his heart. It had been years since his father's house had been filled with the sound of women's laughter and the delicate scent of exotic feminine fragrances.

Nanny was in the kitchen preparing the evening meal and had suggested to Austin that he should invite Howard to dine with them. Howard readily accepted and arrived early.

When the women went to refresh themselves, Austin turned to him. "Has something happened, Howard? You seem a little vexed, or is it a malady of sorts?"

"It's an unimportant work issue, Austin," he replied.

"Well, we should rejoice as Julian De Vore will receive his comeuppance," Austin grinned.

Howard tore his gaze away from the wall and turned to him. "Yes, perhaps you're correct." He smiled, "And of course, Harriet, she is a dear thing, isn't she?"

"Oh yes, she is excited about attending the concert performance tomorrow night."

Howard seemed to have shrugged off his dourness and laughed. "As am I, Austin."

CHAPTER THIRTY–FIVE

Austin's mouth opened in astonishment at Harriet's radiance. He'd seen her dressed for the occasion at Ascot during the horseraces and was taken with her looks then, but now, the way she looked… he didn't know what to say. She was exquisite.

"My dear," remarked Howard with a huge smile. "If you've failed to impress Austin, then I'd be honoured to escort you to this evening's entertainment, as you are positively regal."

Harriet smiled and performed a slow pirouette, emphasising the new trend in lady's dress fashion. Her lilac-coloured dress was a creative masterpiece, tastefully adorned with ribbed silk, trimmed with satin and faced with cotton and brass. Austin had never seen anything like it. Her auburn hair was parted in the centre and smoothly combed back into a chignon, and small curls, like braids, were carefully pinned above her ears.

He managed to close his mouth and beamed from ear to ear, fighting the impulse to rush over and kiss her. "Harriet," he squeaked, "You, you, uh, look nice."

Nanny stood a little back and frowned, inclining her head in disapproval. Austin saw her reaction. "I mean…" he cleared his throat and attempted to dig himself out of the hole he'd dug. "Harriet, you have truly taken my breath away, for never have I laid eyes on such beauty. I feel privileged to be your escort this evening, and Howard be damned, he isn't coming near you," he laughed.

He spared another quick look at Nanny, who was again beaming like a proud mother.

Howard turned to Eunice, who was also smiling. "Forgive me for my thoughtlessness, Mrs Hewitt-Thompson, and had I known you were to be a guest, I would have obtained another ticket for this evening's performance," he dipped his head respectfully in apology.

Eunice laughed. "I have made other arrangements for this evening, and I entrust you as chaperone, Mr Willoughby, to ensure neither of them comes to mischief or harm in my absence. And Austin, you cut a dashing figure," she playfully winked, "and are quite a handsome young man."

Not used to that kind of attention, Austin's face coloured. He wore a black wool frock coat with its defining waist seam, tailored trousers and waistcoat to match. A lilac-coloured cravat, a gift from Harriet, complimented his attire. He couldn't take his eyes off her and couldn't stop grinning.

Howard arranged for a carriage and driver for the evening, and it waited outside. After saying their goodbyes, the three of them climbed aboard, and after some adjustment to her bustle, Harriet was seated and comfortable.

Harriet held his hand tightly as they clip-clopped towards the Queens Concert Rooms at Hanover Square to enjoy a night of music from Bach, performed by the New Philharmonic Society.

Carriages and Hansom cabs were in line, waiting to disgorge their well-dressed passengers as they approached Hanover Square. The mood was festive and jolly, and people could be heard laughing and emboldened by the beverages they'd already consumed, their spirits were high. Austin and Harriet were no different, laughing at some private joke as their carriage arrived outside the venue. Austin and Howard alighted first, and then Austin gently assisted Harriet from the carriage, worried he might damage or ruin her dress. Heads turned to stare as Harriet, with her arm linked through Austin's, walked up to the concierge to present their tickets. Around them, at the peripherals, people gawked out of curiosity at the elegant women and their dapper consorts. Some were opportunists, looking to pick a pocket, and a few lads ran through the attendees, creating mayhem. A constable or two chased them away, but the youthful mischief-makers only returned to further antagonise. It was expected and typical of any event the privileged attended.

Austin couldn't help but grin. He felt proud and happy to be with Harriet. He saw the envious glances from men and the more covert sideways looks from women as they took in her dress and gave him a quick once-over.

Howard was content to walk a step behind, greet a friend or two and allow the focus to be on the young couple. Otherwise, he seemed quiet and a little distracted, Austin remarked to Harriet.

The Queen's Concert Rooms were relatively narrow and long, and Austin was suitably impressed. Their seats were first-rate, in the middle and only a few rows back from the orchestra. Just as Howard described, the seating was perfect.

As expected, the performance was magnificent, and everyone was abuzz as enthusiastic applause filled the hall after two raucous encores. Chatter filled the hall as people began slowly filing out to find their driver and wait for their carriage to pull up.

Beneath the halo of gas lamps in the damp, night-time air, concertgoers congregated. Many stopped to chat with friends, and Austin introduced Harriet to a few acquaintances as they slowly meandered up Hanover Square, where they'd arranged to meet their driver. As usual, the gawkers and hawkers were there; eagle-eyed lads watched, masked behind filthy boyish faces, seeking an opportunity to make off with a valuable pocket watch or money from an inattentive gentleman. Austin kept an eye on them, and they wisely kept their distance. The tall man with his beautiful consort didn't look the type to be trifled with.

Howard walked beside Harriet, discussing the finer points of Bach's musical genius. When the people in front of them unexpectedly stopped, Austin steered Harriet around them, taking them closer to the street.

Austin saw two lads partially obscured behind a wall, watching them as they stepped around the couple. To his horror, and as he made eye contact with them, one raised a wieldy revolver and pointed it in their direction. At the same time, he accidentally stepped from the curb, almost tripped and lunged forward onto the street, pulling Harriet with him.

The single gunshot broke the peace. It could have been a cannon for the commotion it caused, and for the briefest of moments, people froze in silent question. A cloud of blue smoke provided a clue where the sound emanated as all conversation stopped, and time seemed to freeze before screams and panic set in. Horses reared and spooked by the unexpected noise, tugged brutally against harnesses as people scattered.

Howard jerked unnaturally as the bullet entered his midsection, then collapsed with a grunt. Austin looked up and, through the smoke, saw the lads disappear, but his thoughts were for Howard.

The sound of whistles filled the air as police sought help, but the youthful shooter had long since departed. Howard lay on the footpath with a blanket draped over him, and blood seeped from beneath. Concerned onlookers watched, and even a doctor came, but there was little to be done without medical equipment. He still lived, but only just.

A constable had relayed information about the shooting, and one of London's new ambulance carriages eventually arrived. It looked like a regular carriage but had rollers on the floor and large rear doors so a patient on a specially designed bed could be easily transported. Austin overheard the doctor tell a constable that the last patient the carriage transported probably had smallpox.

Howard was quickly transported to University College Hospital, which conveniently wasn't too far from Austin's home. But before he and Harriet could leave, the police had questions.

Harriet was understandably upset, and he wanted to take her home, but a constable asked them to remain until he'd questioned them both. They sat comfortably in Austin's carriage and repeatedly reviewed the details with him.

"It wasn't an attempted robbery, Constable," Austin implored, "They never looked like they had any intention to approach…"

"Sir, you stated the victim, er, Mr Willoughby, is a solicitor. Are you aware of any recent cases where someone could seek retribution? Do you have anything more to add?" the constable asked.

"Constable, Mr Willoughby doesn't generally discuss his work or clients with me. You would be best to talk to other partners at Walker, Wakefield and Willoughby," Austin answered.

Harriet stared despondently through the small carriage window, and Austin was eager to leave.

"Constable, we've gone over this already, and you've spoken to witnesses, may we leave? Miss Stephenson is distressed, and I would like to take her home. You have my address, and I'm more than willing to answer any further questions you have tomorrow or when it's convenient."

The constable nodded. "Very well, sir. We may have some follow-up questions for you."

As soon as the constable departed, Austin instructed the driver to take them home.

Harriet leaned over and grasped Austin's hand. "Do you think Howard will survive?"

He shook his head. "I don't know Harriet. I've seen minor wounds fester, and before long, they succumb and die. Howard's wound is severe...but I have hope."

"I'm so sorry, Austin. Howard is a good man, and I'm sure he can fight and overcome this," she reassured.

"Why, why?" Austin began. What has Howard done? Why shoot him? It wasn't random, it was deliberate. Those lads were there for the single purpose of shooting him. Someone put them up to it, I know it, but who and why?"

They were silent during their journey home, each lost in thought.

When Austin broke the news to Nanny, she didn't immediately react, but he could see her struggling with her emotions. Her façade was fragile, and within moments, any resemblance of self-control was lost in a torrent of tears.

"My dear Howard..." she sobbed. Harriet helped Austin guide her to a chair, and she slumped down, her tears real and heartfelt.

Austin was surprised at her reaction, but then, as Harriet reminded him, she'd known Howard for many years, and he'd been in this house countless times, he is family.

"I'm going to visit the hospital, Harriet, you stay with Nanny and inform your mother when she returns. I'm unsure how long I'll be, so please don't wait for me. I shall see you in the morning." He crouched down and hugged Nanny, and when he stood, Harriet melted into his arms.

Hospitals were dangerous places to visit and rampant with

disease. Harriet didn't argue with him going, although she had concern for his safety. "Be careful," she whispered and tenderly stroked his cheek.

Newgate Prison's towering black stone walls didn't have to look ominous to persuade people that prison life was harsh. Newgate's portentous reputation had been established in previous centuries, and without favour to gender or age, it was the unwilling home to murderers, the mentally sick, and those awaiting trial. Men, women and children were its inhabitants, and Julian De Vore was one of its latest guests as he awaited trial at the Old Bailey for the murder of Major Miles Siles.

Julian De Vore had a few days to adjust to the nuances of incarceration and learned surviving behind bars certainly wasn't easy. Filth and overcrowding made life hazardous, however, the opportunity to purchase alcohol did offer some relief from ever-present hardship. Never one to shy away from a drop, Julian purchased the crude beverage made by inmates and decided to remain permanently intoxicated to avoid having to dwell on the practical and unwelcome realities of why he was at Newgate Prison in the first place.

If you could afford it, guards were willing to take a coin or two for a favour, whether they passed on information, purchased food or even weapons. What else was there to do except scheme and plot to rob another inmate for no other reason than for self-betterment and survival.

News of the shooting in Hanover Square had only just begun to trickle in, and most inmates couldn't care less what happened to the toffee-nosed, high and mighty, but Julian, in an alcohol-induced daze, and as far from sobriety as he was from freedom, wasn't in much condition to pay attention to any news much less defend himself.

While slumped in a filthy corner, a skinny pickpocket named Magnus had approached the gangly solicitor with a knife. This wasn't a crude prison-made weapon, it was a very sharp, thin-bladed stiletto handed to him by a guard along with simple and specific instructions, including a threat.

The threat was quite explicit: if he didn't do as told, he would be killed. His instructions were to use the knife to kill Julian De Vore, and the guard had kindly pointed out the victim and then swaggered away, chuckling to himself.

Magnus, ever fearful, took his undertaking seriously and approached the near comatose form of the solicitor, leaned over and drove the knife between his ribs, not once but four times. Julian offered no resistance and probably died utterly unaware he'd been murdered.

Not long after, guards came across the body and carried the limp form of Julian De Vore away to be incinerated.

Except for Mrs De Vore, no one mourned the loss.

Le Taureau was pleased. The murder only cost £3/6.

CHAPTER THIRTY–SIX

Austin revisited Howard on Monday morning. The poor man was in enormous pain and wasn't responsive, however, at least he still lived, and that was some consolation. Medical staff coldly informed him of the prognosis, adding there was only a slender probability of survival if they couldn't fend off infection.

He returned home before luncheon, and just as Nanny was preparing to serve their midday meal, a knock on the door announced an unexpected visitor.

"Sir, it's Detective Sergeant Roggin," announced Nanny.

"More bloody questions about the shooting," Austin grizzled. "I'll see him in the library, Nanny." He turned to Harriet, "Would you like to come?"

They'd just seated themselves when Nanny showed the detective in. "Detective Sergeant Roggin, sir."

Austin stood. "Thank you, Nanny. Hold lunch for us, as I hope this will be quick." He gave the policeman a long, penetrating look. "Please, have a seat, Detective, and how can we be of help?"

Detective Sergeant Roggin sat on the edge of a chair and looked a little uncomfortable. "Forgive me, Captain Willems, Miss Stephenson, I didn't mean to intrude on your luncheon."

"We were questioned by police on Saturday evening. What more information can we provide?"

"I, er, I'm not here about the shooting, but please accept my sympathies. I hope Mr Willoughby has a quick and full recovery."

Austin inclined his head as his heart rate increased. *Not here about the shooting*, he thought. *What's going on?* He composed himself and smiled. "Thank you, Detective."

Harriet nodded in acknowledgement and remained silent.

Detective Sergeant Roggin wasted no time in delivering his news. "Were you aware Julian De Vore was killed Sunday morning?" He carefully observed Austin for a reaction.

In bewilderment, Austin quickly turned to Harriet. "Killed?"

"Murdered," informed the young detective.

Austin again faced the detective and looked shocked. "Where was he, at home?"

Detective Sergeant Roggin shook his head, "No, sir, at Newgate Prison, he'd been remanded there until his trial."

"Then he was arrested for the murder of–"

"Major Miles Siles," interjected the detective. "I was hoping you may have information about it," he added.

Austin shot to his feet. "Do you suspect I had something to do–"

"No, not at all. I find it unlikely you broke into Newgate to murder an inmate and then escape without being seen. However, Captain Willems, hiring someone to perform a task in prison isn't unheard of if you have the contacts and money."

Austin wasn't happy and returned to his seat, fuming.

Harriet spoke before Austin could say something unkind. "We weren't aware Mr De Vore was incarcerated, Detective. We don't even know the man and have no, er, um, mot–"

"Motive?" asked the detective.

"Exactly." Harriet smiled.

"I didn't think you did, but I needed to ask." He cleared his throat. "I have a couple of other questions, Captain," Detective

Sergeant Roggin continued. "Do you think Mr De Vore's death and Mr Willoughby's shooting are connected?" The detective pulled his notebook from his pocket, flipped a few pages before licking his pencil tip and waited for a response.

Austin forced himself to relax. The detective caught him unaware and was deliberately needling him, trying to provoke him into saying something he shouldn't. "I, uh, I honestly don't know. Frankly, I hadn't given it any thought because we've only just found out. What do you think, Harriet?"

"I can't see how they're related, Detective," she replied.

"Both Mr Willoughby and Mr De Vore are both solicitors, and Mr Willoughby's shooter didn't shoot him by accident. It was very intentional, and I want to know why," stated the detective.

The detective's words… Austin stared distractedly at a painting on the far wall. All eyes were on him as they waited for him to speak. "Unless the shooter shot the wrong person."

Detective Roggin's eyebrows furrowed. "Sir?"

"I'm beginning to wonder. I think I was the target… but I stepped off the footpath immediately before Howard was shot. That step I took made the shooter miss, and he may have hit Howard in error," Austin said. "I think he shot the wrong person."

Harriet raised a hand to her mouth and looked astonished. "Dear God."

"Can you draw a diagram and detail where everyone was standing," asked the detective as he tore a page from his notebook.

With Harriet's assistance, Austin drew a diagram showing the position of Howard, Harriet, himself and the shooter. He added the two people who stopped before them and drew a line representing the curb. Detective Sergeant Roggin placed his pencil along the axis, connecting Howard and the shooter.

"Had I not taken a misstep, then I would have been standing

there." Austin stabbed at the drawing with his finger, pointing to where he stood. "Because of that misstep, Howard ended up in front of me. It was me – I was the target," he stated as he leaned back in his chair.

Harriet glanced over and saw his grim expression.

Detective Sergeant Roggin folded the paper, placed it in his pocket and looked at Austin. "Now, Mr Willems–"

"Captain, Captain Willems, Detective Sergeant Roggin." Austin hoped the correction would disrupt the young detective's thoughts. To Austin's mind, the young detective was becoming very self-assured, a bit too cocky.

"I stand corrected, sir." He cleared his throat. "Er, Captain Willems, please explain why you would be a target?"

Austin shrugged, "I really wouldn't know. I saw the shooter's face, but he is unfamiliar to me." He turned to Harriet, "Do you know who would want me dead?"

She was already upset and dabbed at her eyes with a small handkerchief. "No, I do not."

"No one?" asked the detective.

"I've been plain with you, Detective. I cannot think of anyone who would want to kill me."

Detective Sergeant Roggin tapped his notebook with his pencil. "Could Sir Ronald want to kill you because you stole two of his racehorses? Revenge, sir?"

"I beg your pardon, Detective, you are–"

The detective glared at Austin, but his youthful face remained impassive.

"–You have over-stepped, and unless you have evidence, then I suggest you apologise." Austin risked a quick sideways glance at Harriet, who cleverly hid her reaction behind her handkerchief."

The detective scribbled onto his notepad. "There is a witness who has come forward. You were seen, Captain. Is your stepfather behind the attempted murder, Miss Stephenson? I understand the horses are worth a fortune, and if he suspected Captain Willems, then it might be enough for him to seek retribution."

"Even if you are correct, Detective Sergeant Roggin, which you aren't, I doubt he would want me dead only because of two stolen horses."

Austin saw a subtle change in the young detective. *That's why he's here. He came here to arrest me for stealing the racehorses.* It was time to deflate the detective's ego.

"Captain Willems, I have evidence." He took a deep breath. "Admit to it and tell me what happened; the court could look favourably at your admission."

Austin momentarily held the young detective's unwavering gaze and leaned forward in his chair. "Detective Sergeant Roggin, before you formally accuse me of stealing two racehorses owned by Sir Ronald Hewitt-Thompson, think carefully. Can you accuse me of theft or even arrest me if no crime was committed?"

"Of course not, but this charge is not inconsequential, Captain Willems. It's a serious offence, and if found guilty, the penalty will likely be custodial."

"Then let me be clear, you can only accuse me of breaking the law if a crime has actually been committed, am I correct?"

The youthful detective nodded.

"And in this case, the *alleged* crime is the theft of two horses?"

Clearly annoyed, Detective Sergeant Roggin sighed loudly. "Yes, you are correct. Now might be a good time to conf–"

"In that instance," Austin interrupted, "I suggest to you, Detective Sergeant Roggin, that no crime has been committed. Perhaps you should be more thorough in your investigation before you make unfounded accusations."

The detective's expression changed to puzzlement, and he looked unsure.

"Detective Sergeant Roggin, my home is at Windhaven," began Harriet, "If two racehorses were stolen, I would certainly know about it. Perhaps you should check with your associates in Chieveley, as I don't believe any horses are missing at all."

A look of uncertainty flashed across the detectives face, and wasn't sure what to do. He'd been about to arrest Captain Willems for horse theft, but now? *This was absurd.* He stared at his feet as he tried to compose himself. "The theft of two thoroughbred racehorses was reported to Chieveley police..." Finally, he looked at the captain. "Very well, sir, I will confirm the horse theft from Windhaven and may call on you tomorrow."

"The horses may have been temporarily moved. Mistakes like this happen all too frequently, wouldn't you agree?" Austin paused to give the detective time to digest the news. "But of course, Detective. I shall be here," Austin smiled and then rose from his chair. "And now, if we may enjoy our luncheon. Will that be all?"

"I uh, I apologise for intruding, Miss Stephenson. Good day to you both."

Austin wiped his mouth with a napkin and turned to Harriet. "Do you think your stepfather could have wanted me dead? That he hired someone to kill me?"

"I'm sure if he suspected you of stealing his horses, he may have wanted you dead, but he does not have the mettle to see it through. No, it wasn't him."

Austin placed the napkin on his lap. "Then who had Mr De Vore killed? I believe Detective Roggin is correct, both events are linked."

"Then we are in danger, Austin, as they will try again," she warned.

He lost his appetite and pushed his plate away. "Perhaps it's one of the other directors of London Private Acquisitions. It cannot be difficult to determine. After your stepfather, there are only three others, Virgil Hartmann, George Dillington and Oscar Baker. George has no money, so that limits it to two."

Harriet was looking at him with a peculiar expression.

"What is it?" he asked.

"Austin, I recall telling you there are five directors of London Private Acquisitions, there is one more."

"No, there are only four. Howard confirmed that with me," he replied.

"I believe he is wrong, Austin." She took a sip of water from a glass. "About two years ago, my stepfather held a directors meeting at Windhaven for London Private Acquisitions. It was a board meeting, and I will never forget. The table setting was wrong, and he was quite upset and spoke harshly to the majordomo and the estate manager. It caused a commotion, and the chef was dismissed."

Austin dabbed at his mouth with a napkin. "And what was the correct place setting?"

"Five."

"Five... Are you sure, Harriet?"

"Absolutely. It was definitely five, not three or four, it was five."

"If they had a board meeting, then you would have seen the directors," Austin stared at her with a measure of hope.

"No, stepfather insisted that we were not to make an appearance, and we were to remain in our rooms or stay outside until they departed."

"Why would he do that? Seems rather unreasonable."

Harriet shrugged. "That's what I thought at the time," she replied.

Austin rubbed his chin. "Why did Howard tell me four?"

"He made a simple mistake, Austin. It happens all the time."

"No, Harriet. Howard is a solicitor, and experienced solicitors don't make that kind of error." Austin took a sip of wine as he gave the matter some thought.

"Do you think it's important?" Harriet asked.

He looked at her directly. "I thought I knew who was trying to kill me and believed it could only have been one of the four directors. Now, I have no idea who it could be, which is a little disconcerting."

"Then you believe me when I say there are five directors?"

Austin nodded. "In a way, it makes sense because none of the four directors I know about are the type of people to hire an assassin. They're greedy, objectional men, that is all. But hiring someone to kill another, that takes some courage. Whomever he is, he is a ruthless and dangerous man."

"Should you tell Detective Sergeant Roggin?"

Austin shook his head. "Not yet. If this other unknown director discovers the police are looking for him, then he will become desperate and desperate men do reckless things. I shall inform the detective when I learn who he is."

They were again eating in silence and mulling over what they'd discussed when Harriet spoke. "Will the detective confirm what we told him about the racehorses?"

Austin looked up, grinning. "I believe he will."

Harriet smiled in return. "It was thoughtful of you to have Peter return the horses."

"Yes, a little earlier than I planned, but for the better, eh?" he laughed. "I only hope your stepfather doesn't learn of their return."

"The stable master said he wouldn't tell him."

"Good, otherwise we will steal them again," Austin added with a laugh as Nanny appeared to clear the table.

"Nanny?"

She turned to face him. "sir?"

"Where are all of Father's business papers stored?"

"I put them in the upstairs storeroom." She looked puzzled. "Has this to do with Howard –er, Mr Willoughby being shot?"

"Perhaps, Nanny. I want to look through them, as there might be clues."

"If it pleases you, sir, I shall move the boxes to the library after I've cleaned up from lunch."

"No, that isn't necessary, Nanny. I will sort through the papers in the storeroom."

"And I shall help, Austin," stated Harriet with finality. "As long as you tell me what we're looking for."

CHAPTER THIRTY–SEVEN

From within a nondescript rooming house on Dean Street in Soho, a dim circle of yellow light from a paraffin lamp challenged the oppressiveness inside the dingy room and failed to add any cheer. Deep within the room's shadows, peeling wallpaper and a stained, threadbare rug were partially visible. Still, the darkness did little to mask a musty odour that permeated through everything, a reminder of unwashed bodies and hasty sex. Mould on walls and ceiling were like scabs on a festering wound and revealed themselves at the fringes of the lamp's effectiveness, but if it bothered the assassin, he never let on. He was hunched over a wobbly table, composing a letter to his employer—a missive he didn't want to write.

A half bottle of French wine sat at his elbow, and a nearly empty glass beckoned. He replaced the cap on his fountain pen, leaned back in his chair and stretched, letting out a satisfying groan as his hands reached upwards to ease the tension in his neck. He lowered his arms and continued to stare distractedly at the ceiling, trying to imagine the faces of the people he knew from the dark abstract blotches of mould that covered most of the area. After a moment, he cursed his time wasting and lowered his head to re-read his half-completed letter.

Sir Felix expected an explanation as to why Captain Willems

survived the attempt on his life. *Le Taureau* couldn't offer any reasonable excuse; the boy had been paid well, and the description of his target had been carefully explained, even down to the colour of the cravat he wore. Yet the boy had missed the single shot and, most unfortunately, had instead struck an innocent elderly gentleman accompanying the captain.

One of the main reasons *Le Taureau* had such an illustrious career was that he avoided putting himself in harm's way. Most frequently, he always hired another person to do the killing and then distanced himself so that he could never be associated with the crime. But he was still accountable and handsomely compensated – a fact that his employer had coldly reminded him. Yet completion still evaded him, and he'd assured the man he was up to the task.

Now, Captain Willems was forewarned, and as a military man, he would take steps to ensure he wasn't caught unaware again. However, maintaining vigilance was unsustainable, and if he allowed a few days or a week to pass, the captain would eventually let his guard down, and when that happened, he would strike. Now was the time to focus on the other target, a non-military man who'd be oblivious to a threat on his life until he drew his last breath.

Austin was upstairs with Harriet, sorting through boxes of papers pertaining to his father's business, Midlands Collieries Company. He was searching for any documentation about Grand Overland Rail that, he hoped, may provide a clue to the identity of the mysterious director. So far, they'd had no luck, and while Austin knew his father kept meticulous records, finding any useful document about the rail company was no easy task.

Their search was interrupted when Nanny appeared.

"Sir, you have two gentleman callers."

"Detective Sergeant Roggin?" Austin griped.

"Oh no, sir. A Mr Jeffrey and Harrison Watson, from, er, Watson–"

"Watson Brothers Coachbuilders?" he confirmed.

"Yes, sir, that's what they said."

He looked at Harriet, "This is interesting. I wonder what they could want?"

"Then you should do what is polite and greet them," Harriet offered with a smile.

"Show them to the library, Nanny. I'll be right there."

Nanny clomped down the stairs, and Austin eased himself upright from the floor. "I saved these men a fortune by persuading them not to invest in Grand Overland Rail, and now they're here – most intriguing, Harriet. Will you come?"

"You go, Austin. I'll continue to search," she smiled.

Austin welcomed the Watson brothers to his home, sat in his favourite chair, and looked at both men. "How can I help you?" he asked.

Typically, it was Harrison who spoke. "Again, we would like to thank you for apprising us about Grand Overland Rail, Captain Willems."

"You are most welcome, sir, but I presume your visit here is not only to offer gratitude... there is another matter?" Austin smiled warmly.

Jeffrey sought a more comfortable position and adjusted a pillow as Harrison again spoke. "Correct, Captain. Our sources have informed us that Grand Overland Rail is experiencing major financial difficulties. It appears they might be close to being insolvent and are looking to liquidate assets, Midlands Collieries Company being one of them."

This wasn't news to Austin as he'd been following anything and everything about Grand Overland Rail. "Yes, I'm aware of that."

Harrison nodded. "Perhaps you are not aware that the directors of Grand Overland Rail are secretly looking to sell their rail company. They all want out. The company is struggling, ultimately brought on by the labour strike. One motivating factor is that most key directors have all privately succumbed to their own financial challenges and require cash."

Putting Grand Overland Rail on the market was news to Austin. "How did you come by this information?"

"I was approached by one of the directors, Mr Virgil Hartmann. He essentially offered to sell Grand Overland Rail to us," stated Harrison.

Austin shrugged, "And what does that have to do with me?"

Jeffrey leaned forward. "If I was you," he pointed a calloused stubby finger at Austin, "Then I'd want to buy back Midlands Collieries Company from them and…" he looked to his brother.

Harrison continued, "And perhaps invest with us as partners to purchase Grand Overland Rail."

"Gentleman, we are talking about a great deal of money." Austin's head swivelled from one brother to another. "I don't believe I have that kind of capital available to me."

"Let me explain, Captain Willems. If you purchased the coal company from Overland, that would reduce Overland's selling price, would it not?"

"Somewhat, but yes, agreed," Austin stated.

"If you had access to more funds to contribute with purchasing Overland, then that would enable us to invest and become partners. We can't do it alone."

"It's a sum well above my means," Austin insisted.

"And ours," Jeffrey admitted.

"We might be able to make some referrals on your behalf to er, assist you with obtaining suitable lines of credit," Harrison offered.

This development caught Austin entirely off guard, and he was ill-prepared. He wished Howard was with him. "I, uh, I'm not sure, and it depends on what it could cost me to purchase Midlands and what Grand Overland Rail is valued at." Austin turned to each of the brothers and made eye contact. "And, of course, anything we say is purely speculation until we determine the ultimate selling price."

"Would you be interested in exploring this further, Captain Willems?" Harrison asked.

Austin rose from his chair and began pacing the room. "Gentlemen, in principle, I'm not averse to this and would like to keep all my options open. We must remember that Grand Overland Rail requires funds to complete its expansion. In addition to purchasing the rail company, we must ingest capital into the business." He stopped in front of the brothers and faced them. "You are correct. I do want to regain ownership of Midlands Collieries Company, but the thought of becoming a partner in Grand Overland Rail was something I'd not considered. Without making any commitment, I can tell you I'm interested. Of course, I am, however, that interest extends only to what I can afford."

The brothers smiled. "That's what we hoped for, Captain Willems." They stood and shook Austin's hand. "We shall keep you informed, Captain. Thank you for seeing us." The brothers turned to leave.

Austin had a thought. "One moment, gentlemen. Do you have a list of all Grand Overland Rail directors er, past and present?"

Jeffrey's eyes narrowed. "What possible reason could you have to want those names?"

Harrison turned to his brother in puzzlement, then looked at Austin. "I suppose I could get that list, it shouldn't be difficult. I will ask Mr Hartmann for it," he replied with a final glance at Jeffrey.

"I want to know more about the directors. Due diligence, gentlemen," Austin offered. "However, if you speak to Mr Hartmann or any other Grand Overland Rail directors, do not tell them you've been communicating with me. I think it best they don't know my interest in purchasing Midlands Collieries Company from them. If they know of my involvement, they might try to increase the selling price, which won't serve either of us well."

"I agree." Harrison nodded.

Austin was upstairs back in the store room and explained to Harriet the nature of the Watson brothers visit.

"Are you interested in being a partner with the Watson brothers to purchase Grand Overland Rail?" she asked.

"Honestly, I don't know, Harriet. Father always felt partnering with a rail company would benefit Midlands Collieries Company. But we're talking a large sum of money, and I'm not sure I can afford that luxury. Harrison Watson was here to inquire about my interest, and I told him I was interested but did not make any commitment."

"Do you trust them?"

"The Watson brothers?" he asked.

"Yes, what do you know about their reputation and business practices besides your past and recent dealings with them?"

Austin looked at her and shook his head. "Virtually nothing."

She smiled. "I'm not convinced about them."

"Then, m'dear, we shall take steps to remedy that." He looked down at what she held in her hands. "What do you have there?" he asked.

"I found it at the bottom of a box," she held up the folder. "It's a prospectus for Grand Overland Rail and some other documents, mostly legal. I wanted to show you." She handed it to him

Austin opened the folder and found a handful of brochures and papers, primarily sales-related pamphlets enticing potential buyers to invest in the rail company. They contained general information about the company's assets, income and expenditures. Nothing remarkable, and they didn't reveal anything that he didn't already know. But the other documents were copies of permits and permissions by government departments relating to building a railway through undeveloped and developed land.

He sat on a box and quickly read through the permits. After a few minutes, he looked up at Harriet. "I'm impressed, all these documents show that Grand Overland Rail was diligent and had obtained all the required approvals they needed for their Swindon to London rail expansion."

"But nothing to help us find the identity of the mysterious director of London Private Acquisitions?"

"No, apparently not. These copies are instructions on what, where, and how Grand Overland Rail can build their railway line, and they are all signed and approved by a dozen dreary bureaucrats."

He returned the folder to her, and she began to look over the paperwork again. "I don't think so, Austin. Why has the same person signed all the documents, isn't that a bit peculiar?" She handed the papers back to him.

"Actually, it is odd," he said after confirming what she said. "The same person has signed each permit or authorisation. Are there any more papers like these?"

Harriet shook her head, "I've looked, but this is all I can find."

"Let's go downstairs and look through these in more detail."

Papers were laid out over the floor, and Austin sat amongst them with legs stretched, reading through each document. They'd spent the best of the afternoon reading, writing notes, and summarising their findings.

Eventually, with his bottom numb, he stood and turned to Harriet, giving it a vigorous rub. She raised her eyebrows at his lack of manners and laughed.

"It's sore, and I need to improve circulation. Since I'm a gentleman, I would never request you to do it." He gave her a wink. "Now then, what have we learned, Harriet."

A knock on the door preceded Nanny's entrance. "If you'll be excusing me, sir. I'm going to visit Mr Willoughby. I shan't be long, and is there anything you need while I'm out?"

"No, Nanny, if he is lucid, tell him I will visit tomorrow."

"Very well, sir." She closed the door; moments later, they heard the front door close.

Eunice was upstairs in her room resting, and they were almost alone. Harriet interrupted the silence, "Er, it seems Nanny has a fondness for Mr Willoughby."

"Aye, she has. I learned that years ago when I was a boy. I find it endearing."

"Endearing? The woman has no man in her life and is a barren spinster. You keep her caged up in this house, Captain Willems, and have never encouraged her to socialise and meet people, you should feel ashamed."

Austin saw the twinkle in her eye. "Aye, and perhaps I shall do that to you, too. Keep you barefoot, childless and locked up in this fine home forever."

She swung an arm at him and missed.

"Now that you've got that out of your system, Miss Stephenson, perhaps we should address the matter at hand," he laughed.

She held his gaze, then looked down at her notes and composed herself.

The doorbell chimed.

"I shall return," said Austin as he headed towards the front door.

"Detective Sergeant Roggin, how lovely to see you. I was expecting a visit from you," said Austin by way of a greeting.

The detective removed his hat. "Captain Willems. I was just passing and thought I would stop and give you a brief message. I won't be staying."

Austin looked at the boyish detective with curiosity. "Of course."

"It appears, and I can confirm, sir, that no crime was committed at Windhaven. The reported theft of two racehorses was a false claim, the er, horses were found as you suggested.."

Austin did his utmost to keep a straight face. "I'm pleased to hear that, Detective Sergeant Roggin."

"And on behalf of the Metropolitan Police, I would like to extend our sincerest apologies for any misunderstandings…" he paused.

Austin inclined his head and waited.

"…And for suggesting you may have had any involvement. I was wrong."

He knew the detective struggled to deliver the apology and felt terrible for him. "Think nothing of it, eh, and thank you," said Austin graciously.

Detective Sergeant Roggin dipped his head in acknowledgement but gave no indication he was leaving.

"Good day, Detective." Austin went to close the door.

"Uh, Captain Willems, You wouldn't know anything about artwork stolen from Finch and Gossett, would you?"

What? Austin saw the detective's chaste facial expression and knew it was a deliberate ruse. Obviously, the detective had cultivated an expression to make him appear young and naïve when he was far from that. In that moment of clarity, he understood how he could have made an enemy. The young detective wasn't impressed with his overconfidence. It might have worked in the past with others, but this young detective was too astute. *I've made an error in judgement*, Austin realised. He felt a chill run up his spine. He had to take a different approach with the man.

Rather than display a haughty, self-assured reaction, Austin was more or less honest with the detective. He shook his head, "I have heard of Finch and Gossett, most people who have the resources are aware of them, however, my father was not a collector of fine art and nor he and certainly not I, have ever had occasion to store anything at their facilities," Austin truthfully admitted and held the detective's unwavering gaze. His heart beat furiously as he waited for the detective to respond.

Detective Sergeant Roggin deliberately gave no outward reaction to Austin's reply. But he wasn't sure if the captain was being truthful– he had doubts. The captain's response wasn't what he had expected, and his answer was almost identical to responses by other members of the gentry when he asked about the company. He smiled. "Good day, sir." He replaced his hat, turned and walked down the steps and back onto the street.

CHAPTER THIRTY–EIGHT

"I do know that a railway cannot be built without an Act of Parliament. Look here," Austin pointed to a document titled Railways Regulation Act 1844. "And many other requirements that need to be met are all administrated through the Board of Trade."

Harriet nodded, and so Austin continued. "And The Railways Inspectorate, for example, and you can see they have signed off on all their paperwork. All the documentation is perfect, and everything approved…"

"Except," Harriet added, "They've all been signed by the same person."

"And is that normal? It doesn't appear to be standard, and I imagine a departmental supervisor's job is to oversee and manage the various requirements for their area of authority. There shouldn't be one person signing everything." Austin paused and looked at the signature. "Cecil W. Bishop. Who is this man, and whom does he report to?"

"He must be important for no one to question his signature, therefore, he must have a position of responsibility."

"I think so too, but Harriet … so what?" Austin raised his arms in despair. "We need to find the name of the mystery board member of London Private Acquisitions, and all we are doing is looking at Grand Overland Rail permits, which has brought us nothing."

"Except a gentleman who signed papers that should have been

signed by a dozen other individuals," she reminded him.

Harriet's mother, Eunice, entered the library and looked around the room at the scattered paperwork. "Oh, am I disturbing something?"

"Not unless you are familiar with Mr Cecil W. Bishop. And if you were, Mama, we would be eternally grateful," Harriet added.

She shook her head. "I'm sorry, I don't know this name. Should I?"

"No, it was a question steeped in hopelessness, Mrs Hewitt-Thompson. But can I ask, was your husband always secretive around meetings involving Grand Overland Rail?" Austin asked.

"Everything he did was secretive, and he claimed commercial sensitivities," she frowned. "To be honest, his businesses held no allure for me because he didn't want me to become interested." She raised a hand to her cheek, and Austin could see how even talking about the man reminded her of the injuries she'd sustained.

"I apologise, it was thoughtless of me to discuss him."

"It's quite all right, Austin," she smiled.

He wanted to change the nature of their conversation. "Well, then, I can only hope you shall enjoy dining out as my guests," he announced to everyone's surprise.

"Then we're dining out?" Harriet asked.

"Indeed. Nanny has the day and evening off, and I invite you both to dine with me," he said with a huge smile.

"Then perhaps we should get ready, isn't that right, Mama?"

"I'm not sure, Austin," Eunice replied. "Thank you for your kind offer…"

Harriet stepped close to her mother and took her hands in her own. "Mama, you need to go out, you can't continue to hide from him. "With Austin, we are safe, and no one can harm you."

"And no one knows where we will dine," Austin interjected.

He had no fear of Ronald Hewitt-Thompson, but privately, he was concerned about being hunted by an unknown assassin and potentially putting Harriet and Eunice in peril. He'd been checking constantly, and no one was watching the house or stalking them, and he was careful not to advertise where or what he was doing. Other than the three visits he'd made to see Howard, he'd deliberately stayed at home and avoided going outside since the shooting, but now he needed to continue with his life and venture out. The walls were closing in. "We won't accept no as an answer."

Eunice relaxed. "Very well. Let's enjoy a lovely meal together."

Palmer Southbridge loitered in the shadows, well away from any light that could illuminate his face. Across the street, about fifty yards away, his son, Penny, also hid in a doorway. Penny was just a nickname. His real name, Leslie, was never used, and thankfully only his mother had ever called him that. He could never understand why he was burdened with a girl's name, although the irony of his adopted nickname was lost to him.

Penny was trying to redeem himself with his father after bungling the job he'd been tasked with almost a week ago when he'd been given a gun and told to shoot the toff with the purple cravat. Penny knew he should have shot the man, but the fool had tripped when he stepped off the footpath, and the shot had missed and struck another toff walking beside him. The bruises still showed from where his father had beaten him. He had contusions on his arms where his dad had gripped him tightly and shook him in a drunken rage. He had a welt on the side of his face, and his arse was still tender where his father's belt had inflicted humiliating pain. But no more, Penny decided. If his father ever lifted a hand to him again, he'd stab him with the knife he now carried. But for the time being, the importance was on the job and appeasing his volatile dad.

Palmy, as Palmer was known by his friends, had spent most of the last few days preparing to kill his next target. His gaffer had gone over the route the target would take and, between the two of them, had decided how and where the killing would take place.

Le Taureau had meticulously explained his reasoning and preferred the death appeared to be an accident. A plan was quickly formulated, and *Le Taureau* insisted they rehearse to minimise errors and calculate timings. Afterwards, Palmy was quite pleased and accepted that the gentleman's death was possible with little chance of either of them being caught.

Palmy reached for his battered fob watch, pried open the lid, extended his hand beyond the doorway, and from the yellow light of a gas street lamp, saw it was almost time. He signalled with a single wave to his boy as he snapped the cover shut and returned the watch to his pocket.

A small group of men exited the building, and one said goodbye, separated from the group and walked along the footpath towards them. Their mark was habitual and always departed for home at the same time. They'd also been given his description. With his identity confirmed, Penny would follow and immediately begin to harass the toff for money. The distraction was crucial and allowed Palmy to approach unseen without arousing suspicion.

Palmy blended into the darkness, and he could hear Penny begging for a coin or two from the man as they approached. At this early time of evening, coaches and cabs were everywhere as they delivered passengers to their destinations or picked up a fare. Ahead, a major crossroad was what held Palmy's real interest.

As expected, their target was already losing patience with Penny. Palmy smiled, the man had a short fuse and very little tolerance. He waited a moment longer, then after gauging distances, he stepped from concealment, crossed the road and converged with his target. As hoped, the man was too busy yelling at Penny, threatening to hail a constable and never saw him approach.

Palmy and the gentleman stopped at the intersection waiting to cross as Penny continued to rile him. He grabbed the man's coat, tugging on it as he begged for a handout. Palmy and the gentleman both saw a pause in passing traffic. The target was only too eager to cross the busy road as Palmy made eye contact with his son, a prearranged signal. In response, Penny tugged even harder on the gentleman's expensive coat.

In some desperation, the gentleman threw an arm at the boy and missed; if he didn't cross now, it would be a long wait for another gap to appear. The boy was strong for his size and age, but the gentleman had weight. He gathered himself, and with a curse pulled hard at the same time Penny released his hold on the target's coat.

All his energy was focused on pulling his coat from the boy's grasp. Now, suddenly unencumbered, he lurched onto the street and directly into the path of a two-horse carriage trotting rapidly towards him. He had time, perhaps a second at most, to regain his balance, leap to the side and avoid being run over.

To observers, it appeared a pedestrian came to his rescue when a man unexpectedly stepped onto the street to offer assistance. However, Palmy wasn't there to help.

Only a few paces from the Old Bailey on Fleet Street was a small public house called 'The Bar', frequented mainly by the legal fraternity. Barristers, solicitors and law clerks generally filled the place. Occasionally, a magistrate could be seen swilling back an ale or three, but it usually was the barristers who filled the smallish venue, their loud, uncouth antics driven by ego-inflated self-importance. Bragging and impromptu re-enactments of past courtroom oratories provided enough entertainment to amuse most patrons.

Le Taureau wasn't drinking at The Bar because he had an interest in law – he had none. Nor was he there because of loose and available women. While no rules said women couldn't frequent the public house, they just weren't generally allowed to visit.

He drank there so he could be recognised. He'd talk to a few barristers, even obtain a business card, and if in the unlikely event he was implicated in a crime, then he could always say, 'I was at The Bar,' and prove it. But it wasn't like he was a complete stranger, he was known to a few regulars as he'd been there a few times in the past.

Le Taureau discretely looked at his pocket watch around the same time as Palmy looked at his and ordered another ale, loudly asking if anyone knew the time. He settled onto his chair and quietly hoped that Palmer Southbridge and his boy, Penny, wouldn't have any difficulty this evening.

And Palmy wasn't there as a bystander, nor to help; he had a job to do. With remarkable quickness, he gave the man an extra shove in the back, propelling him directly into the path of the oncoming two horses pulling the heavy carriage before turning and quickly striding away. No one saw him leave, and no one paid him any mind as all the attention turned to the coachman who screamed in warning, at the horses shrieking in protest as their heads were savagely jerked back by the coachman pulling desperately on the reins. When he had a free arm, the coachman hauled a wooden lever beside his seat and yanked hard. Wooden blocks attached to the lever slammed into the wheel and helped to slow the heavy coach. Alerted by the screams and yelling, all pedestrians in the area turned in disbelief to witness the horror unfold as Palmy and Penny disappeared.

A flailing hoof from the nearest horse struck the gentleman on the thigh, and he immediately crumpled. Before he had collapsed to the street, another hoof struck him in the abdomen, deflecting his fall beneath the hooves of the second horse. The weight of the heavy carriage, still moving forward, forced the horses to keep moving, and they couldn't turn away or even stop. It was unavoidable, and the horses trampled over the body, causing incalculable damage. The gentleman was still alive, but only just as the horses stomped over him. It wasn't until the front wheel of the carriage ran over the body and crushed his skull that the gentleman finally died. By the time the distraught coachman managed to pull the carriage to a complete stop, Palmy and Penny had already been forgotten.

Within seconds, police whistles could be heard, and a large crowd gathered at the scene. The coachman was beside himself and told anyone who'd listen how he never saw the man until he was almost underfoot. "Ain't my fault, it ain't my fault, honest," he repeated, shaking his head in anguish.

"Is he responding to treatment?" Austin asked Nanny.

She shook her head. "No, sir. He isn't dead, but he isn't alive either. The physician said the wound had been corrupted after the bullet had been removed, and they could do little more. We have to wait." She clasped her hands together and lowered her head while she composed herself.

Austin stepped up and wrapped his arms around her. "Howard is a strong man, Nanny. If anyone can overcome this, he can. I've seen men with worse battlefield wounds survive, and they only had field attention. Howard's a survivor, Nanny, and I will see him this afternoon and talk some sense into him, eh? He leaned back, placed a finger beneath her chin and gently lifted her face to him. "Chin-up, eh."

"Thank you, sir," she replied with moist eyes. "And, er, if you'll excuse me."

He watched her leave the room, then turned to Harriet. "She is taking this hard."

Austin and Harriet were seated in the offices of solicitor Simon Walker, a partner of Howard's in his law firm, Walker, Wakefield and Willoughby, Barristers and Solicitors. Austin knew all the partners well but particularly liked Simon, a jolly, no-nonsense fellow who always seemed to have a different and refreshing perspective on life than most people.

Howard's business partners needed to be kept apprised of Howard's medical condition, and visiting Simon seemed to be the decent thing to do. Austin and Harriet sat on a settee inside Simon's office and were about to leave after enjoying tea and updating Simon.

"Simon, I have an unusual request, and I'm hoping you might be able to provide some guidance," Austin began.

Simon Walker peered over the rim of his spectacles that perched at the end of his nose. "Continue," he replied and habitually reached for paper to write notes if required.

Austin detailed the discovery of all the paperwork his father had received from Grand Overland Rail that had been signed by one person.

"Extraordinary," quipped the solicitor. "Highly irregular and improper, If I may add. And do you have this most important gentleman's name?"

"Cecil W. Bishop," Austin answered.

"Never heard of the man, but that is no surprise," Simon responded. "I know few people and have even fewer friends." He looked at Austin with a grin. "But there are people who can help. Let me impose on these good folk and let them learn who this Mr Bishop is and who he reports to, eh?."

"Thank you, Simon." Austin turned to Harriet. "And we must return home." They stood. "And we will keep you updated on Howard's condition."

Simon stood and extended his hand to Austin and then to Harriet. "Lovely to meet you, m'dear, and keep a close eye on this one, don't let him slip through your fingers."

CHAPTER THIRTY–NINE

Austin was reading through Grand Overland Rail documents in the library when Nanny knocked on the door and entered. "Sir, Detective Sergeant Roggin is at the door–"

Austin groaned. "What does that confounded man want with me now?"

"Beggin' your pardon, sir, but he asked for Mrs Hewitt-Thompson and Miss Stephenson."

Austin's eyebrows furrowed. "Did he say why?" He rose from his chair.

Nanny shook her head. "No, sir."

"Alright, inform Mrs Hewitt-Thompson and Harriet, and I will see to the detective in the parlour."

"Detective Sergeant Roggin, perhaps you should move your office here," Austin suggested in the way of a greeting.

"Perhaps that would be prudent, Captain Willems," replied the detective without a smile. "But it is your good fortune that I'm not here to speak with you this time."

"So I'm told. Please, come inside, this way," Austin invited.

He thought the detective looked tense and wondered why he needed to speak with Eunice and Harriet. He could hear them descending the stairs and directed the detective to a seat.

Austin introduced Mrs Hewitt-Thompson to Detective Sergeant Roggin, and no introduction was needed for Harriet, whom he'd met on his previous visit. "I shall afford you some privacy," Austin offered, "and shall return to the library."

"Please stay, Austin," Harriet said. She looked at her mother. "I'd like Austin to stay, Mama."

Eunice was as puzzled as anyone because of the detective's unannounced call. "Is that permissible, Detective Sergeant Roggin?"

"Of course," he replied.

Austin noticed the young policeman had not smiled. *This didn't portent well*, he thought.

Three expectant faces turned in question to the young detective.

He cleared his throat. "I apologise for my intrusion, however, I felt it appropriate that I come here today instead of someone else because of my past visits and ongoing investigation that Captain Willems has been helping us with."

Barnabus Roggin fidgeted with his hands, and Austin could see the detective was distressed.

The detective turned to Eunice. "Unfortunately, I am the bearer of bad tidings, Mrs Hewitt-Thompson. At approximately 7.35 p.m. last evening, your husband, Sir Ronald, collided with a carriage on St James Street. He, er, ah – did not survive."

Eunice's hand flew to her mouth, Harriet gasped, and Austin leaned back in the chair in shock. No one uttered a word.

After a moment or two, Eunice looked at the detective. "What happened, Detective?"

If Detective Sergeant Roggin expected tears and two hysterical women, he would have been disappointed. While shocked at the news, both women were relatively composed.

He took a deep breath. "Witnesses have confirmed that your

husband was attempting to cross St James Street when he stumbled and fell beneath a swiftly moving carriage. Unfortunately, it was unable to stop in time."

Austin leaned forward. "He stumbled?"

"There is an account where a witness saw Sir Ronald distracted by a beggar, a lad, before falling. They were tussling."

Austin made eye contact with Harriet.

"Has the body been identified … is it Ronald?" Eunice asked.

The detective nodded. "His identity has been confirmed, Ma'am."

"Dear God," she managed.

Harriet reached out and held her mother close.

"Do you believe there are suspicious circumstances around his death?" Austin asked.

"Captain Willems, I'm unable to discuss any particulars around an ongoing investigation. It's standard procedure, sir, and I'm sure you understand."

Austin completely understood. Ronald Hewitt-Thompson was murdered.

The detective maintained eye contact with him but didn't elaborate further.

Eunice sat straighter and looked at the detective. "I'm sure you will forgive me, Detective Sergeant, but my husband and I have not been close of late, and we have had our share of disagreements…"

"He was a brute, Detective," Harriet suddenly interjected.

"Harriet!" warned her mother.

"No, Mama, I will not be silent, and he needs to know. Detective Sergeant Roggin, my stepfather, was a violent and despicable man who beat Mama around the head with his fists. You will understand if we do not weep for his loss."

Austin watched as Harriet turned to Eunice, offering comfort as her mother succumbed to a flood of tears.

Detective Sergeant Roggin coughed. "I er understand, thank you for sharing." He turned to Austin before standing and facing Eunice. "I really must be leaving. Mrs Hewitt-Thompson, I'm sure you have arrangements to make, and er, your husband's body is in the care of the morgue. Please accept my sincerest condolences."

"Thank you, Detective," Eunice offered behind her handkerchief.

"Let me show you to the door," Austin offered.

On the doorstep, Detective Sergeant Roggin lowered his voice. "Mr Willems, I think we need to have a wee chat. I believe Ronald Hewitt-Thompson was murdered, and you may be next. We may have our differences, sir, but I need you to be forthcoming, not just for your safety but for the protection of Miss Stephenson and God knows who else. Do I make myself clear, sir?"

The detective's message was perfectly clear, and Austin knew he spoke common sense. He looked out, past the detective and into The Regents Park. "Tomorrow, 1.00 p.m., if that time is convenient."

Detective Sergeant Roggin turned and looked over the park and pointed. "By that seat, 1.00 p.m., sir."

Eunice quickly decided that she needed to make funeral arrangements and see to the affairs of her late husband. Temporarily moving back to her old home in Mayfair, where Ronald had been living, seemed the most straightforward and logical thing to do.

Harriet wasn't thrilled about moving from Austin's home, but she needed to be supportive and be near her mother until she adjusted to her new life. Austin's home was a hive of activity as cases were packed, and a carriage was called to take them the short one-mile drive to Upper Brook Street in Mayfair.

Three hours after the detective departed, Eunice stepped into the carriage as Harriet hugged Austin before leaving.

"You do not need an invitation, Austin. Please come whenever you can." To his surprise, she kissed him on the lips. "Neighbours be damned," she winked and stepped into the carriage.

"You did well," complimented Sir Felix to *Le Taureau.*

The splash of three ducks landing on St James Lake accented the rare accolade afforded to the assassin.

In acknowledgement, *Le Taureau* inclined his head but said nothing as his employer adjusted his tie and ensured his coat sat as it should. *Vanity will be your undoing*, thought the Frenchman. He waited patiently for Sir Felix to continue and touch on the subject of this unscheduled meeting.

Sir Felix gave his polished shoes a quick rub on the back of his trousers before speaking again. "That leaves one more, and your work is done. However, I want you to take your time and plan carefully so you can complete your final task in a week or two."

"What? *Monsieur*, I cannot do this. I have expenses and costs, waiting is a luxury I can ill afford." He tore his gaze from the lake and focused on the man beside him. "Why the delay, perhaps you should tell me this, *non?*"

"I find St James Lake tranquil this time of year, don't you, *Le Taureau?*" He didn't wait for an answer and continued. "A sense of well-being promotes clarity of thought, and we all should make informed decisions with complete lucidity, especially when other people's lives are at stake."

"You have second thoughts. Do you wish to cancel our agreement?" *Le Taureau* shook his head vigorously. "I am unable to return your money. *Non*, it is not possible."

Sir Felix maintained his stern expression. "Things have changed, and I've been instructed to wait until–"

"–Wait? Wait for what?" interrupted *Le Taureau,* who was becoming agitated.

The tone of Sir Felix's voice changed. "You *will* wait for further instructions – is that understood, Mr Taureau?" He reached into his coat pocket and extracted a rolled wad of bank notes. "This should be ample to cover your expenses, and while you wait, I suggest you learn more about Captain Austin Willems's habits. Just ensure you are not identified or seen. Be discrete, eh."

Le Taureau took the proffered notes and studied them before folding them away. "Well, er... this helps, *monsieur,* but it would be useful to know why you insist on a delay."

If Sir Felix had known the reason, he might have told *Le Taureau;* however, he was entirely in the dark and did not know why Fin wanted him to wait. "All in good time, all in good time," he smoothly reassured with measured and practised authority.

Le Taureau knew then that Sir Felix didn't know. "I will do as you ask as long as I am compensated." He stood, looked at Sir Felix like he would say something more, changed his mind and strode away.

An errant ball landed near his feet, and Austin kicked it back towards the three boys under the supervision of a nanny playing a short distance away. He returned to his seat in The Regents Park and enjoyed the sunshine while waiting for Detective Sergeant Roggin.

Harriet and her mother, Eunice, had departed late yesterday afternoon to attend to the affairs of the late Sir Ronald Hewitt-Thompson, and he felt lost. He missed her already and had spent the evening moping around the house, thinking of nothing else but her.

A couple, arm in arm, walked past, and he envied their closeness. Her escort leaned down and whispered into her ear, and he imagined her blushing. It brought a smile to his face, and he longed to hear

Harriet laugh and feel the softness of her skin beneath his touch. He exhaled loudly as Detective Sergeant Roggin sat down beside him.

"Am I that much of a bother, Captain Willems?"

"No, no, my mind was elsewhere, it wasn't intended at you."

Austin watched the amorous couple wander away, and the detective saw where the captain's attention was focused. "Matters of the heart?"

"Are you married, Mr Roggin?"

"Er, no. I've not been fortunate to find a woman who'd be content to marry a policeman, sir."

Austin laughed. "Is that the excuse you tell yourself, or just others?"

"What do you mean?"

"I don't think that genuine love cares about the profession of a partner."

The detective removed his hat and patted his hair with a hand. "If love is the criteria, Captain."

"Then you seek a faithful woman who can cook and clean and be a good mother to your children?"

"Yes, of course. Why wouldn't I?"

Austin turned to the young detective. "Then I wish you well."

"Thank you."

Austin knew the detective had no understanding of love and probably had never experienced the tide of varied emotions brought upon by such a powerful gift. "How can I assist you, Detective Sergeant Roggin?"

"Captain Willems, I have been instructed to open a murder investigation into the death of Ronald Hewitt-Thompson."

Austin didn't react, as the detective had said as much yesterday.

"I believe that the death of Miles Siles, Julian De Vore, Ronald Hewitt-Thompson and the shooting of Howard Willoughby are related. What I find most peculiar is that you have a connection to each one of these men. At this time, I don't believe you are behind their deaths, but you do know a lot more than you have divulged to me." He paused and held eye contact with Austin. "Who is next, Captain? Miss Stephenson, her mother, your housekeeper?"

Austin remained tight-lipped.

"Who will be the next victim in this madness?"

Austin watched another couple pass by pushing a perambulator. They looked so happy and content. He shook his head. "If there is going to be another death, then I believe it will be me, Detective. The shooting of Howard Willoughby was an error – I was the intended target."

"And so you have said. But tell me, Captain, are you closer to discovering who is orchestrating these murders? I surmise you haven't, and that is why I asked to speak with you today." The detective knew he had the captain's attention and continued. "My superiors are unaware I am speaking to you about this and asking for your help. I know you were involved in some dubious activities involving the directors of Grand Overland Rail, although I am not concerned about them at present, but I need to put an end to these killings."

Austin remained reserved.

"Have you nothing to say?"

After a dozen heartbeats, Austin responded. "Detective, I don't have any notion as to who is behind these killings, and I've tried to look at this from every conceivable angle, but I don't know where to begin."

"But you've enquired and sought answers... what have you learned?"

"That it wasn't that brute, Sir Ronald."

This time, the detective remained quiet.

Austin took another deep breath and exhaled loudly. "I believe London Private Acquisitions are somehow involved."

"Who are they?" asked the detective as he half twisted on the seat to better see Austin.

"I'm still uncertain, but I believe London Private Acquisitions is a private company who, in tandem with Grand Overland Rail, have successfully and repeatedly schemed to bilk Grand Overland Rail shareholders of a fortune."

The detective's eyebrows furrowed in puzzlement.

"Four directors of Grand Overland Rail, in addition to one other, whose identity eludes me, are also the principals of London Private Acquisitions, and they purchase assets and on-sell them at an exorbitant profit to Overland and keep the difference."

"One other?"

"Yes, a fifth director who is unknown. And I believe that his anonymity is deliberate."

Detective Sergeant Roggin's eyes hardened. "And how do their activities equate to murder?"

"That's because I seem to have caused them a spot of bother."

CHAPTER FORTY

The day began with good news. Howard's condition finally turned, and he was now recovering. The doctors had beaten the infection, and Austin decided to hire a nurse and have Howard convalesce from home. Nanny became quite distressed and insisted that only she could accommodate Howard's needs while he recovered. She said, "A hired nurse is nothing more than a waste of money when I can do the job myself." It wasn't negotiable, and arrangements were made for Howard to relocate from the hospital, and to keep the peace, Austin informed her the nurse s wasn't required.

Nanny was in a tither and, like a seasoned General, took charge and began preparations for Howard's arrival. Austin wasn't allowed to interfere and, to avoid conflict, looked for an excuse to leave the house. It didn't take him long.

The letter from Walker, Wakefield and Willoughby, Barristers and Solicitors arrived by messenger, and Austin curiously tore open the envelope to read. The sender was Simon Walker, whom he and Harriet had visited only days ago.

> *Walker, Wakefield and Willoughby,*
> *Barristers and Solicitors*
> *14 Essex Street,*
> *Temple, London.*

My Dear Austin,

I hope this letter leaves you in healthy spirits, for a rather good turn of fortune brings about these tidings. You asked for my assistance to inquire on your behalf and locate an individual named Cecil W. Bishop. Mr Bishop wasn't difficult to identify as he has a distinguished and senior position within the government here in London.

Previously, he was employed by the Her Majesty's Railways Inspectorate and now recently promoted to the capacity of a senior manager within the inspectorate's governing body, The Board of Trade at Downing Street. According to my source, Mr Bishop reports to The Permanent Under-Secretary of State of the Home Office, Sir Felix Dampierre. I wish you well in your endeavours.

I hope Howard has a full and speedy recovery, and please pass on my thoughts and best wishes if you can converse with him.

With the highest regard,
Simon Walker

It was turning out to be a splendid day, and Austin decided he'd take the opportunity to leave Nanny to her devices and visit The Board of Trade on an exploratory, information-gathering exercise to learn more about Mr Cecil W. Bishop and his master, The Permanent Under-Secretary of State of the Home Office.

As he was apt to do, Austin stood against the window with his chin cradled in his hand, staring out over The Regents Park. Couples strolled, children played, a lone man sat on a park bench reading a newspaper, and people, happy to be outside enjoying a glorious day, ambled by. Austin ignored them, thinking about Cecil Bishop and Sir Felix Dampierre and how he could learn more about them. He had nothing, no information or anything to help with his enquiries. *But his name... Felix Dampierre... it was familiar.*

He ensured he was suitably attired and caught a cab for 1 Downing Street, just off Whitehall, where The Board of Trade had their offices.

His visit turned out to be almost a complete waste of time. All he confirmed was that Mr Bishop was a senior manager, and his superior was Sir Felix, as Simon Walker had already detailed. He was none the wiser and in a quandary. He had no connections to anyone who could provide him with an introduction to either of these men nor did he have any legitimate business interests that could facilitate a meeting.

Feeling a little disillusioned, he went to Covent Gardens to see Ollie and have him inquire into the Watson brothers.

Ollie wasn't available until late afternoon, and Austin left a note with instructions and returned home feeling disappointed.

Howard was lying in bed and tended by Nanny. When he entered the guest room, she was seated beside his bed, spoon-feeding him soup.

Howard looked emaciated, pale and frail. He'd been through quite an ordeal, and for a moment, Austin felt overwhelmed by guilt. The bullet that almost killed his trusted and dear friend was meant for him.

Howard managed a weak smile, and Austin sat on the edge of the bed and grasped his hand. "Your condition brings me cheer, Howard, and it is good to see you well on the road to recovery."

Nanny wiped Howard's mouth.

"Is good to be here," he croaked. "Lizzy is taking good care of me."

Lizzy? Austin smiled at the familiar use of her given name, Elizabeth. "Of course she is, and you'll be up and about in no time, eh."

Austin saw her cheeks redden as he stood.

"He's tired, sir, and needs rest," Nanny advised.

"I'll come visit you this evening, Howard." He didn't wait for a reply and quietly returned downstairs to lean against the window and look out over the park while he thought. It was late afternoon, and fewer people were about. But the man with the newspaper was still there. Austin felt his heart rate increase. The man with the paper was spying on him.

He pulled himself away from the window and felt his anger rise. Originally, Julian De Vore had sent Miles Siles to follow him, but De Vore and Siles were both dead. When Howard had been shot, he believed Ronald Hewitt-Thompson had been behind it, but he had been killed under suspicious circumstances. *Who sent this man to watch him, and why?*

He changed clothes and left the house through the rear entrance, just as he'd done when he first confronted Major Siles. He walked down the lane, turned into the park and approached the man with the newspaper from behind where he couldn't be seen. This late in the afternoon, most people had returned indoors, and this suited him perfectly as the park was mostly deserted. The stranger was unaware that Austin stealthily advanced towards him.

Did he carry a weapon, a knife or a gun? Did he have an associate nearby? At the last moment, with increasing concern and doubt, Austin turned away from the stranger to survey his surroundings.

With Miles, he'd been rash and attacked the man without ensuring it was safe. He'd been driven by emotions and could easily have been killed because he'd not made sure it was safe to confront him, and now, he'd almost foolishly done the same.

The stranger was unaware that Austin was stalking him and continued to keep a watchful eye on Austin's home. Meanwhile, Austin walked in a large circle and kept his eyes open for others who may be loitering in the lengthening late afternoon shadows.

Feeling more confident, he approached the stranger a second time and silently walked directly up to the seated man to stand behind him. Before the man could respond, Austin's left arm encircled the man's neck, and he pulled hard, choking him.

In desperation, hands clawed at his arms, and the man squirmed, trying to break the death grip around his throat. Austin held fast as the man's panicked struggle intensified. It was a losing battle, and he felt the man's strength ebb.

After a moment or two, Austin released the pressure and allowed the man to breathe. Understanding that he was beaten, the man gave up resisting but still hopelessly held on to Austin's arm.

"Why are you here watching the house?" Austin asked. So far, the stranger had not seen his face and had no idea who his assailant was.

The man chose not to respond.

"I asked you a question." He felt the stranger tense and knew it was in preparation for a counterattack. Austin pulled his right arm back, then powered his elbow forward into the side of the man's head. He groaned and briefly went limp. Only seconds passed before he felt the man stir.

"I'll ask you again, why are you watching that house?" Austin relaxed his hold on the man's neck to allow him to swallow and speak.

"Don't know why," he grunted, struggling to suck air into his lungs. "Am just here – to watch and follow the toff – who lives there, that's all," wheezed the man.

"Why?" repeated Austin.

"Told ya, I don't bleedin' know."

"Who do you work for? Who paid you?"

The man didn't respond, and Austin drew his arm back to deliver another jarring blow to the side of the man's head.

"No, no, wait." The man swallowed again. "*Le Taureau,* he paid me.

Le Taureau? The bull? "Is that his name?"

"T'is what he wants to be called," replied the man. "Don't know 'im by any other name."

"How do you contact this bull chap?" Austin asked and applied more pressure to the man's neck.

"He'll bloody kill me," he croaked.

"So will I if you don't start talking." He eased his arm a little.

"It's arranged, a'fore hand, and always somewhere different."

Austin thought quickly. He needed the help of this man. Without him, he couldn't identify this *Le Taureau* fellow. "When and where will you meet next?"

"You ain't a mutton-shunter, who the bloody hell are ya?"

Austin tightened his arm.

His response was quick. "Two days from now, at 8.00p.m.."

"And where?"

"Saint Anne's church in Soho. I can hardly breathe, mister, can you take yer bloody arm away? Promise not to do a runner," the man appealed.

"What's your name and where do you live?"

"Look, mister, I told yer enough, do with me what you want or let me go."

The man was regaining his confidence, and Austin pulled his arm back.

"For Christ's sake… upstairs at 10 St Martin's Lane in Covent Garden."

"Your name?"

"Floyd Harris."

Austin knew St Martin's Lane wasn't far from Ollie's Lamb and Flag public house. It gave him an idea. "Where do you do your drinking, Mr Harris?" Austin asked in a more conciliatory tone.

"What?"

"What alehouse do you drink at when you're at home?"

"What sort of–"

Austin applied more pressure to Floyd's neck.

He coughed and began struggling but was no match for Austin's strength and superior position standing behind. "The Lamb and Flag," he sputtered.

Austin had so many questions and had no idea if the man spoke truthfully. He could walk away, and Floyd Harris would be none the wiser who had assaulted him, or… the other option had more appeal but had risk associated with it. He thought quickly as he decided his best course of action.

"If I release you, I want your word that you won't run. If you run, I'll catch you easily because you don't look like the sort of man who runs often."

The man began nodding his head despite having Austin's arm around his neck.

"Do you promise not to run?"

"Aye, I promise,' wheezed Floyd.

Austin withdrew his arm, nimbly stepped around the bench seat, and stood before the stranger, who began rubbing and turning his head to restore circulation to his neck. He looked up with a scowl.

"You!" he exclaimed and began coughing. "Captain Willems," he managed to croak when the hacking fit subsided.

Austin had his fists clenched and was ready to leap onto the man if he as much made any sudden moves. "Empty your pockets."

The man looked unremarkable. He was slightly overweight, approximately in his late thirties, and his well-worn clothes were clean—no wonder he'd easily fit into the neighbourhood without arousing any suspicion.

He carried no real weapons except a sand-filled leather sap, a few coins and nothing else. Austin pocketed the sap. "Now, I think after such an exciting afternoon, we should go and have an ale together, what say you, Mr Harris?"

Floyd looked at Austin like he was a madman.

"Come now, we're off to Covent Garden."

Floyd Harris eased himself to his feet while still rubbing his neck. "Don't tell me, we're goin' t' the Lamb and Flag."

"Indeed we are, Mr Harris. I worked up quite a thirst, and I'm sure you are parched as well, eh?"

The Hansom cab dropped them near the intersection of St Martin's Lane and Garrick Street, a short walk to the Lamb and Flag. As expected, Austin saw Ollie's lads loitering in groups of four from various strategic locations. He saw Cat and Lenny amongst them, and Lenny gave him a subtle nod and ran ahead, ostensibly to alert Ollie of his arrival with a stranger, thought Austin.

When they entered the alehouse, Austin and Floyd were immediately guided upstairs. Lenny opened the door, and Austin gave Floyd a gentle shove when he paused.

"Oh my, look what we have here, if it isn't Floyd, 'th' Griff', Harris." Ollie looked at Austin in question but held his tongue. He knew Austin would explain.

Floyd remained silent and stared at his feet.

"Griff?" questioned Austin.

"Mr Harris fancies his self as a bit of a grifter[17]. Been nicked a few times, but now he knows better. Ain't that right, Floyd?" said Ollie.

Floyd grunted.

"This calls for an ale, Ollie, including one for Mr Harris, who is probably quite thirsty, and then I'll fill you in on what I know and why I brought him here," Austin said and waved an arm, indicating Floyd should be seated.

---

17   *Grifter – The perpetrator of a confidence trick, with a grifter being more of an opportunist than a conman.*

CHAPTER FORTY-ONE

St Anne's Church in Soho was surrounded by residential buildings and streets on all four sides. Austin admitted it was a clever place to meet because if anything went wrong, the man who called himself *Le Taureau* or The Bull could escape through any of the tenements, then onto a street and disappear.

Ollie expressed his concern after they took a cab to reconnoitre the area. The church had trees and a well-tended garden where *Le Taureau* could conduct his clandestine meeting in privacy and, when finished, vanish into the shadows.

"Then how do we capture the man?" Austin asked in frustration.

"Five lads on each street might do it, Cap'n, but I'd need 'bout twenty lads. What happens if he goes into a building and doesn't come out? We can't search each bleedin' flat, can we."

Ollie echoed Austin's sentiments. That sat morosely back at the Lamb and Flag nursing an ale. Earlier, they'd allowed Floyd Harris to return home after some direct threats not to speak to anyone about their chat. Ollie had a couple of lads escort Floyd home and then have them watch him to ensure he kept his word.

"I think this Bull fellow is cunning, Ollie, and I need to be careful," remarked Austin. "I can't let him slip away because I won't get another chance."

Ollie looked at his friend over the rim of his glass and said nothing.

"Even if I had thirty people surrounding the church, they would arouse suspicion."

"But two lads on each street would go unnoticed..." Ollie suggested.

"Then what? If the Bull pops out onto a street, what do we do? We can't contain him with your lads, and if he takes a cab, we can't follow. I think we have to take him inside the church grounds."

"Then we'll need suitable men," suggested Ollie.

"Along with me, we'll need at least three trustworthy, agile men. If the need calls for it, solid chaps who aren't afraid to mix it up and can hold their own in a scrap. Could you get such men, Ollie?"

Ollie wiped his mouth with the back of his hand and nodded. "And we'll need a swift carriage; a single carriage on the street ain't gonna attract attention."

Austin looked thoughtful. "We will need to take precautions, Ollie. My instincts tell me this *Le Taureau* is a clever fellow and could be dangerous, so we must out-think him. If we do grab him, can we bring him back here?"

"Right here will do, Cap'n," Ollie grinned. "St Anne's can't be more than half a bleedin' mile away from the Lamb and Flag. No one here gives a toss what we do."

Austin leaned back in his chair. "Sergeant Oliver Nagle, I do believe we have the makings of a plan."

Ollie refilled both of their glasses. "Tomorrow evening!" He raised his beer in a toast.

"Tomorrow evening," repeated Austin as their glasses clinked.

Austin had just finished breakfast and was thinking about this evening's mission to confront *Le Taureau* when Nanny entered the dining room.

"Detective Sergeant Roggin is here to see you, sir."

Austin looked puzzled, "Er, show him in, Nanny."

Moments later, the detective and a constable entered the room. Austin wiped his mouth and hands on a serviette. "Good Morning, Detective Sergeant Roggin, and how may I avail myself to you this dreary morn?"

"Captain Willems, I'd like you to accompany us to the police station to answer some questions."

Austin noticed the detective was being particularly formal. *Something is up*, he thought. "Am I being arrested?"

The detective took a step closer, followed by the constable. "Not yet." Roggin raised an arm, "If you please, sir."

"Allow me to retrieve my coat and hat, Detective." Austin's head spun. *Why was he bringing him in for formal questioning?* Being interviewed at the police station was somewhat serious, and if they decided to arrest and charge him with a crime, then, amongst other things, this evening's escapade at St Anne's church wouldn't happen.

The constable followed him. "If I don't return by early afternoon, tell Howard, he'll know who to contact," he instructed Nanny after she handed him his hat and coat. She looked concerned as he was led from home to the waiting wagon.

Detective Sergeant Roggin and the constable were uncommunicative and wouldn't answer any questions during their journey to the Bow Street Police Station. On arrival, the constable escorted Austin to a sparsely furnished interview room with bars over the window, and he was told to sit on one of the three chairs at a table while the constable stood guard at the door.

Almost thirty minutes later, Roggin returned, along with another constable carrying a sheath of papers in multiple folders and sat at the table facing Austin.

With absolute formality, the detective began questioning him and confirmed his identity, address, occupation and a host of other insignificant details while the constable transcribed his answers. Eventually, the questions became specific. Roggin wanted to know about his relationship with the directors of Grand Overland Rail, where he was the evening the sailboat *Belusha* caught fire and whether he had been down to the Tower Bridge Moorings at any time recently.

After an hour of questioning, the door to the interrogation room opened, and another man, in full uniform of a senior officer silently entered. The constable at the door straightened his posture and Detective Sergeant Roggin lost some of his confidence, Austin observed. The officer remained standing, leaned against the wall with his arms folded and silently assessed them.

The questions changed, and Roggin wanted to know about the art robbery at Finch and Gossett's warehouse and Sir Ronald Hewitt-Thompson. Oddly, the detective had asked him all these questions at previous interviews at his home, and now he was asking them again as if for the first time. For Austin, the temptation was to act indignant and be cocky, but a sixth sense warned him to be polite, helpful and respectful.

After another hour, Detective Sergeant Roggin seemed to have run out of questions when the superior officer leaning against the wall straightened and stepped closer.

"For what purpose did you communicate and reveal to Mrs Pearl

Dillington of her husband's lurid pastimes and the identity of his mistress, Mr Willems?"

Austin looked down at his hands rather than make eye contact and appear insolent. After a few heartbeats, he looked up to face the unknown officer. "I'm sorry, sir, I believe we are unacquainted. To whom am I speaking? I am Captain Austin Willems, previously of the 67th South Hampshire Regiment of Foot, and you are?"

The officer was unsure if his suspect was just being polite or audacious. Determining that the young military officer had not demonstrated hostility and had been courteous throughout the interview, he replied accordingly. "I know who you are, but forgive me, Captain Willems, I am Chief Detective Inspector Bird."

Austin nodded in acknowledgement. "I have never had the pleasure of meeting Mrs Pearl Dillington, nor have I ever stepped upon her doorstep or into her home, sir."

"That isn't what I asked, Captain," the Chief Detective replied with an edge, "I asked, and let me be quite plain and repeat – Why did you communicate and reveal to Mrs Pearl Dillington about her husband's lurid pastimes and details about his mistress?"

"You must excuse me, Chief Detective Inspector Bird, I am unaware of what you are referring to." Austin shrugged. "But to answer your question, no, I have never communicated in any form to Mrs Dillington." Austin couldn't help himself and responded to the question with one of his own. "But is communicating to her or anyone a crime?"

Detective Sergeant Roggin's superior took another step closer. "Could be, Captain, especially if the intent is to extort or commit blackmail."

Austin maintained eye contact with Chief Detective Inspector Bird and said nothing more. After all, he hadn't lied. On his precise instructions, Ollie had drafted the letter and sent it by messenger to

Mrs Dillington.

After a moment or two, the chief returned to the door and exited, leaving the door ajar. The guard followed after him.

Detective Sergeant Roggin slid his chair back and stood. "That will be all, Captain Willems, thank you for your time."

The constable gathered all his notes and left the room, leaving the two men alone.

"What was all that about, Detective Sergeant Roggin? I previously answered all your questions at home, and then you drag me here to be interrogated like a blaggard. For what reason?"

Roggin's eyes darted to the open door, and he lowered his voice. "Because, Captain, Chief Detective Inspector Bird realised that I had not formally interviewed the prime suspect in a host of crimes and insisted I do so."

The explanation made sense to Austin, and he now understood. "I see."

"But I'm still convinced you're not entirely innocent in all this, are you?"

Austin looked away.

They were silent a moment before the Detective spoke. "Er, have you learned anything more?"

Austin looked back at the young man and even felt sympathy for him. His superior was meticulous, and his lack of faith in the young detective was telling. "Perhaps, Detective Sergeant Roggin, I will contact you when I learn more. Am I free to go?"

"Yes, I apologise for appearing so brusque this morning, but it is quite likely the constable who came with me will report back to Chief Detective Inspector Bird on my performance."

Austin patted the young detective on the shoulder and walked from the room.

By nature, *Le Taureau* was a cautious man, and he'd remained alive all these years because he was vigilant, didn't take unnecessary risks and never stayed in one place too long. However, this job was pushing the boundaries of his comfort zone. He should have already gone, departed English shores, and returned to Europe to enjoy the spoils of another successful mission. Against his better judgement, he'd agreed to his client's demand to delay the final task, where in the past, he wouldn't have even entertained the idea of waiting. It was absurd, but the financial reward had been the deciding factor, and greed had overcome common sense and habitual caution.

Darkness had descended over London, and *Le Taureau* waited near the southeast corner of one of the surrounding streets that encircled St Anne's church, hoping to see the lone figure of *Monsieur* Harris walking towards him. He'd already been to the church, checked the doors and walked around the grounds, ensuring no surprises lurked in any doorways or sprung from behind a bush. Deciding it was safe to continue, he positioned himself near the corner of Dean Street and Shaftsbury Avenue, where he could observe anyone approaching from the direction of *Monsieur* Harris's residence.

Le Taureau took nothing for granted, and his head swivelled constantly for anything that seemed untoward or broke the natural rhythm of street life. People hurried past, and a cab clip-clopped down the street, everything was as it should be.

Ahead, he could make out the dim outline of a solitary man strolling along the street. *Le Taureau* melded into the darkness and waited. Eventually, the man passed him, crossed the road and headed towards the church grounds. Assured Floyd wasn't being followed, he walked down a bordering street, crossed over and entered a tenement building, walked through and appeared near the entrance to St Anne's, ssurprising Floyd Harris with his silent appearance.

"Oh, you gave me a start," exclaimed Floyd as he brought a hand to his chest. The Bull slowly walked around Floyd, who seemed more nervous than in past visits.

"Is something wrong? asked *Le Taureau* as he paused before Floyd.

"All is well," remarked Floyd.

Le Taureau could see that Floyd's eyes darted everywhere. He hadn't been like that during other meetings. The Bull wanted to leave. "What information do you have for me? Quickly."

Suddenly, the two stout wooden doors to St Anne's Church crashed open and slammed into the wall. Before *Le Taureau* could react, four men ran from inside the church. *Police*, he thought in growing alarm. He wanted to run but wasn't fleet of foot, and the men who quickly approached were young and quick. He kept his hands in his pockets and waited, he hadn't committed a crime, and there was no law to say he couldn't meet a friend inside the church grounds.

A bag was thrown over his head, and he was led to a wagon and placed inside. Within seconds, the wagon headed off. Not a word had been spoken which seemed most peculiar, and for the first time, he felt the inklings of fear. *Le Taureau* knew these men were not the police.

CHAPTER FORTY-TWO

The pillowcase was removed from his head, and *Le Taureau* sat blinking in the private upstairs room of the Lamb and Flag public house. Austin and Ollie watched as the man they knew to be *Le Taureau* adjusted to being held captive in the unfamiliar surroundings.

"Why am I here?" he began. "Why have you done this to me?" he asked whilst looking around the room and testing the bindings that secured his wrists, his inquisitive gaze stopped at the faces of the two men before him.

Austin studied the man carefully. He was unremarkable in every way and could have been a teacher, clerk, or merchant and looked far from being a killer. Even now, the man's demeanour appeared to be of surprise and indignation at being kidnapped but fearful he wasn't. That in itself was telling.

"I must apologise for whisking you away with a hood over your head without even a word of explanation," began Austin. "And if there has been an error, we will release you immediately." He smiled warmly. "It would be most impolite to chat with you without knowing your name?"

"I am outraged, and this is most improper, please untie my hands… I have done no wrong and committed no crime," he appealed.

To Austin's way of thinking, the man sounded quite convincing. "Your name?"

"Er, Louis, Louis Bardin." Again, *Le Taureau* looked from Austin to Ollie with puzzlement. "And you are?"

"Forgive me for my rudeness, Mr Bardin. I am John, and my associate is James."

Le Taureau laughed, and Austin saw behind the façade. It was the eyes – dark, deep wells of malevolence and deviousness.

"Of course, they are not your names," replied their captive.

"Mr Bardin, why did you seek a meeting this evening with Floyd Harris? Or rather, if I could be so forward as it would save both of us considerable time, who is your employer?"

Le Taureau managed to look aggrieved. "You must have me mistaken for someone else," he shrugged. "Untie me, release me, let me go, and we can put this unpleasantness behind us, *monsieur.*"

Austin made eye contact with Ollie. They'd expected this. "Why was Sir Ronald Hewitt-Thompson killed?"

Again, for the briefest of instances, the eyes gave him away. "I do not know this man, I did not kill him. Please, you have me confused for another person."

Austin pressed on and gave *Le Taureau* no time to think. "Perhaps you can explain how you had Julian De Vore killed."

"Wha, what is this? How dare you–"

"Tell me about Captain Austin Willems," Austin interrupted.

It was a bit much for *Le Taureau,* and he lowered his head to look down at the floor and not respond.

Ollie shook his head. He wasn't happy with the progress they were making.

Austin tried a more direct approach, *"Monsieur Le Taureau,* either answer my questions or suffer the unpleasantness of what's to come. I can inform the constabulary that we have you here, or as my friend would prefer, we can resort to more unconventional methods to persuade you to talk."

Using his preferred professional name, *Le Taureau's* expression hardened, and he looked up at Austin. "You will not go to the police because that would implicate you in a kidnapping." He laughed, "You can hurt me if you so choose, but regardless, I will not talk to you or anyone. *Non, non*, this will not happen."

"Very well. James, outside."

Ollie rose from his seat and clomped to the door.

"You can't escape. Remain where you are; don't move," Austin glared at the man and turned to follow Ollie to the only door in the room.

"I can beat it out of 'im, Cap'n. Give me a little time, and he'll be squealing real quick," Ollie stated once they could talk without being overheard on the landing by the stairs.

"I'm tempted, Ollie. My problem is that once we have the information I need, he should be turned over to the police and face justice for murder. If we beat him badly, then we face the risk of being charged ourselves."

Ollie looked disappointed, "What do you suggest, Cap'n?"

Austin took a deep breath. "That I have a quiet word with my favourite policeman, Detective Sergeant Roggin and let him interrogate *Le Taureau.*"

"And you trust Roggin?" Ollie looked unhappy.

"I'd insist that he share with me all he learns. Once *Le Taureau* talks, then it is assured that he will be charged and suffer for his crimes."

Ollie sighed. "And what about kidnapping?"

"Kidnapping? Ollie, the man is here of his own free will," smirked Austin.

Ollie grinned. "You knows best, Cap'n. But I can have 'im singing in no time at all."

Austin laughed and clapped his friend on the back. "I'll spend the night here with *Le Taureau,* and in the morning, I will see the detective."

Austin's appearance at the Bow Street Police Station caused Detective Sergeant Roggin to smile. "It is a pleasure to see you here, Captain Willems, are you here to confess?"

"If I was so inclined to confess, then I would seek a priest, but as I'm not Catholic, then that is most unlikely Detective."

The detective laughed, and to Austin, he seemed more likeable. "May we talk in private, Detective Sergeant Roggin?"

"One of the interview rooms is available."

"And risk your superior walking in, no, I don't believe that would be acceptable," Austin smirked.

"Perhaps we should go for a stroll outside?"

There wasn't anywhere pleasant to walk near the police station, but privacy mattered, and there wasn't any other option other than to walk on the street, Austin nodded.

"I presume you have a development, some information to share?" asked the detective once they were away from the station.

Austin didn't answer the question. "Are you having any success in identifying who murdered Ronald Hewitt-Thompson and Julian De Vore or who shot Howard Willoughby?"

"Now you sound like Chief Detective Inspector Bird. Unfortunately, we've had no luck, Captain. We have nothing to go on. According to Chief Detective Inspector Bird, you are the closest we have to a legitimate suspect."

He ignored the long, hard look the detective gave him. After half a dozen steps, Austin paused and faced the young detective. "If I could find you a *real* suspect, Detective Sergeant Roggin, would you be willing to share with me what you learned during interrogation?"

"We do not interrogate, Captain, but we do question with, er, some persistence," replied the detective. "However, as it would be doubtful you would take the law into your own hands to investigate those murders, then I find it a preposterous notion that you could ever locate a real suspect."

"Of course, Detective. But if you happened upon such a suspect in the course of your duties, then would you share any and all information with me?" Austin clarified.

"No, that would be deemed highly improper. Although, from time to time, copies of interview transcriptions have been misplaced," Detective Sergeant Roggin tut-tutted.

Austin turned and began walking back to the station, the detective fell into step beside him, and they returned without speaking. Once outside the station, Austin stepped closer to the detective and lowered his voice. "If I were a detective, such as yourself, I'd be very curious about two men, Mr Cecil W. Bishop and his superior, Sir Felix Dampierre, the Permanent Under-Secretary of State of the Home Office." I'm sure with some persuasion, an actual suspect in a murder investigation could reveal valuable information about them."

"The under-secretary...?" mumbled the detective. He pulled a small notebook and pencil from his pocket and began writing.

"Mr Floyd Harris, who lives at 10 St Martin's Lane, in Covent Garden, was watching my house and spying on me, Detective. I'd recommend you speak to him as he will reveal how he was employed by a gentleman who calls himself *Le Taureau*. The Bull. I believe he will be quite useful to you with your inquiries."

"London is a big city, and finding such a man could be difficult."

"You will find Mr Harris quite accommodating, Detective, and he is expecting a visit from you."

Detective Sergeant Roggin's mouth opened as he furiously wrote.

Austin waited for two constables to walk past and chose his words carefully before continuing. "From time to time, I'm told, *real* suspects in murder investigations have been known to make an appearance at the upstairs room above the Lamb and Flag public house in Covent Garden. Such a suspect could be a vital link to solving those murders, Detective. I'd guess such a suspect may be called *Le Taureau,* and like most professional criminals, they probably have an aversion to talking and require considerable encouragement to be forthcoming. Wouldn't it be a turn of good fortune if two policemen were to arrive at the Lamb and Flag, er, an hour from now. I imagine there wouldn't be any resistance." Austin smiled. "Have a good morning, Detective." Austin hailed a cab and was gone, leaving the detective with his mouth still open.

Everyone of a dubious nature had temporarily departed the Lamb and Flag public house when two policemen entered the establishment. Unusually, no unkind words were said, although a few unsavoury looks were directed at them.

Detective Sergeant Roggin approached the barman, who pointed to a doorway and the stairs beyond which led upstairs. "Don't know why you'd be goin' up top, no one is there," advised the barman with a knowing shake of his head. "Bleed'n Peelers, he muttered as the detective and constable headed towards the stairs.

Austin and Ollie were seated at a table drinking ale when Detective Sergeant Roggin entered and walked past them without even a hint of acknowledgement.

When the detective opened the door to the upstairs room, *Le Taureau* was untied, alone, and sitting on a chair with an empty ale glass before him. Any accusations he made of being kidnapped would have been laughed at, as it was plainly evident to the detective the man was there of his own accord.

Austin watched the detective leave with his prisoner and let out a long sigh.

"Do you think the detective can get *Le Taureau* to talk?"

"I'm sure he will."

The man, who called himself Louis Bardin, was left in an interview room with a guard outside the door while Detective Sergeant Roggin and a constable visited Floyd Harris. The young detective had learned that keeping a suspect waiting for considerable time made interviewing them easier. The longer they waited, the more stressed and anxious they became.

As Captain Willems accurately informed him, Floyd Harris was quite talkative and answered every question put to him. Based on what he'd learned from the interview, he was keen to return to the Bow Street Police Station and begin interviewing Mr Bardin or *Le Taureau.* And if Mr Bardin talked, it would solve more than two murders and one attempted murder, it could uncover a host of crimes leading to the highest offices in government. He'd need to speak to Chief Detective Inspector Bird first.

"How did you come by this information, Detective Sergeant?"

"Captain Willems, sir. He came to me with the name and address of Mr Floyd Harris. I believe Mr Harris was spying on Captain Willems outside his home when apprehended. Mr Harris divulged the name of his employer, Mr Bardin, or *Le Taureau,* who we picked up at an alehouse."

"Have you begun to question Bardin yet?

No sir. I thought I would inform you first, er, as you required, sir."

The Chief Detective Inspector looked thoughtful. "What is your impression of the man?"

"He's a wily one, sir. He claims to be stitched up and demands to be released, but his mannerisms and attitude are not typical of an innocent man."

"Doesn't mean he's guilty, though," added Roggin's superior.

The young detective said nothing.

"Have you had his residence searched?"

"I dispatched two constables, sir."

"Good. I believe your intuition, Detective. Interview him as you deem fit, but if he is not yielding, then call for me, perhaps I can change his mind. Understood?"

"Aye, sir," replied Detective Sergeant Roggin.

The suspect was quite agitated when Detective Sergeant Roggin entered the interview room and immediately demanded to be released. His protestations were somewhat typical, although Roggin felt it was just an act.

Detective Sergeant Roggin began with simple questions designed to make the suspect participate in a conversation, and when asked about his work and income, Mr Bardin became vague. He had answers, but nothing was verifiable. As the interview progressed, Detective Sergeant Roggin believed Captain Willems's assessment of the man. After an hour, the detective had nothing. Mr Bardin had not said anything which could implicate him in any wrongdoing.

The two constables who searched *Le Taureau's* flat returned, and Detective Sergeant Roggin stepped outside the interview room to speak with them.

"Find anything of interest?"

They both shook their heads. "The flat was clean," said one constable. "No guns, nothing to suggest the gentleman was up to no good, sir."

Detective Sergeant Roggin didn't believe them, and there was always something, one insignificant detail the suspect forgot about that didn't make sense that could prove to be useful. He shook his head. "Did you search everything, question the neighbours?"

"As you asked, Detective Sergeant."

"What about his rubbish, did you check through that?"

"One constable nodded. "Nothing, sir."

Detective Sergeant Roggin scratched his head, searching a room that was devoid of clues was in itself suspicious, it meant the room had been sanitised. "Thank you, both." He turned away to re-enter the interview room.

"The only thing we found was a half-completed letter," volunteered the youngest constable. "But it had no relevance and may have been from a previous tenant, so we assumed it wasn't important."

The detective froze and slowly turned back to the constable, "Where is it now?"

The constable shrugged, "Probably where we last saw it, sir. But it won't be of any use it was all scrunched up and likely discarded by a previous occupant. We found it behind the desk. That is why we didn't bring it."

The young detective tightly closed his eyes to control his anger. When again calm, he looked at both men and spoke slowly. "I suggest you return to that address with some haste and bring me that letter immediately. Am I understood, Constables?"

"Yes, sir," they answered in unison.

"And, anything else you believed to be of unimportance that you didn't bring with you."

CHAPTER FORTY-THREE

Austin had just finished dressing in preparation for dining with Harriet and her mother at their home in Mayfair when Nanny handed him a message.

"This just came for you, sir."

"Thank you, Nanny." He looked at the envelope and recognised Ollie's untidy scrawl. He slid a fingernail under the envelope flap and tore it open.

Captain Willems,
You asked me to look into the Watson Brothers for you, and I done as you asked.

One brother is Harrison, he'd be 38 years old, with a wife called Sarah and have three children. They live at 41 Welbeck Street in Marylebone. Harrison manages the Watson Coachbuilding Business.

Brother number two is Jeffery, 40 years old. He is less personable but has the tradecraft skills. From what I was told, he is quite the talented artisan. He was married, but his wife passed away many years ago, leaving him childless and grumpy. He lives in flat 5 at 8 Weymouth Street, also in Marylebone.

This is where it got tricky. Brother number three, Phineas Grosley, 45 years old, plays no outward role in Watson Brothers Coachbuilding or in the lives of his other two brothers, they'd be like strangers. He is a half-brother to Jeffrey and Harrison, but as I learned, he has a big interest in trains. Phineas lives at 1 St James's Street, in St James. He never married. However, his occupation came as a surprise, Phineas Grosley is Governor of the Bank of England.

If you need more, always happy to oblige.

At your service,
Ollie

The letter slipped from his hand to the floor as he eased himself down to sit on the bed. Ollie's message was astonishing. A third brother... Could he be involved with Grand Overland Rail or London Private Acquisitions... the mysterious director, or was it nothing more than an innocent coincidence?

"Already, I have no fondness for the man, Austin. Tell me, what man has an important job and could provide handsomely for his family and never married or had children?" stated Harriet.

Austin had just dined with Harriet and her mother, Eunice, at their home in Mayfair and was having an after-dinner digestif [18] Earlier, he had shown Harriet the letter that Ollie had written.

"Who is this man, Dear?" asked Eunice after pausing from her embroidery and sipping her cream sherry.

"A man Austin has linked to his father's business dealings," she replied.

18   Digestif – an alcoholic beverage taken after a meal to aid in food digestion.

"Perhaps you're familiar with him or know his name?" asked Austin.

Eunice placed her glass back on a side table and looked at Austin. "Phineas Grosley?"

"Yes."

"Yes, what, Mama?" Harriet clarified.

"Of course, he was a frequent guest of Ronald," she added and picked up her embroidery.

Austin sat forward in his chair.

"Here, in Mayfair?" Harriet asked excitedly.

"No, always at Windhaven, but not recently, though, ah, perhaps the last must have been two years ago."

Austin couldn't help himself. "Did you know the reason for his visits?"

"Rail, it was always rail," Eunice replied. "I had no interest, nor was I invited to partake in their lengthy discussion and debates on the finer points of English rail."

Austin could barely contain himself. "Er, what can you tell me about the man, can you recall much about him?"

Eunice put down her embroidery hoop, took another sip of sherry and looked at Austin. "A good question. I never took to him, as I found him peculiar. He behaved oddly at times and was very uncomfortable around people, especially with women. Yet he had an extraordinary gift with numbers and calculations. Something Ronald remarked about countless times." She paused a moment. "I believe he was a banker, a good profession if you find numbers agreeable. But there was something else about him, I can't recall exactly."

Austin and Harriet exchanged glances.

"Continue, Mama," Harriet urged.

"Oh yes, I remember now. His interest in rail. He knew

everything about trains and rail and was an unrivalled authority; it was his passion and a lifelong hobby."

"Anything else?" Harriet asked.

Eunice shrugged. "No, not really. I avoided him because he had poor social skills, and I found him rude and insensitive, so I can't give you more." She returned to her embroidery and intricate stitching.

"Austin? You are thinking, I can see your mind twirling around inside your head."

Austin rose from his seat and walked towards the fire. "Could Phineas Grosley be the mystery person we've been looking for?" He tore his gaze away from the flames and made eye contact with Harriet.

Eunice had retired for the evening, and Austin was at the door saying goodbye to Harriet. "Something your mother said about Phineas Grosley," he began. "I think he might be an acquaintance of loverboy George Dillington. I may pay Mr Dillington an unexpected visit and see how he responds when I ask him about Mr Grosley."

Harriet had her arms around him and looked up into his face. I care not for loverboy George or Mr Grosely, I am more interested in other things, Austin," she whispered into his ear.

Austin pried himself away from her, removed his hat and coat, grasped her hand and led her back into the drawing room.

"Captain Willems, you scoundrel."

The following morning, with nothing to fear, Austin announced himself at the residence of Pearl Dillington and presented a letter of introduction written by Howard Willoughby. A maid escorted him to the parlour, where he waited for George Dillington's wife to attend to him.

It wasn't a long wait before she appeared. Pearl Dillington was a robust woman with round, fleshy cheeks and clear, sparkling eyes that hinted at intelligence and a keen wit. She greeted Austin cordially, but he could see she was understandably puzzled about his visit.

"And how can I assist you, Captain Willems?" she asked after concluding pleasantries.

"Mrs Dillington, I apologise in advance if my visit here causes you any distress. It is not my intention to do so, but I seek only information that may help me."

She nodded, which Austin took as permission to continue.

"My father was a director of Grand Overland Rail for a short time before he passed. His name is Enoch, and you may have heard the name."

"No, I'm not familiar with the name, Captain."

"I'm presently arranging my father's affairs, a complex matter had he been alive, but in his passing, it has proven to be an arduous task at best. I have questions about Grand Overland Rail that your husband can answer, and I seek to speak with him."

Her eyes bored into his. "Who recommended you speak to Mr Dillington, Captain Willems?"

Austin smiled, hoping to appear more personable. "My solicitor, Howard Willoughby, Ma'am. Initially, my questions were to be directed at Sir Ronald, but his untimely passing has made that impossible."

She gave no reaction and Austin could see her thinking. Finally, after an age she responded.

"Captain Willems, Mr Dillington no longer makes his home here."

"I understand. Can you direct me to where I can locate him, Mrs Dillington?"

Again, her face was impassive. *She'd make a great poker player*, he thought.

She sat primly in a chair that wasn't designed for such a substantial woman. Her hands were clasped in her lap, and he couldn't help but notice that a single large breath was all that prevented her ample bosom from being liberated from the confines of her dress.

"Far be it for me to share personal information, Captain Willems, but it is relevant. Mr Dillington is not currently in favour and has sought lodgings elsewhere. I believe he is staying with an acquaintance, and you will find him at 14 Montague Street in Bloomsbury. To maintain harmony, I'd prefer you didn't disclose that you'd been to see me or that I provided the address where he currently lives. Do I make myself understood, Captain?"

By the miracles of modern dressmaking, her dress held together after a large inhalation before she successfully managed to hoist herself from her chair.

The meeting was over, and Austin stood. "Of Course, Mrs Dillington. I won't say a word. Thank you."

Austin departed the Dillington residence and felt that, somehow, he'd escaped from a potentially cataclysmic event. He was pleased to be back in a cab headed to Montague Street, as his short visit had been stressful under her unwavering scrutiny.

George Dillington wasn't as polite or as considered as his wife. He stood in the entranceway of his temporary home coldly glaring at Austin and had spoken only one word, "You!" when he saw Austin.

"Mr Dillington, I am Austin Willems, my father is Enoch who you are familiar with, and I seek some answers. I'm hoping you can spare a few moments with me."

"Are you responsible for the crisis at Grand Overland Rail?" he grizzled. "You give me one good reason why I don't slam this door into your face."

Austin shook his head. "I think you may have mistaken me for another, sir. I know nothing about rail, and what I do know, I learned from my father, and that is about coal."

"What do you want to know?" George stood a little straighter, but similar to Pearl, the tailoring of his clothing was tested as the buttons on his vest miraculously held fast, such was the expanse of his belly.

A good tailor, Austin surmised. He cast aside any questions he had about how George managed to be intimate with a woman when his belly prevented him from closeness and took a stab in the dark with his first question. "Mr Dillington, are you acquainted with Phineas Grosley?"

The reaction was immediate. George's eyes opened to double their normal size, and his face coloured. "No, never heard of him. Why is he important?" George recovered quickly and inclined his head in question.

"I believe he may have been involved with purchasing Midlands Collieries Company."

George shook his head in denial, and his jowls flapped from side to side.

"Does the name Sir Felix Dampierre mean anything to you?"

Again, his cheeks flushed red. "Absolutely not. He, he, means nothing to me," stammered George.

Austin could see that George had become agitated and looked like he would explode. He needn't have lied about denying knowing those two men, his reactions were proof enough.

George Dillington raised a fleshy hand and pointed a finger at Austin. "If you're on a fishing expedition to gain gossip on my, er, uh, social activities, then you've just landed in hot water, lad. Drop it, and don't mention their names ever again. The door slammed shut.

Austin could have laughed. George Dillington had assumed his questions about the two men were about his sordid lifestyle choices and not Grand Overland Rail. But on reflection, did George's reaction mean those men had no involvement with governing Grand Overland Rail or London Private Acquisitions? He was in a quandary and needed to talk with someone who understood. Unfortunately, Ollie wasn't available this evening, so Austin decided to visit him tomorrow and then discuss everything with Harriet on the best way to proceed.

He returned home and went upstairs to see Howard and report to him on his visit to see Mrs and Mr Dillington and seek his wisdom. When he entered the house, Nanny was nowhere to be seen, and he assumed she was tending to Howard, who, under her strict orders, was still confined to bed.

Austin knocked on the door and entered Howard's room to find Nanny lying on top of the bed beside Howard in his arms. He froze momentarily. "Uh, excuse me," he stated in embarrassment and retraced his steps, shutting the door behind him. He heard Howard call out his name.

He was stunned. It was unfathomable, *Nanny and Howard*? He made his way downstairs to the library to pour a drink. He wasn't angry or upset, only surprised. He stood near the window, gazed over The Regent's Park, and thought about them both.

How silly and blind he'd been? The signs were there... how often had he arrived home in the morning to find Howard already having breakfast with Nanny? The flirting and the occasional innocent peck on the cheek... Howard's overt compliments about her cooking. Austin laughed. He thought it was fantastic, but why keep it a secret?

He emptied his glass and returned upstairs to apologise for his intrusion and to give them his blessings.

When he entered the room, Nanny was in tears and being consoled by Howard.

She looked at him and tried to stand, but Howard held her firm. "I'm so sorry, sir. I feel that I have failed you…"

Austin raised a hand. "That's enough, Nanny. It's quite alright," he spared a look at Howard, who kept a comforting arm around her. "I apologise for barging in, but I didn't expect this, er," he remarked with a smile. "I am not upset, nor am I against any relationship you both choose to have. Frankly, it's not my business or concern." He was trying to be respectful to them both. "However, I do have one question," he looked at Howard. "How long, for how long, have the two of you, er, been together?"

Nanny blew her nose into a handkerchief.

"Many years," Howard sheepishly replied.

"Many…?" Austin shook his head in disbelief.

Nanny nodded but didn't elaborate.

"Did father know?"

Howard looked at Nanny. "If he did, then he never said anything. I suspect he knew."

Austin walked around the bed towards Nanny, who sat on the edge of the mattress and warmly embraced her. "I'm truly happy for you," he whispered into her ear. "For me, it changes nothing."

He smiled at them both and quietly left the room. He knew they'd probably have a lot of talking to do.

CHAPTER FORTY-FOUR

Late the following afternoon, Austin decided to visit Ollie at the Lamb and Flag to discuss what he'd learned from loverboy George Dillington and Harriet's mother. Afterwards, he arranged to call on Harriet. He'd been thinking about Howard and Nanny and couldn't wait to tell her about his recent discovery about their relationship. He caught a Hansom Cab, and after paying the driver, he stepped from the coach near the crossroads of Covent Gardens and began walking down Garrick Street, where he would turn left on Rose Street to the Lamb and Flag.

Howard may invite Nanny to move in with him. The thought gave him a chill. *They might even marry, move elsewhere and disappear from his life.* Whatever they decided to do, he hoped they'd be happy, and he would give them his blessing. The thought of Nanny and Howard not being part of his life was a little disconcerting, and he tried to cast those selfish thoughts from his mind.

Without warning, a man stepped aggressively from a doorway to block his path. He recoiled in surprise, taking a backward step to avoid a collision. Lost in thought, he hadn't been paying any attention to his surroundings and was caught entirely unaware.

Unseen, another man silently stepped behind him and gave him a hard shove. He stumbled forward, and the man in front drove a fist hard into his stomach. He doubled over in pain, retching and gasping for breath. Again, the man in front struck him and drove a fist hard up into his face. He saw nothing but a bright flash and lost his balance to collapse heavily onto the footpath

The unprovoked attack was relentless as both men savagely kicked. In defence, Austin brought up his knees and curled into a ball, but the brutal blows continued and took their toll. They kicked his face and every exposed part of his body. A hard kick to the back of his head was the last he remembered before succumbing to blackness, but the beating didn't stop.

The sound of an angered yell caused one of the assailants to look up, and he saw them coming. At least six men poured out from Rose Street wielding clubs, led by at least another six lads.

The man tugged at the sleeve of his associate. "Time to scarper."

"Aye, better finish 'im off." He reached inside his trouser pocket and extracted a small revolver.

"Better bleedin' hurry," anxiously cried his associate as he saw the men and lads quickly approaching. For good measure, he drove another foot into the body that lay motionless on the footpath.

His associate looked nervously at the attackers, lowered the revolver and hurriedly squeezed the trigger. Before the smoke dissipated, both men had gone.

When his lads reported the altercation on Garrick Street with Captain Willems and the two strangers, Ollie responded quickly, rallied his men and sent them out urgently where they streamed onto Garrick Street. Unfortunately, his wooden leg prevented him from keeping up with them, or he would have been the first to defend his friend. He heard the gunshot and then rounded the corner to see Austin lying in a spreading pool of blood. In response to the sound of the gunshot, police reacted, and distant whistles echoed through the streets, but of the two men who assaulted Austin, there was no sign. Later, his lads informed him that they'd clearly seen their faces, but the men were strangers, and no one had ever seen them before.

Unconscious and bleeding from multiple abrasions, contusions and a bullet wound, Austin was gently carried to the upstairs room of the Lamb and Flag. Police were already on the scene trying to piece together what they believed to be another simple robbery gone awry and suggested that Austin should be taken to the hospital, but Ollie wasn't having any of it, believing his friend had a higher chance of survival under his care and protection. Already, he'd sent out lads to the home of a retired army surgeon he knew. Ollie knew enough about gunshot wounds and injuries to test any physician, and while he impatiently waited for the surgeon to arrive, he instructed his lads to boil water and find clean cloth for bandages as he began carefully removing Austin's clothes.

The constables were a nuisance and constantly underfoot while they asked silly questions, and Ollie cursed them, urging them to leave.

When the crusty old surgeon arrived, he barked at them, "You gather like rabid wolves impatiently waiting to feast on a warm corpse. Be off with you," he scowled in annoyance. "Let me do my damn job."

Soon after, Detective Sergeant Barnabus Roggin arrived, quickly made his presence felt, and order was established as the surgeon went to work on Austin. Ollie led the detective downstairs to a place they could talk unhindered, leaving the surgeon and a couple of local women to tend to Austin.

Ollie noticed the detective looked disturbed. "Are you unwell?" he asked.

Detective Sergeant Roggin looked at Ollie. "I admit, I'm a little taken back," he paused a moment, "I've come to know Captain Austin quite well, and this incident is a little upsetting, and I hope he can survive."

Ollie grunted.

The detective seemed to pull himself together. "What do you know, Sergeant?"

Ollie's expression changed, and he stared coldly at the detective. "I'm a retired sergeant, previously and most proudly with the 67th South Hampshire Regiment of Foot, sir, and I'm not entitled to use my rank. You can call me Ollie, Mr Nagle, or anything you bleed'n like, but you may not call me Sergeant – sir." The word 'sir' was delivered like an insult.

Detective Sergeant Roggin's face coloured, and he looked away. "I, er, apologise, no harm intended, er, Mr Nagle."

Ollie's look softened, and he shook his head. "I saw nuttin'. The nobblers[19] ain't from 'round here. No one I spoke to seen 'em a'fore."

"Any thoughts as to why he was attacked? Was it an attempted robbery or linked to the deaths of the others?"

Ollie laughed. "Not a bloody robbery. Someone wants Cap'n Willems dead."

Detective Sergeant Roggin saw his superior, Detective Chief Inspector Bird and two other constables enter the public house and pause at the entrance as their eyes adjusted to the interior gloom of the near-empty public house. He raised an arm and waved, perplexed why his superior would be here, and curiously waited for an explanation.

"Afternoon, Ollie," greeted the Inspector.

Ollie nodded, "Tobias."

Detective Sergeant Roggin was shocked; not only did they know

19   Nobbler – Victorian era slang for a person who inflicts grievous bodily harm.

each other, they were familiar.

"What do you have for me, Ollie?"

"Same as I told 'im." He pointed to Detective Sergeant Roggin, "Nothin'. Two men beat Cap'n Willems to a pulp, then shot 'im. May have killed 'im, don't know yet, the surgeon is with him now."

"Targeted?"

Ollie nodded.

Detective Chief Inspector Bird turned to his subordinate. "Did your interview with Mr Louis Bardin, the bull chap, fare well? Has he provided you with the information you sought?"

Detective Sergeant Roggin was puzzled. Here he was at the Lamb and Flag public house investigating an assault and shooting, possibly even the murder of a man who may be involved in a case currently under investigation, and the chief inspector was asking about another suspect. "No, sir, we have yet to learn anything, he hasn't talked. I believe he is implicated in the murders of Sir Ronal Hewitt-Thompson, Julian De Vore and perhaps the attempted murder of Captain Willems, sir."

"I see, but your Mr Bardin was in our custody at the time of Captain Willems' assault and shooting?"

Ollie looked from one man to the other in disbelief. What he heard was absurd. *Of course, the bull, is involved.*

"I believe so, sir, when I saw him last, he was in our custody," replied Detective Sergeant Roggin.

Detective Chief Inspector Bird looked around the interior of the Lamb and Flag before speaking again. "You sent constables back to his room for a partial letter, did that provide results?"

Detective Sergeant Roggin shook his head. "No, sir, it was a waste of time."

"Then Mr Bardin can't be involved, can he?"

"But sir–"

"– If he was in custody, then it wasn't possible for him to assault and shoot Mr Willems. Am I correct, Detective Sergeant Roggin?" continued Detective Chief Inspector Bird.

Detective Sergeant Roggin's mouth opened to reply.

"Do you have any reason to hold him in custody, Detective?"

"He is a suspect in a homicide investigation–"

"Detective?"

Detective Sergeant Roggin shook his head.

"I want Mr Bardin released. It is impossible that he could be behind the attack on Mr Willems, and you have no evidence linking him to any crime."

The detective sergeant knew his superior was technically correct. However, instincts also led to sound deductive reasoning, and his gut feeling was that Louis Bardin, also known as *Le Taureau,* was the mastermind behind the murders. If he released him as ordered, Bardin would disappear, and they would never find him again. He looked at his superior and saw that he was resolute. "Aye, sir, I will see Mr Bardin released today."

Detective Chief Inspector Bird looked around the room. "Very good. Where was the victim attacked?"

"Out here, sir," replied a constable. "This way."

The Inspector followed the constable outside.

Ollie turned to Detective Sergeant Roggin the moment they couldn't be overheard.

"I know, Mr Nagle, I agree. I have no choice in the matter. If the inspector wants him released," Detective Roggin shrugged. "I can do nothing unless new evidence comes to light."

"And the sod will 'ave scarpered," replied Ollie with a shake of his head. "I knew that turn'in him over to th' constabulary was wrong. I could have had a wee chat with Mr Bardin, and he'd a sung like a whore in heat."

Detective Sergeant Roggin's head whipped around, and he stared at Ollie for a dozen heartbeats. "I suppose I must follow orders, Mr Nagle. As instructed, I will release Mr Bardin at 6.00 p.m. this evening. He will undoubtedly seek a cab or other transportation to take him to his lodgings."

Ollie looked puzzled. The detective continued to hold eye contact, and then it dawned on him, and he smiled. "You said six?"

"On the dot, Mr Nagle."

"Oy, Ollie!" shouted one of the women helping the surgeon, "You might wanna drag yerself up 'ere, then."

Ollie saw the woman who stood on the stairs waving at him to come over, and he looked back at Detective Sergeant Roggin. "Tonight at six, you say?" he started to clomp his way to the stairs. "You comin' Detective?"

Harry Ramsbottom, the surgeon Ollie called to attend to Austin, was a disagreeable fellow who found fault in most things and felt it his duty to point out and vocalise his displeasure at every available opportunity, which was frequent. He was also a gifted and highly respected battlefield surgeon, now retired, and availed himself to help those in need when he could. When Ollie and Detective Sergeant Roggin entered the upstairs room, Doctor Ramsbottom was wiping his hands and admonishing both his temporary nursing assistants for their lack of sobriety.

"What say you, Harry?" asked Ollie as he looked at the still form of his friend lying on the table.

"I've seen worse after a Saturday night brawl, Ollie. The problem with young men these days, is they have no grit, eh? They get roughed up a bit and cry for their mama. They're soft, the bleed'n lot of 'em."

"Then he'll live?" Ollie clarified.

"Of course, he'll bloody live," he poked Austin in the side and received a grunt in response. "He's got a couple of cracked ribs, a severe brain commotion and a few minor scrapes from trauma."

Ollie had stepped up to the table and saw the rise and fall of Austin's chest, but his eyes were closed. "What about the gunshot?"

"Oh, hardly worth mentioning," scoffed the physician. "The bullet, from a child's firearm, was small calibre and entered the abdominal external oblique. Bloody poor shot, really. Missed the intestines and passed through muscle. More inconvenient than harmful. My wife suffered more severe injuries doing embroidery."

"What about his recovery?" asked Detective Sergeant Roggin.

"Who the bloody hell are you?"

"This be Detective Sergeant Roggin, he's investigatin' the, er, the assault," Ollie replied.

"Oh, the polite thing to do is introduce yourself, eh," admonished the surgeon. "No bleed'n manners. However, your patient may want to rest for a day or two. The ribs may be a tad uncomfortable; change the bandage on the gunshot wound twice a day, and for the head knocks, a couple of brandy's and a good night's sleep will work wonders." With his advice dispensed, Harry Ramsbottom wiped his surgical instruments and packed them away.

Ollie arranged for a carriage to take Austin home. He knew Nanny would be beside herself when she saw him – but at least he's alive, Ollie thought. While the physician may have downplayed the severity of the injuries, Ollie knew Austin required care while he recovered, and no one was better suited than Nanny.

When the carriage arrived at The Regents Park, Ollie clumped up the few stairs, knocked on the door and waited. It wasn't long before the door opened, and Nanny took one look at Ollie, then rushed down to the carriage and saw Austin. Her hand flew to her mouth. "Oh, my Austin," she cried. In the space of two heartbeats, her disposition changed. "Careful, Ollie, bring him upstairs. Don't move him unnecessarily, and take your time." She hurried back inside, scooped up vases and ornaments that could be knocked over and raced upstairs to prepare the bed.

"You heard the' lady," Ollie bellowed in his parade ground voice to the two men he brought with him. "Nice an easy, break anything, and you'll be need'n to call back the bloody crocus[20] to see to the injuries you'll be getting from me!"

As shocked as she was at seeing Austin in his current state, Nanny remained calm and composed and within a short time, she had Austin on the bed, where she began cleaning congealed blood and applying salves and ointments to cuts and scrapes. By early evening, Austin was between crisp, clean sheets and in a restless sleep.

---

20   *Crocus – Victorian slang for doctor/physician. Crokus – to croak (Die)*

CHAPTER FORTY-FIVE

Retired Sergeant Oliver Nagle wasn't going to blow this opportunity given to him by Detective Sergeant Roggin and, at some considerable expense, had secured the help of four able-bodied men. Two were retired soldiers from the 67th South Hampshire Regiment of Foot and were still more than capable, while the other two gentlemen were known to be extremely violent and typically conducted their shady day-to-day activities outside the peripheries of the law. A coachman, another frequent customer at the Lamb and Flag, assisted by providing his services and an enclosed coach.

They loitered near the Bow Street Police Station, and Ollie's four men were divided on each side of the station entrance, waiting for Louis Bardin to emerge. Ollie rechecked his fob watch and saw it was almost 6.00 p.m.

To Ollie's immense relief, at 6.01 p.m., Louis Bardin appeared outside the station looking somewhat dishevelled and paused briefly. Coming to a decision, he began walking towards where Ollie was hiding in the coach, craning his neck and looking for a cab. From a safe distance, two of Ollie's men followed while the other two waited for him to walk up to the parked coach. The plan was to snatch him as he passed by. To avoid being recognised, Ollie was inside the coach and peeking through a curtain just as his men made their move.

Ollie thrust open the door, and immediately, Louis Bardin was thrown inside, and the two thugs climbed in after him. The coach only had seats for four, and the two retirees would return to the Lamb and Flag as their services were no longer required.

"Evenin'," greeted Ollie, "Remember me?" he grinned.

The coach headed away from the Police Station just as Detective Sergeant Roggin stepped outside for fresh air. He smiled as Ollie waved behind the coach's window as the horses clip-clopped by.

While Ollie had bragged to Austin about making Louis Bardin talk, he took no pleasure in inflicting pain on another individual. Torture was something he despised. However, sometimes it was necessary, and he hoped that Bardin would be forthcoming to avoid any real unpleasantness.

Le Taureau, or Louis Bardin, was roped securely to a chair, again in the upstairs room of the Lamb and Flag, and he didn't look thrilled at being held captive after being detained by police for a few days. One of Ollie's thugs wielded a wooden club and stood confidently in front of their prisoner while Ollie did all the talking.

Ollie warned Louis what would happen if he chose not to answer his questions, and he affirmed that he understood. Ollie was keen to begin. "Are you called, or do you call yourself *Le* bleed'n *Taureau?*"

Louis didn't look at all happy. He nodded. "I am," he replied hesitantly.

Ollie exhaled. "That's a good start. Now, did you arrange for Captain Austin Willems to be shot outside Hanover Square when the shooter missed?"

Bardin swallowed but remained silent, preferring to stare at the thug with the club.

Ollie nodded, and a thick rag was tied around Bardin's mouth. He didn't repeat the question and waited as the thug drew the club back and then swung it powerfully into Bardin's knee.

Bardin screamed, and even with a rag stuffed in his mouth, it was a loud, painful cry, and Ollie knew it hurt.

The question was repeated, and Bardin glared at Ollie, choosing not to respond. Sweat dripped from his forehead and sprayed around the room when the thug struck his knee a second time. Bardin threw his head back and shrieked in agony before passing out.

The second thug threw water over him, then slapped his face a few times until he was again conscious. His bloodshot eyes stared malevolently at Ollie.

"Answer the bloody questions, an' we'll stop this nonsense," Ollie implored. Bardin gave no reaction. "Will you answer now?"

Bardin's eyes narrowed, and he shook his head.

Ollie nodded.

The club was a blur as the thug swung with all his might. Ollie knew for certain that *Le Taureau* would never again regain the full use of his right leg. The impact of splintering bone was drowned out by the inhuman scream that followed. Ollie could smell urine as Louis's bladder released.

Give 'im water," ordered Ollie to the thug, who immediately removed the rag and gave Bardin a mouthful of water from a pitcher. The rag was re-tied.

Ollie took another deep breath. "You'll be need'n a cane from now on, you know this, don't you, Louis?"

Bardin nodded weakly.

"Are you ready to answer my questions?"

Le Taureau held eye contact with Ollie and remained steadfast. Ollie knew he wouldn't talk unless… "Now, the other knee," said Ollie in a conversational tone.

Immediately, Bardin's eyes opened wide and followed the thug as he walked to the other side and positioned himself to strike Bardin's good knee cleanly. The wooden club hissed through the air as the thug took a couple of practice swings.

Ollie nodded, and the thug positioned himself to strike the other knee. Immediately, Bardin cried out, and Ollie raised a hand to stop the swing. "Gonna talk?"

Bardin nodded, and his head lolled forward. Like earlier, he was doused in water, his cheeks slapped, and within moments he was again cognisant. The rag was removed, and he was given water to drink.

Blood seeped through Louis Bardin's trousers, and his mangled lower leg hung at an unnatural angle. He'd bitten his lip, and his eyes were red. Ollie knew the man was in considerable pain, and if he didn't talk now, he doubted he ever would.

"Louis, are you gonna answer my questions?" Ollie repeated.

The bull nodded, and even the thugs looked relieved.

Ollie leaned forward in his chair. "Did you arrange for Captain Austin Willems to be shot outside Hanover Square?"

There was a lengthy pause. "I did."

"Alright, let's start at the beginnin', shall we," instructed Ollie with relief.

Austin cautiously opened his eyes and felt the stab of pain from his chest, side and from a multitude of places – he was sore and parched. His eyes were almost swollen shut, and his lips weren't much better. He groaned and quickly shut them again. Immediately, he felt the soothing, gentle touch of a wet cloth on his lips. "Can you drink?"

Nanny. He grunted and opened his mouth as much as he could. Water trickled in, and he swallowed with discomfort, but the cool liquid helped. "Don go, Nan," he mumbled.

She leaned forward, her hair almost brushing his lips to hear him better. "What did you say?"

"Don go, Nan," he repeated.

"Don't go? Oh, sir, I'm not leaving your side. Don't speak anymore, rest and sleep if you can, I'll be here," she assured.

"With Howd," Austin added.

"Howd? Oh, you mean Howard."

If Austin had his eyes open, he'd have seen her face colour slightly.

"I'm not going anywhere, this is my home." She reached out and held his hand and gently squeezed. She felt his breathing settle, and within a short time, he was asleep. She sat with him, occasionally dabbing his brow and lips with a wet cloth, and silently wept.

A short time later, she arranged for a message to be delivered to Miss Harriet Stephenson at 25 Upper Brook Street, Mayfair. She knew if Austin were to recover quickly, he would need Harriet at his bedside.

Ollie was alone and sat at a table in the upstairs room of the Lamb and Flag and thought about the unpleasant experience he'd had with Louis Bardin and all that he'd learned from his little chat with him. Professionally, *Le Taureau* ceased to exist; he was a broken, dispirited man who no longer threatened anyone. Although reluctant at first, Louis Bardin eventually told Ollie everything and gave up his precious secrets along with the names of privileged and powerful employers who needed his exclusive and discrete services.

Finally, when he had nothing more to offer, Harry Ramsbottom had been recalled, and the old surgeon grizzled and griped while he treated Louis Bardin's rather severe leg injury. He'd done all he could by resetting the bone and binding it firmly around a splint before Bardin was taken to the rooming house where he lived.

Ollie felt he had a moral obligation to inform the police about what he'd learned from Louis Bardin and would contact Chief Detective Inspector Tobias Bird, who he'd known for years and provide him with the relevant information on the assassinations of Sir Ronald Hewitt-Thompson, Julian De Vore and the two attempt on Austin' life. But he wouldn't tell him everything; some things Louis spoke of, the police didn't need to know about.

Ollie was exhausted. It had been a long and tiring day. He up-ended his ale and placed the empty glass on the table when the unbidden thought struck him like a mortal blow. "Jesus, Mary and Joseph – No!" he yelled in anguish as he thumped the table with his fist.

Brandy snifters were refilled, and conversation temporarily halted until the attendant completed his duties and left the card room at Whites Gentlemen's Club. George Dillington stared morosely into the amber liquid in the glass he held while Oscar Baker watched Virgil Hartmann reviewing his notes.

Virgil closed his notebook with a snap and met the curious looks of the other two men with him. "Gentlemen, I shall make this quick as it is late." He took a deep breath and slowly exhaled. "It appears more bad luck has befallen us."

George rolled his eyes. "What now?"

Virgil ignored the comment. "In our wisdom, we initiated severe cost-cutting measures at Midlands Collieries–"

"We? It was Sir Ronald's idea, not mine," remarked George.

"And I believe you agreed, George," replied Oscar Baker.

"–and as a result, employees, unused to the rigours of hard labour, have begun talks with the union to strike."

"Bloody lazy layabouts," George added.

"What should we do? Certainly, we can't acquiesce," Oscar suggested.

"I agree. Perhaps our only option is to sell and walk away," offered Virgil.

George stopped fiddling with his brandy snifter and looked at Virgil with interest.

"We haven't lost money, as our capital investment in Midlands Collieries has proven to be a sound decision, and we have enjoyed considerable dividends. If we sell Midlands now, at the very least at our initial purchase price, we will not incur losses nor face the burden of expenses if the labour union wins the support of the workers and they strike. May I remind you that coal contracts must be honoured, and failure to deliver on those contracts will incur monetary penalties."

"Has the Chairman weighed in on this?" Virgil asked.

"No, we haven't heard from him at all. George, have you had contact with the Chairman recently?"

George shook his head.

"Then I suggest we place Midlands Collieries on the market immediately," Oscar suggested.

"The sooner, the better," quipped George.

"And that brings me to my next point." Virgil opened his notebook and ran a finger down a page. "A few weeks past, and according to Sir Ronald's notes, he received correspondence from a solicitor inquiring if we were interested in selling Midlands Collieries Company. Accordingly, he did respond and told the solicitor that Grand Overland Rail wasn't interested at this time. The solicitor responded and stated that if our situation changed, we should contact him, and he would present us with an offer."

George smiled for the first time that evening. "Then what are we waiting for, send the toff a letter, and we'll accept his offer and be done with it."

Virgil glanced at George. "I agree with George, let's not dilly-dally and inform the solicitor that we will accept a reasonable offer."

Oscar nodded in agreement.

Virgil wasn't finished. "Gentleman, while the sale of Midlands Collieries Company will temporarily stem the haemorrhaging of our hard-earned money, it does not cure all. Grand Overland Rail is in a financial spot of bother. We have no capital to invest in our expansion, and any company profits will not be disbursed because Grand Overland Rail needs the funds to operate and meet overheads. We walk a fine tenuous line."

"Can we borrow?" George asked.

"That was something the Chairman normally arranged, but through my inquiries, we no longer have the credit to borrow, George," Virgil advised.

Oscar picked up his brandy snifter and downed its contents. "Bloody Grand Overland Rail, she's been good to us, but now is the time to move on. She's like an expensive mistress, eh, George. By golly, we had some fun, but the old girl is now showing her years."

George laughed. "She has the pox."

"Think upon it, Gentlemen, I am going home," said Virgil as he wearily rose from his seat.

CHAPTER FORTY-SIX

It was late when Harriet arrived; a member of her mother's house staff safely accompanied her in the coach ride from Mayfair and brought her baggage upstairs to the guest room before departing. Nanny did her best to explain the crisis that had befallen Austin and how they could take turns nursing him.

"Howard, who now has the strength to walk short distances, is sitting with Austin while he sleeps," informed Nanny. She could see that Harriet had been weeping, so she took her hands in her own and spoke softly. "Now is our time to show strength, and this is when he truly needs you. Your love and care will help him in his recovery."

Harriet seemed to respond to Nanny's little talk and pulled herself together.

"Come," she led Harriet to Austin's room.

An oil lamp on a dresser provided enough light for Harriet to see, she gasped. "Dear God. Austin, what have they done to you?"

"He will recover, m'dear," Howard stated. "Many of these injuries look worse than they appear. Please, be seated, and we shall leave you for a while and afford you some privacy." He rose unsteadily from his chair and shuffled to the door. "He needs you."

Harriet stood beside the bed looking down at Austin and his horrific injuries. She felt his pain and it took all her willpower not to burst onto tears again. Howard patted the bed. With care she slowly sat and reached for his hand. "I'm here for you, Austin and will do all I can to help."

The chime of the doorbell broke the silence.

"Mr Nagle!" exclaimed Nanny when she saw Ollie at the door. "It's rather late to visit Captain Willems. His condition hasn't changed since you brought him in this afternoon." She looked at him quizzically.

"Nanny, Cap'n Willems, he'd be in danger, and we needs to talk."

With a look of worry, she stepped back and allowed him inside.

Ollie took a step, paused and looked over his shoulder into the darkness before clomping into the hall. "Who'd be here at the moment?" he asked.

This was too much for Nanny, and she became flustered. "Er, Mr Nagle, please come into the drawing room, er, would you like a cup of tea?"

Ollie followed her into the drawing room and turned to face her. "Other than you, Mr Willoughby, and the Cap'n, who else is here?"

"Oh, er, Miss Stephenson arrived a short time ago, just before you, she is tending to Captain Willems," she replied. "Er, how can I help you, Mr Nagel, it is rather late?"

Ollie took a deep breath. "Nanny, can Mr Willoughby make his way down here, or should I go upstairs? I needs to speak with him urgently."

"Let me ask him, Mr Nagle. One moment." With that, she made her way upstairs.

Ollie fidgeted nervously while he waited for Howard.

It wasn't long before he heard Howard slowly descending the stairs with Nanny assisting him.

"Ollie, what is going on? Nanny informs me you are worried.

I'm sure Austin is in good care. I don't believe there is any need for concern," he said when he entered the drawing room.

"Mr Willoughby, sir, while I have concern over the Cap'n and his well-being, this ain't just 'bout his injuries."

Howard's expression changed, and with Ollie's help, he lowered onto an armchair. "Alright, you have my attention, Ollie."

"Sir, I've been help'n th' Cap'n with his, ah, enquiries. Earlier today, he was com'n to see me when got hisself shot. It weren't no robbery. It was an attempt to kill 'im. The Cap'n had information he wanted to tell me about and never got the bleed'n chance."

Howard nodded. "What does that have to do with your visit here this evening, Ollie?"

"Ah, well, you see, Mr Willoughby. The police had a suspect they tried to question, didn't they. Didn't do them any bloody good, and the fella never talked."

"A suspect?"

"Aye, sir, a suspect in the murder of that toff, Sir Ronald, and the bent solicitor, De Vore. The same fella who had you shot."

Howard sat up straighter.

"The police let me have 'im, and the fella talked his bloody head off, didn't he." Ollie took a step closer to Howard. "Whatever the Cap'n learned and wanted to tell me about, and what was told to me is enough to scare these toffs. They want to kill the Cap'n a'fore he tells the police what he knows. They'll come 'ere, sir. They'll come to this house and kill the Cap'n and anyone else who gets in their way."

"How can you be so sure, Ollie?"

Ollie's shoulders slumped. "I ain't sure, sir, but what would you do if you were in their shoes? Would you wait until the police were told, or would you do something 'bout it?"

Howard stared into the distance as he digested what Ollie told him. He had no reason to doubt the man, Austin trusted Ollie with his life. "I think we need to wake Austin and see if he can talk. But first, er, Ollie, let's pour a whiskey, eh." He pointed to the bottle on a credenza.

Ollie helped Howard climb the stairs, and they entered Austin's room. Harriet was delicately dabbing Austin's face and turned in surprise. "Ollie."

"Miss Stephenson, we need to ask the Cap'n a couple of questions, his life depends on it."

Her eyebrows furrowed together. "What's happened, Ollie?"

"Ollie believes men will come here to kill Austin and anyone who stands in their way, Harriet. We need to ask Austin his opinion if he can answer," said Howard, speaking for Ollie.

"I don't know if he can," she replied.

Ollie clumped over and sat on the bed. He reached out and placed a hand on Austin's shoulder. "Cap'n, Cap'n, can you hear me?"

Austin stirred.

"Cap'n, Ollie repeated.

"Austin, can you hear me?" Harriet asked and squeezed his hand.

Austin's eyes blinked open, and he groaned.

"Cap'n, what did you learn from George Dillington?"

Austin looked like he would drift off.

"You must of upset them as they tried to kill ya today. Will they come back? Cap'n, do you think they'll come here?" Ollie pressed.

Austin's eyes opened to their fullest. He groaned again, and Harriet felt him squeeze her hand. "Not – safe – here," he croaked and turned his head slightly to look at Ollie. "Phineas - Grosley – and Felix – Dampierre…b, bad men."

"Do you know these men?" Howard asked Ollie.

"Aye, *Le Taureau,* the man I interrog– er, I chatted with today.

He told me that Sir Felix Dampierre was the man who hired him to kill Sir Ronald, Julian De Vore and the Cap'n. The other man, Phineas Grosley, is a brother to the Watsons and is the Governor of the Bank of England, I don't know his involvement, sir."

Harriet gasped.

"Dear God!" Howard exclaimed, just as they heard the sound of someone climbing the stairs.

All heads turned to the door as Nanny entered.

"Mr Nagle, two young boys are at the door, and they say they must speak to you."

Ollie opened the door to see Cat and Lenny waiting. "Sarge, tis as you said," volunteered Cat immediately. "We saw 'em, at least two nobs just entered th' park down the far end." Lenny nodded enthusiastically.

Ollie shook his head as Howard and Harriet entered the drawing room.

"Where are they exactly?" Ollie asked.

"Oh, they'd be havin' a natter near the Rose garden. They were point'n an waving their arms in this direction. Seems they were waitin' for somethin', perhaps for others to arrive," Cat added.

"Bad news?" Howard asked.

Ollie nodded. "Aye, seems like it. They'll be comin' for Austin soon."

Harriet looked at the faces of Ollie and Howard and saw they showed uncertainty. No one had any ideas, but she knew that staying in the house wasn't the smartest thing when men were coming. She wondered what Austin would do in this situation. In his current state, he couldn't guide them or offer a clever solution… but she could. She squared her shoulders.

"Ollie, can you have the boys hail a coach and a wagon and have them come to the service lane behind the houses? I'll have Nanny light a candle so they know which house to come to. We all should leave here and travel safely to Mayfair with Austin in the wagon. Luckily, they won't see us depart from the service lane." She looked at both men hoping they couldn't see how frightened she was.

"Aye, Ma'am. Be best if the lads disappeared out the back door, eh?"

"Howard, are you able to travel?" she asked.

"If Austin can, then so can I," he smiled. "I'll inform Nanny and pack a few things."

"Thank you, Howard. We also need to inform Detective Sergeant Roggin. I will write a note, and Ollie, can Cat and Lenny deliver my message to the Bow Street station when we all leave here? I'll give them some money. I doubt he will read it before morning, but there isn't anything else we can do."

"Y'hear that, lads, you'll be doin' the lady a big favour."

Both lads nodded shyly.

"Wait here." Harriet rushed from the room to find her purse.

Ollie was giving the lads instructions when she returned.

"If the coachmen give you trouble, wave this pound note at them." She handed the money to Cat, including a few coins for cab fare, before sitting and composing a message for the detective. When finished, she placed it into an envelope and gave it to Cat.

"Ya know what has to be done?" Ollie asked.

Both lads nodded as Nanny came down the stairs carrying a hold-all.

While they waited for the coach and wagon to arrive, Ollie peeked through an upstairs window into the darkness. The Regent's Park was enormous and not lit at night, but he saw nothing of concern. He didn't doubt Cat and Lenny's observations, he trusted them implicitly. If they said men had gathered, then that was good enough for him. He moved downstairs, ensured the bags were near the doorway to the rear entrance and stepped outside. With relief, he heard a wagon and coach approach.

"Wagon's a-comin'," he shouted.

With a cash incentive, both coachmen were conscripted to carry Austin on a blanket down the stairs and onto cushions placed in the wagon by Nanny and Harriet. A short time later, the house was locked, and the coach and wagon departed for Mayfair.

Their late and unexpected arrival at the house previously owned by the late Sir Ronald Hewitt-Thompson caused some consternation, and with Eunice's support and instructions, house staff were frantic in arranging bedding for Austin, Howard and Nanny.

Once Austin was again comfortable and resting, Harriet called everyone together in the drawing room. "I believe whoever seeks Austin will not know, for tonight at least, that he is here in Mayfair. Our hope lies with the police and the willingness of Detective Sergeant Roggin to investigate Sir Felix Dampierre and Phineas Grosley and prove their involvement in a murder conspiracy."

She looked around the room, and all heads nodded in support. Her gaze settled on Ollie. "Do we have the home addresses of those two men?"

"Aye, Ma'am," he replied.

"Good. Can you write their addresses so we can give them to the police?" She handed paper and pen to Ollie, who scribbled away.

"What is the likelihood we could have both their homes watched? Do you have anyone you trust who could do that and report to you any significant findings?" she asked.

Ollie blotted the ink and handed the paper to Harriet. He looked uncomfortable and then shifted awkwardly on his chair. "Ma'am, it isn't that I don't have people do this, it's just that I need's to pay 'em for their time."

"How much do you need, Ollie?" Howard asked.

"A pound should cover a coupla days, sir."

Howard reached into his blazer and extracted some money. "Here are two pounds. Ensure they do a good job; Austin's life depends on it." He handed the money over. "Best you get some rest, eh? It's time we all went to bed."

CHAPTER FORTY-SEVEN

Detective Sergeant Roggin arrived bright and early and was seated in the drawing room. While Nanny was tending to Austin, Harriet, Eunice, and Howard had just finished explaining the events of the previous evening to him.

He closed his notebook and sighed. "This is a most delicate matter, and while I fully understand the nature of your concerns, there is no evidence to support your accusations that Sir Felix Dampierre and Phineas Grosley are implicit in any illegal activities, let alone a conspiracy to murder as you outlined, Miss Stephenson."

Harriet went to speak, and the detective raised a hand. "One moment, please, allow me to finish."

Harriet sat back in her chair with her arms folded.

"Both these gentlemen hold important positions and presumably have a large sphere of influence. If I aggressively question them, there will be consequences." He shook his head. "The fact of the matter is, I believe you, I truly do. But how can I obtain evidence to link these two men to the murders of your, er, stepfather, Mr De Vore and the attempt on Captain Willems' life outside the theatre and again yesterday?"

A knock on the door interrupted Harriet before she could reply, and a house servant appeared. "Excuse me, Milady, Mr Oliver Nagle is here to see you."

"Thank you. Mary, see him in if you please."

Moments later, Ollie appeared. When he saw everyone staring, he looked uncomfortable. "Morn'n all." He acknowledged Eunice with a respectful dip of his head.

"Please, Mr Nagle, have a seat," she instructed.

"Detective Inspector Roggin has just informed us there is little he can do about the two gentlemen whose names you provided unless he has evidence linking them to crimes," volunteered Harriet.

"Thought as much," Ollie replied. He looked at the young detective. "May I have a word in private? What I needs to tell might not be appropriate like, for, er, ladies."

Harriet knew Ollie was going to tell the detective about *Le Taureau*. She rose from her chair. "We can check on Austin, come, Mama."

Ollie informed Howard and Detective Sergeant Roggin about what he'd learned from Louis Bardin, *Le Taureau*. The detective looked thoughtful. "Doesn't change much, really, Mr Nagle. It only bolsters unsupported theories, and my superior will not permit any police action unless we have proof. However, I feel vindicated that my instincts on Mr Bardin were correct."

"Oh, he's a piece o'work, he is. A real scoundrel, tough bastard in all," Ollie added.

When Harriet and Eunice returned, Harriet sat on the edge of her chair and looked intently at the detective. "Tell me, Detective Sergeant Roggin, how long must Captain Willems remain in hiding? When can he return home and be assured he will not have strange men forcibly enter his home and try to kill him?"

The young detective wished he'd never come to this house this morning, and his facial expression echoed his sentiments. "Miss

Stephenson, regardless of my opinion or recommendations, my superior, Chief Detective Inspector Bird, will not authorise any police resources to protect a gentleman who was a victim of a robbery gone awry. It won't happen. What Captain Willems decides to do to protect himself, you or his friends is completely up to him. That is what I will tell my superior when I report back."

The room was deathly quiet.

"Could you take him to Chieveley, to your country estate?" he added.

"Yes, we could," Harriet replied in a whisper.

The silence was awkward.

Detective Sergeant Roggin stood. "I must get back to the station, good day. And please, if you have any developments, send word immediately."

Nanny and Howard went to rest after their long night, and Harriet allowed Austin to sleep. She spent the remainder of the day contemplating how she could protect Austin and find a way to implicate Sir Felix Dampierre and Phineas Grosley, but she had no success.

The following morning, she entered Austin's room to check on him, and she was surprised when he seemed alert and greeted her.

"I'm not an invalid," he said.

"No, but you were shot and severely beaten," she responded.

"My chest hurts, and the gunshot wound doesn't feel so bad." He touched the swelling on his face. "The sensation is uncomfortable, but I can talk - just," he said with a hint of a smile.

With some difficulty, she managed to prop him against the pillows so he could sit up, and they spoke for a while recounting the drama of two nights ago and how the police couldn't do anything.

"I have no solution, Austin, and don't know what to do."

"It has been bothering me too, however, there may be a way, Harriet. I need to find someone suitable for the task I have in mind because I can't do it."

"And you think it will prove to the police how those two gentlemen are behind the murders?"

Austin shrugged and then winced from the movement. "I don't know, but it's the only option," he said. "I can't think of an alternative."

"Then tell me, what have you schemed?"

He explained his idea in detail to her. When finished, she looked at him. "Who do you think can do this? Not Ollie, he doesn't have the social distinction. Howard's professional reputation could be at risk, and he is still physically recovering. You need someone trustworthy who is willing and capable, with the intelligence to pull off this daring escapade."

"I don't think Detective Sergeant Roggin would be willing, as it implicates him in a crime," Austin added. "That only leaves Charles Newbury. Unfortunately, the regiment has been deployed, and he won't return for another eight weeks or so. I don't think we can wait two months, Harriet. Perhaps in a few days, I might have recovered enough…"

"Absolutely not Austin Willems!" Harriet exclaimed. "You're in no shape or condition to do much of anything for at least two weeks. No, you can't do it."

"Ollie may have some ideas. He found that actor, who was superb when confronting Julian De Vore," he wanted to laugh at the recollection but couldn't.

"Just because he could convince De Vore doesn't mean he could do what you need him to do. He may not be able to adapt, and you cannot take the risk, Austin."

Austin looked despondent, and Harriet felt sorry for him. His face was swollen and discoloured, he had cracked ribs and been shot. He felt helpless to do anything, and she completely understood. "So be it, Captain Willems, then I shall do this task."

Austin's eyes opened wide in horror. "You shall do no such thing, Harriet," he implored.

"Why not? Give me one good reason why I couldn't do it?" She glared, daring him to offer a valid reason.

"Because you're a–"

"A woman? Austin, I think that works in our favour. You'll have to do better than that," she said with a smile and a shake of her head.

In all honesty, Austin couldn't think of a reason, and the more he thought about it, the more he realised Harriet probably could do what was needed. "There is always a chance this plan could fail, Harriet, and if it does, you may have to stand before a judge and face charges."

"And if you were to do this deed, then the same applies to you, you could face criminal charges. But you accept that regardless, and so–do–I."

He knew it was pointless to argue, and he'd never win. He looked down at her hand that tightly held his and thought about what she meant to him. If anything happened to her, he couldn't live with himself. He exhaled slowly.

"We need to get Ollie here and plan this out, Harriet. You need to rehearse and prepare for every contingency. I think even Howard can contribute. His outlook and experience could be most useful."

She felt a flutter in her stomach. *What have I got myself into*? she wondered. She looked at the beaten, swollen, bruised face of the man before him and felt the emotion. *I will walk to the ends of the Earth for this man.* "I love you, Austin," she whispered.

His mouth opened then closed as he swallowed and opened again. "Harr–," he croaked, and he tried again. "Harriet…" He wanted to hold and smother her in kisses. He couldn't, it hurt. "I, uh, I love you too, and always have, from the first day we met – and I always will love you."

She leaned down and kissed his forehead.

Austin sat in a chair in the guest room of Eunice's home in Mayfair. He wasn't able to walk down the stairs yet, as it had only been five days since the shooting and the physical exertion was too much. Howard sat in another chair along with Ollie and Harriet, who also sat comfortably on chairs brought in.

Austin had spent the last thirty minutes detailing his plan, and when finished, all heads nodded in agreement.

"It's brazen, but I think it will work," said Howard in support.

"I don't think they will expect that, Cap'n. The more I thinks 'bout it, then I reckon it will work," added Ollie with a grin.

"Except Austin," continued Howard, "Who will do it? You never mentioned that, and presumably, it isn't going to be you."

Austin looked at Harriet. "Harriet wants to do it. Against my wishes, she volunteered, and before you tell me what a foolish idea it is, hear me out." He looked into the curious faces of his two friends. "You have to agree, there isn't a valid reason why she shouldn't."

After a pause, Howard spoke. "Does Eunice know?"

"No, and I'm not going to tell her, and neither will either of you," Harriet sternly warned.

Ollie shrugged. "That be your business. I ain't sayin' a word." He winked at Austin.

"Very well, mum's the word," responded Howard a moment later.

Austin grinned. "Thank you, gentlemen. Now, we need to plan and cover every possible contingency. The way I see this, there are various possible outcomes, and we must be ready."

Howard turned to her. "Harriet, are you sure you wish to do this?"

"There isn't anyone more suited, Howard," she smiled.

Sir Felix Dampierre blew a thin stream of cigar smoke upwards between pursed lips and watched the bluish smoke succumb to the draft before dissipating. When the smoke completely disappeared, he turned to his companion. "And what do we do now, Fin? Captain Willems has survived and vanished, and truth be told, I am rather concerned–"

"Concerned?" repeated Phineas. "You've made a hash of it, and now we both face the possibility of life behind bars. Incarceration won't suit me, Felix, my constitution is not up to it. We must make a more concerted effort to locate Captain Willems, as what you've done so far has proven ineffectual. We have to remove all links to us, only then can we move forward."

"I've had people looking for him and had no success," stated Sir Felix, with a hint of petulance creeping into his voice.

"Then we will have to invest further," Phineas added.

"I have men scouring London as we speak, and this is becoming a rather costly exercise."

"Would you rather be in jail?"

"No, no, of course not," replied Sir Felix. "But Grand Overland Rail is no longer the cash cow it once was–"

"It's over. God damn it, Felix! We must divest ourselves from Grand Overland Rail, London Private Acquisitions and any other business associated with them. Yes, men have died, and it put us in a precarious and unenviable position, but it was necessary. Do not forget these men knew what they were doing and weren't innocent bystanders. For us, self-preservation is the key. Captain Austin Willems should be the last obstacle we face. Beyond that, we can do what we bloody like," Phineas reached for his cognac and took a sip. He licked his lips as he replaced the glass at a small table near his elbow and looked at his friend. "We have had some good times, though."

"You refer to George's er, social activities, his get-togethers?" asked Sir Felix.

Phineas smiled. "How could such a man be so depraved and have such stimulating guests?"

Sir Felix felt a stirring in his loins as he recalled the countless parties. He looked at his friend and reached out to grasp his hand. "The fun has yet to begin."

Phineas Grosley savoured the intimate touch for a moment before removing his hand and reaching towards the table, opening the cigar box lid, extracting a cigar, and carefully examining it. Satisfied, he picked up a cutter to snip the head of the *puro* and then grabbed a box of matches. He took a cold draw to savour the pure taste of the expensive cigar and then lit a match, holding it beneath the cigar foot and gently drew in. The ritual was completed in silence, and when finished, just as Sir Felix had done, he tilted his head back and blew a stream upwards. He watched the smoke curl away before speaking. "You know, my dear Felix, perhaps as was reported, Captain Willems isn't in Chieveley because he is at Ronald's home with his new sweetheart, Miss Harriet Stephenson, in Mayfair. Has anyone looked there?"

"There's a thought," replied Sir Felix. "No, I don't believe so. I will pass on instructions tomorrow to investigate."

CHAPTER FORTY-EIGHT

Grand Overland Rail director Oscar Baker saw no cause to deny a request by Sir Ronald Hewitt-Thompson's step-daughter, Harriet Stephenson, to see him. Of course, he was puzzled about the reason for her visit, and he presumed she was organising her stepfather's estate and had questions. He readily agreed.

A private coach with curtains fully drawn arrived outside Mr Baker's home in an exclusive part of Kensington, and a house servant received Miss Stephenson as she descended from the coach with the assistance of the coachman.

If she felt nervous or anxious, her outward demeanour gave no sign. On the invitation of the house servant, she entered Oscar Baker's home and was escorted to the parlour, where she waited a few moments for her host to appear. Her eyes flicked over the walls where artwork hung in unapologetic museum splendour. She decided that many of them were gaudy, vulgar, and garish, not her taste, and she wondered what drove wealthy people to spend a ransom on distasteful wall hangings they called art.

The door opened, and Mr Baker entered. She'd met him once in Chieveley and still found him dull and dry, and he seemed no different now as he took her proffered hand.

"Miss Stephenson, please accept my condolences for our loss.

Sir Ronald was a wonderful, kind and generous man who will be missed."

"Thank you, Mr Baker," she replied, masking her true sentiments.

"Please be seated. Tea will be brought in," he tittered and sat in an expensive Howard and Sons chair as Harriet returned to a comfortable settee and presented him with her warmest smile.

"Now then, I presume you are seeing to the affairs of Sir Ronald and have questions?" He raised a single eyebrow.

The room seemed to be closing in on her; the obtrusive artwork and décor didn't help, and she felt trapped. She took a deep breath. "Mr Baker, I have some questions about Grand Overland Rail that I'm hoping you can help me with."

"Of course."

Just then, a maid entered carrying a silver platter with a tea set.

"Good timing, eh?" he tittered again.

The tea helped her nerves and settled her stomach.

"I understand that Grand Overland Rail has recently been beset by a, a financial crisis of sorts that has extended to its directors."

Oscar Baker inclined his head and remained silent as he stirred his tea.

"I'm also led to believe that the company is floundering, has no capital reserves, poor to no credit, and that the directors will be liable for any debt, especially if the labour strike gains traction. How would you respond to that, Mr Baker?"

He placed the spoon in the saucer with a clatter. "I would say you are well informed, although I wouldn't admit to that in public." Mr Baker shifted position on his chair. "Miss Stephenson, Grand Overland Rail is experiencing growth, and as a result, there will always be financial challenges. It's a matter of comprehending financials and the precepts of commercial enterprise, and I wouldn't expect you to understand, it is quite complex."

Harriet ignored the slight and nodded. "And you suffered a significant loss and had several pieces of valuable artwork stolen…"

Oscar's expression changed. "Yes, most unfortunate, really."

"Combined with the recent theft of your art and Grand Overland Rail's current financial position, then you continue to suffer considerable financial hardship. Am I correct in assuming that your fine art indemnity has failed in its obligation for reimbursement?" She took a sip from her teacup.

"Miss Stephenson, I thought you were here to discuss questions around Sir Ronald's estate concerning Grand Overland Rail, not the state of *my* finances. I find your enquiries to be extremely personal and somewhat offensive."

Harriet could feel her heart pounding in her chest and hoped her anxiety didn't show. "Let me change the nature of our discussion, Mr Baker."

Oscar looked relieved.

"Let me pose a question to you. Would you rather remain a director in Grand Overland Rail, in its current position, or would you prefer to have your stolen art returned?"

He shot to his feet and glared at her before speaking. "What is this? What nonsense do you speak? How dare you come into–"

"Mr Baker, please answer the question, it isn't rhetorical."

His head shook from side to side. "I don't understand."

"How important is it to you to have your art returned?"

"Of course, it's imperative, the value of the stolen art is incalculable, its–"

"Would you be willing to provide testimony to the police about the criminal behaviour of Sir Felix Dampierre and Phineas Grosley?"

Oscar slowly lowered himself back onto his seat. His face drained of colour, and she thought he would faint. "Phineas Grosley?"

"Mr Baker, look at me," she instructed.

He turned his head and stared with mouth agape.

"The criminal and unethical activities of Grand Overland Rail, London Private Acquisitions, and its Board of Directors, including Sir Felix Dampierre and, yes, the mysterious Phineas Grosley, are coming to an end, Mr Baker. You can assist the police by providing witness testimony to aid in a formal investigation that will undoubtedly lead to criminal charges. If you agree, then I believe I can arrange to have your artwork returned."

"You stole my artwork!" he stabbed a finger in her direction.

"No, Mr Baker, I did not steal your artwork, nor was I involved or knew about it. But I am in a position to help you. For your full cooperation, all your artwork will be returned."

"How...? What... ? How do I know you're being truthful?"

This was the question she'd been waiting and prepared for. She leaned forward. "Mr Baker, my coach waits for me on the street. Ask a servant to go outside and knock on the coach door."

She could see the disbelief on his face. "Humour me, Mr Baker. Go on, call a servant and have them knock on the coach's door. What do you have to lose?" She offered a pleasant smile.

He reached behind for a tasselled cord that hung from the wall and pulled it once. Then bent over and rubbed his face with both hands. Within moments, a servant entered the room, and she looked to her master for instructions.

"Please, go outside and knock on the coach's door," Harriet urged.

The housemaid looked to her master for confirmation. He nodded meekly, and the maid walked from the parlour into the hall. Harriet heard the outer door open.

Harriet placed her hand on her chest to quell her frantically beating heart. Knowing that Ollie and one of his men were in the coach gave her some peace, but her mission wasn't over yet. Oscar Baker glowered as if he wanted to kill her.

Footsteps resounded from the hall, and the maid returned carrying a smallish wrapped object. It was easy to see it was a painting and she reverently handed it to Oscar, who cautiously removed the wrap.

"My God!" he exclaimed, "A Vase of Flowers... How did you obtain this?" He caressed the painting with sinuous fingers as he marvelled at its appearance. "Do you realise the value of this fine artwork? Do you?" It suddenly dawned on him, and he inspected it for damage.

"Mr Baker, do you agree to the terms of the exchange?"

Finding no damage, he slowly stood, walked to an empty chair and lovingly placed the painting on it before turning to face her. "I'm not totally convinced."

Harriet stood, "Mr Baker, if you agree to the terms, I will ensure you receive half the artwork taken from you tomorrow, and when your unfiltered witness testimony results in the prosecution of Sir Felix Dampierre and Phineas Grosley, you will receive the other half. Do I make myself clear, sir?"

Oscar Baker took an intimidating step closer to her. "What prevents me from going to the police and having you charged with extortion and theft?"

"You may do that if you wish, but as I explained, I was not involved in the theft of your art, and today, I'm here to compel you to do what is morally right by assisting the police," she waited a moment before continuing. "However, if you refuse, I can promise you'll never see the remainder of your collection again." Harriet turned and gestured at the paintings on the parlour wall. "Be a dreadful pity if something untoward were to happen to your artwork, Mr Baker, you'll always be at risk. Any deviousness and deception will forever haunt you."

She turned back to face him. "It's been a lovely chat, Mr Baker. It's a shame we can't come to an agreement. I can see myself out." She walked from the parlour and immediately heard hurried footsteps behind her. She tensed, fully expecting to be attacked.

"Tomorrow, you say? Tomorrow, I will receive half my paintings back?"

Harriet kept her back to him and smiled. "Half, Mr Baker."

"Then I agree to your terms," he said.

"Have a pleasant afternoon." She walked outside expecting Oscar to have doubt and chase after her. From within the coach, the door opened, and a hand extended out to assist her inside.

"How did th' toff respond?" Ollie asked.

"I feel faint, Ollie," she said as the coachman urged the horses into a trot. She fanned herself with her hand. "I do believe we have come to an amicable agreement."

Ollie turned to Peter, who sat beside him. "I guess we'll be havin' us a busy morn'n, eh?"

"Detective Sergeant Roggin is here, sir," informed Mary.

"Thank you, Mary, see him in." Austin had been helped from his bed and carefully down the stairs, and now he sat uncomfortably on a chair in the parlour of Eunice's home. The discomfort of the gunshot wound was manageable, however, his cracked ribs were another matter, and as long as he kept movement to a minimum, he could endure the pain.

"Miss Stephenson," the detective acknowledged when he entered with a respectful head bow. "Mr Willoughby, it is good to see you recovering, sir," he added before turning to Austin. "Captain, shouldn't you be in bed? And if I may say, you look dreadful."

The bruising and swelling on Austin's face had yet to heal, but like his other injuries, he felt he could cope.

"I told him to remain in bed," Harriet responded. "However, typically, he wouldn't listen." She gave Austin a harsh look followed by a smile. "Please be seated, Detective Sergeant Roggin," she invited.

"Detective Sergeant Roggin," began Austin in a voice barely above a whisper. "You promised that if you obtained evidence, you would act on that information and begin a formal investigation that could hopefully lead to a prosecution."

"I do recall that is what I said, Captain." The detective turned to Howard and Harriet. "But you have no–"

"We do."

Roggin's eyes opened wide, and his head whipped around to stare at Austin. "You had better explain."

Austin finished detailing how Mr Oscar Baker had a sudden change of heart and was willing to do his civic duty and be interviewed by police. On cue, Nanny brought tea, which allowed the detective time to consider what he'd just been told.

When Nanny left the room, he looked at each face individually and shook his head in disbelief. "How did you manage it, Captain Willems?"

"The same way these unscrupulous men became involved in crime in the first place – we appealed to their greed," Austin answered truthfully.

The detective took another sip from his cup. "When is he expecting me to interview him?"

"I'd suggest tomorrow morning, er, he will be a little preoccupied this afternoon, Detective Sergeant Roggin," Austin replied with a pained version of a smile.

The detective placed his teacup on its saucer. "Have any laws been broken? Did you threaten violence or some other horrific act to coerce him to talk?"

"No, no, Detective Sergeant. Far from it. Although, if through the course of your official inquiries, you discover that Mr Baker has committed a crime, then through his willingness to be interviewed, he may seek some leniency on your part."

Detective Sergeant Roggin was quiet as he thought about this new development. After a few moments, he looked at Austin. "I fear you are still in danger, perhaps more than ever. If what you say is true about Sir Felix Dampierre and Phineas Grosley, and they learn about Mr Baker, he and all of you could still be at significant risk. It won't take long to discover you are currently in Mayfair."

"Detective Sergeant Roggin," began Howard, speaking for the first time. "We are cognisant of the fact that these men want our heads, and wisely, once it is dark, we will relocate this evening. Where we go will not be disclosed, and we hope that you can keep us appraised of developments of those two despicable men by sending a message to Mr Nagle at the Lamb and Flag. Once they are in custody, we can all return home and put these unpleasant experiences behind us."

"Are you sure you'll be safe?" the detective asked.

Howard nodded. "For the time being."

"If my interview with Mr Baker proves fruitful, then I can justify assigning a constable for your protection," added the detective.

"Thank you, Detective Sergeant Roggin," Austin said. "We'll accept all the help we can."

CHAPTER FORTY-NINE

Ollie delivered the message to Austin, preferring to convey it himself rather than rely on someone else.

Deciding they could no longer stay in Mayfair, Austin, Harriet, and Nanny had temporarily moved to Howard's flat the previous evening, and no one other than Ollie knew its location. However, his unscheduled arrival caused some concern, and Austin was keen to understand why.

Howard's home was a spacious three-bedroom, Holborn flat not far from his office. Austin believed no one would think that's where he'd hide while he recovered, and if all went to plan, they might only need to stay two or three nights before returning home.

Howard was about to leave for his office as he had numerous legal documents to sign, and he felt strong enough to spend the afternoon at work when he heard the door knock and discovered Ollie outside.

"You have news, Ollie? Hopefully, you bring news that Detective Sergeant Roggin has arrested Sir Felix Dampierre and Phineas Grosley," greeted Austin.

"Er, I wished it'd be, Cap'n." Ollie shook his head and self-consciously held his hat in both hands as everyone stared at him. "It'd be the toff, Baker, sir. He was killed last evening and 'is 'ouse burned."

"No!" Austin cried out, then winced at the involuntary movement. "It can't be." He shook his head.

"Do we know did it?" Harriet asked.

"Not so that I'd heard, Ma'am."

Austin's mind was working frantically. "Was he burned to death, Ollie?"

"T'was a knife, he bled to death. Other than house staff, he was alone," Ollie added. "Then they torched the place."

"My God," Austin whispered.

"Family??" queried Howard.

"Mr Baker has no family, Howard," Austin added.

"Aye, and he had 'is throat slashed while he slept," Ollie added. "Murder."

"Good heavens," Harriet exclaimed in horror. "That is tragic, and how sad for him," she began. "But that changes much, and Austin, you and I are in considerable danger."

"I reckons so too," Ollie stated.

"Probably safest here," said Howard.

"I can't imagine Detective Sergeant Roggin will be thrilled. Means no investigation," said Austin. "Now I have to think of a new plan."

"Any ideas?" asked Howard as he rose from his chair to look down at the street through a window.

Austin slowly shook his head. "No."

Howard departed soon after, leaving Austin, Harriet and Nanny with Ollie. Collectively, they could think of no solutions, and Ollie returned to the Lamb and Flag.

It was late afternoon when Howard returned from his office and was exhausted.

"I think I should retire, Austin. I never realised how taxing my work is," suggested Howard after slumping in his chair.

"Signing papers is strenuous," quipped Austin with a smile.

Howard didn't react. "Which reminds me. You and Harriet visited one of my partners, Simon Walker, while I was convalescing," Howard began.

"Yes, I asked Simon to keep me appraised if Grand Overland Rail was liquidating their assets and put Midlands Collieries up for sale."

"Seems they are, Austin. Not only Midlands Collieries, but the directors of Grand Overland Rail have strongly suggested they'd be very interested in selling their rail company."

Austin didn't respond.

"Austin, did you hear me?" Howard asked.

Harriet was looking at Austin. "I believe he is thinking, Howard."

"Austin! Did you hear me?"

Austin slowly turned his head and looked at Howard, then at Harriet. "I think that is it – our solution."

Harriet's eyebrows furrowed.

"I will make an offer on Midlands and buy back father's business," he grinned. "But, will inform them that I will also purchase Grand Overland Rail."

"You don't have the capital," advised Howard. "If you purchase Midlands, you fall far short of what you'll need to make an offer Grand Overland Rail will accept as legitimate."

"Even if you don't buy Midlands, then that adds to the value of Grand Overland Rail. You still don't have the means," Howard added.

Austin looked thoughtful.

"Not if I contribute," said Harriet.

Austin and Howard turned their heads to look at her. "What did you say?" Austin asked.

"I will partner with you to purchase Grand Overland Rail and provide the shortfall after you purchase Midlands Collieries."

"Are you serious? Austin asked.

"Of course," she replied. "When father passed, I inherited a great deal of money, as did Mama. I have more than enough on my own."

Austin knew that when her biological father, Ambrose Stephenson, had been enormously wealthy and endowed his wife, Eunice and only child, Harriet, with his entire estate. While he didn't know the extent of Harriet's wealth, which they had not previously discussed together, he determined it was enormous. That is probably why Sir Ronald Hewitt-Thompson married Eunice in the first place.

"I think we should discuss this, Harriet. I don't feel you need to put your inheritance at risk for my sake," he explained.

She shrugged. "Of course, we should discuss it, but I shall not change my mind, Captain Willems." She poked her tongue at him.

"Simon needs your authorisation to begin negotiating on your behalf," Howard instructed

"As an anonymous purchaser, I hope."

"That's what I'm led to believe, Austin. And he gave me some contracts for you to sign so he can proceed."

"I just hope they haven't run Midlands down to the ground. And we can't go snooping around to find out, or word will spread."

"I think it's good news, and your father would be pleased," added Howard.

"I don't have Midlands yet, but fingers crossed, eh."

"If Grand Overland Rail's directors knew, do you think they would sell the company to you?" Harriet asked.

Austin tried to laugh and grabbed at his chest. "Don't make me laugh." Suddenly, his expression changed. "Oh dear God."

Howard, Harriet, and Nanny, who had just stepped into the room, stared.

"Austin?" Harriet asked.

"It just dawned on me. One by one, all of London Private Acquisitions directors are dying, except–"

"Virgil Hartmann and George Dillington," stated Harriet.

"That is the motivation for Sir Felix Dampierre and Phineas Grosley to see the remaining two dead as well. With them dead–"

"And us," reminded Harriet.

Austin grimaced. "Then it most unlikely that any criminal charges will be filed against Dampierre and Grosley."

"Unless they are caught," suggested Howard.

Jeffrey and Harrison Watson were seated in the parlour of Eunice's home in Mayfair. Austin sat in an armchair with a blanket draped over him, and Harriet sat on a chair beside him while Howard was also present and was currently the focus of the Watson Brothers' attention.

"We don't understand, Captain Willems, why is your solicitor here?" asked Harrison.

"He is a trusted friend, and I value his counsel," replied Austin.

"Doesn't explain why you wanted to see us, although I realise your injuries make travelling difficult," added Jeffrey.

"My injuries are somewhat serious, and physicians have told me they will have a long-term effect on my life," lied Austin.

The Watson brothers exchanged glances.

"I no longer have the energy or desire to purchase Midlands Collieries Company or partner with you in Grand Overland Rail."

"We had an understanding," Harrison appealed.

"I apologise, we did have a loose agreement of sorts, however, that was before I was attacked and shot. As a courtesy, I wanted to explain to you personally, and I'm sure you understand."

"This changes much," added Harrison and spared his brother another quick glance.

"Perhaps I have saved you from pursuing a bad investment. I understand that Grand Overland Rail requires significant capital to move forward with its expansion, and quite frankly, I do not have access to those funds needed nor the motivation to continue."

The room was silent as everyone digested what Austin revealed.

"This does put us in a difficult position, Captain Willems. We have made assurances and formalised a line of credit to purchase Grand Overland Rail in partnership with you." Both Harrison and Jeffrey looked unhappy at Austin's disclosure.

Harriet was looking at her hands in her lap while Howard sat with legs crossed and stared at the far wall.

"I do understand, gentlemen, and again, I must apologise to you both for wasting your time," Austin continued.

Jeffrey looked morose while his brother lowered his head in obvious disappointment. After a moment, Harrison raised his head. "Captain Willems, would you reconsider if you had access to a line of credit?"

Howard's eyes shifted imperceptibly towards Austin, but his head didn't move.

Austin silently exhaled. "I fail to see how any financial institution would grant me credit, as I don't have the assets."

"I told you at a previous meeting that we could help in that regard," said Harrison.

"Yes, I recall. But…"

"You haven't answered the question, Captain."

Austin tried to shift position, and his face took on a pained expression. "I wouldn't be interested unless I knew the credit was honoured by a respected institution."

Harriet raised her head and turned to look at Austin.

"What Captain Willems is trying to say," interjected Howard. "He will not enter into any financial agreements unless he is assured that there is no impropriety and the organisation is sound and credible. Who is your credit source?"

All heads turned to Harrison Watson.

"Bank of England."

"Nonsense, they of all banks wouldn't touch Captain Willems unless he had assets and a borrowing history," Howard exclaimed with a vigorous shake of his head.

"I couldn't agree with you more, Mr Willoughby. However, we have a source inside the bank to establish a suitable line of credit in Captain Willems's name."

"Unless Mr Willoughby and I can meet with the lender to establish bona fides, I'm not interested. Unfortunately, and due to my injuries, coach travel is problematic, which does make such a meeting improbable. Who is your source, Mr Watson?"

"I'm not at liberty to disclose that information to you yet. However, if you agree, I will disclose his name and arrange a suitable place."

Austin turned to Howard. "Have you an opinion?"

Howard cleared his throat. "I think meeting this person face to face is prudent. If he is indeed in a position to provide the credit line, then I think it is something to consider seriously."

Both Watson brothers smiled for the first time.

"Harriet?" Austin asked.

"I agree with Mr Willoughby. But I do believe that consummating this arrangement should be done with haste as I have heard that Grand Overland Rail has had another expression of interest from an interested buyer."

The Watson brothers smiles were short-lived. "Is this true?"

"I heard through my mother, as a board member informed her," Harriet added.

Austin began coughing, which caused chest pain. He held his chest tightly until the urge subsided.

"Be advised, gentlemen, Captain Willems will be relocated and convalesce at Windhaven, our country estate in Chieveley, where clean air and rest will serve him well. Unfortunately, any meetings must be at Windhaven. I understand it is inconvenient, but a minor one at worst."

The Watson brothers exchanged glances. "Very well, we understand," replied Harrison.

"Captain Willems needs rest, gentleman," suggested Howard, who slowly eased himself to his feet and smiled at the guests. "We look forward to seeing you and your financial expert at Windhaven."

Harrison and Jeffrey rose to their feet. "We will send word of our arrival," Harrison confirmed.

CHAPTER FIFTY

Large decorative murals of Roman men and women frolicking naked in a bathhouse were painted on marble tiles, adding authenticity to the Turkish Bathhouse on Jermyn Street, just around the corner from White's gentleman's club. The bathhouse catered exclusively to the privileged, where privacy and pleasure were expected if not assured.

After submitting to traditional hot, dry air to cleanse their bodies that Turkish bathhouses were renowned for, Sir Felix Dampierre and Phineas Grosley were now, like various murals depicted, soaking naked in a heated sunken bath before receiving a sensual massage afterwards.

Phineas was admiring the form of a scantily clad attendant as he sauntered past, his bare feet pattering softly upon marble floor tiles as he placed fresh towels on a bench behind them. "Something about these places is just so invigorating," he wistfully said to his friend as they watched him leave.

The attendant closed the heavy door behind him, and the two men were again alone and could talk without fear of being overheard.

"The night is still young, Fin," replied Sir Felix with a grin.

Phineas laughed, "And we may yet share the pleasures such a nubile and eager participant is willing to provide."

"He is indeed a vamp and knows we hunger," added Sir Felix.

The sound of their combined laughter echoed around the cavernous space.

"And speaking of hunger, have you given thought to Captain Willems? I believe you said we need to provide an answer by tomorrow morning," reminded Sir Felix. His eyes closed as he rested his head on a pillow while his body was submerged beneath the hot water.

Phineas nodded. "I have given this some considered thought, Felix."

Eager to learn more, Sir Felix sat upright and turned to his friend.

"I will accept Miss Stephenson's invite to visit Windhaven. I know it to be an impressive estate, and I care to see it for myself again, as who knows, perhaps it will fall into my hands soon. I will bring all required paperwork and insist that Captain Willems provides me with his signatures immediately, which will activate the line of credit Grand Overland Rail seeks."

Sir Felix's eyebrows furrowed in puzzlement. "Is that wise, Fin? Exposing yourself to Captain Willems... do you think he knows of your existence and our plans? Perhaps I should come too."

Phineas grinned and rose from the pool's heat to sit on the side with his legs dangling in the water. "As you fully know, I have no problem exposing myself, dear boy." He snickered and clapped his friend affectionately on the shoulder. "Captain Willems has no knowledge of who I am, although he may know of you. He will learn I am a banker who can approve a line of credit, nothing more. But while your company would be most welcome, I think it best if you remain in London and arrange for Captain Willems and Miss Stephenson to receive a visit from your friends. A visit that results in a permanent solution to our problem."

"He will find it peculiar that the governor of the Bank of England is personally delivering papers a subordinate could easily do."

"I will tell Captain Willems, that I have a personal association with Grand Overland Rail and my presence will assure the captain of the legitimacy of the credit line."

"Indeed, a prudent course of action," agreed Sir Felix with a nod.

"Once the credit doccuments are signed, I will immediately leave Windhaven, and on my departure and safely on the train, your gunmen friends should enter the estate and shoot Captain Willems and Miss Stephenson until they are dead," again sniggered Phineas. "I don't foresee any complications, and Captain Willems is invalided, unable to offer resistance or even flee. After all, it is a country estate, and it is unlikely farmers have the courage or motivation to defend their masters," Phineas chuckled. "I believe Captain Willems erred when he suggested Windhaven as a place to meet. Its isolation is perfect for us to finalise our plans."

Sir Felix's face relaxed as he broke into a smile. "Which means the Willems estate becomes liable for the credit line, and we may end up again being the owner of Grand Overland Rail by default."

"Yes, that is one way of looking at it, Felix. More importantly, we remain unburdened of any wrongdoing. I will be on the 1.00 p.m. train headed for London and when Captain Willems and his lady friend are killed, I will not be considered a suspect. Remember Felix, both of them are the last people who could implicate us."

"But then we still have Virgil Hartmann and George to consider," added Sir Felix.

Phineas broke into a smile. "I no longer believe Virgil will be a problem. I hear he's at the end of his tether, it's all become a bit much for the poor fellow."

Sir Felix sighed.

"And dear George... I have such fond memories of his social get-togethers."

"And what of your brothers?"

Phineas Grosley's head whipped around to glare at Sir Felix. "What of them?"

Sir Felix shrugged. "Do you fear them talking?"

Phineas laughed. "No, not at all. They were the architects of our windfall, and we have all benefitted immensely.

Ollie placed his glass on a coaster and rubbed his leg above where a leather boot was attached to the stump. "From what you'd be tellin', these coach builders are bent?"

Austin sat with Harriet, Howard and Ollie in Howard's spacious flat and took a sip of port before replying. "They are, I have no doubt whatsoever. I made the mistake of going to them for help and, by doing so, allowed myself to be manipulated, and without your investigation of them, Ollie, I'd either be dead or destitute."

Harriet shivered, but not from the cold. "But we must plan accordingly now that the banker has agreed to meet us at Windhaven."

"And so we shall. When did Detective Sergeant Roggin say he would arrive?" asked Austin.

"Later this afternoon, as soon as he could leave the court, he was at the Old Bailey," offered Ollie.

Howard twisted in his chair to face Austin. "Have you considered what you will do if the detective is unwilling to help?"

"I have, and we carry on regardless. I don't believe we have an option to do otherwise. We cannot continue to run and hide forever, they will find us and see us all killed. If the police don't help, we are forced to take matters into our own hands unless anyone has a better idea."

No one did.

Detective Sergeant Roggin pinched the bridge of his nose with a forefinger and thumb. After a moment, he removed his hand and raised his head to look at Austin. "What proof do you have that this Phineas, er–"

"Grosley, Detective," Austin added.

"–Will commit a crime at Windhaven? All you can tell me is that Grosley is coming to Windhaven in three days, as he believes you will sign a line of credit to enable you to purchase a rail company. If I'm not to be misunderstood, gentlemen and lady, I don't believe that is a crime."

Austin sat with a blanket over his lap and faced the detective seated opposite. With some discomfort, he leaned forward. "Detective, Phineas Grosley and his partner Sir Felix Dampierre want to see my death, perhaps even Harriet's or Howard or Ollie's. Why? Because we have learned about their scheme. They have already killed Julian De Vore, Sir Ronald Hewitt-Thompson, and Able Baker and made two attempts on my life. Grosley will, in all likelihood, send men to Windhaven because they believe the remoteness offers them an opportunity to kill me and, or others. Once we are dead, they can continue with their plans to bilk investors of thousands of pounds." He spared Harriet a look.

"And you are certain of this?" asked Detective Sergeant Roggin.

"I'm putting my life on the line. How much more proof do you require?" Austin's voice rose in frustration. He slowly leaned back in his chair as the outburst hurt his healing ribs.

"Tell me again, when is this meeting?"

"On Friday, in three days," informed Austin. "Approximately 11.00 a.m., which will coincide with train schedules.

"And what am I to tell Detective Chief Inspector Bird when I ask for authorisation to assign constables to assist me in the arrest of an influential businessman who you suspect is involved in multiple homicides – outside my patch?" Detective Sergeant Roggin made eye contact with everyone in the room while waiting for a response.

"You will tell him that the brief reassignment of men will prevent further murders, Detective," Howard suggested.

"Detective, this Phineas Grosley has no idea we know that we are on to him. He will bring Jeffrey and Harrison Watson, his two half-brothers, who are complicit in this conspiracy. The last remaining conspirator is Sir Felix Dampierre—"

"Another influential government bureaucrat who can affect my employment status," the detective reminded them. "I believe he has already applied internal pressure to Detective Chief Inspector Bird to resolve the investigation."

Austin grimaced, the constant discomfort of his injuries was fatiguing. "If everything goes according to plan, we hope to extract a confession from Mr Grosley, who will implicate Sir Felix Dampierre and any others in this conspiracy, if they exist."

Detective Sergeant Roggin looked thoughtful. "I'm sorry, Captain, I'm not convinced. Although circumstantial evidence supports your theory, it isn't enough, and even if I wanted, my request to assign staff to Chieveley will, with absolute certainty, be denied." He shook his head. "Again, I'm sorry, Captain."

All heads turned to the door when someone hammered on it. Ollie eased himself to his feet. "I'll get it, Nanny," he said as she entered the room. Detective Sergeant Roggin stood, and Austin saw how his hand went to his belt where his revolver was secured.

Ollie opened the door to find a constable standing awkwardly outside. He looked down at Ollie's wooden leg. "Beggin' yer pardon, sir. I needs to speak to Detective Sergeant Roggin."

The detective rushed to the door as everyone watched.

"Sorry to disturb you, sir, but there's been another death related to this case. Detective Chief Inspector Bird requests your presence."

Austin turned to Harriet and whispered, "Virgil Hartmann, I wager."

"Who died?" asked the detective as he rubbed the back of his head.

The young detective shrugged, "I wasn't told, sir. There's a carriage outside waiting." He turned and pointed.

The detective turned back to Austin. "I apologise. Forgive me. It seems I am needed elsewhere."

"Detective, remember what we discussed. I implore you to think carefully. And if the victim is Virgil Hartmann, as I believe, that only adds credence to my request for police assistance."

Ollie shut the door and scowled after the detective stepped out. "I reckon we need to gather our forces and regroup in Westhaven, wherever the bloody hell that is, and as soon as bleedin' possible, or we be next."

"Go, Ollie," instructed Austin as Harriet handed him an envelope. Ollie looked at the thick envelope and placed it in his coat pocket.

"Everything you need is in there," said Harriet. "Please hurry."

"We are no longer safe here." Austin closed his eyes at the thought of how much discomfort a lengthy train journey would provide. "All of us must leave."

Harriet and Nanny went to pack their few belongings as Austin and Howard reviewed their plan.

St Saviours Estate was not far from Tower Bridge in Bermondsey, on London's south-east side, and the police carriage made good time. On arrival, Detective Sergeant Roggin hurried inside the house and found Detective Chief Inspector Bird contemplating the morbid sight of a man hanging by a rope from a rafter.

"No doubt the gentleman had a bad day, eh Detective?"

He couldn't see the man's face from where he stood. "Who is he?" asked the young detective, ignoring the smell of faecal matter and the unsavoury comment from his superior.

"He was Virgil Hartmann."

At the disclosure, Detective Sergeant Roggin's eyes opened wide, but tactfully, he chose to remain silent and took a closer look. A sturdy nautical line, similar to what you'd find on a sailboat, had been attached over the only exposed rafter in the room, and the other end was looped over the head of an approximately forty-five to fifty years old, prematurely grey, haired man. He recognised the face as a director when he visited Grand Overland Rail.

"Suicide," simply said Chief Inspector Bird, folding his arms. "Same chap whose yacht was torched not that long ago. Must have been too much for him, and he decided to end it all."

A sideboard had been moved from the wall into the middle of the room, and Detective Sergeant Roggin assumed the deceased had stood on the furniture, thrown the rope over the rafter, affixed it around his neck and then stepped off. Judging from the angle of Mr Hartmann's neck, it was broken.

Chief Detective Inspector Bird exited the room to stand outside, where the air was fresh, while the young detective continued investigating. He stepped around the excrement that dripped from the body onto the expensive thick rug and studied the area carefully. He bent down, opened the sideboard drawers and cupboard, and saw books on boats, yachts and marine navigation.

It was an unpleasant scene, and Roggin's had seen enough. He joined his superior outside as undertakers waited for permission to remove the body.

"Just log it as a suicide, Detective. The man certainly had a motive to take his own life as his businesses failed and his beloved yacht was destroyed."

"Suicide, Chief Detective Inspector?" clarified Detective Sergeant Roggin.

His superior turned to face him. "Of course."

"Sir, Mr Hartmann was murdered," Roggin responded. "Come, I will show you." Both men re-entered the house and asked the undertakers to leave briefly. "Sir, can you move the sideboard and put it back against the wall."

Bird grunted, his displeasure evident as he scowled. He bent down, placed both hands on the furniture and pushed. It didn't move. He turned around and tried to use his back, but the sideboard was too low. Again, he faced the furniture, and with his shoulder and both hands, he tried to push the sideboard. It moved slightly, leaving a furrow mark on the rug.

"If you look here, sir, you'll see where the sideboard was originally placed against the wall, and then you can also see where it was pushed for about six inches. Then, the indentation on the rug stops. I suggest to you, sir, that more than one man, possibly two large or three men, moved the sideboard and hanged Mr Hartmann in such a way that it would appear to be a suicide. The weight of the sideboard makes it almost impossible for Mr Hartmann to move it by himself." Detective Sergeant Roggin squared his shoulders and faced his superior. "Chief Detective Inspector, this is a murder investigation."

Detective Sergeant Roggin thought back to Captain Willems's last comment before he left earlier in the day.

The chief detective inspector loudly exhaled. "Very well, Detective, good work, I concur. Carry on," said Chief Detective Inspector Bird with word efficiency before turning to leave the premises.

"Sir, before you leave, may I have a word?"

CHAPTER FIFTY-ONE

On arrival, with Austin supportively at her side, Harriet told house and ground staff that for their safety they should leave Windhaven immediately. Some asked to remain, including Elias Pickenbury, the stable master, Stacey, the staff cook, one maid, and a groundsman, Bartholomew Loomis, a retired soldier who felt he could contribute and pleaded to stay. After a conversation with him, Ollie agreed, and Bart didn't have to go.

Elias Pickenbury felt only he could look after the horses, and Stacey, who worked in the staff housing, had nowhere to go, and she reminded Harriet someone was needed to provide meals and care for the strangers who would be sleeping there.

Bartholomew, or Bart as he was known, had specific knowledge about the estate and, combined with his military expertise, proved invaluable. He assisted Ollie when assigning the ten men he brought from London to various tasks and positions around the estate. None of the men strongly objected to their *faux* work assignments, although some initially griped a little. Ollie sternly reminded them that they were being paid handsomely.

There was a tenseness around Windhaven; the normally serene country estate belonging to Eunice Hewitt-Thompson was not operating normally. It was odd for the few remaining staff to see so many strange men assuming duties usually completed by friendly and familiar faces. Their presence was an unkind reminder that all was not well and danger lurked.

Ollie was in his element, and his voice boomed across the estate as he instructed his small force to make defensive preparations. Adding to the unease, no one fully understood what they were actually preparing for.

Austin believed that an attempt on his and Harriet's life was inevitable, and by association, Howard and Nanny could also be targeted. In what form that attempt would be made was anyone's guess. Ollie and Bart believed men would come at night from the main road, spread out and enter the house and simply shoot anyone who stood in their way.

They still had two days before Phineas Grosley arrived with the other Watson brothers. However, Austin wasn't sure if that was a ruse, and they had no intention of travelling to Windhaven and send killers instead.

Frustrated by his injuries, Austin couldn't do much except issue instructions and think.

He implored over and over again that everything had to appear normal. Nothing or no one should appear out of place to a casual observer or an assassin.

Harriet suggested sending a man with a horse to Chieveley's railway station as a lookout and providing warning, but as Austin pointed out, none of the emplyees knew who to look for or what the Watson brothers looked like.

It was unanimously agreed that everyone, including Austin and Harriet, would sleep in the staff quarters, no one would sleep in the manor. During darkness, lamps would burn inside the estate mansion to create the impression people were inside. Adding to the deception, a guard would wander through the house and a few men would be hidden in strategic locations nearby.

Austin was understandably anxious, the constant apprehension and responsibility he felt for the safety of Howard, Nanny, Harriet, and, of course, other people who were at Windhaven sat heavily on his shoulders. He needed fresh air to think more clearly, and with some difficulty, he eased himself from the chair to slowly wander outside.

The moon, suspended protectively above Windhaven, sat high in the evening sky. Its full brilliance in contrast to the darkness behind and the shimmering stars beyond. Austin gazed upwards into the heavens at the celestial splendour offered by a peaceful and cloudless night. He felt Harriet's presence, and without turning, he reached an arm outward and guided her into his side. The movement caused him to wince, and she tensed. "I'm healing but tend to forget," he whispered, lowering his chin to rest softly on her head as she gently nestled into him. They remained silent, unmoving, yet fully aware of each other's unspoken thoughts.

He breathed in her fragrance that he'd come to know so well. He could feel the light rise and fall of her chest as her breathing settled and she slowly relaxed. The past week had been stressful for everyone, and yet, through the adversity, Harriet endured and remained steadfast and supportive. She loved with an openness and directness that was not just endearing - it drew him in, enveloping and ever consuming. This was a new experience for him, and he welcomed it.

Above them, the dependability of the stars to sparkle was like the love he felt from her, immediate, reliable and constant.

And, as a result of two unsuccessful attempts on his life, he'd questioned his fragile mortality and simultaneously accepted Harriet as now being part of his being. He was fully aware that she sparked the light that manifested from within. She'd changed him, not physically, but intellectually and emotionally; his future was bound to hers, as permanent as a distant star and the glittering eternal companionship of its neighbour. He closed his eyes, ignored the threats and danger that would soon surround them, and reflected on the positive changes she brought to his life.

She must have known his thoughts because she spoke two words. "I know," she simply breathed. He heard them clearly, his senses finely attuned to her as hers to him. It moved him, and he opened his eyes to clarity.

Slowly, he separated and looked down at her face, lit precisely by the moon. She glowed. Her beauty, so absent of flaws... She didn't question his silent appreciation; her last spoken words said it all. She knew.

"I love you, Harriet Stephenson, and I'd be honoured if you'd be my wife – will you marry me?"

She didn't reply, her expression unchanged, and like his own, her eyes welled—that moment of acceptance and understanding frozen in time.

"You needed to ask?" her face broke into a smile, and ignoring the pain, he pulled her back into his embrace.

He felt her hot breath on his cheek.

"Yes."

Day two at Windhaven saw everyone relax as they became accustomed to what was to come, and Austin and Harriet tactfully decided to delay the news of their engagement until this unpleasant business was over.

Men were strategically placed around the grounds, and weapons were always within easy reach. Some of the men who came from the filthy streets of London warmed to the quiet, peacefulness of country life, but those same men were also attentive to the perils still to come and were no strangers to violence and death.

Against all his military training and years of experience, Austin began questioning his judgement, and doubt crept into his frequent discussions with Ollie. His physical fragility was never more apparent than now, and he felt frustrated that he couldn't defend Harriet and those close to him if the need arose.

Everyone sensed Austin's vulnerability, and each took time to offer support or talk.

It was just after 3 o'clock, and he sat alone while Harriet took Howard to see the thoroughbred racehorses he'd heard so much about. Nanny came into the sunroom with tea and biscuits. She placed the tray on a table, poured two cups of tea, and sat beside him.

"You haven't had time to grieve," she affirmed.

Austin was perplexed, Nanny never did this. She never sat with him to just chat. She'd bring tea, pour a cup for him and leave. He thought about Howard conveniently asking Harriet to show him the horses and knew Nanny had this conversation planned. He looked at her and smiled. "No, Nanny, I haven't."

"I miss him too, Austin. Enoch played a big part in my life, even long before you were born. He was a lovely, warm-hearted and generous man."

She called him Austin, and even though he'd asked her repeatedly to address him familiarly, she never did.

"I have memories, Nanny, and I'm grateful for them. We had good times together, didn't we – you, me, father and even Howard?"

She nodded.

"Of course, how could I ever forget those good times, Nanny?

You and Howard would take me out when Father was busy at work."

"Yes, Enoch was always busy," she said reflectively with a wistful sigh. "I loved him dearly, Austin."

"I didn't know," he replied honestly.

"You weren't supposed to, Austin."

She called him Austin again. It was the way she spoke, her choice of words… He sipped from his tea and felt his face colour. He knew it then, or perhaps he'd always instinctively known. The immediate realisation, as if awakened by a surprise thunderclap wasn't frightening, it was wholly unexpected but, at the same time, welcome. His heart rate increased, and fearing spilling tea, he placed the teacup on the saucer. She reached across and patted his hand and then self-consciously withdrew it.

He inhaled deeply and turned to look at her. Tears ran freely down her face, confirming what he felt. He opened his mouth to speak but couldn't. Overcome with emotion, he raised his hands to cover his face and, as a boy before his mother, wept without shame. He never felt her lean over to embrace him, and he didn't know how long they held each other. It was the touch of a mother he'd never felt or acknowledged.

Eventually, she pulled away and wiped her eyes. "I was a spirited and rebellious young girl and constantly disobeyed my parents. My father, bless him, was a coal miner and worked hard alongside Enoch. When Midlands Collieries Company began to make money, Enoch offered to take me in as a maid. He promised my father he would care for me and ensure I could read, write and learn my numbers. He even told my father I would learn self-respect."

Austin listened with rapt attention. He couldn't believe what he heard, but he knew everything she said, supressed for years, was true.

"Enoch Willems was more than a good man, Austin; he was

noble and true to his word." She sighed as her memories and emotions, unspoken and stifled for so many years, surfaced. "We fell in love, and then … I was with child. Enoch was a gentleman, and I, unmarried and a mere maid," she shook her head. "It wouldn't do. Enoch wanted to marry me, but I wouldn't have it. People would gossip, his reputation and standing would be affected, and his developing business would suffer. He pleaded with me to marry him."

She paused, and Austin gave her the time to collect her thoughts – what she'd revealed was astonishing.

"I wanted to marry him, and I knew we could be happy together, but my past and social standing would eventually take its toll. I knew it, and deep down, so did Enoch."

This time, Austin reached over and held her hand tightly, and he wouldn't let go.

"We came to an arrangement. Once I gave birth, he sold his small home and purchased the house at The Regents Park, and I became your Nanny and raised you."

Austin swallowed and shook his head at the revelation. "But, but where, how did Howard…?"

"Austin," she squeezed his hand, "Enoch and I ended our relationship permanently. If I was going to be a Nanny to a mischievous young boy, then that was what I would do. I couldn't do it and be in a relationship with your father." She smiled at him.

"My affections with Howard began some years later, and we kept it to ourselves, but Howard and I suspected Enoch knew and approved. He said nothing, and we were, er, circumspect. Howard and I love each other, Austin, and to me, you have always been my son, and I am so proud of the man you've become, even if you are still mischievous."

Through the blur of tears, Austin saw her smile. "Why keep it a secret for so long?"

She nodded. "Now is the right time. Because of Enoch's death, your relationship with Harriet… Howard and I fear for your well-being. It was time, Austin, and you needed to know."

Austin was stunned; thoughts and notions filled his head, and memories surfaced, linking everything together. The more he thought about it, the more he realised what Nanny had told him was unbelievable, but it all made sense. He wiped his eyes and saw Harriet and Howard standing in the doorway. He never heard them return.

Harriet rushed over to sit beside him. "I know."

He found his voice. "When?"

"Just now at the stables, Howard told me."

Austin exhaled. "Good heavens." He looked down at his hand, which still held Nanny's, then up at her expectant face. "Can I call you Mother?"

Shadows lengthened as the sun descended, and the four of them talked of the past, the present, including the engagement, and the future. Talking and sharing was an elixir, and despite the emotional fatigue, Austin felt invigorated. The more he thought about his mother and their life together, the more accepting he became. He wanted to call her Mother, and when he did, her face brightened with pure joy. A simple word she'd waited years to hear from her son.

However, tomorrow would be telling, and Austin knew he needed to be mentally alert and thinking clearly. Phineas Grosley had planned well, and Austin needed to be a step or two in front if he and those he cared about would survive.

Ollie did the rounds and checked all his men one last time before turning in. Tomorrow could be a long day.

CHAPTER FIFTY-TWO

The waving white cloth signalled that the Watson brothers were arriving and quickly and the news quickly relayed to Austin and Harriet, who were in the rear garden. Immediately, he felt his heart racing, and he took a couple of deep breaths to steady his frayed nerves. It was imperative that he appeared calm and composed when the brothers arrived.

Still feeling a little anxious, he turned to Harriet. "How are you?"

"As well as can be expected," she said, smiling at him. "We will all be fine, Captain Willems."

Phineas Grosley, accompanied by Jeffrey and Harrison Watson, stepped from their rented coach which remained waiting for them to conclude their business. A maid received them at the door and brought them into the parlour, a large, open and comfortable room where Austin, Harriet and Howard sat. Unusually, no refreshments were offered to their guests after their long journey.

"Your estate is spectacular, just as I remember it," began Phineas. "And thank you for receiving us." He dipped his head but did not offer his hand in greeting.

Austin took an immediate dislike to the man. His sense of dress style was garish, his mannerisms silky and insincere, and his eyes wandered everywhere except where they should.

"Thank you for coming," Austin replied, turning his attention to Jeffrey and Harrison. "Is good of you both to come all this way, but I needed to be in the country to convalesce due to an unfortunate injury, so excuse me if I do not stand. I'm forever in debt to Mrs Hewitt-Thompson for her generosity. She's been most kind for allowing me to stay here." He waved them to three chairs. "This is my solicitor, Howard Willoughby, and beside me is Miss Harriet Stephenson."

All men nodded politely, but Phineas' eyes inappropriately lingered on Harriet longer than was deemed polite.

It was game time, and Austin had thought long and hard how he would approach this get-together. This meeting put his adversaries in his domain, on his terms, and he would take full advantage and confront the three brothers face to face. He silently exhaled to ease his apprehension and then turned to Harrison Watson. "You never told me you had another brother."

Harrison's face flushed, and Jeffrey looked down at his shoes. Phineas turned and glared at the audacity of his host's impropriety.

Harrison recovered and cleared his throat. "I never had the occasion to mention it," he began.

"Or that your brother is also the Bank of England's governor. A lofty position that affords certain privileges."

"What is your point, Mr Willems?" Phineas asked as he crossed his legs and leaned back in his chair. "We have made time in our busy schedules to attend to you and present you with an opportunity to purchase substantial shares in a rail company. What is your purpose with these abrupt statements? We have business to discuss, do we not?"

"Address me as Captain, as I'm entitled, Mr Grosley."

Phineas just glared.

"And to answer your question, it is my purpose to inform you that I know that you and Sir Felix Dampierre are responsible and orchestrated the deaths of Julian De Vore, Mr Oscar Baker, Virgil Hartman and," Austin turned to Harriet, "Miss Stephenson's stepfather, Sir Ronald Hewitt-Thompson."

Jeffrey Watson shot to his feet, "Bollocks! What nonsense is this? Captain Willems, I strongly object–"

"You have no proof, Captain. Do you recall that you came to us? We did not initiate this relationship," Harrison loudly interjected.

Phineas looked uncomfortable, uncrossed his legs, and looked away briefly before turning to face Austin. He opened his mouth to speak.

Austin spoke first. "And once you have enticed me to sign your line of credit documents, then I expect that I, and anyone else whom you believe knows about your unlawful acts, will also meet an untimely death. After all, Mr Grosley, you have already made two unsuccessful attempts on my life, or do I stand corrected?"

The perpetual smugness on Phineas Grosley's face disappeared.

"Time we left, Harrison," said Jeffrey, rising to his feet.

Howard leaned forward in his chair. "The both of you are implicit," he pointed to Jeffrey and Harrison. "You both knew what Grand Overland Rail was doing to its shareholders was morally wrong, and you both conspired and were party to the deception. And you, Mr Grosley, why would the governor of the Bank of England lower himself to present loan documents that a subordinate could so easily have done?"

"Is this true, Fin? Did you have those people killed?" Harrison turned to his half-brother in disbelief.

Jeffrey remained standing, glaring at Phineas, who wouldn't make eye contact with his brothers, instead, he dismissively brushed lint from his trousers.

"I expect an answer," Jeffrey demanded.

Phineas regained his composure and again looked confident as he looked at each brother in turn. "Do you honestly believe that the amount of money that came your way was through virtuous means?" he laughed without mirth. "Where do you think it came from?"

"But to kill people?" Jeffrey shook his head in disgust.

"We have to protect our interests, your interests, Jeffrey," Phineas stated.

"This is just a game to you, isn't it? Nothing more," Jeffrey added. "This man, Felix, that Captain Willems mentioned, who is he, and what is his involvement?" He shook his head. "You've done nothing but lie to us."

Austin's mind raced. The admission could only mean one thing, Phineas Grosley had every intention to murder him, Harriet and Howard and to leave no one alive that could implicate himself or his associate, Sir Felix Dampierre.

"It was necessary, damn you. Those directors were greedy and running amok. They had to be stopped, or we'd lose everything." Phineas turned away from his brothers and looked at Austin. "Your father was the worst. It was he who first began to question our practices. He spoke up and created discord. Had he left well enough alone, he would have been wealthy beyond his dreams, but he had to be damn righteous and ruin it for everyone." He rose from his chair.

Everyone in the room glared at him in stunned silence.

"Don't you see, all the legalities, all the permits, permissions, and approvals were taken care of? Lines of credit were approved. Nothing stood in our way except one elderly gentleman, your meddling father, and now... God damn it, you!"

Harrison stood. "That's enough, Phineas. He turned to Jeffrey, "We should leave."

Phineas reached into his blazer and extracted a revolver. It was an ugly black thing with a long barrel, and with slender manicured hands, raised the weapon confidently.

"No, Fin, this is wrong!" Harrison cried out.

Austin was closest to Phineas, but there wasn't any way he could rise from his chair and disarm the man without being shot. Howard was furthest away, and Ollie was near the road, ensuring no one crept unseen onto the estate. The closest armed man was now positioned outside the main door.

"Wrong? No, dear brother. We are not linked to any improprieties or illegalities. With the Captain, his solicitor and Sir Ronald's daughter out of the way, we can continue. What *is* wrong is this meddlesome man." He waved the revolver at Austin. "All because of that fool Enoch Willems!" The solid metallic click of the hammer being pulled back was an obtrusive statement. Austin was frozen. There was nothing he could do as he stared down the unwavering barrel.

Phineas smiled as he levelled the firearm to point directly at Austin's chest two yards away. He couldn't miss.

"God, no!" yelled Jeffrey while Howard cried out in warning.

Inside the house, the discharge was loud. Harriet screamed, and the room was partially filled with blue smoke.

In immediate response and alarm, Ollie's men ran towards the house. Bart Loomis, posted outside and near the main door, charged in with his firearm held at the ready. He skidded to a stop in astonishment when he entered the room.

All heads turned to Nanny, who stood with a handgun hanging by her side. Austin sprung to his feet with a cry of pain from his ribs while Howard leapt up and ran towards Nanny.

"I, I had no choice, he, he was going to shoot…" Nanny stammered.

Phineas Grosley lay unmoving on the floor, his expensive blazer now adorned with a growing dark stain. "Jeffrey bent over him, looking for signs of life. "He's bloody dead," was all he managed to say.

Harrison, in shock, slowly stepped up to his half-brother and stared down at the lifeless body while his mouth moved in silent admonition.

Harriet and Howard took Nanny upstairs to a bedroom while Austin dealt with the aftermath.

Ollie finally arrived and clomped into the room. He looked at Bart. "You?"

Bart shook his head in denial, "Was Nanny, she did it, Sarge."

Ollie cursed.

Harrison and Jeffrey decided not to wait for the constabulary to arrive and hurriedly departed in their coach back to the railway station without speaking to anyone. They were content to leave their dead brother for the police at Windhaven.

Ollie dispatched a rider to report the death to Chieveley's police, and Phineas remained where he fell.

A sergeant and a constable arrived by wagon and spoke to Nanny, Austin, Howard and Harriet. The police were distressed that Jeffrey and Harrison Watson fled the scene but told Austin they would be interviewed in London. With some hesitancy, they felt Nanny acted within the legal interpretation of self-defence. As Howard insisted to the sergeant, if Nanny had not shot Phineas Grosley, Captain Willems would now be dead.

The corpse was loaded onto the police wagon, and the sergeant and constable departed soon after with Phineas's revolver in their care.

The day hadn't begun as Austin hoped. If his mother hadn't

shot and killed Grosley, he would have been killed. It felt peculiar thinking of Nanny as his mother, but he'd get used to it.

While waiting for the police to arrive, he'd spoken to her, and she explained how she had been listening to Grosely's disgusting rant from the hallway and was genuinely fearful he would shoot someone when she heard he'd extracted his handgun.

Earlier that morning, Austin had placed the handgun in the drawer of a hallway cabinet for the explicit purpose of easy access and defending themselves if the need arose. Wisely, she acted on her feelings and was ready when Phineas was about to shoot.

"Is it over, Cap'n?" Ollie asked.

Austin was inclined to believe it was over, but then he recalled what Phineas had said. "You know, Ollie, I don't think it is over. Phineas Grosley confessed to the murders, and he wouldn't have done so if he hadn't made plans. Shooting me this morning was never part of his plan, that was nothing but his rage and frustration."

"Why? What's so important about signing those documents?" Ollie asked.

"That's what I asked Howard. He believes that once my signature was on those papers, my estate would have been responsible for repaying the credit line in the event of my death. As the amount of money is significant, then it is most likely that my estate and Grand Overland Rail would have reverted to the bank and Phineas Grosley and probably Sir Felix Dampierre."

Ollie scratched his head. "Not the Watsons, Cap'n?"

"No, I don't think they were involved in that part of the scheme or knew about the murders. Just Phineas and his partner Sir Felix Dampierre."

"Seems bloody complicated."

"It's an age-old swindle, Ollie. You lend someone money and

extract a promise they'll pay it back. Then you ensure they can't make the repayments and then place unreasonable demands on them, insisting they do. Ultimately, they hand over assets, including what they purchased in the first place. Then you do it again."

"Ah, I see. Like a gift that keeps on bleed'n giving, sir?"

"Very much so."

Ollie looked thoughtful. "S'cuse me for say'n, but how will Grosely's partner, that other toff, Sir Felix, know you never signed them bleed'n papers and that Grosely be dead?"

Austin turned to look at his friend in growing realisation. "Good heavens, Ollie, Dampierre wouldn't know. Jeffrey and Harrison Watson admitted to not knowing about Sir Felix, so they won't be able to inform him. That means if Phineas and Sir Felix hired someone to kill Harriet and me, then they're still coming. Grosely didn't come here to shoot me himself. He wanted me to sign the line of credit documents, leave and then have someone kill us when he was safely away and could have deniability."

Ollie rubbed his face in his hands. "I'll get the men back in their positions, Cap'n. I suggest you stay indoors."

CHAPTER FIFTY-THREE

Amos Blackwell wasn't particularly concerned about the task he'd been hired to do. He had no conscience or moral objections to killing three or four people as long as he was paid the agreed-upon fee. He'd been well compensated for this particular job and received half the money in advance and the remainder when all the deaths had been confirmed. The only thing about these killings that made it different was that the targets were on a country estate and might have some light protection – a few guards, he'd been told. To ensure success, he needed to hire two other experienced shooters.

While all his previous jobs had been successfully completed, mainly because they'd been simple and uncomplicated and he hadn't encountered any real difficulties, Amos had developed a rather cavalier attitude and approach to his work. It wasn't because he lacked the required skills; he was, in fact, quite experienced. He'd had years of military training, faced an enemy on the battlefield and held himself to good account. He was better than average with a long rifle and, by some, even considered a marksman of sorts.

He wasn't fazed when given details about who, where and when he had to kill these people; he was keen to complete the job as quickly as possible so he could receive payment because he was broke – and to Amos, this was just another job.

The two additional men he hired had served with him in the

military, so he knew and trusted them both. He'd hired them before, individually, one at a time. This was the first time he'd hired them to work together.

Amos had reconnoitred the Windhaven estate the previous evening and driven past in a rented coach, then walked back and assessed how he would enter and exit the property. He diligently looked for anything suspicious indicating the targets had taken any defensive measures and counted three men. There might be one more, two at the most, but he determined the odds were certainly in his favour, and typically he wasn't worried.

Including himself, he and Iain carried a long rifle; the other man, Frank, had a double-barrelled, break-action shotgun. Additionally, each carried a handgun and a sharp knife tucked into their waistband.

Outside and in the open, a rifle was ideal. Once inside the estate house, rifles were cumbersome and restricted quick movement and a handgun was better suited, although not as accurate. It wouldn't be a factor because the distances were less. The knives were helpful if they became involved in any close-quarters action.

With the waning moon high in the sky, Amos, Frank, and Iain climbed a fence some distance from Windhaven and walked, single file, away from the road and alongside hedgerows towards the estate. They made no noise, didn't speak, and kept low. They encountered no one and heard nothing. As far as they were concerned, they were entirely alone.

Once they were on Windhaven estate land, they slightly spread out and then paused to listen. Amos knew one of the guards he previously identified last evening was near the trunk of a large tree a short distance ahead on a slightly elevated rise. It wasn't a hill but more of a low mound that gave the position a strategic advantage.

He couldn't see or hear him, but Amos knew he must be hiding.

Positioning his long rifle on his back and quietly removing his knife from its sheath, he signalled for the other two to remain while he lay prone on the ground and inched forward. He was skilled in tracking and could traverse great distances undetected.

With the help of moonlight, he saw the guard on his knees and cleverly hidden by the tree trunk. Amos was patient and slithered closer to the unsuspecting man. When two yards away, he silently rose to a crouch, with an arm extended and still holding the knife, he launched himself at the guard with his arm encircling his throat. Before the guard could cry out, he clamped his hand over his mouth then with the knife, slashed his throat from one ear to the next and expertly lowered the body to the ground. He hardly made a sound. A low whistle drew the attention of Frank and Iain, who crept to the tree where Amos waited.

Ahead, about one hundred yards away, the impressive estate mansion cast a dark outline against the sky. Yellow light seeped from behind drapes, and Amos indicated that Iain should attend to another guard at the eastern end of the house before entering the mansion from a rear entrance. He and Frank would look for an open window near the east, front side of the large home to gain access, but Amos wouldn't walk up the steps and knock on the door to announce his presence. He wanted to stealthily enter the mansion, kill the targets and quietly leave before anyone noticed they'd been there.

Iain crept away, heading towards the guard as Amos and Frank waited. They both knew Iain wouldn't fail. After Ian disappeared into the night, Amos turned his attention to the possibility of another guard, who he believed could be located at the far, opposite and western end of the house. He saw nothing and decided to push on towards the estate.

As it turned out, Amos felt most fortunate as he discovered many open windows. Within moments, he and Frank were inside. They waited until Iain appeared from the rear before all three silently moved upstairs to where they expected their targets to be. Iain guarded the top of the stairs while he and Frank searched for targets in the many upstairs bedrooms.

Amos would have been whistling if it weren't for the need for silence. His confidence was high, he enjoyed his work, and they were undetected and about to enter the first stateroom where light seeped into the hallway from beneath the door. With care, Frank twisted the door knob and gently pushed open the large, heavy door. It didn't creak and swung noiselessly open as Amos, with only the sound of his rustling clothes, entered the large room. It was empty.

So far, Amos and Frank hadn't exchanged any words, and now Frank looked at him in puzzlement. His expression echoed Amos's thoughts. He pointed next door.

The second stateroom, of equally impressive size, was also empty.

"Amos, what's goin' on?" whispered Frank.

Amos shrugged. It was a large mansion with many rooms. "We keep lookin'," he replied.

They re-entered the hallway and were reassured to see Iain still at the top of the stairs.

There was no one in the third and fourth bedrooms, and when they stepped back into the hallway, they heard the sound of footsteps from downstairs, confirming they were not alone inside the house. With his rifle held ready, Iain was still pressed against the wall in the shadows.

The temptation was to hurry and for each of them to split up and begin searching the rooms, but Amos resisted the notion. When they found someone sleeping, there might be more than one person in the bed, and Amos knew it would require two people to kill their targets quietly. They stealthily continued and didn't find a soul. The upper storey was empty.

They regrouped near the top of the stairs.

"Somethin' ain't right, Amos," Iain warned. "We be gettin' setup."

Amos looked back down the hallway and then down the stairs. "Did ya see who is down there?"

Iain shook his head.

Amos quietly cursed. "I think we need to get out of here and bloody quick."

Frank nodded, and Amos and Iain could see the fear etched on his face.

"Just like we practised, we leave together, quietly, eh, boys," Amos grinned, but his heart wasn't in it.

They descended the stairs one by one and headed towards the rear door Iain originally entered through. They were like ghosts slipping noiselessly from shadow to shadow. Once outside, they rounded the end of the house, and they were lit up by the brief flash of a rifle discharge. Iain was leading and dropped like a rock when the bullet entered his chest, killing him instantly. In the confusion and without hesitation, Amos ran with Frank following close on his heels.

Ollie yelled and instructed three men to run down the carriageway onto the road and block the escape route of the killers.

'In pairs, damn you! You two, go around the south side of the tree," Ollie bellowed before turning to another two men. "And you lot go around the north side of the tree, then head back parallel to the road. Hurry!"

Another pair of Ollie's men ran up.

"They've dun a runner, that way," he pointed. "That's where they came in. But they ain't nowheres to go but north. The only cover for 'em is the horse water trough. Hide and wait there, boys, just don't shoot the wrong bleed'n people. Go quickly now!"

There wasn't much more Ollie could do. He was as livid as Austin had ever seen him when he clomped over to the staff housing to check on him, Harriet, Howard and Nanny.

Austin stood holding a revolver and didn't look happy either. "How many did we lose, Ollie?"

"Two! Gunter had his throat slashed, Michael was stabbed and gutted. We'll get the bleed'n sods, Cap'n, even if I have to run down the road after em meself."

Howard stepped up. "Are we safe, Austin?"

"I don't think we need to worry for the time being. Tell everyone else to go to the kitchens and wait there."

Howard nodded and disappeared.

Ollie started into the darkness. "They're bastards, sir. But we'll get 'em, we will."

"I need to sit," Austin said after Ollie left.

Harriet and Nanny eased him into a chair.

"Just a little tired," he whispered.

As Ollie predicted, his men had cut access to the road and the neighbour's property and the only direction the two gunmen could run was in a northerly direction. Wisely, Ollie had two men waiting and hiding behind the large horse water trough and sure enough, throwing caution to the wind, the two gunmen ran directly towards them.

Frank fired both barrels of his shotgun in quick succession, but he was hasty, running, and his shots went wide. He dropped the gun as Amos tried to level his rifle and shoot at the two waiting men.

Both Ollie's men were in position, ready, and experienced. They fired at almost the same time, and Amos was blown backwards by the impact of two bullets from high-powered carbines. In panic, Frank growled and hopelessly charged at Ollie's two men, but he was tired and didn't stand a chance as the two ex-soldiers, again, calmly fired in tandem.

With lanterns, Ollie sent his men searching through Windhaven. They checked the estate house, stables, staff housing, coach house, farming outbuildings and gardens all the way down the carriageway to the road.

"Cap'n, t'was only the three of 'em. We searched everywhere."

Austin was relieved. "Good work, Ollie, I knew I could rely on ya."

The eastern horizon was already turning grey as dawn approached. The three bodies had been wrapped in cloth and placed in the coach house in readiness for when the police were notified and came to investigate.

"Do you recognise them, their faces?" Austin asked.

"Is hard to tell Cap'n. I'll look again when it's light, but so far, I can tell ya, I ain't seen em afore."

"Get some sleep, Ollie, it's been a long night," said Austin.

Harriet walked over, and Austin saw she looked exhausted.

"Ollie, when you send a man to the police, tell them not to come until 11.00 o'clock. We will sleep for a few hours."

Austin and Harriet were having a cup of tea with Howard and Nanny, recounting the events of the previous evening, when they were informed the police had arrived.

"See them in, please," Austin told the maid.

"And here we go again, more endless questions," stated Howard with a sigh.

Two uniformed constables were escorted into the parlour, followed by Detective Sergeant Roggin.

"Detective Sergeant Roggin, I dare say this is an unexpected surprise and not an unwelcome one," Austin greeted. "Please, gentlemen, be seated."

The detective greeted everyone and introduced the two constables before turning to Austin. "I had concerns, Captain Willems. After our last chat and what you told me about Phineas Grosely, Sir Felix Dampierre, and the attempts on your life... I couldn't let it rest. I sought permission to travel here to Chieveley, which, er, was denied." The detective looked sheepish. "But I persisted and had Chief Detective Inspector Bird re-read the case notes. He finally agreed, and I rushed here as soon as I could. However, upon my arrival this morning, and as a professional courtesy, I visited the police station to announce my visit, and they informed me of the death of Phineas Grosely and that you had more trouble last evening. What happened?"

The constables extracted notebooks and began to make notes, as Austin explained. Ollie was called, and he was also asked to recount his version of the events. One by one, each person was laboriously interviewed. Ollie took the two constables to the coach house to view the bodies while the detective remained inside.

"Other than chatting with Sir Felix Dampierre in London, this entire fiasco is over. I can close the files on multiple homicides, and you can return to your life, Captain Willems," assured the detective.

"Yes, something I'm looking forward to. Uh, Detective Sergeant Roggin, are we safe? Do we need to be concerned? I mean, until Sir Felix has been apprehended and all loose ends tied up..."

"No need to worry, sir. I believe Sir Felix doesn't soil his own hands, he employs others. I shall return to London this afternoon and immediately seek his arrest. He has no way of knowing that his scheme failed and that Mr Grosely and the killers are deceased, does he?"

"No, I expect he doesn't," replied Austin.

"I'm just pleased this torrid affair is over," added Harriet.

"I will require you both to come to the station in London when you return, sir. We will have further questions for you and Miss Stephenson before we can complete our investigation. I'm sure you understand. I will notify you when Sir Felix has been detained."

"Of course," replied Austin wearily.

CHAPTER FIFTY-FOUR

Sir Felix Dampierre had two sleepless nights in a row. He was more than worried, he was beside himself with anxiety. Fin had failed to communicate the outcome of his visit to Windhaven and he'd not yet heard from Amos Blackwell. They'd arranged that Fin would send a telegraph to London after the successful conclusion of his meeting with Captain Willems and before he departed Chieveley by train.

The expected telegram had never arrived. Using reliable sources through the ministry, Sir Felix learned, only this morning, that Phineas Grosely had been shot and killed at Windhaven.

The telegram was vital. Phineas had cleverly determined that in the unlikely event that something went wrong during his meeting with Captain Willems and Sir Felix never received the telegram, then the game was up. If he received a telegram, all was well, and everything went according to plan. Using the new telegraph system gave Sir Felix advance warning, and he could make necessary plans to flee. His source also informed him that the police would come for him this morning.

His despair manifested into a rage. Fin was more than just a dear friend, he was an intimate. A cherished confidante who was immeasurably loved. They had shared more than ideas and gallant implausible dreams, they'd bonded as one, like a single and powerful entity. Their emotional connection surpassed that of his droll, bored wife and spoiled children. Fin made him feel special, different and most of all, loved – and now the man was dead. The loathing Sir Felix felt, manifested and consumed him. Captain Willems was toxic, like a festering growth that required severing.

As he sat inside a coach, with his suitcase on the floor beside him, he planned through the blindness of grief and untethered rage.

Windhaven was returning to normal. Staff were recalled, and everyone had fanciful thoughts and beliefs on what transpired in those few days they had been away. To stem the idle gossip and inevitable prattle, Harriet had gathered all staff and explained concisely what had happened. It was over, she said, and everyone could return to their work and feel assured their safety was paramount and any danger had been averted.

Ollie and his men departed for London. They'd been well compensated and thanked for their loyalty. Along with his sincerest condolences, Austin ensured the families of Gunter and Michael were taken care of and that they would be without need or want.

Austin was exhausted and needed rest. While his ribs and gunshot wound healed, he was weak and far from his usual self. Harriet's concerns were justified, and a local physician called and prescribed the cure-all remedy, laudanum. Under its immediate effects, Austin succumbed to the opiate, and Harriet and Nanny watched him closely. They both disapproved of the tincture and were fearful he could become dependent on it if he sustained prolonged use.

Harriet wrote a letter to Detective Sergeant Roggin informing him that Austin's frail condition precluded them both from travelling and delayed their return to London. She would advise him of any changes.

With Windhaven now safe, Eunice arrived, and life at her country estate returned to normal.

Driven by the pain of his emotions and recent losses, Sir Felix Dampierre arrived in Chieveley without discernment or conscience. In his vaunted and inflated opinion, Captain Austin Willems was solely responsible for losing his ranking government position, his fortune, his family and, of course, his lover Phineas Grosely. His unhealthy obsession with the captain was inimitable and consumed every moment, whether sleeping or awake. Believing alcohol could dull the sharp pangs of his unfortunate disposition, Sir Felix found some solace in a potent bottle of the finest Irish whisky money could purchase in Chieveley, but after a forty-eight-hour binge, self-pity and desperation arose victorious.

Harriet was far from content, and similar to Sir Felix, she thought of almost nothing else but Austin. Something tugged at her consciousness and percolated beneath her composed exterior – the unease chafed.

She sat on the edge of Austin's bed as he slept in an opiate-induced state, and she looked up at Nanny when she entered his room.

Nanny silently watched her son as he slept for a few minutes before speaking. "You are troubled, Harriet" she simply stated.

Harriet nodded and pointed to the Laudanum bottle on the nightstand beside the bed. "This is wrong, and I feel Austin slipping through my fingers. What can I do?"

Nanny inclined her head. "Don't give him any more, but what then? Your worry is more than just the doctor's remedy. What is it, Dear?" She sat on the other side of the bed and looked intently at

Harriet.

"I don't know. We have not heard anything from Detective Sergeant Roggin, and I feel we are still threatened, I think Austin is in danger."

Nanny didn't reply as she thought about Harriet's comment. "I agree," she replied after a lengthy pause. "But I don't know what to do."

"What does Howard think?"

"He believes Austin is recovering, and nothing is untoward."

"And you don't believe him?" Harriet asked. "And he isn't worried that Sir Felix may still seek retribution?"

Nanny shook her head. "No."

"Then it is up to us."

"Do you have any ideas?

With some difficulty, Sir Felix Dampierre alighted the coach outside the main entrance to Windhaven. In contrast to his expensive, well-cut clothing, his dishevelled appearance disturbed the maid who came to the door, and she accurately determined the man was inebriated. She refused him access, and fearful of the repercussions, she immediately reported it to Mr Harkness, the estate manager who came to investigate.

Mr Harkness was no fool, and he saw immediately that the intoxicated stranger seated on the step at the door was a gentleman of some importance. The dilemma was to find out who he was, and so far, he'd made no attempt at volunteering his name. Protocol dictated that no one should be admitted inside Windhaven unless their identity and the purpose of their visit were verified and approved. As the mistress was otherwise occupied, that left Miss Stephenson.

But first, Mr Harkness decided to try one last time. "Begging your pardon, sir. May I have your name, a business card, or a letter of introduction? Who is it you wish to see?"

Still seated comfortably on the step, Sir Felix looked up at the estate manager and belched. With some effort, he tried to stand, and helpfully, Mr Harkness lent a hand, grabbed an elbow and assisted the gentleman to his unsteady feet. He released the man and appropriately adjusted his shirt sleeves, then pulled the sleeves of his jacket to where they should be positioned and clasped his hands behind his back. With all the seriousness he could muster, Mr Harkness leaned forward slightly and looked enquiringly at the stranger, "Can I arrange a coach for you, sir?"

Sir Felix looked blankly at the man. In his trouser pocket lay the comfortable weight of a Hopkins and Allen .32 calibre, five-shot revolver. It was a small gun with a spur trigger originally designed for defence purposes. It had been a gift from Fin. As if remembering he had it in his pocket, Sir Felix raised a finger as if to say, one moment, and then reached inside his trouser pocket to extract the weapon.

Mr Harkness believed the stranger was delving into the recesses of his finely tailored trousers for information that could assist and then direct him to where he should be headed. Instead, and at the horrid sight of the revolver, Mr Harkness froze. He didn't appreciate the fine, extraordinary workmanship of the pistol or the delicate ivory grips, nor did he care that the gun had been a treasured gift.

While Sir Felix was suffering the effects of his Irish whiskey and, therefore, impaired, he was still able to lift the pistol and squeeze the trigger. In the resulting explosion of smoke and the unexpected impact of the .32 calibre bullet on the forehead of Windhaven's estate manager, Mr Harkness instantly died.

The maid who stood behind the door screamed.

Sir Felix stepped uncertainly around Mr Harkness, opened the door and began looking for Captain Austin Willems, Miss Harriet Stephenson and more Irish whisky. As he'd been to Windhaven as a guest of Sir Ronald Hewitt-Thompson for a meeting, he had a rough, if not vague, idea of the interior layout.

At the sound of the gunshot, house staff fled. They understood Mr Harkness was dealing with an unwelcome visitor at the door, so they knew where to run.

Eunice was upstairs taking a nap and woke instantly. She slipped on her shoes, grabbed a shawl and, assisted by house staff, was led safely down the servant stairs near the rear of the building. Nanny and Howard were strolling in the garden when they heard the shot. In indecision, they waited until fleeing staff, with warnings of a gunman in the house, urged them to run.

"No, Howard. The stables," she corrected him.

Harriet had just departed the stables and was heading towards the house when she heard the unmistakable report of the .32 calibre revolver discharging. Her hand flew to her mouth, and she paused.

Elias Pickenbury stepped up to her. "Miss Stephenson, best if you move away."

He meant well, but she wasn't having any of it. "Thank you, Mr Pickenbury, please ensure others manage to get to safety, I'll be fine. Go, help them, please."

He looked at her with uncertainty. However, her expression left him in no doubt. "Of course, Ma'am."

As quickly as she dared, she ran toward the house and saw a maid leaving. "What's happening?"

"Ma'am. Mr Harkness is dead, he shot him, he did."

"Who, who shot him Amelia?"

The maid shook her head. "Don't know, ma'am. A stranger, a gentleman, and he be drunk."

"Only one man?"

Amelia nodded. "The mistress is safe, Miss."

Harriet was relieved. "Go, get to safety and make sure everyone is out of danger."

After Amelia ran off, Harriet cautiously entered the house and listened. She heard yelling and doors slamming and presumed it was the gunman. With utmost care, she headed towards the library.

Sir Felix went from room to room and found no one. With every successive empty room, his fury increased. He stopped... *perhaps the captain is in the sunroom or garden,* he thought and turned back towards the staircase, cursing his misfortune at every step.

The stairs proved to be an obstacle. Ascending had been easier, however, climbing down was another matter, and with the endless patience of a drunk, he eventually made it safely to the bottom.

Encouraged, he began searching through the rooms on the ground floor. There were many, and again, his anger simmered and threatened his lucidity when he discovered they, too, were empty.

He found a scullery maid in the kitchen hiding in a pantry. "Where is he, damn you!" he shouted. Spittle flew from his lips, and his face glowed red.

Her eyes were wide in terror, and she was too frightened to answer. She cowered and raised her hands to cover her face.

"Damn you to hell, wench!" He raised the revolver, pointed the revolver at her chest, jerked hard on the trigger and missed.

In a brief moment of temporary sanity, he realised he had limited bullets and shouldn't waste them. Leaving her hysterical, he reluctantly stormed from the kitchen.

As before, each room was empty, and he yelled at the top of his voice. "Where are you? Where are you?" he repeated over and over.

Inside the manor and hidden behind a wall, Harriet heard the pitiful cries and knew it was Sir Felix who'd come to her home. He'd entered her home uninvited, but one way or other, he would be carried out.

His shouting grew louder, and she knew when he exited the parlour, the next room over was the library where she hid. From the uneven cadence of his steps on the highly polished hardwood floor, she heard him approach.

She stepped from concealment as he stumbled towards the open library doorway. He stopped in surprise and looked at her in astonishment then raised Fin's gift. "Where the hell is he!"

"He is safe," she replied and raised her father's shotgun, pulled the stock firmly into her shoulder, levelled it and pulled the first trigger. He flew back from the impact, the vulgar red mess of his shredded chest exposed as he fell to the floor. Then she pulled the second trigger when she saw him move.

She dropped the shotgun, ran out of the house towards the stables, and entered the stall where Prince was usually kept. Austin lay on a bed of straw as Howard, Nanny, and Eunice watched over him.

EPILOGUE

Simon Walker, a senior partner at Walker, Wakefield and Willoughby, placed the document folder into his case and smiled. "Congratulations, Captain, you are the proud and sole owner of Midlands Collieries Company, and I'm sure your father would be proud and pleased." He extended his hand, and Austin shook it with a grin.

"Without your help, Simon, I never expected it could ever happen." Austin turned to Harriet, who was beaming. " And for your help too, Miss Stephenson."

The sound of her laughter filled the room. "You deserve it, Austin. As Mr Walker said, your father would be proud and as thrilled as I am."

"You'll both be busy," added Simon with a smile as he slowly gathered his things. "With both of you partners in Grand Overland Rail and your ownership in Midlands Collieries Company, you'll have no time for each other."

Harriet reached out and took hold of Austin's hand. "That will never happen. Austin has promised to leave Midlands management in place and not be involved in the day-to-day running of the business, isn't that correct, Captain?"

"Apparently so," he laughed.

"If I may ask, and if it's inappropriate, forgive me, but I am curious. Is it true your mother, Mrs Thompson-Hewitt, is purchasing Watson Brothers Coachbuilders?"

"She has already, Mr Walker, all we need to do is finalise our supply and demand contracts between Midlands Collieries, Grand Overland, and Watson Brothers. We should be able to provide new quality coaches and low-cost coal to Grand Overland Rail for years."

"Again, congratulations." Simon stood. "I really must return to the office."

Simon departed, and before Austin and Harriet could continue their day, Amelia, Austin's new housekeeper, sequestered from Windhaven, knocked on the door and entered. "Excuse me, sir, Detective Sergeant Robbin is here to see you."

"Don't let him hear you call him Robbin, Amelia, he may become quite upset. His name is Barnabus Roggin. And yes, please show him in."

"Miss Stephenson, Detective Sergeant Roggin politely dipped his head and turned to Austin, who stood to greet his visitor. "Captain Willems, you look much healthier than when I saw you last."

"I wasn't in the best shape, Detective Sergeant Roggin."

"He overdid it, Detective," volunteered Harriet. "He had us worried for a bit."

"Please be seated, and how can we help you with your investigation?" asked Austin as he returned to his seat.

"Is it over, Detective? Is it finally over, or must we continue to watch over our shoulders?" Harriet asked before Detective Sergeant Roggin could reply.

The detective sighed. "I believe it is over, Miss Stephenson. Although the amount of paperwork you created for my team was astonishing."

Harriet and Austin exchanged glances.

"The death of Sir Felix created some internal strife, but our investigation proved the man had blackmailed many people who came forward to provide us with valuable information. Phineas Grosely and Sir Felix were devious and corrupt. It's unfortunate they both died because had they faced trial, it would have drawn a lot of attention to the failings of government processes."

"What of George Dillington, does he still live? Austin asked.

Detective Sergeant Roggin fought to control his emotions. He coughed to clear his throat. "Uh, yes, Mr Dillington," he began. "His wife, Pearl—"

"She controlled his finances, if I recall," Austin interjected.

"Yes, cleverly through a trust to which Mr Dillington had no legal access. However, it appears Mrs Pearl Dillington has had a remarkable change of heart, as has her estranged husband. They've rediscovered their affections, and both have avowed everlasting love, and she has taken him back."

Austin couldn't help himself and burst out laughing. "Lover-boy George, the most despicable of all the directors, the most unlikely repulsive man you could ever imagine, has found love." Austin shook his head. "I would never have guessed."

"Perhaps you should talk to him, Captain Willems, he may give you some instruction on the finer points of romance," offered Harriet, fighting to keep a straight face."

Detective Sergeant Roggin coughed. "Er, it appears he has you to thank, Captain, and the last thing he is interested in is pursuing any kind of vendetta. He and Mrs Dillington departed for Greece earlier this week for a romantic holiday." He looked to Austin. "Which brings me to the reason for my visit, sir. Upon the instruction of Chief Detective Inspector Bird, we have closed the case. You will no longer be investigated for your alleged role in the personal calamities that befell each director. As no directors remain alive who can assist us with our enquiries, we have no option but to close the file. Case closed, sir."

Austin kept his expression impassive, but inside, the relief was enormous. 'Thank you for the update, Detective Sergeant Roggin. Continuing to investigate those occurrences would have proven to be a waste of police resources."

Detective Sergeant Roggin leaned forward with both elbows resting on his thighs, looked down at the floor briefly, then up and met Austin's deadpan expression with a single raised eyebrow. "A shame Able Baker's home burned down immediately after you returned half his artwork. What will you do with the remainder of his fine art collection, Captain Willems?" He shifted his gaze to Harriet.

End

AUTHOR'S NOTES

This novel is a work of fiction. The characters portrayed in this novel are a result of my fertile mind and creation. Any resemblance to persons either living or dead is purely coincidental and unintentional. I offer no disrespect to the 67th South Hampshire Regiment of Foot or the Queens' Own Hussars of their mention in this novel and hold their legacy in the highest regard.

I have attempted to be faithful to the period this novel depicts. Historical accuracy is important to me, and through extensive research, I endeavoured to represent the Victorian era accurately and touched on sensitive and sometimes controversial topics. However, because this novel is a work of fiction, I conveniently exercised my writers prerogative and altered the historical timeline of actual events to advance the plot. Any and all mistakes are my own.

The legal rights of a husband over the finances of his spouse in the Victorian era were astonishing. Thankfully those draconian laws have since been repealed, but within the context of this story what I outlined is essentially true.

In today's modern world, sending a complex message across town or to a faraway country is effortless and something we can easily take for granted. However, only a handful of years ago, our letters and postal mail were delivered daily, and postal services were essential.

In Victorian times, mail was delivered as many as twelve times a day and six days a week. In 1889, in many of the largest cities in the UK, the first mail delivery began at 7.30 a.m. and the last at 7.30 p.m. At the turn of the century, deliveries slowed to six a day, and in London, if mail were not delivered within two hours, people would complain. In this novel, I write often about sending and receiving messages. The method of dispatch could easily have been through the post or by a messenger, but delivery within a short time was assured and crucial to this story.

In the early 1800s, ice was mainly imported from the USA, and by the late 1800s, harvesting ice had become a vast industry, with ice being transported from Switzerland and later, Norway, to satisfy the appetites of the wealthy. At the height of the ice trade, over 90,000 people were employed across Europe, and 90 million kilos were shipped from Norway. With a healthy rail network, transporting ice became easy and readily available to the wealthy.

According to the UK National Archives, Britain's railway network proliferated in Victorian times. In the 1840s, 'Railway Mania' saw a frenzy of investment, speculation, and fortunes earned or lost. From 1845 to 1900, *£3 billion was spent* developing English rail. In 1870, 423 million passengers travelled on 16,000 miles of track, and by the end of Queen Victoria's reign, over 1100 million passengers were using trains.

The railway system offered new opportunities for travel, holidays, transporting goods, developing businesses, and growing towns and cities. However, with more people and goods on the move, crime increased. The first carriages were unlit and unconnected by corridors, which provided criminals with easy opportunities to rob or attack isolated passengers. Railway stations were often busy, which made theft commonplace. When the first passenger was murdered in 1864 on the North London Railway, the public began to raise concerns about travel safety. This was a topic I chose not to pursue in this novel.

However, a crucial component of this story was the absence of limited liability protection for shareholders. I conveniently altered the timeline as The Limited Liability Act was passed by the UK parliament in 1855, a few years before the period in which this story takes place.

It was compulsory for those in English military service to sport a moustache, and it had been mandatory for 60 years. Various explanations detail that a clean and shaven face is 'boy-like' and that it is hard to instil fear into your enemies when you look like a youth. French soldiers in the late 17th century wore moustaches and were said to be 'appurtenances of terror', while another explanation states that growing a moustache has health benefits. WWI was the last war when English service members were required to cultivate a moustache.

Thank you for reading,
Paul W. Feenstra

Other historical fiction books
by
Paul W. Feenstra
Published by Mellester Press

Boundary

The Breath of God (Book 1 in Moana Rangitira series)

For Want of a Shilling (Book 2 in Moana Rangitira series)

Gunpowder Green

Into the Shade

Falls Ende short story ebooks

     1. The Oath

     2. Courser

     3. The King

Falls Ende full length novels.
Falls Ende – Primus (ebooks 1,2 & 3)
Falls Ende – Secundus
Falls Ende – Tertium
Falls Ende – Quartus
Falls Ende – Quintus

Leonard Hardy's
A Sinister Consequence
A Questionable Virtue

A Gentleman at Heart

Milton Keynes UK
Ingram Content Group UK Ltd.
UKHW021604050724
445023UK00012BA/150/J

9 781991 182494